INHU

CW00394437

A M PAYNE

To Ella!
Thank you for reading
Inhuman!
I really hope you
enjoy it.

Adam

This book is dedicated to

My wife, Sophie.
My inspiration, my world and the force that drives me. Without her, I could not write about love and the happiness it creates.

My fellow author and lifelong friend, James.
A fantastic writer, who proved to me that you should never give up on your dreams. Without him, this book would never have been published (he was also the editor, so that really is true!).

My unborn child.
Nothing would make me prouder than for you to read this book one day and think your dad is a pretty cool dude.

FOREWORD

To see this book published is the most surreal feeling in the world. I had planned *Inhuman* over thirteen years ago whilst I attended college. The book started as something very different, but fundamentally it has always been the same people, Terry and Amy, who, in my opinion, have characteristics that I aspire to have. I started *Inhuman* during a depressing stage of college; I never enjoyed my time there, and everything I had hoped it would be turned out to be very different. I created the world in this book as an escape and wrote about the world I wanted to live in.

I strongly believe in a happy place in your inner mind, a place that creates equanimity. As I wrote *Inhuman*, I started to realise that Byanbythe (*buy-an-buy-the*, in case you were wondering how to say it), was my happy place. When I try to describe Byanbythe, it captures all the places where I find peace; it's almost like Center Parcs, the beautiful forest with the houses spaced out, next to the beach and sea, all hidden behind a great big mountain. Nothing could be a greater success to me than you reading my story and sharing a little bit of this happy place. Among the chaos in Amy and Terry's life, Byanbythe is a comfort, a place of love and a home.

Thank you for taking time to visit my world and reading the story I have to tell. I hope you enjoy it as much as I enjoyed creating it and hope you finish this book wanting more. Who knows? There may be more to come …

PROLOGUE
MILKAIA

I watched the small boy lying in the middle of the road, in a pool of blood, dying before my eyes. The forest was pitch-black, surrounded by thousands of trees, only broken by the small road in the middle. Many of the surrounding trees were now on fire, lighting up the scene of chaos like a spotlight. Around a hundred metres in front of the boy's body lay the cause of the chaos, which was a car on fire; the people stuck in the car were dead.

Every fibre of my body knew this was a bad idea. I wanted to run over and save that boy's life, but the man I thought I knew, who stood right next to me, cool and calm as if he was watching a TV show, wouldn't let me move. I inched forward and he grabbed my wrist.

'No,' he simply said.

The fire spread quickly and it felt like hours before the sound of sirens began to penetrate the sound of the crackling fires.

'We're done here,' he said.

'Please …' I begged.

'No,' he repeated.

A mixture of fire engines, police and ambulances were visible in the distance, all flashing red and blue lights, illuminating the black forest as they raced to the scene.

I walked away from the chaos I had caused, knowing that my life would never be the same. I cried and slowly turned around to catch up with the coldest man I knew.

I hoped the boy had lived.

I hoped he didn't remember.

AMY

'And in other news, a tragic scene early this morning, in the middle of Mynydd Road and forest. We are still at the scene awaiting more information, but it appears that a severe car crash has occurred. Three casualties have been rushed to Penstantyhe Hospital.'

I entered the kitchen and saw Mom standing in the middle, watching the news with great interest. As always, the kitchen smelt amazing, as Mom was just about to finish her final batch of bread, cakes and pastries for her shop. The most amazing part of having your mom as the one and only baker in town were the smells that came from the kitchen.

This morning was like no other morning, as Dad wasn't at the kitchen table, drinking his usual coffee and reading the paper.

'Where's Dad?' I asked.

Mom was still standing there, staring at the TV.

'Mom?'

She blinked as if just awoken by a horrible dream, suddenly looking at me.

'Sorry, Amy. He's had to rush out on an emergency call.'

Dad was a children's social care worker and was extremely busy, sometimes travelling all over Wales to see clients. It was very rare he was called out for an emergency, especially so early. I should have put two and two together to work out that this was why Mom was so worried.

'Eat your breakfast before your nan comes,' Mom ordered and carried on glazing the final pastries.

Nan came over every morning to look after my baby brother, Tim, who was just over one year old. With my parents' busy work schedules and my school work, she was a helping hand as Mom tried to manage her career and such a young baby. I didn't need a babysitter myself, but of course, like Mom and her career, I had a career at school too, so I was far too busy to look after a baby.

Apart from Dad not being there, it was just another boring Tuesday in Byanbythe. I was seven years old and yet I could write down the whole of my future. Byanbythe was a beautiful, unique town. It was very big, hidden away from the world behind a mountain with a forest on the one side and the seaside on the other. Whilst the town had character, beauty and lots of people, it was predictable. I should not be seven years old thinking this, but by the age of five, I realised all my classmates' parents went to school together and so did their parents and their parents and so on and so forth. It was a huge tourist attraction to come to the town and thousands of people would visit every year; after a few years, you started to recognise the same people coming back, always to the same locations, same shops, doing the same thing. No one seemed to have dreams and most kids ending up working with their families and taking over the family businesses. I didn't want to be a social worker like Dad, I hated kids and resented the fact that I was one (but for all intents and purposes, my brain was a very adult brain). I also didn't want to be a baker like Mom, who woke up every day at four a.m (four a.m!), to start baking. I simply didn't fit in at Byanbythe. I had big dreams, I wanted to do big and crazy things and I wouldn't achieve that living in this town. I once tried to explain this to Mom and Dad, who explained that things were changing for the future of the town.

'They are building a college and university,' Mom would say with pride, 'The biggest in the country, right on the side of the mountain. And lots of new houses! That's going to bring hundreds of fresh people and jobs into the town!'

'And the town's becoming the new Sandbanks!' Dad would chime in. 'Lots of celebrities are having mansions and houses built at the top of the forest and on the beaches!'

I didn't care about college, university or celebrities. I wanted to explore! They simply didn't understand; they met in primary school, went to high school together, bought a bakery business together, a house, got married and then had kids ... they were boring and predictable. Indeed, by the age of five, I realised my life was falling into an infinite repeat, written like a book, knowing how it would end up. *Nothing* happened exciting in Byanbythe.

*

Dad arrived home the next day, but he didn't stay long. If I asked Mom what was happening, she would dismiss the conversation. I was *not* stupid, but they still treated me like a child and I hated it.

About a week after Dad's emergency call, I was slowly getting used to him being out of the house. I missed the nights where I would watch TV with him or a film. It was funny how much he tried to make me watch American football; he would never admit it, but he loved American football because he didn't understand English football and wanted to be different. It was our quality time together and I was happy to spend my whole night with him; he always let me watch programmes Mom wouldn't allow me to and he never forced me to do homework.

On this particular night, something was different. Mom was on the phone for a long time, talking fast and sounding very concerned. She stared out of the kitchen window and would look outside and up the street, but I wasn't sure what she was looking for. The tone in her voice suddenly changed and whatever she was looking for no longer seemed to matter. She quickly ended her conversation and put the phone down and I pretended to watch TV in the living room, acting like I hadn't been listening at all.

'Amy,' she said, 'I need you to go upstairs and watch Tim, please.'

'He's asleep, Mom!' I replied.

'Amy, go upstairs - please. I need to sort something out.'

I could tell she wasn't up for an argument and seemed firm in her word. I slowly got up, turned the TV off and dragged myself upstairs. I knew she was listening to me, to make sure I wasn't hiding at the top of the stairs or trying to eavesdrop, but to play the part, I actually walked to my baby brother's room and watched him sleep in his crib. My plan was to wait here for a small amount of time, then creep downstairs to see what was happening.

I waited some time and then waited a little bit more. I slowly sneaked out of the room and crept to the top of the stairs. I knew if I sat on the third step down, I would be able to hear anyone talking in the living room and kitchen. Our living room was huge, almost the size of the whole house, with a single door to the kitchen and the front door of the house. I needed to stay quiet, as the big room sometimes echoed when I ran down the stairs. I closed my eyes tight and listened as hard as I could to the conversation in the kitchen.

'Lisa, what else could I do?'

It was Dad! He was home.

'Michael, this is huge,' Mom said very quickly, and by the sounds of it, she seemed very angry. 'This isn't policy. This should be for a foster carer. Your job has always been out in the field, to look after, care and offer support. But this is a whole different level. We're not qualified!'

'He has no one, Lisa. He's extremely scared and vulnerable ... He will only talk to me; he won't talk to the police, the doctors, nor the nurses. Only me. What could I do?'

Mom didn't reply.

'He has lost everything and practically performed a miracle recovery,' Dad continued. 'He had third degree burns, practically should have been scarred for life. He's now sitting in the living room healed, looking like nothing has happened at all. He needs support and a chance to get away from the hospital.'

'And work has said this is okay?' Mom questioned. 'Michael, I'm not sure about this ...'

The conversation continued, but my attention had drifted away. I was suddenly wondering about who was sitting in our living room. I crept down the stairs a little bit more. I peeked around the stairway banister and looked into the seating area. Someone was sitting in Dad's armchair with their back to me. I took a step further, making sure a step wasn't heard by my parents, who were still arguing in the kitchen. I crept a little further and finally made it into the living room.

'Hello?' I whispered.

The person didn't move.

'Hello?' I repeated.

Still nothing. I felt angry that this person was ignoring me, so I decided to jump in front of the chair to get their attention.

'Excuse me! Oh …'

I stopped, as I now understood why they hadn't replied. A small boy, who now looked petrified at the sight of me, sat in the armchair with Dad's headphones and phone. The boy must have been watching videos on the phone when I suddenly jumped in front of him. Whenever Mom and Dad argued, I was either sent to my room or, if they really wanted to make sure I wasn't listening in, Dad would make me listen to music or videos on his phone.

The small boy stared at me, but didn't say anything. He had really light brown hair, almost grey like Nan's. His eyes were bright brown, with a tinge of yellow like a wolf from one of Tim's nursery rhymes. He was skinny and quite small (much smaller than me). He slowly took the headphones off, but remained silent.

'Hey ... who are you?' I asked.

He still didn't reply. I felt angry again.

'It's rude to ignore someone! Who are you?'

My voice must have raised louder than I had intended, as Mom and Dad suddenly entered the living room from the kitchen.

'Amy!' Mom shouted. 'I told you to stay upstairs.'

I looked at the small boy in front of me, who was staring at my dad.

'Amy, I see you've met Terry,' Dad said. 'Terry's going to be staying with us for a bit whilst he gets better. He hasn't been well in hospital, have you, Terry?'

Terry didn't reply and I was relieved to see that it was not just me he ignored.

'Terry, dear, my name's Lisa; I'm Michael's wife. I'm so glad you're feeling a little bit better,' said Mom, who quickly came over and placed her hand on his shoulder. He flinched and shuffled away from Mom, who gave Dad a quick look of concern.

'Everyone's tired. Why don't we all have an early night?' suggested Dad, who faked a yawn and stretched out his arms.

'Good idea!' agreed Mom. 'How does that sound, Terry? We have a lovely room upstairs for you.'

Terry didn't reply. Mom quickly escorted me to bed whilst Dad took Terry to our spare bedroom (my dressing room, which I had now obviously lost access to).

I didn't think I would sleep, as my mind was wild with questions. Who was Terry? What was Mom and Dad's argument about? One question led to another, but I must have fallen asleep at some time.

'Hey …'

I suddenly woke up and saw Terry standing next to my bed. Did he actually just talk to me?

'Did you say something?' I asked.

'Hey,' he repeated.

We stared at each other and I was starting to feel really confused.

'Are you okay?' I asked.

'Yeah,' he whispered. 'I'm sorry. I just … wanted to say sorry for before.'

'Sorry for what?'

'For being rude. You said I was rude.'

'Oh … I didn't mean it.'

Terry just stared at me.

'Is something wrong?' I asked.

'I don't know where my mom and dad are,' he replied.

I didn't know what to say.

'I'm sorry,' I finally replied, 'but hey! My dad will find them. Until then, you can stay with us.'

Terry gave a small smile, but continued to stare at me.

'Do you want to sleep in my bed tonight?' I asked. 'If you're scared, we can sleep together.'

'I'm not scared!' he replied.

'Shhh! You'll wake my mom and dad up! Do you want to stay in here or not?'

His face frowned, but he didn't reply, simply climbing into my bed and rolling over onto his side. He didn't say another word and I could only presume he had fallen asleep. After trying not to get too close to him, I slowly drifted back to sleep. I had never had a boy sleep in my bed before.

*

I woke up the following day to Mom and Dad acting awkward with me, and for some reason, they didn't want Terry sleeping in the same bed with me. Dad must have spoken to Terry and made a compromise to set up a camping bed in my bedroom, if that made him feel more comfortable.

The next few weeks were weird. I had to go to school still, but Terry didn't. Dad stayed at home a lot more now, but left the house with Terry all the time. Terry didn't talk much, but if he did, he only spoke to me and Dad, ignoring Mom and my nan. Mom was really kind and caring, not bothered that Terry wouldn't talk to her and treated him like her own son.

I tried to get to know Terry and asked him lots of questions. What music did he like? What did he watch on TV? Did he like sports? He never gave me a real answer and always said he didn't know. He was really strange. We talked the most at night when we were supposed to be sleeping in my room. He would ask me questions about school, my friends and about Byanbythe. The most information I found out about him was his last name, which was Haynes.

Mom and Dad had lots of secret conversations about Terry, but they were no longer arguing. Every time I tried to listen, they quickly realised I was hiding somewhere close by and changed the subject to something boring. As days passed, things strangely started to feel normal with Terry living with us. It wasn't normal, but it became part of the usual pattern. I finally had my nights back with Dad, but with the addition of Terry. He didn't talk, but he would listen to everything we spoke about or any story my dad told. I was starting to get used to things, but unfortunately, the new normality didn't last long. On one particular night, I heard Mom and Dad arguing again.

'He won't want to go!' Mom shouted. 'Michael, you need to put your foot down!'

'I have no choice, Lisa.'

'The poor boy's already crying.'

I hadn't seen Terry for a few hours, as I thought he was out with Dad. He wasn't in the living room, so I slowly crept upstairs to see if he was in the room. As I got closer, I could hear crying.

'Terry, why are you crying?' I asked as I walked through the door.

He was sitting on the bed with his head in his hands, but suddenly stood up as I entered the room.

'I'm not crying!' he snapped back.

'You are. What's wrong?'

'I … I have to go live with someone else.'

'What do you mean?'

'Your dad said I had to go live with someone else.'

'My dad wouldn't say that. He's looking for your parents, remember?'

He stared at me, tears still streaming down his face.

'I have to move out.'

'I don't understand, why?'

As I asked this question, Mom and Dad appeared behind me and joined us in the room.

'Ah, Amy … Terry …'

'Dad, why is Terry leaving?!'

'Amy …' Dad replied; I had never seen him this upset before.

Mom placed her hand on his shoulder and cleared her throat.

'We don't want Terry to go, Amy,' she said. 'We care about you, Terry, we really do. It's just … the law says that Terry needs to have a proper family to live with.'

'Why can't he stay here until his mom and dad come back?' I asked.

Mom and Dad gave each other a look of concern, which resulted in Dad walking out of the room.

'It's just the rules, Amy, we have no choice,' Mom explained. 'Terry, I am so sorry, my dear. We really want you to stay here.'

Terry continued to cry and followed my dad by walking out of the room.

'Mom?' I pleaded.

Mom sat on the bed and grabbed me into a hug. She too was now crying.

'Amy, your dad's job isn't to foster or take children into care. He really cares about Terry and so do I … but it's time for Terry to get real support.'

'What about his mom and dad?' I asked again.

'They aren't well …' she slowly replied. 'Amy, I need you to trust me … We really care about Terry. This isn't something we have any control over.'

I believed her. Terry really did feel like he was part of our family now. It had only been a few weeks, but he spent every moment with Dad. Mom was super caring and treated Terry like a loving son of her own. I too loved spending every night talking to him and he now felt like a new best friend, even if he didn't say much.

The rest of the night was awful. Dad was so upset that he didn't spend any time with us, using his time to pack up Terry's things. Mom was baking in the kitchen, but she seemed to be baking a lot more than usual; she wasn't even talking on the phone, which was strange for her, instead remaining very quiet as she baked.

Terry sat with me in the living room as we watched TV; even though he stared at the screen, I could tell he wasn't really watching it.

'Want to talk?' I asked.

'No, thank you,' he replied. 'I'm okay.'

Our bedtime soon arrived and Terry still didn't want to talk. Normally we would wait for the lights to be turned off and listen for my mom and dad to fall asleep before we started to talk. Unfortunately tonight, Terry stayed quiet and I presumed after a while that he had just fallen asleep. I closed my eyes and felt very upset that this was Terry's last night with me.

*

I was suddenly woken up by a bang, somewhere downstairs. I looked over towards Terry's bed, but he wasn't there. I quickly jumped out of bed and crept downstairs, looking for the source of the bang. As soon as I was in the living room, I noticed that the front door of the house was open slightly. I ran to the door and onto the drive, looking down the street to see a small figure in the distance; it was Terry! I ran as fast as I could, and quickly caught up with him.

'Terry!'

He quickly turned around and looked at me in shock.

'Amy, go back home!'

'Where are you going? It's the middle of the night, we'll get in trouble!'

'I'm going to find my mom and dad.'

'Dad said you needed to wait for them to get better, Terry. Please come back home.'

'I'm not going to live with another family!' he shouted. 'I don't want to. I was happy with your family.'

'I know. We were happy with you … I don't think we have a choice.'

'I know, I'm not blaming any of you. Your mom and dad have been super nice to me … but it's time I was back with my own mom and dad.'

'How, though?' I asked. 'It's the middle of the night! Do you even know where they are?'

'Yes. I looked it up before I left, I promise. Now go back to bed!'

'Terry …' I pleaded.

'I promise I'm going to be okay, Amy. You gotta promise me you won't tell your mom and dad either. If you tell them, we'll both be in trouble! I'm gonna be okay, I'll find my mom and dad and everything will go back to normal. I'll even ask them to bring me over sometime!'

I didn't think he was telling the truth, but this was the happiest I had ever seen him. What could I do?

'Okay,' I finally replied.

We stood there in silence. I smiled at him, but felt really sad.

'Thank you,' he finally said. 'You've really been a good friend to me, Amy.'

He slowly grabbed me and gave me a hug. As the hug ended, he kissed my cheek. I felt myself going extremely red. We didn't say anything else and he turned around with his big backpack and carried on walking down the street. I watched him until he disappeared into the distance, thinking what the right thing to do was.

And suddenly, it dawned on me. What had I done? Never mind the trouble we could have been in, it was nothing compared to the trouble of Terry actually running away! I suddenly felt scared and stupid. I ran back to the house to tell Mom and Dad what Terry had done.

But it was too late.

Terry was gone …

10 YEARS LATER

AMY

I hated college and I could never express how annoyed I was that I still had two years left to complete. Today would be the first day of my second year and while most would feel excited to go back, I dreaded it. I would not be staying on for university and I would be moving away from this town once and for all. Yes, lots had changed over the last few years, but were they really changes? We had a lot of celebrities living here now, big houses, posher restaurants, more people, tourists and I was in the biggest college/university for over a hundred miles. But you could put glitter on shit as much as you wanted … it was still shit.

I was harsh and ungrateful but, to be honest, I couldn't have cared less. Whenever Mom and Dad would remind me that people were queuing up to move to Byanbythe, I reminded them that I was queueing up to move away. This town felt like an episode of *Twin Peaks*, because it felt frozen in time. I wanted to escape, to see the world and what it had to offer. I knew so many people that had never gone past the forest, never mind the other side of Mount Cudd (Byanbythe's giant protector from the world). How could people never travel? I simply did not understand it.

'Amy, you're going to be late for college!' Mom shouted from the kitchen.

I gathered my bag and books and dragged myself downstairs.

'Is Nick picking you up?' she asked.

'No, I told you we split up weeks ago,' I growled.

Nick was my ex-boyfriend and I hated him dearly. I had dated Nick since the last year of high school and to many girls he was the finest example of "husband material" you could bag. He was the best rugby player in Wales (his words), extremely fit and strong (many girls' words) and most of all, he was a 16th century male. His plan was simple: marry me, play for the rugby team until he was too old to get a real job and then coach it. I would of course stay at home and make his breakfast, dinner and tea and should he desire it, provide him with sex on demand.

IN. HIS. DREAMS!

This fantasy of his, like many Byanbythe boys for generations, was a Byanbythe girl's dream. I felt isolated in this town because I had ambition to have my independence and not rely on a man for a future. I was so proud of my mom, who seemed to be one of the only women in the whole of the town who had her own dreams and succeeded without the financial dependency or permission of any man. She was a baker all of her life and started to save for her own bakery long before she married Dad. Most of her friends who had businesses were bought by their husbands to keep them quiet. I had grown up to be a fearless feminist, I hated the idea of women being "put in their place" to provide a man an easy life. My relationship with Nick was six months of fun, followed by almost two years of regret, prolonged by my inability to end it until recently.

'Ah, I expected you to be back together by now,' said Mom, who was loading up cakes into crates ready to take to her shop.

'You know I hate him,' I replied.

She laughed and began to carry crates to her car.

'Can I catch a ride with you?' I asked.

'Sorry, Amy, I'm going straight to Anne Moodligh's house! Can you believe it? She commissioned me for a gender reveal cake. If you cut my cake on the left side, it's blue cake and on the right, it's pink! How fun.'

Anne Moodligh was one of the many celebrities occupying the forest and mountain mansions. At one point in my life, I would have loved to have met her, told her I loved her acting and her films … Now I was a moody, bitter teenager, just wishing my life away.

'Okay, maybe Dad can take me?'

'Sorry, Red, I'm training early this week.'

Dad suddenly emerged through the front door. I hated his nickname for me, which was due to my bright ginger hair. It was so unfair that I was pale-skinned and ginger-haired with green eyes, whilst Mom had blonde hair and Dad and Tim had dark brown hair … It was like a family club and I wasn't allowed in.

'Don't call me that!' I barked.

Dad laughed and grabbed his lunch from the fridge. He was so ecstatic for work I could never begrudge him for sometimes putting his job before my need for a personal taxi. For almost nine years now, he had successfully run an American football team and made them so successful that they were now competing against actual American teams! The biggest success around his team was converting rugby players into American football players, something he was immensely proud of. Rugby was almost like a religion in Wales and therefore to even talk of another sport was borderline suicide and a quick way to isolate yourself. Dad was the greatest man I knew and single-handedly with his charm and warm heart had converted his hobby into a success and inspired others to join him.

I was forced to get the bus to college and left the house after saying goodbye to everyone and stealing a custard cake from Mom's car; the worry that Anne Moodligh may have one less cake was outweighed by my need for breakfast.

The bus stop was no further than a ten-minute walk and I was surprised to see my best friend, Laura Hoskins, waiting for the bus too.

'Why are you getting the bus?' I asked.

'Ryan's a dick,' she replied.

I rolled my eyes and we both laughed.

Laura was slim, short and blonde, but had big boobs and a big bum, so she was obviously popular with guys. She was the complete opposite of me and deep down I knew we were only friends because of nostalgia, not because we shared anything in common. She was a typical boy's girl and everything I hated about boys, she loved. She had slept with so many people that she was known as being an easy target at parties; each week she had a new boyfriend and one week later, she would split up with them. Laura's life, like so many people, was written in the unwritten book that foretold the future. Her mom was a nail and spray tan technician and Laura wanted nothing more than to take over that business. I had nothing against that career choice, but my own personal hatred stemmed from people's inability to have ambition. I was completely ignorant to what made people happy and thought everyone else had to think like I did. It was a horrible trait to have, but one I held onto dearly, as it was my only guarantee that I would move away as soon as possible. We talked throughout the whole bus ride, and as always she questioned me about my split up with Nick.

'You were the luckiest person to be with him,' she claimed.

'Take him, he's yours,' I replied.

'Oh, Amy, you have no idea. You are the first girl to ever reject Nick, so he will forever be chasing you. He wants what he can't have.'

'And that is one of the many reasons I hate him. He loved the *idea* of me, not me.'

She laughed. She clearly did not understand why someone would want to be with someone for something more than sex and fun.

'Hey, have you heard about the penthouse on Great Western View?' she said.

'No, why?'

'It's finally been sold!'

I understood her excitement. The penthouse was possibly the greatest house anyone had ever seen. It was secure, private and had a full view of the town, beach and forest. It could see everything, but could not be seen by anyone. No one lived there for long, but many, many bands rented it out to record albums, citing the views as huge inspirations.

'Any idea who rented it?' I asked.

'No, but rumours are it's someone really young whose *bought* it.'

'Oh great, some trust fund kid, then?'

Someone with millions of pounds had most likely spent millions of pounds to come and live in the place I wanted to escape from. Why didn't they contact me first? I could have sold them my bedroom for a fraction of the price.

I had to say one thing for Byanbythe; it was beautiful to travel around and so extreme with the change of scenery. Most of the houses were situated throughout the forest, in little congregations. As we travelled on the bus, we left a small cluster of houses, to the dark, dense and vast forest, almost blocking out the sun with the extremely tall grand fir trees that stretched for miles and miles. Occasionally, as we would follow the winding road, we would sometimes see a glimpse of the seaside in the distance, but then it would disappear and we would climb the road higher into the forest and then see a glimpse of Mount Cudd. Then it was back to a small cluster of neighbourhoods and houses. Sometimes it was huge houses and then it was houses more like the natives and the locals - smaller three and four bedroom houses. As Laura continued to talk, I stared out of the window and basked in the beauty.

It was a warm September, something they called an Indian summer. In less than one year, I would finally be in my last year of college, ready to finish off courses and take exams in subjects that would never benefit me when I had to get a real job.

I was a fool, because I took subjects in stuff I was passionate about, not subjects that would easily get me a job. If I was honest, I had no idea what I wanted to do, I just knew I wanted to travel and see the world. One of my subjects was English Literature, because of my deep love for novels and analysing. To balance English, I also studied Media and Film, which everyone thought were easy subjects of watching videos and making films. I remember the novelty wearing off after four months, when we started to study social realism in film and TV. When you've heard the same northern accent and the same stupid, sad piano over a million times, you realise the course wasn't easy - it was torture.

A saving grace of the subjects I chose was the fact that I didn't have to be with Laura all day, who did Hair and Beauty, and I didn't have to see Nick, who did Physical Education and played rugby. I know I sounded like a bitch, but I genuinely did find solace in my own company and really invested myself in college work. If Laura or Nick were there, I would have been distracted for all the wrong reasons.

The bus turned the final corner and the college was in view. Byanbythe College and University was enormous and consisted of one giant building, around twenty-five smaller buildings and a huge campus of student accommodation. It could easily have been mistaken for its only village, as it currently had five thousand students.

I bid farewell to Laura as we left the bus and took the five-minute walk to my form room, the first point of call for any day.

Form was the usual excuse of a mess and around thirty students from various classes piled into the classroom. No one paid attention to our form tutor, Roberta Hush, who was a moody, self-important woman, who possibly cared less about college than we did. Roberta took the register and ignored the fact that I was one of the only people who replied to their name being called.

'Amy Doorey?'

'I'm here -'

'Jack Tosland?'

She didn't even let me reply. If there was a fire drill and they needed the registers to realise who was on campus or not, we were doomed if anyone was missing. After registering the class (those who were present and even those who weren't), she gave a huge sigh, rolled her eyes and banged her desk with a large book.

'Shut up, all of you. I have your timetables here,' she said in her dreary, monotonous voice. 'Get out of my classroom and collect yours on the way out.'

One of the greatest wonders of the world was Roberta Hush; no one knew what she taught, she didn't seem to have any emotion other than misery and if truth be told, no one had ever seen outside of the college.

I took my timetable and saw what classes I had and when. I had English most of the week, as it was my main subject. The rest of the hours and timeslots were equally split between Media and Film Studies. With great pleasure, I strolled over to the English and Arts building, which was west of the campus. I was so excited to see what book we would be learning first! Would we cover Shakespeare again (my absolute favourite) or perhaps poetry? Last year we had a mix of Philip Larkin (the most miserable poet of all time) and William Burke, a visionary.

I took my usual seat and caught up with a few people that I liked in the class. No one really knew me that well outside of English, so this was the one class I wouldn't get questions about Nick, who, for all intents and purposes, was illiterate by choice and had never read a book apart from a porn magazine in his whole life.

One of my favourite teachers was a lady named Louise Thenes and I had hoped, out of the five possible teachers we could have had, it would have been her. Louise was young, but so, so wise. She had read every book in the world and back in the day was a punk rocker, so had this beautiful colourful vibe in her style and aura. Louise had become my lecturer mid last year, after our first teacher, Janine, stormed out of our class and never returned. Janine was a self-professed hater of children and indeed people. If people did not understand books or if people did not have the same intellectual level as her own, she hated them. I knew she was going to be weird when the first statement she made was about her idol being the character Miss Havisham from *Great Expectations*. In one particular term, we were learning a very depressing book, which Janine was reading in her boring, dreary voice. When she read out loud, it was for the benefit of her own voice and not for students to learn. One unfortunate boy, Colin Robinson, had fallen asleep and once she realised, she burst into a huge rant of idiots, her hatred of children, how we were all doomed to work in fast food and then, for her standing ovation, told us all to colour books before storming out. We never did see Janine again and something told me she either quit or got fired. Louise was the complete opposite, she loved students, loved to interact and made *any* book to come to life. As she walked into the classroom, with a summery dress and long pink hair, she smiled at the class and took a deep breath. My heart felt elated knowing she was my teacher again.

'Welcome back, everyone. I'm glad I have the same class as last year!' she said in her gentle, husky voice. 'This year we are going to be studying a mixture of things … but we'll start with a personal favourite of mine, *Paradise Lost* by John Milton.'

I had heard of *Paradise Lost*, so that was a good start. Louise suddenly looked around the room.

'Oh … I thought we had someone new in our class today?' she said as she read some papers on her desk. 'Has anyone seen him?'

People shrugged and she quickly wrote something down before carrying on with her lesson. She handed out copies of *Paradise Lost* and the term started with a flurry of passion and deep-dive analysis of a book. I was happy, for once.

*

The first day of college was pleasant but uneventful. My day was mostly English and the last part of the day was Film Studies; my first term for film was fully focusing on music used in film, which seemed like an interesting subject. Jeremy Finch, our lecturer, played a scene from a horror film with the original suspense music, but then replayed the same scene with fun music, then romantic music, then fast music, which was amusing and an eye-opener to the power of music.

I was pleasantly surprised that my dad was waiting for me by the bus stop in his car, and as we drove to pick up my brother from school, he asked me hundreds of questions about my first day back at college. When we eventually returned home, Mom then asked me the same questions as Dad had and I gave the same replies.

The next day at college was dedicated to Media Studies for the first half, which was taught by a lady called Lindsey Chalmers. Lindsey was a small, intelligent, fierce lady and had a teaching style that did not let you rest for a moment. Our first assignment was to focus on British soap operas, which I really could not stand. Mom would have been ecstatic, because when she wasn't baking, she was watching crappy soap operas; I was almost tempted to ask her to do my coursework.

College always seemed to have something going on, and as I finished lunch with Laura, I looked around at the hundreds of kids that attended, all doing their own thing. In the middle of the campus was a huge park-like area and this was where most people would try and hang out during their free time (if there was space). I remember skipping lessons a few times just to sit in this park and read a book or to listen to music; it was such a beautiful place to hang out. I said goodbye to Laura and returned to my favourite lesson, English, which would take up my Tuesday afternoon. I hated to admit it, but I felt like I had already read a third of *Paradise Lost.*

I took my seat, not really paying attention to my surroundings. I started to write some notes I had suddenly thought of in my notepad, when Louise finally entered the room.

'Welcome, class!' she said and took a quick look around the room. Her face suddenly lit up, and she beamed a large smile. 'Ah! You're here!'

I looked to where her eyes were staring and at the back of the class was someone new, the same person who must not have turned up yesterday.

He was tall (which was easy to tell by the way his legs almost reached the chair in front of his). He had light brown hair, with flecks of white in it and his eyes were a light brown, which almost seemed yellow. He was slim, a little stubble on his face and, without judging too much, dressed quite normal compared to most people at college. College kids wore bright, vibrant clothes; some were designers, some were fashion and most were just plain weird - this new kid wore simple blue jeans, a white t-shirt and plain white trainers. I couldn't place my finger on it, but he looked a little familiar.

'I am that teacher that will make you stand up in front of the class and embarrass yourself, so I'm really sorry, but...' said Louise, who was now waving her arms towards the whiteboard at the front of the class, indicating the new kid to move there. He smirked and slowly stood up following her direction.

'Hi, everyone ... I'm Terry Haynes.'

My eyes widened and I dropped into a state of shock. Terry Haynes? It couldn't be? Really? I mean, he was my age, he was new ... but surely it was a coincidence? It looked nothing like him. He left ... Why would he come back?

'I've just moved back to Byanbythe,' said Terry.

Moved back? Oh no ... maybe it was.

'I actually didn't stay here for long when I was a kid ... but I guess I was drawn back to this beautiful town. Apart from that, I am extremely boring and have nothing else to say,' he finished and gave a small bow to the room. A few people laughed and Louise welcomed him to class.

'And where were you yesterday, Mr Haynes?' she asked.

'I was lost! Have you seen the size of this place? I should have moved into the college, it would be quicker to find my bearings,' he replied and more people laughed.

Terry returned to his seat and as I turned around to stare at him, he smirked and winked at me.

It was him. I was freaking out. I felt like I couldn't breathe.

'Louise, I'm not feeling so good. Can I be excused?' I asked.

Without waiting for an answer, I stormed out of the class, down the stairs and quickly out of the building. I walked without thinking straight and suddenly found myself at the college park. I sat down on a bench and started to take deep breaths in.

Was that really the same boy who stayed in my room ten years ago? I can't believe he's here. I felt angry, I felt shocked, I felt like this was a really strange dream.

'Amy?'

I snapped my head around and saw Terry behind me.

'Oh my god … it really is you,' I whispered.

'Hey …' he said.

I quickly stood up and looked him up and down. He really was tall.

'What are you doing here? When did you come back?' I asked.

'I've only been here a few days.'

'Why are you here?' I demanded. I started to sound angry.

'I … wanted to come back.'

'Do you know the problems you caused running away?!' I was now shouting. He looked petrified.

'Amy … I'm sorry, I had no idea,' he stuttered.

'My dad lost his job because of you! My mom and dad spent weeks looking for you. They were so worried. So scared. So upset! They really cared about you and you just ran away!'

He was suddenly lost for words and any sign of a smirk was long gone.

'I'm … sorry. I really didn't know.'

'You wouldn't, would you?! It was okay for you, you ran off and you left your problems with us.'

His face suddenly changed.

'Hey, wait one second. I LEFT MY PROBLEMS WITH YOU?" he barked back. 'My mom and dad were dead and no one told me. I was happy with your family, I was safe … and after losing one family, I was going to lose another. What choice did I have? No one cared what I wanted. I did the best thing for me and left before I was put with a random family.'

I knew I had spoken out of turn. I had no idea at the time because I was a kid, but there was a lot of information I didn't know about Terry's circumstances. Terry's mom and dad were moving to Byanbythe, but unfortunately died in a car accident at the top of the forest, not far from the tunnel that was built underneath the mountain and the only route out of town. They died during the crash, but Terry survived. I never really understood why Terry had stayed with us at the time, as my dad was a social carer, but it was because Terry recovered in a matter of days. As they had nowhere to keep Terry whilst they sorted social carers (and the fact he only spoke to my dad), they allowed Terry to stay with us.

I didn't want to sound weak and I still felt angry, so I changed the subject.

'Where did you go?' I asked.

He didn't answer straight away, but still looked furious.

'I travelled for a bit, then found my uncle.'

'Uncle? My dad said you had no family.'

'Well, I did. They didn't search very well.'

There was suddenly an awkward silence.

'It was never my dad's fault ...' I finally said.

'I would never blame your dad. He was one of the only people who was there for me. He made me feel happy and I trusted him. If I had my choice, I would have happily stayed with you and your family forever.'

'Why didn't you come back sooner?'

'I was scared. I didn't think anyone would want to see me.'

He was so wrong. I was heartbroken when Terry had left ... but nowhere near as much as my parents. I remembered that it felt like years before everything seemed normal again, and when my dad lost his job, his world was upside down for a long time.

'Why did your dad lose his job?' asked Terry.

'Because you were under his care,' I slowly replied. 'He was blamed for not keeping your safe.'

'I really am sorry, Amy.'

I didn't reply, but turned around to walk away.

'Please don't hate me,' he begged.

I stopped walking, but didn't turn around.

'We were so worried about you … and now you're suddenly back like nothing happened?'

'I have done nothing else but think about you since I left,' he said, and when I suddenly turned around to look at him, he quickly added, 'You were such a good friend.'

I remained silent. After what felt like a huge moment of awkward silence, Terry sighed and continued to talk.

'This wasn't the reunion I planned in my head. I'm sorry, Amy, I really didn't think.'

Terry looked like he wanted to say more, but simply walked away.

*

I didn't stay at college that day, instead deciding to go home early and have some time alone. I had never expected to see Terry again, but certainly never thought a reunion would be like that. Had I overreacted?

I had dreamed that Terry would be found for a long time after he disappeared when he was younger. My dad was in so much trouble after the initial search for him was over, it caused him months of pain … but in those months, he wasn't worried about his job, he was worried about Terry. This was an awful time during my childhood ... but did it end up so bad? I mean, my dad finally got the courage to create his dream job, after all. Yes, the emotional pain was there, but what I failed to see was what Terry was feeling. He had lost his family, was stuck with a strange family and was then being forced to ship to another. He was already quiet and didn't say much - what was going through his mind? I was so upset, then angry, I failed to see his point of view. I suddenly felt guilty and ten years on, nothing had hardly changed; I was still acting ignorant.

I decided not to say anything to Mom or Dad, mainly because I had *no* idea how to approach this subject. What did I say? "Hey everyone! Remember Terry? He's back!" They all knew something was wrong with me, as I was quiet for the remainder of the night, but thankfully my brother, Tim, had won an award at school that day, so all eyes were on him.

In times like these, I didn't feel like I had many people to turn to. I was not an open book and I resented the idea of people sharing their problems on social media. With the subject of Terry not one for my parents, I thought of Laura ... but she wasn't a great shoulder to cry on.

Laura would always find a way to change the conversation to be about her. If I spoke about Terry, she would most likely say something about someone she knew like that and then change the subject to something going on in her world.

I sat in my room in silence and mulled everything over in my head. Eventually, I came to the conclusion that there were no right answers in this scenario, but I certainly was harsh to Terry. I wanted to talk to him again, maybe alone somewhere and really talk this out. I had English again tomorrow morning, so I would wait outside the door for him to appear.

I had planned the conversation in my head and was fired up, ready to confront Terry again. All my efforts were wasted, though, as he didn't turn up for college for the rest of the week.

I felt sick, I felt like I had really fucked up. Had he left? Maybe he had moved away? I must have really upset him and I suddenly felt an infinite amount of guilt in the pit of my stomach. I tried to think outside of the box and for ways I could track him down. I had only just found out that Terry was alive, never mind knowing his mobile number, who his friends were, any potential new family, nor other classes he took? It took until Friday for my one and only plan to form and it was a stupid plan at best. I walked into the Administration and Reception building for both the college and university, debuting my very bad acting skills. A lady at the reception looked up at me whilst she was typing and effortlessly showed me she had no interest in speaking to me. When she didn't say anything, I blurted out my plan.

'Hi! I study English Literature, second year. A new student, Terry Haynes, has missed some crucial coursework and needs the reading material. Our teacher, Louise Thenes has asked if I can take the work to his house?'

The receptionist stopped typing and gave a small sigh that I was sure she was trying to disguise.

'And?' she snapped.

'Well, I don't know where he lives,' I replied.

'Well, Louise Thenes should know better. We cannot simply give out student addresses willy-nilly. It's data and security! Let me check something here,' she said and began furiously typing on her keyboard. 'He hasn't reported his absence, are you sure he's off?'

'Yes, he hasn't been to class since Tuesday. He was also off Monday.' I was starting to feel irritated by this creature of a receptionist.

'Fantastic first week at college, then ... Right, have you got the books? I'll ring his parents or something.'

Parents? Was he adopted? I didn't have time to think much more on this, as I now had to back out of my stupid plan.

'Yes, they are in the class ...' I lied. 'Shall I bring them down?'

'Well, I can't post them to him if I haven't got them?'

I bit my tongue ... I really bit my tongue.

'Thanks,' I sarcastically replied. 'Sorry to have wasted your time.'

Plan failed. What was I going to do now? I had no one to ask, no one to talk to about what had happened and no where to start looking for him. Just like ten years ago, I was going to lose Terry, but this time it was my fault entirely.

Friday had ended and I should have felt elated for the weekend and the fact my first week was over. Instead, I just felt awful and had a headache from everything that had happened. I now truly understood what "sick with worry" felt like.

That night, Laura and a group of friends were going to hit the game arcades in town, then drink underneath the pier on the beach. The arcades were a central place of happiness for tourists, but locals would go there in irony to watch tourists waste money on the rigged machines. I didn't want to go out and had many times in the past made excuses up to not partake in nights out in town. But I also knew if I had stayed home, I would have driven myself crazy over Terry.

Most of the second-year students were all still seventeen, so we couldn't drink legally, but those who drank illegally drank the worst concoctions of alcohol possible. I personally didn't see the appeal in alcohol, but did not push my opinions on others (as I was very much alone when it came to staying sober). Around twenty people were out and I knew most of them from school or college. There were a mixture of boys and girls, and like some mating ritual dance, the boys would mess around in the arcade and the girls would watch and laugh. Some of the boys, ironically in Nick's friendship circle, were all taking turns on the boxing machine, where you would punch a boxing bag and gain a score based on how hard you punched it. I must have had the mind of an eighty-year-old woman, as I just didn't have the patience for boys my age.

We eventually reached the pier and there was a mixture of smoking, drinking, kissing and messing around going on. The sky and sea were black, but the pier was illuminated with bright lights and music. Things were pretty secluded underneath the pier, so anything could go on without the police breaking up the small gatherings. As the night went on, I felt like I couldn't hold in my thoughts any longer and finally reached out to Laura.

'Laura, I think I really fucked up this week …'

She was texting on her phone, but suddenly looked up at me.

'What do you mean?' she asked.

'I fucked up … Do you remember that kid who ran away from my house when I was young?'

She paused, but her face suddenly lit up with realisation.

'What about him?'

'He's back.'

'What?! When? How?'

'I don't know … but he's at our college'

'Oh. My. God! Amy, this is huge! Why haven't you said anything?'

'Because I fucked up.'

'What do you mean?'

'He's in the same English class as me. He tried to talk to me and I just bit his head off. I hadn't even given him a minute to talk and I got nasty.'

'Oh …'

Laura knew the troubles we had when we were younger and it must have dawned on her that she couldn't give an easy reply.

'Have you spoken to him since?'

'No, he hasn't been to college since.'

'I'm sure it's nothing to do with what you said. You know, Beth Blakedon was off for six weeks last year and her boyfriend thought it was because of an argument they had … but she was actually cheating on him with another guy that I was dating at the time, so she was just too embarrassed to turn up to college.'

I looked at her with a pained expression on my face and she immediately knew that what she had said was possibly the most stupid thing she could have said.

'How does that relate to Terry?' I asked.

'Because sometimes people disappear from college and it's not always the reason we think.'

We both laughed and I changed the subject quickly. As I predicted, her reply was as useful as a cat flap on a submarine.

'There you are!' called an unwelcome voice from behind me. 'Hey, babe!'

My night had changed from bad to worse. This voice made me shiver from the bottom of my spine, causing goosebumps from my head to toe. I turned around to see my ex-boyfriend, Nick, standing there with the same vacant expression.

'Oh … hi,' I replied, trying to hide all disdain from my voice.

'I didn't think you liked coming down here!'

He grabbed me into a hug and attempted to kiss me. I quickly turned my head so he just caught my cheek.

'Well,' I said, 'I'm out tonight.'

'Great! Let's have a drink.'

'You know I don't drink.'

'That's fine, you can tell me about your first week of college.'

He led me away from Laura, who chuckled at the look of horror on my face.

Nick tried not to acknowledge that we had split up. He was also very hands-on and attempted to flirt with me whenever he had a chance. I had never had sex with Nick, but he liked to tell everyone that we had. Half of the time, I thought he wanted to be with me because I was the only girl he hadn't slept with; I was a challenge, one he was adamant he was going to conquer.

I was very vague about college and treated the conversation like I was talking to an auntie that you hated to speak to at a family party. I could have told Nick that I had murdered a man and he wouldn't have listened.

'Cool, sounds like you had a good week,' he said, pretending to listen. 'I've missed you, you know.'

Very creepily, he grabbed me around the waist. I pulled myself away.

'Nick, we're not together.'

'Amy, I have no idea why we split up, but I'm sorry. I know we're a great couple, let's just give it a go again.'

'No, Nick. Please just take no for an answer.'

'I know you want to be with me, Amy, you're just shy. I see you staring at me all the time.'

He was right, I did stare, but purely because I questioned why I ever went out with him. He grabbed my hand and I started to get angry, thinking of ways I could easily escape.

'Look, Nick …' I started, 'I'm sorry, you're great and everything -'

'See! You do like me!' he shouted. 'Look, we haven't got to rush back into things. Just go on one date with me? Let me take you for a drink and show you how much I want to be with you.'

I reminded myself how I had ended up staying with him for so long. It was because I suffered from an extreme case of being socially awkward, terrible with difficult situations and mostly took the easy options, instead of doing what was right.

'Okay, whatever. Look, I need to go.'

I quickly pulled my hand away from his and walked back to Laura. I heard his friends cheer in the background, as he must have walked over and made up a victorious story of getting back with me; I instantly regretted my decision and now had to think of a new excuse not to see him …

After the shit turn of events with Nick and the lack of inspirational conversation from Laura, I texted my dad around eleven o'clock, and like the amazing parent he was, he drove down to the arcade to meet me and take me home. My parents were so relaxed about me going out and never wanted me to get taxis or buses late at night, so I never stayed out too late and they never minded picking me up. They never set curfews, never asked what I was doing and never once worried I was going to do something stupid.

'Hey, Red, good night?' he asked.

'It was fine - and don't call me that.'

'Drank much?' he asked (it was a running joke because he found it highly amusing that I didn't drink with the other kids my age).

'Loads. I'm so drunk I had to take drugs to balance it out.'

'That's my girl!' he laughed.

We sat in silence as we drove out of town and into the pitch-black forest. Against my better judgement, I decided to test the water with my Dad.

'Dad?'

'Oh no …' he laughed again.

'Do you ever think about Terry?'

I watched his smile fade and he strained his eyes as he tried to think.

'All the time. I still worry about him,' he replied. 'That's a really random thing to ask. I haven't heard you say his name since you were little.'

'No reason, it's just … something reminded me of him the other day. I just wondered if you still thought of him.'

'Of course.'

The silence returned and I could tell Dad was now deep in thought. I decided that it was for the best that I wouldn't tell him about college and my encounter with Terry.

'I bet you he drinks with his friends, though,' he said and began to laugh once more.

I began to laugh, but quickly stopped myself; I had promised myself that I would never acknowledge one of my dad's bad jokes.

*

I somehow managed to survive that weekend. I received constant texts from Laura about Terry, which angered me enough to forget about my own worries. Her questions never seemed to be out of concern, more out of interest and gossip.

Monday was my main day dedicated to English and as I entered the class room, I dropped my books on the floor. It was Terry! He was sitting at his desk! Everyone was now looking at me, but I quickly picked up my things and walked over to his desk.

'You're here!' I said, my voice embarrassingly high-pitched.

Terry looked confused, but slowly smiled as he stared at me.

'Yeah, we have English on Mondays don't we?' he asked.

Louise walked into the room and called for the class to sit down. Before I could answer

Terry, I begrudgingly returned to my desk. Unfortunately, the morning was dedicated to Louise talking at the front of the class, with very little opportunity to talk (specifically, me talking to Terry). Eventually, it was my first break and I bolted over to Terry's desk.

'Where have you been?' I asked, not giving him a chance to speak.

'Are you always this bossy?' he replied with a smirk.

'I thought you had left.'

'Left?'

'College. Town. You were off almost all week.'

'Wow, this college is really strict on attendance. I had five missed calls from the Truancy Team ... someone was trying to send homework home.'

'Where were you, though?'

The classroom was now empty whilst everyone was on break.

'I had a migraine,' he replied. 'I get them a lot.'

'Oh ...'

I suddenly felt stupid.

'Why?' Terry asked. 'I got the impression you weren't happy to see me the last time we spoke.'

'Yeah … about that. Terry, I'm really sorry.'

His expression changed and he looked surprised at what I had said. Did he know me so well already that he knew I didn't say sorry often?

'Thanks … I guess I have a lot to apologise for too.'

'Look … I didn't give you a lot of opportunity to talk. I was hoping we could maybe talk … maybe somewhere private?'

This conversation felt awkward, on both parts. He raised an eyebrow and didn't reply straight away.

'Okay, yeah. What did you have in mind?'

'Maybe a walk? I know some nice trails in the forest.'

'Yeah, sounds good,' he agreed. 'I can drive if you want?'

'Wow, you drive?' I asked, a hint of jealousy in my voice.

'Yeah. Why, don't you?'

'No, I crashed the car on my first lesson. Kind of put me off.'

We both laughed and people started to return to the classroom as the breaktime ended.

'Okay, after college?'

He winked at me … and I felt a very quick flurry of something in my stomach. I quickly ignored the stupid thought that popped into my head and returned to my desk.

TERRY

Get those thoughts out of your head, Terry.

But … she was so beautiful. I remembered feeling the same as a kid, but nowhere near as much as I did now. She was the most beautiful person I had ever seen. Her long red hair that almost reached her waist, her dark eyes (almost black), the freckles on her pale white skin. She was angry, spirited and everything about her made her unique. Even the way she dressed made me lust for her - she didn't dress like the other college girls. She dressed grungy and a bit goth, like the best bands of the '90s. I had thought about her every single day since the moment I took those headphones off in her living room and now it felt like a dream to finally be near her again.

Get those thoughts out of your head, Terry!

I reminded myself over and over again that I had already fucked up any kind of friendship with her. How could I have been so stupid and not thought about the consequences of running away?

And regardless of my relationship with her … things were already complicated. The last thing I needed was to drag others into my mess. No … I was going to keep things simple, be her friend again (if she let me) and keep my distance.

I thought I was going to love studying English Literature. I had spent most of my life reading books, really investing in characters and stories of faraway lands … but this poetry stuff and especially this extremely intense list of poems we were having to study wasn't my thing. The only benefit to this class so far was being close to Amy and like some weird twist of fate, we were talking to each other again, right where we left off.

My only problem now was, what did I tell her? Did I tell her a story? Part of the truth and mostly story or … the truth?

AMY

College finally ended and I walked with Terry from our classroom to the huge car park at the front of the campus. We did small talk and I asked him how he was finding college. He told me how much he was enjoying English and all the amazing poems, but something told me he was being sarcastic.

The car park was huge (and it had to be for the amount of pupils and staff on campus). Most cars for people our age were old, retro and mostly beaten up, as they had been passed down from parents. It was obvious if someone's parent was a celebrity, as their cars would stick out amongst the crowd.

'So, which one is your car?'

'It's not a car, it's a truck,' Terry replied and pointed in the distance.

It was not what I had expected. Had I not known Terry, I would have associated that truck with someone who worked in construction or did some extreme sport. It was a huge, bright orange pick-up truck, complete with the cargo bed at the back; it looked brand new.

'Wow ...'

'What's wrong?' he asked.

'I did not expect that. That's a huge car - truck.'

'I know, I love it so much.'

'Whose is it?'

He paused and looked at me with a confused expression.

'Mine. Who else's would it be?'

'It's just ... so big and so new! You could live in there!'

Terry began to laugh and we climbed into his giant army tank of a car. Inside was extremely roomy and could easily have been a small camper van.

'I have lived in it. I travelled over the summer and pretty much slept in here every night.'

'Wow … that sounds like a dream. Who did you go with?'

I noticed that every time I asked him a question, he took his time to answer, almost like he was thinking about what to say.

'Just me.'

'Oh, didn't you travel with your uncle?'

He began to laugh again and we drove through the forest.

'I have a lot to tell you,' he said. 'How about you tell me where to drive and I'll tell you everything from the start?'

I agreed and guided him to a National Trust trail around ten miles away from college and deep into the forest. We mostly sat in silence until we parked up at the small car park for the trail. It was empty and it seemed like no one else was around as we started to walk.

'Okay, let's start from the start,' he finally said.

'Where did you go the night you ran away? I heard you went to the hospital?'

'Ah yeah … that's a good place to start. I was a fool that night, I thought I could walk straight into the hospital and find my parents waiting for me. The nurse I asked about my parents put me in a room and went to call social services. I quickly put two and two together and realised my parents were dead. So I ran away again.'

'Where did you go?'

'I overheard a couple travelling back to Saundersfoot, which was a few hours away. I decided to sneak into their boot.'

'What? They didn't notice.'

'No, I did it with great sneaking skills,' he joked.

I didn't say anything, which prompted him to carry on.

'I won't bore you with too many details, but I knew I had an uncle in the West Midlands, so kept hitching car rides until I made my way there.'

'Didn't people find it suspicious that a young boy was hitch-hiking?' I asked.

'Apparently not.'

'Why didn't you tell my dad? Or me? If we knew you had an uncle, things would have been different?'

'Because I was happy staying with you, I didn't want to go to my uncle's.'

'I'm sorry, Terry.'

'Don't be. When I found my uncle, it was a long process with social services, but he became my legal guardian. I lived in the Midlands until I was old enough to move away.'

'Terry, we had no idea. Social services never told us any of this, neither did the police! We worried you were dead.'

'I'm sorry, I really didn't intend to do that. I think because of safeguarding, a lot of details were not disclosed.'

'Were you happy with your uncle?' I asked.

'He was okay. He was pretty quiet, didn't really like kids, so left me to it.'

'Does he live with you now?'

'No.'

'Who lives with you?'

'No one.'

'What? Terry, you can't live alone!'

'I can, actually, I'm eighteen.'

'But … you're alone.'

'I actually like being alone, I've gotten used to it.'

'Where is your uncle? Back in the Midlands?'

'No, he died early in the summer. They agreed to not re-home me as I was going to turn eighteen not long after he died.'

'Oh, Terry, I am so sorry to hear that.'

He smiled at me and we continued to walk through the forest. Poor Terry, he had lost everyone around him.

'Are you okay, though?' I asked. 'How are you managing to survive? Do you have money?'

'Yes, luckily my uncle was quite well off. He left all his money to me, hence the nice car.'

He seemed really detached from his uncle, like he wasn't bothered at all about his death. I didn't want to pry or push the subject any further, especially after how I had acted when I first met Terry at college.

'So, you decided to come back here?' I asked.

'Yes. I spent most of the summer travelling around in my truck, but ultimately I always wanted to come back and see you,' he said, but quickly added, 'And your family.'

'Did your uncle never want to bring you here when you were younger?' I asked, forgetting that I had just made a mental note not to ask about his uncle.

'No, he was worried he would get in trouble with social services … and I suppose his brother died here, so it wasn't a great place.'

'I'm sorry.'

'Please stop saying sorry,' he pleaded.

'Sorry.'

We both laughed.

'Why does this feel so awkward?' he said. 'I genuinely have missed your family so much, I dreamed about coming to see you for years.'

We stopped walking. We stared at each other and both smiled.

'I really am sorry for shouting at you on that first day,' I finally said. 'I was in so much shock.'

'Well, it sounds like I caused a lot of pain, Amy. Maybe it's time I asked you some questions? Like what happened after I left?'

'Well, not much more than I already told you. Social services really gave my dad a hard time, they said he should have been watching you and the house obviously wasn't "safe". He lost his job.'

Terry looked awkward and suddenly faced away from me, looking into the forest.

'Your dad is such a great man,' he said. 'He was the only person I wanted to talk to in hospital, that's the only reason they let me stay with your family. He put so much at risk and I threw it back in his face.'

'I don't think you meant to, Terry, you were going through a lot. And now we've spoken, it makes a lot more sense.'

He didn't reply and I still couldn't see his face, so I carried on talking.

'You did him a favour, he now has his dream job!'

'What do you mean?'

'He started up his own American football team. He's been a huge success.'

Terry gave a small sigh of relief.

'I would love to see him and your mom. Do you think that's possible?'

'Of course,' I replied. 'I just don't know how to start that conversation.

'Maybe I could burst out of a cake or something?'

We both laughed and it suddenly felt a lot less awkward. I was starting to feel comfortable around Terry again.

'I really have missed you, Terry. I never stopped thinking about you. I'm so glad you were safe and with family.'

'I missed you too.'

He grabbed me into a hug and he held me tight. This was the nicest hug I had ever had and I felt warm just being close to him. I kept feeling things that I should not have felt and I kept pushing them to the back of my mind. We let go and just smiled at each other.

'At least I have a friend here,' he said. 'Byanbythe's too big!'

We began to walk back towards the car park, as it felt like we had been walking for some time.

'Where are you living, anyway?'

'Up in the forest,' he replied.

'Wow! You must have a fancy house.'

'I don't really like it. My uncle actually bought it for me before he died.'

I looked confused and he must have sensed that, as he continued to talk.

'We had always agreed that I could move out when I was eighteen and he would buy me a place to live.'

'Wow, that's a lot to take in,' I replied.

We had walked back to the truck. After climbing in, we both sat there in silence.

'Do you want me to take you home?' he asked.

'If you don't mind? I guess my family will start to wonder where I am.'

We began to drive and I gave him directions to my house. As he drove, an impulsive idea entered my thoughts and I spoke without giving it much thought.

'Maybe you could come in? Maybe the best way is to just get it over with?'

He turned white as a ghost and did not answer. He started to fidget in his chair and avoided looking in my direction.

'Okay,' he finally said.

'We don't have to,' I said and added, 'Sorry, I didn't mean to put you on the spot.'

'No, you're right. I'm just worried they will hate me.'

'They won't, they both think about you all the time. Plus, you survived my rampage on your first day of college … If you can survive that, you can survive anything.'

He smiled, but concentrated on the road ahead, suddenly looking extremely serious. Was this a good idea?

TERRY

I felt sick; I was extremely scared and had no idea how this was going to pan out. The conversation with Amy had gone really well, better than I expected. The hug felt so warm and a little too good … but to see Michael and Lisa again? That was a whole new level of fear.

As we parked on her drive, she asked me to sit in the truck and wait while she walked inside and spoke to her parents. I agreed and sat nervously waiting for her to come back to me. I looked at the house and it still looked the same as before. Beautiful old bricks and lots of dark wooden panels that covered most of the house, complimenting the dark brown windows. Most houses looked similar in Byanbythe and they all seemed to blend well with the colour of the trees and the mountain and forest.

I stared down the street and my eyes fixated on the spot where I had stood that night, where Amy had chased me before I ran away. How naive and stupid I had been. I really should have stayed ... would things have turned out differently?

I wasn't expecting Michael to walk onto the drive ... but he did and he slowly looked at me, like he was looking at a ghost. I opened my truck door and approached him. Neither of us said anything and tears were streaming down his face. I couldn't tell if he was super angry or really upset.

'Is it really you?' he asked.

'Erm ... yeah,' I replied.

He still looked the same; light brown hair, thick-rimmed black glasses and a thick moustache. He had a warm, gentle look about him that complimented his warm, gentle personality.

'What was the first thing you ate in the hospital when I sat with you?' he asked.

That was a strange question and I really had to think back. What had I eaten? Michael sat with me in the hospital from the day I had woken up from the accident, right through to the moment we left to stay at his house.

'Tomato soup and bread and butter pudding?' I finally replied.

He let out a small weep and suddenly grabbed me into a tight hug. He was now sobbing uncontrollably. Behind him stood Lisa, who was also crying. She too had not changed, with her short blonde hair, bright green eyes and the most gentle smile you could expect from a mother. When Michael finally let me go, she too grabbed me for a hug.

I had no idea what came over me, but I too started to cry and then Amy started to cry and we all stood on their driveway crying.

*

The evening consisted of me telling all of my stories that I had told Amy and answering lots of questions about my life over the last ten years. I tried to apologise so much, but neither Michael nor Lisa would accept it, telling me I had no reason to apologise and they should have been there for me. I tried to reject this idea, but they insisted that they regretted their actions when I was expected to move to a foster family.

We laughed, we cried, we drank lots of tea and Lisa kept feeding me cakes. I did not expect this and could not have imagined this scenario to have happened in a hundred years. They kept asking me questions and showed huge concern when I told them I was living alone.

'You can't live alone, Terry,' said Lisa. 'You have to come back and live with us!'

I insisted I was okay, but promised I would be visiting them every week now that I lived here. They insisted that I visit every day and I cried. This was the first time since I ran away that I felt like I was part of a family. Michael and Lisa just felt like parents and all of those feelings before I ran away came back; I felt safe, I felt protected and I felt like I belonged.

I just continued to apologise and they tried to not make me feel guilty; they acted like loving parents and it was obvious how much they cared about me.

'I thought you were both going to hate me,' I admitted.

'Hate you?' said Lisa. 'My boy, we loved you like our own child … We worried about you every day. Just to know you were okay is enough for us.'

'But I caused you so much trouble. Michael, you lost your job!'

'That doesn't matter,' said Michael. 'Your safety is what matters. Plus, I didn't really enjoy my job … I ended up pursuing my dream instead.'

The vibe changed and from sadness came enthusiasm, happiness and passion; Michael explained his full American football career and all the successes he had achieved.

Amy sat there and listened and she didn't stop smiling. I caught her eyes a few times and she continued to smile at me. When Michael had finished, I was invited to stay for tea, which I accepted.

I finally met Amy's baby brother, Tim, who was only a couple of months old when I lived here. He was now ten and very small for his age. He was quiet and didn't really say much, instead playing on a portable game console throughout the night.

Michael and Lisa asked me lots of questions about college and then Michael asked about my truck. When they asked where I lived, I gave the same short reply as I did to Amy and they didn't seem to pick up on what I had said.

It was starting to get late and even though I didn't want to leave, I decided it was time to go back home.

'I don't want you to leave,' pleaded Michael.

We laughed, but he grabbed me into another hug.

'Terry, please treat this house as your second home,' said Lisa. 'I want to see you here every day.'

'I will. I promise, I'm not going anywhere this time,' I replied and I truly meant it. I felt happy for the first time in many years.

I left the house and Amy walked me to my truck on her own, which I was grateful for.

'Wow, I didn't expect that to go so well,' I admitted.

She smiled and beamed up at me.

'Well, it's official, let's forget the last ten years,' said Amy. 'You're now part of the family again.'

'Does that make us brother and sister?' I asked, but suddenly regretted what I had said.

'Erm … I don't think I like the idea of having you as a brother,' she admitted. 'I certainly don't see you in that way.'

'Friends?'

She hesitated, but finally agreed.

'Friends,' she mocked and extended a hand out to shake my hand.

I grabbed her into another hug and again, absorbed that feeling of pure euphoria, just by holding her.

'Do you have a phone?' she asked. 'Maybe we could text each other?'

We exchanged numbers and it suddenly felt awkward. Why did it suddenly feel awkward to say goodbye to her?

'I'll see you at college, then?' I asked.

'Definitely. Text me later?'

I agreed and after lingering for a few moments, I realised I was just making things more awkward.

I waved and finally got into my truck. I drove away and started to think about Amy immediately. I felt so happy, and things felt so right. I drove through the dark forest … when it suddenly hit me.

Oh no …

That sickening feeling in my stomach. The same feeling every time was back … but it had never happened this fast before? I had to get home, as quickly as possible. I put my foot on the pedal and sped like a police car through the forest, trying to find my way back home. I started to sweat, I felt like I couldn't breathe and my arms started to twitch. I drove faster and more erratically, which made the sharp and tight forest roads extremely difficult to manoeuvre around. I didn't care what I hit, I just knew I had to get home - and fast.

And all my thoughts of the Doories, of Amy or any perfect life had gone, as the world around me started to black out. The roads were getting darker, I felt weak and I suddenly felt tired. I just about managed to park my truck on the drive and dropped out of the passenger seat and onto the drive, wriggling around like a helpless cripple. I blacked out and I entered the nightmare.

AMY

I felt over the moon. Things had turned out so well and, if honest, I had never seen my mom and dad so happy before. I had sat and watched everyone talk all night and watched Terry become more comfortable as the night carried on.

I had these feelings that I was trying to ignore. It was plain and obvious that Terry was really attractive. The colour of his hair was unique, his eyes were bright and he seemed more of a man and less of a boy. He was gentle in the way he spoke and he was the kind of person who would rather listen to someone speak, instead of talking himself. Yes, I did find him attractive, but after all the emotions of the last week, it was easy to mistake my feelings, as I felt so overwhelmed. Even if I did find him attractive ... it would be too weird. My family thought he was family ... and once upon a time, I guess I did too. To think of him as anything more would be wrong ... wouldn't it?

After Terry had left, I caught up with Mom and Dad and explained the events of the last week.

'Poor lad,' said Dad. 'You really gave him a hard time at college, Amy.'

'I was in shock!'

We all agreed how it felt like fate that Terry had returned and we had to do everything we could to make him feel like family.

'I don't like him living alone,' Mom stressed.

'Give him space, Lisa, he's obviously used to it,' said Dad. 'I don't think he was very close to his uncle.'

'No ... I don't think he was either,' I agreed.

'First thing tomorrow I am calling Jerry Jones, my old boss. I think he still works at social services.'

'Why?' I asked.

'I think they should know. It doesn't matter now, but they all thought he was dead ... The police searched for years. I also think they deserve a kicking too; how did they not know he had an uncle? How did they not locate him in the Midlands?' he ranted.

I also thought it was strange, but I was also worried that it would scare Terry away if we brought up old wounds. I think Mom also agreed, but she didn't say anything.

We all went to bed quite late and as soon as I lay down, I decided to text Terry.

My mom and dad were so happy seeing you..
Looking forward to next time. Xx

I waited for his reply; would he text me back straight away? I waited for an hour, pretending that I wasn't bothered if he replied or not ... but there I was checking my phone every few minutes. By the time I had finally fallen asleep, I still had no reply.

*

I had woken up the next day and immediately checked my phone; Terry had not texted back. Whilst I felt a little disappointed, I tried not to let it bother me. It was late and no doubt the emotional visit had exhausted him.

I quickly got ready for college and caught the bus. Did I text him again? Would that make me look too keen? But then again, how could I look keen if I didn't have feelings for him? I lied to myself.

As I crossed the road from the bus stop, I didn't walk through the main entrance to the campus. Instead, I took a detour to the car park. I looked for his bright orange pick-up truck … and for the second time that day, felt disappointed when I couldn't see any sign of him.

The day dragged until it was finally time for English, but a small feeling in my gut told me he wasn't going to be there … and alas, I was right. Where was he? I decided to cave in and send him another text.

Hey, where are you? Have you got another migraine?
Xx

He didn't text me back and as the day ended, I slumped out of college, feeling more upset that I cared to admit.

'What's wrong with you?' asked Laura on the bus journey home.

'Nothing.'

'Have you seen Terry yet?'

I could have told Laura about last night … but I really didn't feel up to it, so I lied and said I still hadn't seen him.

I continually checked my phone and he still hadn't texted back. Maybe he did have a migraine? I had heard they were extremely painful and the last thing people did was look at bright lights (especially mobile phones). I admitted defeat and accepted I wouldn't see Terry for a few days.

'Hey, Red,' called Dad as I walked into the house.

'Stop calling me that,' I grumbled.

'You wouldn't believe the day I've had!' he declared.

'Why?'

'I rang Jerry Jones, the smug prick. He's now a director! Well, he simply did not want to believe me about Terry, said he had seen the report in person that he had no family! Well, I drove down there and wiped that smug smirk off his face. They checked the system again and lo and behold it was all updated with Terry's life in the Midlands and his uncle, John Haynes, becoming his guardian. He simply could not believe it!'

My dad continued to rant and I felt like he had some closure giving his old boss some grief; he deserved it and it was now a fact that my dad had well and truly been mistreated and unfairly dismissed.

I continually checked my phone, even though I knew he wasn't going to text back.

I sulked for the rest of the week and almost felt like I dragged myself everywhere I travelled. Friday finally arrived and English was my last lesson of the day. To top my mood off, an unwelcome voice called behind me as I was walking towards my class.

'Babe!' called Nick.

'Stop calling me babe.'

'What's wrong?'

Nick was never good at detecting emotions nor tone of people's voices, nor did he think anyone could feel anything other than pure lust for him.

'Just wondering when we are going on that date?'

'Yeah … about that …' I began, trying to muster up courage to finally end this weird relationship once and for all.

'Look, don't back out, Amy. You need to stop trying to run away from your feelings.

Everyone practically thinks we're together anyway,' he said, but his voice became serious.

'And why do they think that?' I growled. 'Because you lied to your friends?'

'Amy, I don't know why you are like this. We've been together for a long time.'

'If you added up the actual time we spent together, it would be equal to a week!'

I wasn't lying. Although I had been with Nick for a few years, we didn't actually spend that much time together; our whole relationship was hanging out at parties, with friends or his feeble attempts to persuade me to stay over at his house. We never really dated, we never texted, we never spoke about why the stars floated in the sky … Instead, we spoke about how good he looked playing rugby. Whatever feelings of attraction I had originally were purely physical attraction, which then proceeded to feeling regret and being too socially awkward to split up with him.

'Look, you're not being fair. Let's just go for a drink after college today.'

'I don't want to get back with you, Nick. Why can't you get the message?'

I started to walk away and I could sense he was in complete shock, almost as if this was the first time I had told him that I didn't want to be with him.

'I'll be waiting in the car park for you! Please think about it!' I heard him shout in the distance.

I felt so angry, so frustrated … How stupid could someone actually be? I was so flustered that I hadn't even realised that Terry was back in class.

'Hey, Amy,' he said.

I looked up and looked again; I couldn't believe it!

'Where have you been?' I asked.

'Migraine. Sorry, I only read your text this morning.'

He looked rough. He looked very tired, pale and like he needed to go back to bed.

'I was worried about you,' I admitted.

'Don't worry about me, how could I ever be ill reading *Paradise Lost*?'

We both laughed.

'Are you sure you picked the right class? I don't think you like English very much …' I joked.

'I didn't expect poetry … but I guess I get to be with you. That makes it worth it.'

I felt like I was going red. Was he flirting with me? I decided to change the subject quickly.

'Are you sure you're feeling better?'

'I'm good, I'm used to getting them now. I just need to sit in darkness for a few days and sleep it off.'

'Wow, you sound like a vampire.'

'Oh god, you don't read those kinds of books, do you?'

'If you are referring to Bram Stoker, then yes, I do like those books.'

'Well, I was referring to more modern vampire books, but you have redeemed yourself,' he laughed.

Louise entered the room and everyone began to take their seats.

'Hey, Amy, fancy doing something after college?' Terry asked.

My face must have been as red as my hair now. What was wrong with me? I quickly agreed and returned to my desk. I felt flustered. I really couldn't control my feelings. I needed to suppress them … but I felt like I was being really stupid. I had barely spoken to Terry for less than two weeks, but I felt so anxious around him now; I was self-conscious and to put it simply, I liked the way he looked at me.

I couldn't concentrate during the lesson and I just about heard Louise comment that we were going to be spending one final week on poetry until the next subject began. When class finished,

Terry stood next to my desk, pretending to celebrate at the thought of poetry almost being over.

'Where shall we go, then?' he asked as we walked out of the class.

'We could have a coffee?' I suggested. 'There's a few nice places in town?'

'Sounds like a plan. Let's go!'

We walked out of class and towards the car park. Through the excitement of seeing Terry again, I had completely forgotten about my previous encounter with Nick. As we were walking towards Terry's truck, Nick drove his car and blocked our path.

'There you are!' he said as he rolled down his car window.

'Oh shit …' I mumbled under my breath.

'Where are we going, then, Amy?' asked Nick.

I felt shocked; I had no idea what to say or do. Thankfully, if Nick did something to annoy me, I felt like the anger mustered the right words to say, compensating for my awkwardness.

'Who's he?' asked Nick, as he looked Terry up and down with a face of disgust.

'Oh, sorry, I'm Terry. I'm an old friend of Amy's,' said Terry, who extended his hand out to shake Nick's and introduce himself. This was the first time Terry had met Nick.

Nick didn't shake his hand and instead continued to give Terry a threatening look.

'Amy, come on, get in the car,' said Nick.

Terry looked at me and then back at Nick.

'Sorry, Amy, I didn't know you had other plans. Honestly, we can rearrange?' suggested Terry, who seemed to not realise that Nick was being aggressive towards him.

'No, it's fine, Terry. Nick, I told you I didn't want to go out,' I growled, finding my inner voice. 'Come on, Terry, let's go.'

Terry looked confused, but slowly backed away from Nick's car.

'Oh, I see, you're with someone else? Boy, do I look like a fool!' laughed Nick.

I grabbed Terry's hand and started to pull him away from Nick's car.

'It was over a long time ago, Nick!' I called over my shoulder and watched how he looked disgusted, confused and ready for an argument. As we climbed into Terry's truck, I could see Nick now driving around the car park, not once losing eye contact with us.

'He seems … nice?' said Terry. 'I didn't know you had a boyfriend.'

'I don't, he's an ex. We haven't been together for a while.'

'Oh right … did he know that?' joked Terry and he began to laugh. Suddenly, I began to laugh too and all my anger seemed to fade away. 'I am sure he thinks we can't see him staring at us.'

'Yeah, he's not exactly intelligent.'

'Maybe we should kiss each other just to really piss him off?'

I felt myself going red again.

Terry started up his truck and drove out of college. I told him the directions to a beautiful coffee shop in town I loved to sit in.

'Oh shit, mind if we take a detour home?' he asked. 'I forgot my wallet and phone.'

Terry did a U-turn in the road and started to drive through the forest towards Mount Cudd.

'I'll literally run and get it,' he said. 'I promise I won't be long, you don't even have to leave the car.'

I was going to finally see where he lived, although I got the impression he didn't want to show me his house. I was now intrigued and decided to push my luck.

'It's only fair I see your house, you practically lived in mine when you were a kid,' I joked.

He looked uneasy about showing me, but accepted that I could come in. We were now passing some of the bigger houses of the forest and soon enough passing mansions owned by various celebrities.

'Terry … do you really live up here?'

He didn't reply and he finally turned into the last road before the end of the forest, Great Western View, which was always known to have the most expensive houses of all. As we rode down the small road, I looked in awe at houses the size of my entire street.

We slowed down and Terry drove through some electric gates to the very last house in the street, It was the penthouse on Great Western View, the most amazing house in all of Byanbythe.

'Oh my god, you're the one who bought the penthouse?'

Terry looked annoyed.

'My uncle bought it, it wasn't my choice. I hate it.'

'Why? It's the most amazing house you can buy!'

'Maybe, but I still hate it.'

Was he being modest? The house was a huge stone house, mostly covered in large glass windows. It was built into the side of the mountain and had the greatest view of the whole forest, town and sea. I slowly followed Terry into his house, where the front door led us into a huge open area, the size of which felt like it belonged at college. I was starting to wonder if Terry had brought me here to show off, but as I looked around the house, I quickly figured out that he wasn't showing off at all.

'It's empty?' I asked.

The house was almost empty, there were only three items in the entire room, which could have fit several houses in. In the very middle of the room (which had the most beautiful, oak floor) was a double bed, a box full of what looked like books and a TV on the floor. The kitchen area, at the back of the room, didn't even have plates or utensils that had dedicated shelves waiting on the wall.

'I think I left my phone in the toilet,' said Terry, who ignored my question.

He quickly entered the only other room in the house, which must have been the toilet. I looked at the staircase, which led to a garden terrace on the first floor and I couldn't believe how beautiful it looked.

I slowly walked over to his bed and box of books. The box was huge, and full of classic books and plays. Shakespeare, *Harry Potter,*

Dorian Grey, The Great Gatsby, War and Peace; there were hundreds of the greatest books known to man.

'Got them, let's go!' said Terry, who quickly emerged from the toilet.

'Terry, why is it empty?' I asked again.

'I've only just moved in,' he quickly replied.

'Tell me the truth.'

He sighed and started walking around the room, looking around as if this was the first time he had seen the house.

'I didn't choose this place, my uncle did,' he said. 'And I hate it.'

'Why, though? It's beautiful.'

'It's too much for one person. I would have been happy living in my truck.'

'I know many families who would swap with you,' I joked.

'They can have it.' He continued to walk around. 'I'm happy with just a bed, some books and a TV.'

'Does it get lonely?' I asked.

'Always. It's funny, I was never lonely until I sat in this house.'

It did feel lonely; the house was bare and just didn't feel like a home.

'Shall we go?' I quickly asked.

Terry seemed more than happy to leave his house. Like his uncle, I decided his house was another subject I wouldn't mention again, although it was something else that now worried me.

We drove down to the coffee shop, which was a single square building that sat by the pier. I loved this coffee shop because it was big, quiet and always had comfy sofas to lounge on. I had spent a lot of money and time sitting in here and just drinking coffee whilst I read my books. Terry bought the coffees and insisted that I didn't pay. We sat down together and admired the view from the large window next to us that overlooked the beach and the sea.

'Shame we didn't invite your boyfriend,' he joked.

'Oh great, another boy that doesn't listen. I said he wasn't my boyfriend.'

'He seemed to think so. I must admit, I know we barely know each other, but he doesn't seem your type.'

'He's not, that's why.'

'Why did you get with him, then?' asked Terry.

'Because I was young, stupid and once thought he was attractive.'

'So that's the kind of guy you go for?'

'No, I made a bad choice.'

'So, what kind of guy do you go for?'

'Wow, we're going for these questions already?' I joked.

I felt myself going red again and I was wondering why he was discussing this area of my life. He smirked and stared at me.

'We don't have to go into those questions, I was just interested,' he replied.

'Well … I don't have a type. I've had a few dates, a few boyfriends … but I guess I've struggled to find that spark with someone.'

'You must know something you like in someone?'

'I like people who listen, who have brains and a good conversation.'

'And Nick didn't have those?'

'No, he only likes sports, talks about himself or sports and thinks sex is the definition of a relationship.'

'He sounds charming. I don't think he liked me much …' joked Terry. Everything he said seemed to be playful, but in a nice way.

'Yeah you're definitely not his type,' I answered and Terry pulled a sad face and pretended to cry. 'Do you have a type?'

'I don't know,' he replied. 'I've never had a girlfriend.'

'Really? That shocks me.'

'I didn't really get a chance. I was home-schooled.'

'Wow … you're full of surprises …'

Never had a girlfriend. Lived alone. Home school. No family. I really started to sense a sadness from Terry. He seemed so kind and gentle, but his life had been full of tragedy. Some people never experienced half of the stuff he had already endured.

'It's not so bad, I have money, a house and I feel like I'm starting to build a new life here. It was really good to see your family too. Some might say I'm lucky.'

I felt choked … All I did was complain about Byanbythe, about being stuck here and yet Terry had lost so much, but was simply happy just to be here.

'You're so positive, Terry. I really find it inspirational how happy you act, considering everything that's gone on.'

'Come on, I'm in a coffee shop with you, it can't get much better than this.'

I smiled and for the first time in a long time, it felt like a real smile. I always thought everyone had different smiles, but it was rare that people gave a real smile; one truly full of happiness, and warmth.

'You know, you don't have to stay in that house on your own. I bet my mom and dad would love to have you stay at our house.'

'That just shows how amazing your mom and dad are.'

'They see you as family.'

He smiled a warm smile and stared out of the window at the pier.

'Can I ask you something strange?'

'What's that?'

'Don't tell anyone where I live. Especially your parents.'

I was really taken aback by his request.

'Why?'

'I hate it. I hate people thinking that I'm rich and that I have this great house. I don't want the money and I don't want the house. In fact, when I get a job and earn my own money, I'll buy my own house and give my uncle's house and money to some charity.'

'You shouldn't feel that way,' I argued. 'It's not your fault and it's certainly nothing to be ashamed about.'

'I do, though. I'd happily live with you.'

'Well … I'm sure that's not out of the question … if that's what you wanted.'

His face was serious and deep in thought, but after taking a sip of his coffee, he suddenly smiled and returned to his cheerful manner. I was starting to guess when Terry was about to make a joke, as he would smile a wicked smile, full of mischief and cheek.

'Would we get to share a room again?'

I burst out laughing.

'I don't think my dad would allow that. It's a bit different now I'm seventeen …'

'Was I the first guy you slept with?'

'Of course not, I had hundreds of boy sleepovers …' I sarcastically replied.

'I was so stubborn. I remember you said something about me being scared and I acted all defensive! I'm glad I slept in your room, though, that was really kind of you.'

'I wouldn't have done that for just anyone, you know …'

'I should hope so! Shame, I may have to sneak in again …'

He was flirting again. I felt like I had to ask him now.

'Terry … are you flirting with me?' I felt like I was actually turning into a tomato now, a big, ginger-haired tomato; I was the opposite of sexy right now. He suddenly didn't seem so confident and started to fidget where he sat.

'Erm … I … um … well …' he bumbled.

I couldn't help but laugh. 'Wow, you don't seem as confident now, do you, Terry?'

'Shut up, you've put me on the spot.'

'You're not denying it, though …'

'Well … I think you're beautiful. I thought so when we were kids.'

'And now you're just inviting yourself into my bed again …' I wanted to joke around *and* get answers out of him the same time; it was also extremely fun to watch him panic.

'I didn't mean it like that! I'm not like Nick! I promise!'

'Terry, I'm joking, I know you're nothing like Nick.'

He was on the edge of his seat and I was sure he was now more red in the face than I had ever been.

'I'm sorry … I'll stop.'

'Don't.'

He suddenly stopped fidgeting and we both stared at each other.

'You … like me?' he asked.

'I enjoy spending time with you,' I admitted.

'So you want me to flirt with you?'

'Take me on a date and I'll think about it?' I replied.

I had never been this confident with someone. What had come over me?

'I really didn't see things turning out this way … I really am lucky.'

'Terry, you're such a nice person, you deserve to have good things happen to you. But, then again, going on a date with me isn't exactly a good thing, I'm quite high maintenance.'

'How so?' he asked.

'I hate drinking, I hate parties, I hate crowds and all things considered, I like weird grunge music, books and movies with really superficial endings.'

He looked blankly at me.

'I hate drinking too, I've never been to a party, I've always been alone, I love all music and books and I also enjoy really weird films,' he listed off. 'Have you ever seen *Twin Peaks*?'

'I love *Twin Peaks*!'

We continued to talk and we spoke about films, bands and books we loved. He searched through my phone at all the music I had and we laughed at some of my more embarrassing choices. This was one of the nicest evenings I had ever had with someone before. Terry just seemed to listen to everything I had said, he took an interest and asked questions. I felt like I could talk to him and I already felt strangely comfortable around him.

It was starting to get late and we both agreed we would spend the weekend with my family (as friends) and then plan a date for some time the following week. We weren't going to say anything to my parents, as we both didn't know how they would react; they saw Terry like family and it felt out of the ordinary to be going on a date with someone your family viewed as another child to them.

As we got into his car, Terry looked down at the pier, which was full of kids from college drinking and smoking.

'So, that's where everyone hangs out?' he asked.

'Some,' I replied. 'There are lots of different spots all over town where kids congregate.'

As he drove me home, I explained some of the spots that people our age hung out at: the pier, various spots in the forest, infamous houses where parties were held and houses were trashed, the beach, the arcades and an old favourite, the Black Lake, which was a huge lake in the middle of the forest.

'It sounds fun,' said Terry, 'but I'll stick to the coffee shops.'

He stopped his car just before my house, turned off his engine and thanked me.

'What for?' I asked.

'I don't know what this is between us right now … but I want you to know, even if we were just friends, I've really enjoyed hanging out with you. It's been one of the best moments of my life, if I'm honest.'

I felt emotional by his statement and just grabbed his hand, sitting in silence.

'I'll see you tomorrow?' I asked. 'I'll tell my parents that you're coming?'

'I'd love to.'

We both stared at each other and it was an awkward moment. He stared into my eyes and I loved how beautiful those bright eyes of his were. He drew his face closer to mine and we kissed.

I had never felt like this before and I had never kissed someone and felt so many feelings at the same time. I felt like my stomach was full of butterflies, like my body had an electric shock flowing through it and every sense had heightened. He smelt beautiful, his lips were soft and his kiss was gentle.

We slowly pulled away from each other.

'Can we do that again?' I asked.

We kissed again and he held my hand.

'I, most definitely, love going to coffee shops,' he joked.

'I don't kiss everyone I go to coffee shops with,' I replied.

'No, just the ones you shared a bed with.'

He winked at me and I got out of his car, sticking my middle finger up at him in a playful way of saying "fuck you". He smiled and I slowly walked to the front door of my house before waving goodbye to him. I felt my phone vibrate in my backpack.

I think we should have done a third kiss, just to round things off?

I closed the door and had a huge grin on my face. I had dated enough people in my life to realise that I now felt something different. Without doubt, I was absolutely and utterly falling for Terry Haynes.

*

We texted most of the most and it wasn't until three a.m that we forced each other to stop texting each other.

I told mom and dad you would be here at 10am!
Go to sleep

Within seconds I had a reply.

No, you owe me a kiss. I can drive down now?

Go. To. Sleep. Maybe tomorrow?

I thought we were playing it cool in front of your mom and dad? Unless he gives me the kiss I'm owed?

I fell asleep with a huge grin on my face and woke up with the same smile. I had never felt this happy before. As we ate breakfast, I tried to hide my smile, as I didn't want it to be obvious that something was going on. I was always moody at home and any sign of happiness would give something away. I had told my parents that I had spent the evening showing Terry some of the places college kids hung around.

'Oh, Amy, I'm so happy you showed Terry around town last night!' my mom fussed.

'I wanted to be nice,' I explained. 'And he's sort of … family.'

'He is family!' my dad shouted proudly. 'Doesn't matter how long he's been away, I saw that boy like my own.'

Dad had planned a full day of activities with Terry and Mom had planned a huge meal for the night.

'Dad, what have you exactly planned for today?' I asked.

'Well, there are a few things. I thought we could go down to the beach? Maybe try out some surfing?'

'Oh no … Dad … please, no.'

It would have been a strange thing to most people that we were surfing in September, but when you lived by the sea, it was the best time for the waves. I, unfortunately, was awful at surfing, which always annoyed me as *everyone* could surf in this town.

'Come on, Amy,' said Dad. 'If you don't try, you'll never get good.'

'What if Terry doesn't like surfing?' I begged, trying to change his mind.

It was, unfortunately, settled and I now felt my moodiness had come back to its natural form. I dragged myself up to my room and started to dig out my old wetsuit.

I heard the doorbell ring and Terry had arrived. I quickly ran to my makeup table and rushed some thick eyeliner, black eyeshadow and dark red lipstick, which was true to my gothic look.

'I'd love to try surfing!' I heard Terry say downstairs.

Great. I walked downstairs and everyone was practically ready to leave.

'Come on, Amy, we'll miss the best waves!' Dad moaned. 'Why have you put makeup on? We're surfing!'

Terry just stared at me and smiled. I really liked the way he looked at me.

'Hey, Amy, thanks again for last night,' he said in a very formal way.

'No problem. Glad you enjoyed it.'

We acted awkward around each other and everyone carried on loading up my dad's car.

'I don't mind driving, Michael,' said Terry.

'Don't be silly, boy, today is my treat!' Dad replied. 'Even if you do have a lovely truck!'

'Why don't you drive my truck, then?'

Dad stopped at his car and his face lit up like a firework.

'Really?'

'Of course. Do you like pick-ups, then?'

'Oh god, Terry, don't get him started,' Mom warned. 'He won't shut up.'

'Lisa won't let me buy one,' said Dad. 'She said I had no reason to buy one.'

'Hey, now's your chance to see if you like driving one,' said Terry and he threw his keys into my dad's hands (who was now acting like a kid on Christmas Day.)

'Aren't you coming, Lisa?' Terry asked my mom.

'No, I don't surf, plus Tim's got a friend coming over today.'

'Aww, has Timmy got a play date?' I said, putting on a baby voice to my brother.

Tim just scowled at me as if he was super embarrassed.

'Right, enough chat!' Dad called. 'Let's go.'

Just before I opened the back door to the rear seats of the truck, Terry slightly grabbed my hand and as quickly as he grabbed it, he let go, climbing into the passenger seat next to my dad.

We drove down to the beach and my dad constantly raved about the pick-up truck all the way down. If he wasn't swooning "Oh my god, I didn't know it did this!" it was "Bloody hell, this drives beautifully!"

On the beach, we got changed in the small changing rooms by the pier. Terry didn't have any beachwear, so walked to a small shop by the arcades to buy some.

Dad laid down three surfboards on the sand (his own, his spare and my old surfboard). I felt the dread enter my stomach and I was worried about looking like a fool in front of Terry. I didn't even notice when he had returned, as I was picking up my surfboard and trying to remember how to surf.

'Well, this is embarrassing, they haven't got any wetsuits in my size …'

I turned around and didn't know what to say. Terry stood there in a new pair of swimming shorts … but his body … it was incredible. He looked like an athlete, his body ripped, muscled and toned at every inch. I had never been one to ogle at men … but I couldn't help but stare.

'Bloody hell, lad, you'll freeze to death without a wetsuit!' said Dad, as if he had not noticed that Terry had the body of an Olympian god.

'Honestly, I'll be fine,' said Terry. 'I always have freezing cold showers at home.'

Dad stood and debated in his mind what to do, but as Terry insisted, we walked to the water and began swimming out to the waves.

It was a travesty. Waves crashed into me, I fell off my board more times than I stood on it and my makeup and hair must have looked like some washed up sea urchin. I was glad that Terry wasn't that much better and as my dad tried to teach him to surf, Terry spent more time laughing and getting swallowed under the water.

'Wow, I thought I was bad!' I teased. 'You're awful, Terry!'

'Come on, first day…' he replied.

A few hours passed and eventually Dad gave up trying to teach Terry, admitting that he would need to practice a few more times before he could stand on his surfboard. Dad drove the truck home (and again, sang its praises all the way home).

Mom had made a beautiful meal that night again, which was a roast lamb with all the trimmings; lamb was a meat we ate on special occasions and celebrations, which was exactly what tonight felt like. We all talked and laughed the night away; it felt like we had not laughed this much as a family for years and it felt like Terry was the missing key.

My mom had insisted that Terry stay the night and we all agreed to go for a family walk the next day. I just sat in awe and watched Terry and Dad talk like they were best friends; even though I had something going on with Terry, he spent most of his time with my parents and I really admired it. As they all spoke, Terry would occasionally glance over at me and smile; every smile made me feel those butterflies and I would just smile back.

When we all finally went to bed, I found myself again texting Terry, even though he was in the next room. He kept joking if he could sneak into my room again, but then admitted he respected my parents too much and felt guilty to even joke about it. Once again, we both stayed awake late into the night texting each other and once again, I fell asleep with a huge grin on my face.

*

The weekend just seemed perfect. The next day, we all ventured for a family walk through the forest on one of the many trails our town had to offer. We had another family meal, but this time at a restaurant in town. Terry and I had perfected the art of acting like friends, but occasionally he would grab my hand ... or worse. As we left the restaurant, just as everyone else looked to the beach, Terry quickly (and smoothly) kissed my cheek and then joined them to enjoy the view, all within a split second; I couldn't help but laugh.

What the hell was going on? Were we dating? Things were happening so fast. Terry and I agreed to go for another coffee after college on Monday. It was English most of the day, which meant we also had to act like friends in class (although, as usual, there weren't many chances to talk during lesson anyway). I didn't want rumours to begin that I was dating Terry, for no other reason than it was no one's business. I also absolutely hated being the centre of attention and any form of PDA (public displays of affection). When I was dating Nick, he would purposely kiss me in front of his friends or try and hold me inappropriately, basically doing anything to show people that I was his girlfriend. I hated it and he knew it.

When lunchtime came, I had planned to meet Laura at the college park as I had not spoken to her for a few days. I invited Terry to meet her, but he insisted he was too hungry to do anything and was going to go to the canteen first to buy food.

'She's alive!' Laura said as I approached her.

'I'm sorry,' I said. 'It's been a manic few days.'

'Care to explain?'

I told Laura everything apart from the kissing and dating Terry part (as this was a sure way for the gossip to spread around).

'Oh my god, so, he's like basically family now?'

'Erm, kind of,' I replied. 'My mom and dad are really happy to have him back in their lives.'

'Aren't you?' she pried.

'Yeah, he's pretty fun to be around,' I agreed, in a very disinterested tone.

Laura quickly changed the subject to a new boy she was texting, who seemed to be a much older university student that had come from Scotland.

'He actually lives on campus!' she exclaimed.

'Have you ever gone five minutes without dating someone?' I asked.

'Where's the fun in that? I won't be good-looking forever, may as well abuse it now.' she joked.

As much as I did not agree with Laura's philosophy, logic or morals, she was a fun friend to have and some of the stories she would tell me were very funny to listen to. As she recounted the horror of possibly meeting her new love interest's Scottish family, I noticed a commotion going on behind me. I turned around and saw lots of people walking towards the same location. If you have ever been to school or college, you know that this could only mean one thing: a fight. It was stupid how, no matter what age you were, people still fought and even more stupid that people would get excited and crowd around the people who were fighting.

'Oh my god, a fight!' said Laura. 'That hasn't happened for a long time! Shall we go?'

'No, it's stupid,' I replied.

People were walking past us to walk towards the fight and I tried to ignore them until I heard someone say, "It's Nick from the rugby team!"

Nick had been in many fights and had won many fights. This wouldn't have been of any interest to me, nor would I have cared normally … but something didn't feel right. The last time I saw Nick … was when he was giving Terry a look of *"I want to kill you"*.

'Oh, shit …' I whispered. 'Laura, I need to see who's fighting.'

I started to run towards the fight and fought through the crowd. The centre of the commotion seemed to be outside of the canteen building, which only made me feel more anxious. I pushed my way through the crowd, through the kids pushing to get a view of the centre of attention, and through the various chants of "Punch him!" and "'Fight!" I somehow made it to the front row, and my worst fears had come true; it was Nick squaring up to Terry.

'The fuck do you think you were doing?' Nick growled at Terry, his voice loud enough for the crowd to hear. 'Taking my girlfriend on a date, meeting her over the weekend? Yeah, I saw you both, getting cosy with her family! Who the fuck do you think you are?'

Terry didn't look bothered at all; in fact, he looked like he was still thinking about what he wanted for his lunch. He just stared at Nick with a look of amusement. I was really starting to worry; Nick was strong and I had seen him knock someone unconscious with one punch before. Terry still hadn't replied, which only made Nick more angry.

'Too scared to say something?' Nick shouted. 'You need to back the fuck away from Amy, mate!'

I had to intervene; I couldn't let this happen, and I didn't want Terry hurt.

'Nick, leave him alone,' I said and tried to pull Nick away. 'You are not my boyfriend! We are over! You need to get over this!'

The crowd cheered and antagonised the situation with chants of *'He's been dumped!'*

'Go away, Amy, I'm dealing with this!' Nick shouted at me.

'There is nothing to deal with,' I replied. 'You are *not* my boyfriend and Terry is my *friend*. Leave him alone!'

The crowd continued to cheer.

'Hey, Nick,' said Terry. 'Maybe you should leave Amy alone for a bit.'

Nick turned his head in an instant, like a dog who had just heard another dog bark.

'What the fuck did you say to me?!'

It all happened so fast, but when it did, all the shouting, jeering and commotion stopped and the whole crowd fell silent.

Nick had lunged at Terry and threw a punch that looked so hard it could no doubt be heard by the back of the crowd. The sheer power of his punch should have knocked Terry unconscious or at the very least, flying backwards to the ground ... except, it didn't. Terry just stood there, unaffected, unfazed and untouched, as if Nick had not punched him at all. Everyone fell silent and the whole crowd, including myself and especially Nick, looked in shock.

Nick quickly regained composure and threw another punch at Terry, letting out a huge groan as he threw a harder punch; again, Nick's fist hit Terry's face, but Terry didn't move, didn't flinch and wasn't affected.

'What the fuck?' Nick cried.

Terry tilted his head to look around Nick and just stared at me. The look he gave me was a look of seeking approval, like he was asking my permission to do something. Nick again just stood in shock and the crowd, although quiet, started to mumble and whisper, as if they were all scared.

Nick went to throw a third punch, but Terry grabbed his fist to stop him. The crowd's whispers became more excited and people jumped up from the back of the crowd to see what was going on.

'Just stop it and give up,' said Terry, but in a very low voice that could only be heard by those closest.

'What is going on here?' shouted a voice in the distance.

It was Phillip Hussain, the deputy dean of the college and university. The crowd divided and started to lessen as Mr Hussain walked to the centre of the commotion. Terry let go of Nick, who immediately began to rub his wrist, as if he was in pain.

'I don't know, sir, Nick started shouting and then threw a few punches at me,' explained Terry.

Mr Hussain looked from Terry to Nick and looked confused, as Terry had just admitted he was the one who had been punched, but Nick was the one who looked in pain.

'Both of you, come to my office now!' ordered Mr Hussain.

Terry gave me one more look and walked away, with Nick behind him. I stood there in shock and still had no idea what had just happened.

*

Terry did not return to the class for the rest of the day, but there was plenty of gossip and whispers going around about what happened.

I tried not to listen, but the gossip only reflected what I was thinking; "He got punched twice and didn't even flinch!" I heard one girl whisper to her friend.

The only rumour that I didn't want to go around was, unfortunately, inevitable. People were whispering that Terry and I were together, I heard one person say that I had dumped Nick for Terry and one had even gone as far as to make up a story that I had cheated on Nick for Terry. Laura must have felt like she was having a breakdown, as she was texting every two minutes.

Are you with that Terry? Xxxxxxxx

Within moments, I received another text from her.

Did you cheat on Nick? Xxxxxxxx

A few minutes later:

Why did they fight? Xxxxxxxxxxxxxx

And finally...

OMG Amy! Tell me what's going on!

I sunk lower in my chair and just groaned. This was my worst nightmare. The day finally finished and I quickly dashed out of the classroom before anyone could stop and ask me any questions. I walked towards the car park to see if Terry's truck was still there and when I saw him standing against his truck, my heart sank. Why didn't he return to the lesson? Had he been expelled? I quickly ran over to his truck and asked him if we could drive away as quickly as possible to talk.

Terry agreed and thankfully no one saw us (as I could not bear any more rumours being spread). When I thought it was a safe enough distance to stop hiding my face, I turned around and burst to life with questions.

'What happened?'

'Nick's been suspended,' Terry answered. 'They didn't get the police involved.'

'What do you mean?' I said within an instant, my voice full of panic and worry.

'Mr Hussain asked what happened. I told him the truth. I literally just bought a sandwich, walked outside and Nick started shouting at me and pushing me. Nick lied, of course, said I had stolen his girlfriend and tried to provoke him. Thankfully, another teacher was sitting on a bench not far away when it first kicked off and when the crowd gathered, they ran to get Mr Hussain.'

'So you're not in trouble?'

'No. In fact, they made Nick apologise to me and offered to call the police for assault.'

'And you didn't?'

'No, he looked like he had shit himself enough. Was rather funny, actually. I'm upset that I didn't eat my sandwich though.'

I felt relieved and my anxiety was replaced by anger, as I couldn't believe what Nick had done.

'Nick's a psycho,' I seethed. 'I wish the police had arrested him.'

'Yeah, he doesn't do a bad punch either.'

I was then suddenly reminded of the most important question of all.

'Really? You certainly didn't seem to be affected. It's like he didn't even hit you!'

'I didn't want to look weak in front of him, but it did hurt.'

'You didn't even flinch, Terry, his punch should have knocked you to the floor.'

'Maybe, but I can take a punch.'

'You say that like you've been punched quite a few times before.'

'I used to be part of a boxing club by my uncle's house.'

He was lying, I was sure of it, but I knew I wouldn't get any more information on the subject.

'Are you sure you're okay?' I asked.

'If I say no, would you kiss me?' he replied.

'I would kiss you anyway.'

'Then I'm fine.'

We drove to the coffee shop and things quickly felt normal again. We spoke about the rumours that were spreading around and while Terry didn't exactly mind people knowing, he respected my hatred for being the centre of gossip and also agreed that we didn't need to kiss or hold hands in front of big crowds. We sat and drank coffee, we flirted, we got to know each other more and things felt good again. My anger for Nick, the millions of questions from Laura and all the gossip at college could all wait; I was too happy in this moment to care about anything else.

*

September passed and the first month of college had been my best yet. Maybe it was due to the fact I was dating Terry, someone I really liked and got on well with, that I suddenly felt like I was starting to enjoy life. I enjoyed college more, I spoke to Laura more, I hung around with friends more and I enjoyed spending time with my family.

The rumours at college soon died down and eventually it was common knowledge that something was going on with Terry and me, but like most topics of hot gossip, no one cared after a few days. People now knew Terry as some stone-cold fighter, which he found amusing. I satisfied Laura's need for gossip and gave her a very toned-down version of what was going on with Terry; enough for her to know, but not enough for her to gossip or find it interesting. I had heard that Nick returned to college sometime towards the end of the month, but I hadn't seen or heard from him.

Terry and I continued to date, having coffees, going for meals, walks and just generally enjoying each other's company. Every weekend, Terry would visit my family and we would do the normal family activities as a group; walks, board games, meals, movies. I was positive that they still had no idea about Terry dating me and that suited me fine. Dad continued to try and teach Terry to surf (which didn't go well), but they found more success in skateboarding and even more success with American football. After seeing Terry take a punch without flinching, I knew he would be able to play American football without any fears. My dad was in awe when Terry practised with his team and immediately wanted him to join. Every Wednesday night was training night and Terry had agreed to train with Dad's team with the potential of joining as a member.

It was the first Sunday of October and it was the first Sunday since Terry had rejoined our family that we didn't see him. When I asked where he was going, he said he needed to do some shopping, but wanted to go alone. I thought this was suspicious, but we had such a laid-back relationship that I just presumed he fancied a day on his own (we practically spent all of our time together before this weekend). When we met up the next day, I asked if he enjoyed his trip, which he seemed to brush off and change the subject.

I was loving life and we had this new system in our lives that just seemed to work. It was a great mix of friends, family and time together. Whilst we never said we were boyfriend and girlfriend, we were certainly in the "honeymoon period" of a relationship, where everything felt exciting and every kiss was just as passionate as the last.

Wednesday night arrived and as part of our new weekly routine, Terry would drive to my house, eat tea with us and then venture to football practice with my dad. When Terry didn't turn the engine off outside my house, I turned and looked at him, confused.

'Aren't you coming in?' I asked.

'I've left my football clothes at home,' he replied. 'Let me go get them and I'll be back.'

I didn't think much of it, but sure enough, Terry had walked through our front door a little over twenty minutes later. After we ate tea (which was a light salad due to the boys training), Dad and Terry started to stretch and prepare for football.

'Want me to drive, Terry?' asked Dad; he was always looking for an excuse to drive now, hoping Terry would offer his truck.

'Please,' Terry agreed, but his face looked excited, like he was holding a secret he couldn't contain for much longer.

As Dad walked outside, Terry winked at me and slowly followed him.

'Terry, where's your truck?' asked Dad. 'Have you changed your truck?'

'No,' replied Terry. 'This is your truck, isn't it?'

I walked outside and saw the most beautiful truck in the world. It was brand new and a beautifully unique colour of blue, red and silver. It was almost identical to Terry's, with four doors, huge wheels and a huge cargo area on the back. I looked at Terry with confusion and then at my dad, who seemed even more confused.

'Terry, I don't understand …'

'Michael, this is now your brand-new truck.'

Dad was speechless and looked from Terry to the truck and finally to me.

'Terry? I really don't understand.'

'Well, when I ordered this truck originally, my uncle had ordered one too. I thought they cancelled the order when he passed away, but I had a call a few weeks back saying it was ready to pick up. As it was already paid for, I want you to have it.'

Dad was shaking, like he was about to cry.

'Terry, no … I can't accept this.'

'Well, I kind of have no choice,' Terry explained. 'Plus, I had it resprayed in your favourite colours. Blue, red and silver, just like the New England Patriots!'

The New England Patriots were my dad's favourite American football team. Dad continually looked from the truck to Terry, until he finally grabbed Terry into the tightest hug I had ever seen, just before he started to cry.

'Terry, I don't know what to say!' Dad cried. 'I'm an emotional wreck here!'

My mom was now outside and, after figuring out what had happened, started to cry too, grabbing Terry into a hug.

'Terry, you shouldn't have,' she cried. 'This is too much!'

'Just make sure you give me a ride back home later on!' joked Terry, gasping for air as both my parents had him in a tight group hug.

I just stood there in shock and also felt speechless. I looked at Terry, who again winked at me and was slowly let go by my parents. My dad was now going to be insufferable and just like he did when driving Terry's truck, he began to rave about all the features. They eventually left for football training and I spent the rest of the evening talking to my mom, who also was overwhelmed by Terry's gift.

When the boys returned home that night, my dad immediately asked my mom to join him for a ride in his new truck and again was acting like a small boy at Christmas. He continually asked Terry if he was sure about gifting the truck, which Terry continually agreed to. When Mom and Dad finally left the kitchen to look at the truck again, Terry and I were alone, which gave me the perfect opportunity to ask him what was going on.

'Is that truck really your uncle's order?'

'No,' explained Terry, 'but I knew he wouldn't have accepted it if he knew I bought it for him.'

'Terry, that must have cost a fortune!'

'I told you, I don't care about the money. I'd give it all away if I could.'

'But still ... that's such an extravagant gift.'

'Your dad's done so much for me and even after causing him so much pain, he welcomed me back into his life like nothing had happened. It was the least I could do.'

I grabbed Terry into a hug and kissed him. I felt so much love for this guy and to see how much love he had for my parents meant more than I could ever admit. Nick only ever met my parents once and he barely made the effort to talk to them, never mind attempting to make a good impression.

'You are the kindest person I have ever met, Terry, do you know that?' I asked as I hugged him again.

'Not as kind as your family. Just promise you won't tell them I bought it?'

'I won't, although I still don't think you have anything to be embarrassed about.'

Could life really feel this perfect?

TERRY

I had paid a lot of money to buy Michael's truck and even more to get it sprayed in the right colours ... but to see how happy he was just made it worth every penny. Even after a week had passed, he still seemed just as excited as the moment I gave it to him.

American football was fun, but I think some of his team were weirded out when they tried to tackle me and I didn't flinch. If I was honest, I was still weirded out by the fact they couldn't knock me over, as they were extremely large men (whose biceps were bigger than my waist). I guess I was just made for American football?

I couldn't keep up with how quickly things had changed in my life and how perfect things were becoming. I had never dreamed in a million years that I would ever kiss Amy and here I was kissing her every single night.

Unfortunately, things didn't stay perfect for long. It was a Thursday night and I had just returned home after a night with the Doories. For a split second, as if fate was a cruel bitch, I had thought about the length of time since my last blackout and how grateful I was that it had not happened in so long … when the feeling suddenly hit me. Maybe the thought had triggered the feeling? All I knew was that the feeling had hit again and with a vengeance. I was lucky (if I could have called it that) for the fact that I was already home. I wasn't far from the panic room. I rushed into the house and hit the hidden button that opened the hidden staircase. I started to black out, and this one felt more violent than any I had had before. The ground was taking too long to lower and reveal the stairs. I blacked out for a moment, but managed to force my eyes open … When I looked around, I had practically destroyed everything in my house. I was starting to shake all over. I felt hot, like my skin was burning. The secret door to the room finally opened and I threw myself down the staircase. I blacked out, ready to enter the hell that tormented my soul.

AMY

It had been some time since Terry had last had a migraine, so it came as a surprise when he didn't turn up for class that day. On most days, I was lucky enough that Terry would drive me to and from college, but I never expected him to; if he didn't arrive by a certain time, I would get the bus without thinking anything of it, as he turned up late for college and loved to sleep in quite often.

I dropped him a text to ask if he was okay, but did not expect a reply. When college ended, I started to miss him, as I started to realise that it was a rare occasion that we were apart; even when we were apart, we would be texting each other.

The next day, I woke up with a fantastic idea to grab some stuff from the shop for Terry, then get a taxi to his house to look after him. After explaining to my mom and dad about Terry's migraines and the fact he wouldn't be spending time with us that weekend, I walked to our local corner shop, picked up some snacks and drinks and then some over-the-counter tablets that were recommended for migraines and bad headaches. I felt excited and even though he never asked to be looked after, it felt like a kind gesture and an excuse to see him again. I called a taxi, which drove up the steep forest roads until we reached Great Western View.

I approached the gates to Terry house and rang the buzzer. After a few moments of no response, I regretted ringing it, in case the noise irritated Terry's migraine. I pushed on the gates and was relieved to find that they were unlocked. I was happy to see his truck on the drive and thought I would try my luck to see if his front door was open, which thankfully, it was.

'Terry?' I whispered, as I walked through the front door.

As Terry only had a bed, a TV and a box in his house, I didn't have to look far to search for him, but when I looked around, I did not expect to see the mess his house was in. Books were scattered around the floor, his mattress a few metres from the bed and the TV smashed on the ground; Terry was nowhere to be seen.

I felt scared and was now worried as to where Terry was. I grabbed my phone and dialled his number. Suddenly, I heard the ringtone of his phone and felt horrified when I found a smashed phone underneath a book on the floor. What was going on? Where was Terry? I was getting more and more worried by the minute. His car was here, his house was smashed up and he didn't have his phone with him. What could I do?

In a moment of panic, I phoned my mom and dad. Even though Terry had begged me to never tell them where he lived, I felt like this situation was too scary and too concerning to worry about promises.

'What's up, Red?'

'Dad … I think something's happened to Terry.'

*

Mom and Dad had hundreds of questions, but all questions would have to be put aside. The police were called and Mom and Dad drove up to Terry's house within ten minutes of my phone call. When we explained the situation to the police, they immediately began the process for a missing person, as Terry had been missing for almost two days, plus the house looked like it had been broken into.

I had to explain to Mom and Dad why Terry didn't want them to know about his house and they were upset by the fact he felt embarrassed or felt like he couldn't talk to them. Thankfully, my dad hadn't put two and two together and worked out Terry had paid for his truck, as I was already worried that I had broken one promise today. Dad drove around town and searched for Terry, looking at some of the spots we had been to, such as the beach, his football club and some spots in the forest. I had checked the college, although I didn't hold much hope for him being there. We spent the whole day searching, but didn't manage to find him. At the end of Saturday, we all went to bed worrying and I doubted any of us would manage to fall asleep. The plan was to search again tomorrow and the police had promised us they would patrol his house in case he returned. I cried in bed and all these extreme thoughts were running through my head about Terry. Why was his car there?

Why was the house in that state? He didn't have his phone, so I couldn't even tell him how much I was worried about him or missed him. I slowly drifted to sleep.

RING. RING.

I woke up and shot out of bed. It was the house phone! I ran downstairs, meeting my mom and dad on the landing as they rushed along with me. Mom snatched the phone and answered it, shouting a high pitched *'Hello?!'* She continually nodded her head and Dad and I watched with bated breath. When she closed her eyes tight and breathed a huge sigh of relief, I felt like Dad and I did the same in sync. It had to be Terry. He had to be okay …

After thanking whoever was on the phone, Mom put it down and started to cry.

'It's Terry, he's okay,' she said.

My heart felt like it was beating again and I felt a huge sense of relief.

'Where is he?' I asked.

'He's home. Apparently, he went for a walk and tripped, hitting his head on a rock. Knocked himself clean out and had only woken up a few hours ago. An ambulance has checked him over, but he's refusing to go to hospital.'

'But what about his house?' asked Dad. 'Why was it wrecked?'

'He doesn't know, they think it's a separate incident.'

'A break-in?'

'Yes, apparently it's quite common at the bigger houses.'

'Right, we need to go up there. Amy, you need to stay here and watch Tim.'

'No!' I shouted. 'I need to come.'

Mom and Dad looked at each other and, for a moment, they both looked confused.

'Okay,' Dad slowly agreed. 'Lisa?'

'I'll stay,' Mom conceded. 'I can see Terry tomorrow.'

I felt like I had broken character in front of them, but I didn't care. Dad and I were travelling to Terry and I could see if he was okay. At the back of my mind, I knew the story the police had told was utter bullshit … but I didn't need to worry about that for now.

We arrived at Terry's house and the police were driving away from the drive as we pulled up.

'Thank you, officers,' my dad called as the police drove away.

Terry was waiting at the door. He looked worse than ever, like he had just been part of a shipwreck. His eyes were dark, his skin was pale and he slumped in the door frame, looking weak and feeble. Our eyes caught each other, but it wasn't the same exchange they normally had. He looked angry and the same warmth and love I received wasn't there.

'Terry!' called my dad, who walked over and embraced him.

'Michael, I'm so sorry,' replied Terry, but his voice was cold.

'You had us so worried.'

'I'm fine, I promise.'

We all walked inside and I was thankful that the house was still a wreck. One thing my mom and dad hadn't realised was how little furniture Terry had and in this state it was hard to tell what furniture Terry actually owned.

Dad made Terry retell the events of his story and he again lied that he had gone for a long walk, but tripped in the forest and hit a rock. When my dad questioned about the "break-in" at the house, Terry played dumb and didn't seem too concerned at the thought of someone breaking into his property nor his things.

'It's late, my boy,' said Dad, 'but I don't want you sleeping here. Come home with us.'

'No, I really appreciate it,' replied Terry. 'But I just want to tidy up here and sleep in my own bed. I promise I'll be down tomorrow.'

'I don't think I can change your mind … but don't think we've forgotten the fact you were embarrassed for us to know where you live. Terry, you should never be embarrassed to tell us anything. You are part of this family!'

Terry forced a smile that seemed to convince him and apologised again before embracing my dad.

'Come on, Amy, let's leave Terry to rest.'

'Can I stay?' I asked. 'I want to help tidy up. Terry will drop me off after, won't you?'

Terry nodded and Dad smiled and agreed to let me stay. We watched him drive away and I suddenly felt nervous; I looked at Terry, whose smile had faded again and now looked very serious.

'Terry …' I began.

'You told them. You broke your promise. And you called the police.'

'What choice did I have? Your house was a wreck. Your car and phone were here, but you were missing. What could I do?'

'I was fine.'

'And how was I supposed to know that?' I argued back.

He didn't reply and started to pick up books scattered across the floor.

'What actually happened?'

'You heard what I said to your dad,' he replied.

His answers were cold, heartless and this was not the Terry I knew.

'You're lying.'

'Okay,' he laughed.

I felt rage building up inside of me.

'I have watched you be punched over and over again and not even flinch. And you expect me to believe you were knocked unconscious after tripping over?'

Terry shrugged and continued to pick stuff up.

'And how many walks do you go out and trip over on?' I continued. 'Isn't this the third time you've gone missing?'

'I don't know,' he growled back. 'We'll have to ask the police to keep track.'

'Why are you being a dick?! I was worried. I thought something had happened to you. I called my mom and dad because I was worried the worst had happened!'

I suddenly started to cry and I couldn't hold it in. Tears streamed down my face and Terry finally turned around to look at me. For a moment, I thought he was going to hug me, but he looked pained and squatted down like the pain was unbearable. He let out a groan of frustration and hit the floor with his fist.

'Come on, I need to take you home.' he said as he stood, acting as though nothing was wrong.

I paused and stared, but he began to walk out of the front door. We walked to his car and I was still crying. I couldn't stop myself and I felt too overwhelmed to say anything.

Terry didn't say a word to me as we drove home, but as I looked at him, I saw that he was also crying. The sun had started to rise and through the cracks of the trees above, sunlight creaked through a pale yellow and grey sky.

'Terry, I was so scared!' I blurted out.

We approached my street and he slowed down the truck. He turned off the engine and leaned on his steering wheel, as if he was impatiently waiting for something to happen.

'Amy … this isn't working. I thought it could work and it's not.'

If I thought I was crying before, it was nothing compared to now. I was now crying uncontrollably and I felt pain like I had never felt before. I couldn't breathe and it was like Terry was stabbing me in the heart.

'Terry … please … no!' I sobbed.

'Don't make this harder than it needs to be. I don't like you in that way … I think we're better as friends.'

I didn't reply, but just continued to cry.

'Please,' I begged.

'Go to bed … I still want to see your family, though. We can still be friends,' he said, but still wasn't looking at me.

This had to be a nightmare.

'Terry … don't do this,' I pleaded one last time.

I grabbed his hand, but he snatched it away as soon as I had touched it.

'Just go,' he repeated.

I was fighting a battle that was already lost. I loosened my seatbelt and left the car silently, trying to suppress my tears and sobbing.

As soon as I had closed the door, Terry had sped off. I watched his car disappear in the distance and I stood in the street crying, feeling heartbroken, confused, hurt and most of all, like I just wanted to hug the man who drove away from me.

*

I should have loved October, it was my favourite month for so many reasons. I loved the cold wind that crept in after the summer, a reminder that Autumn was here. The trees that were not part of the forest, started to turn gold, yellow and orange and scattered the road with leaves just in case you hadn't noticed it was that time of year. Halloween was my main reason to love October, as I ranked it as the greatest holiday of all, above Christmas, birthdays and Easter. I loved the cheesy decorations, the horror films and how the village would come to life with decorations. Byanbythe celebrated all seasons with great style, but for some reason, the town looked that little bit more beautiful with the orange pumpkins outside every shop.

Unfortunately, I could not be happy this October and the month passed quicker than it had ever passed before. I felt like I had found a piece of happiness that could never have been imagined and as soon as I became accustomed to this new-found joy, it was ripped away from me. I still didn't understand why Terry had left me; yes, I had broken my promise, but I had done it with honest intentions. Anyone would have reacted the way I reacted and yet the most honest, sweet and innocent man I had ever known no longer understood me and no longer had compassion. I had texted Terry several times since the night he ended things, but he never replied. He continued to see my dad and played football at his club; I had heard him on a few occasions talking to my mom downstairs too, but he never stayed long and I certainly never saw him face to face. The only other place I could have seen Terry was college, but luckily, I had managed to avoid him there too. It had been three weeks since we had split up and he hadn't been to college once, which was his longest gap of absence. He must have quit and felt it was too awkward to see me in class ... In a way, I was glad too, as it would have felt painful to sit so close to him and yet be ignored.

People around me knew something was up, but they didn't ask me anything; I was a private person and didn't care to share my emotions or thoughts; even Laura, who seldom did not believe there was another person on earth other than herself, started to feel sorry for me; she continually tried to arrange plans with me and I eventually ran out of excuses to not socialise with her.

'Come on, Amy, you can't mope around for much longer!' she said one Thursday on the bus to college. 'So what if Jerry left college?'

'Terry,' I corrected her.

'Who cares? God me! Look, Emma Chanesse is having a Halloween party tomorrow night!

She has *the* biggest house in all of Byanbythe! *Everyone* is going to be there from college. The last party she had was over one hundred people!'

I bet her house wasn't as big as Terry's, I thought in my head. I hated nearly all parties, with the exception of Halloween parties, but I didn't want to see anyone right now, never mind a hundred people at a mansion on the hills. I unfortunately had very little excuses left to give Laura … and I felt like if I stopped seeing her, I would become some sad recluse … and I certainly wasn't going to be a sad recluse over some boy. I hated girls who thought their life was over because of some boy … and although I felt something so strong for Terry, I knew I had to make an exit plan back to reality and some version of a normal life. I agreed and after a painful, ear-shattering scream of excitement from Laura, the conversation changed to planning the party. What alcohol should we buy? What were we going to wear? Who were we going to see? Well, in my head, my answers were simple; I wouldn't drink, I would wear the same thing as always (check shirt, black vest, ripped jeans) and I didn't care who I would see at this party.

Soon enough, Thursday and Friday had passed and it was almost time for the party. I sat on my bed with a towel wrapped around me after a long hot bath and contemplated putting my pyjamas on instead of my going-out clothes. My phone had not stopped beeping and every text was from a frantic Laura.

Are you sure you don't want booze? Xxx

And then, as usual, the list of text after text from her …

I got you some bottles of archers just in case! Xxx

I need cigarettes, reckon you could get served for me? Xxx

Don't worry, Ricky's going to get me some xxx

I had no idea who Ricky was.

Amazing news! Ricky is going to drive us there and back! We don't have to leave early now! Xxx

I already felt anxious and now we had some stranger driving us there and back. I really didn't feel comfortable going and now I would potentially have to stay out really late, dependent on whenever Ricky and Laura wanted to leave. Emma Chanesse's mansion was at least a forty-minute walk and by that time, there weren't going to be any buses operating. I decided to take the little money I had left in my purse with me, just in case I needed to get a taxi. I slowly forced myself to get ready and it felt like every move resulted in a sigh.

Ricky's car pulled up outside my house and my phone had started to ring; it was Laura and when I answered, she sounded extremely drunk.

'Come on, Amy!' she screamed.

I let out a final sigh and dragged myself downstairs.

'Have a great night, Red!' my dad called.

'Be safe, Amy,' said Mom. 'Text us if you need us.'

Why couldn't they be the type of parents who were strict and forbade me from going to parties? I walked out of the door and was horrified to see a boy racer car waiting outside of our house. It was horrible and each door didn't seem to match the colour of the rest of the car. It had a really shitty spoiler on the back, to try and make it look like a sports car (but failed miserably) and instead looked like one of Tim's mini toy cars. It was a three-door car and Laura stumbled out of her seat to let me in; she was most definitely drunk … and worst of all, she was in costume.

'Why aren't you dressed up?' she laughed.

'You never said it was a fancy dress party!' I growled, seething at the fact I was now facing a party as the only person not dressed up.

'It's Halloween … duh!' she mocked.

Laura was dressed as a slutty clown; she would never have admitted that was the intention, but nonetheless still had clown makeup on and hardly any clothes.

I really didn't want to go. I got in the car and sulked in the back, crossing my arms in rage.

'Yo, you must be Amy?' said the strange man behind the wheel.

'Yes, you must be Ricky?' I replied.

'Yes, babe,' said Ricky.

Ricky looked old, rough and like he had had a lot of drugs. He had a really scruffy suit, which I guessed would have been his best suit, and had a very crappy fake moustache on.

'Do you go to college with us?' I asked, but I knew the answer already.

'Nah, I'm a mechanic in town.'

Great. As Ricky revealed his occupation, Laura quickly turned around to look at me and I responded with a look of furious disapproval.

'He fixed my dad's car! It's funny how people meet these days, isn't it?' Laura bumbled.

'And how old are you, Ricky?' I asked.

'Hey! We need to go to the shop for cigarettes!' Laura cut in, which confirmed that Ricky was much older than us.

Ricky drove fast, playing extremely loud music and I felt sick in the back of his car. We drove to a small paper shop a few streets away and I was relieved when he turned off the engine.

'You got money?' he asked Laura.

Laura frantically searched her small handbag and quickly turned to look at me.

'Oh, Amy, I've left my purse. Can you lend me some money? I promise I'll get it back at the party; Tanya owes me money for the booze.'

I put my hand in my pocket and gave Ricky the only bit of money I had. He left me and Laura in peace and no sooner was he out of view did I begin my speech of rage and judgement.

'He's old enough to be arrested for going to a college party!' I shouted.

'He's barely thirty!' she replied.

'I want to go home, I can't be bothered with this shit …'

'Amy, please … I really want to have a night out with you.'

I didn't even look at her, but sighed and stared out of the window. Laura took my silence as agreement and smiled as she watched Ricky "Steve McQueen" the mechanic climb back into the car. We were off driving again at the speed of light and Laura lit up a cigarette in the car, which choked me as the wind blew the smoke into the back of the car.

Even though I didn't want to go to the party, I was extremely thankful to finally arrive. I had to admit the house was huge and could very well have been as big as Terry's. It was all glass, with a grey frame and a large, lit-up swimming pool that surrounded the whole house. There seemed to be hundreds already inside and outside of the house and everyone was in fancy dress. I climbed out of the car and took a deep breath.

'Let's go and get that money,' I said to Laura, wanting to ensure I had my taxi money as soon as possible.

'No worries!' she replied, and took two large bags out of Ricky's car boot, which sounded to be full of bottles of alcohol.

We merged into the crowd and I recognised lots of people from college. Everyone seemed to either be on drugs or drunk … but surprisingly, the vibe seemed good. The music was loud, Halloween-related and so many costumes were creative and realistic (unlike Laura's). Maybe I was just being a moody bitch? I may have lost Terry, but I needed to cheer the fuck up! As I finally lost sight of Ricky, I suddenly felt more optimistic about the party, and although I wasn't in costume, I decided to try and make the best of this opportunity.

We met up with a few other girls from college and Laura quickly distributed the alcohol around. I politely declined, but did not want to be too judgemental. After a short while, a few dances and talking to different people, I started to feel normal and I was actually enjoying myself a little.

Unfortunately, if you have ever been to a party, you'll know most things that start well don't end well. The night passed quickly and it was soon pitch-black outside. People were getting drunker and drunker and the house started to get destroyed by people dancing or messing around. The pool was soon full of half-naked people and everywhere I looked people were kissing each other and basically had their hands in places that would be deemed as a sex act. I reminded Laura several times that I needed my money, but she just descended into more alcohol, almost to the point of being unconscious.

'Who owes you the money?' I asked. 'I will ask them myself if I have to.'

Laura laughed hysterically and wrapped her arm around me.

'You just need to chill the fuck out, Amy. Have a drink, please! You will enjoy yourself more!'

I pushed her arm off of me and asked again who owed her money ... but it was pointless, and Laura quickly disappeared into the crowd.

I finally admitted defeat and realised I wasn't going to get my money back from Laura. I tried to look around the party for her, as I felt annoyed enough to just ask her and Ricky to take me back home. I looked for what seemed like half an hour, when I started to feel extremely frustrated. I found one of the girls Laura had given alcohol to earlier and asked if she had seen Laura.

'Laura left about twenty minutes ago! With some guy in a shitty car!'

I felt like I had passed the stage beyond anger and stormed out of the house, looking at the cars parked out front in disbelief. Lo and behold, Ricky's car was gone and Laura had left me.

I quickly pulled out my phone and tried to call her, but to peak my anger, her phone was going straight to voicemail. I had no money and no ride home … I felt like I had to call my mom or dad for a ride … but when I saw it was one o'clock in the morning, I felt like it was too late to call them. I had no other choice than to walk the forty minutes home, through the pitch-black forest in the freezing cold. I felt myself getting emotional and tears began to well up in my eyes, when a familiar voice spoke out from behind me.

'Amy?'

It was Nick. I felt like my bad night was now taking an extreme turn to become the worst night of all. I sighed a deep sigh and continued to ignore him.

'Go away, Nick.'

'Amy, please … I just want to talk.'

'I don't want to talk to you.'

'Please …'

This caught my attention. His voice was gentle, it sounded full of remorse and sincerity … and most of all, he had said please. Was this really Nick?

'What do you want?' I asked in a cold tone.

'I just want to say sorry,' he said. 'I cannot tell you how much I regret punching your boyfriend.'

'He's not my boyfriend … but thank you. I didn't expect you to apologise, so it's appreciated.'

I meant it, I really didn't think in a million years that Nick would ever be capable of apologising.

'I mean it,' he continued. 'I didn't realise how much of a prick I was being until after I was suspended. I really have a bad temper and I've started to see a counsellor about controlling it.'

'Wow, I'm happy for you, Nick,' I replied. 'That's good to hear.'

I may not have cared about him, but I was glad he was on some sort of path to bettering himself. He did have the worst temper in the world, so any way of improving that was certainly a route to a better Nick. I looked him up and down and suddenly realised that he also did not have a costume on, and he seemed to be the only other sober person at the party; this was nothing like Nick, as he was always up for dressing up in the most extreme costume to show off his body and he was always the first person to be drunk.

'Aren't you drinking?' I asked.

He looked awkwardly around us before he answered.

'No, I've been told to not drink while I deal with my anger. It might be a trigger that sets me off.'

'Wow, you really are trying, aren't you?'

He nodded and looked to the ground like some naughty school kid.

'Aren't you drinking?' he asked.

I didn't even bother to correct him, nor to remind him that I didn't drink.

'No, I was actually about to walk home,' I replied.

'Walk?' he said. 'Are you mad? It's at least forty minutes from here! It's pitch-black. You can't walk.'

'I have no choice … Laura's left and that was my ride home.'

'I can take you home,' he offered.

I didn't expect this option and now contemplated in my mind what to do. I hated Nick, I really did, and regardless of his new-found path to being a better person, this didn't change how I felt. On the other hand, I really didn't want to walk home … and it would have been a fifteen-minute drive with him, which wasn't too long to endure.

'Are you sure?' I asked.

'Of course!' he answered, now looking upbeat.

'And you definitely haven't been drinking?'

'I promise!'

His promises meant nothing to me, as he had broken so many to me before … but he seemed sober, so I accepted his offer for a ride home. It was a short walk to his car and in no time we were driving away from the party and back to my house. For the first five minutes, we sat in silence, which I thought was a quick win to what could have been an awkward ride.

'Amy, can we talk about stuff?' he finally asked.

I thought too soon and suddenly regretted my decision of accepting this ride.

'Nick … there isn't anything to say.'

'Please …'

I let out a small moan and agreed, but quickly regretted this too, as he took a wrong turn in the road that would have led to my house.

'Where are we going?' I asked.

'I'm just taking the long way home, it gives us time to talk,' he explained.

I sunk lower in my chair and banged my head on the passenger window, hoping that it would knock me unconscious.

'Amy, I know I messed up,' he began, 'but before I hit your boyfriend, I didn't even know there was anything wrong with us.'

'How did you not know?' I barked back. 'We split up long before you hit Terry!'

'I thought we were on a break; I thought you needed space.'

'I did, for the rest of my life, from you!'

'Why are you so hostile towards me? I haven't done anything bad to you!'

'Are you stupid, Nick? You lied to your mates that we had sex two months after we started dating. When I finally squashed that rumour, you told people we had sex in your car the day after you passed your driving test. How can people think that WHEN WE NEVER HAD SEX? You never took no for an answer, you always felt me up and you spread a rumour around college that I had sent you naked pictures. You were horrible to me and everything that's wrong about men.'

'That's just lad things, Amy … I didn't mean any of it.'

'They are vicious lies. You were just embarrassed that I wasn't an easy shag.'

'I'm sorry … I'm not like that anymore. I won't do any of that again.'

'I know that, because we won't ever get back together!'

'Oh, come on, what else did I do wrong? Why are you being a bitch?'

'A bitch? You don't know the first thing about me! You never remember that I don't drink. You don't know any of the classes I take at college. Do you know any of the bands I listen to too? Do you even know anything I like?' I reeled off.

He stopped replying, but I was starting to see past his bullshit façade. He hadn't changed; he was still the same old prick that I once dated.

'I suppose your new boyfriend knew all of that?' he mocked, as he put on a very immature baby voice.

'You know what … he did. He took time to know more about me in one month than you did in almost four years!'

'You're lying. You're playing hard to get and it ain't working, Amy! I'm getting tired of giving you chances,' he said, and this fully triggered a demon inside of me.

'GIVING ME CHANCES? Just take me the fuck home, you arrogant arsehole!' I screamed.

'Fine, go back to your lover boy,' he mocked again.

Nick was driving extremely fast down the pitch-black lanes. It was hard to see what was ahead, but he was now angry and worked up, barely paying attention to the road.

'That smug prick starts college and steals you away from me, and I get suspended? I should have punched the prick harder!'

I looked ahead and I thought I could see the strangest thing in the distance. As we sped towards it, it looked like someone was standing naked in the road.

'If I ever see him around college again, I wouldn't even give him a chance to get the teachers involved!' Nick ranted on.

We were approaching the person standing in the middle of the road far too fast. Whoever it was was definitely naked and I soon realised they were not moving.

'I can't believe you picked him over me!'

I started to panic, but before I could scream at Nick to pay attention, I felt like I was falling into a state of shock. The naked person … it was Terry.

'NICK! LOOK OUT!'

We were driving too fast. Nick wasn't paying attention and I didn't alert him in time. The car smashed into Terry and everything happened too fast. I hit the dashboard and the airbag burst and released. The car felt like it was spinning and we suddenly hit something else.

I was in shock, and after a few moments of breathing heavily and the airbag had deflated, I finally looked down at my body, noticing blood on my shirt and then my right arm that was in an unnatural position. I felt like I couldn't breathe and was panting extremely fast to try and get air into my lungs. I turned my head to look at Nick, whose airbag had also released and knocked him unconscious. Blood was dripping out of his nose and his mouth was open wide.

I felt like I wasn't reacting. I didn't feel pain. I didn't feel the blood dripping on me, nor could I use my right arm at all. The only thing I could feel was my heart beating fast and all I could hear was a pinging noise in my ears.

'Terry ...' I mumbled.

I suddenly remembered the last thing I had seen and tried to move my body. I felt like my legs weren't working, so instead I slowly looked over my shoulder to the road that was behind me.

Without doubt, it was Terry, who still seemed to be standing in the exact same spot, completely naked. I looked over the deflated airbag and saw a huge dent in the bonnet, which must have been where we had hit him. Terry had not moved and looked unscathed ... but our car was definitely destroyed. I looked over at Terry again ... Was he shaking? I was so confused by everything. I didn't know what was real and what was fake, but I was almost certain he was shaking on the spot, almost like he was vibrating or having a seizure.

I took another breath ... and it suddenly started to hit me. I felt the hot blood on my chest and my arm started to sting ... badly. I felt like I ached all over and it was like I was struggling to get air into my chest. I was in a really bad situation and I couldn't think straight. Nothing made sense, and less than a hundred metres away, my ex-boyfriend stood in the middle of the road, naked and shaking. To my right was my other ex-boyfriend, unconscious (I hoped) and covered in blood. I took another breath and hoped I could regain some sense.

TERRY

I took a sudden deep breath and opened my eyes. *Oh, fuck … where was I?* I was naked and in the middle of some road in the forest. It was freezing cold and nothing made sense. I closed my eyes and tried to remember the last thing that had happened to me before I blacked out. *I was walking …* that was right. I was going for a run in the forest. I was close to the seaside, at a part of Byanbythe that was nowhere near the town; it was all forest, sand and sea. I must have blacked out, but I had no idea for how long.

After I blacked out, my senses always took a while to return to me. I could see and would next be able to smell. I took in a deep breath through my nose and smelt smoke. *Smoke?* I looked around and suddenly saw the source of the smell, which coincided quickly with the return of my hearing. A car, which was emitting lots of smoke, was smashed up at the side of a tree a few hundred metres away. As my hearing returned, all I could hear now was the horn of the car, which was groaning away constantly. I ran over to the car, completely forgetting I was naked. As I got closer to the car, I started to piece together what had happened. I had returned from my blackout in the middle of the road ... and this car had a huge dent in the front, which looked like it had hit something hard ... or a freak like me. The car must have crashed into me, and like everything else that tried to hit me, suffered more damage. Oh fuck ... I really was in shit now.

I looked into the car and was horrified to see two passengers badly hurt. There was a guy, and ... Amy? AMY!

I ran around to the passenger side of the car and ripped the door open. I was now crying and frantically panicking.

'Amy! Amy! Are you conscious?'

She turned her head to me and opened her eyes.

'Terry!' she croaked.

'Amy!' I screamed. 'I am so sorry, are you hurt? Talk to me!'

'You need to get out of here.'

'What? No, Amy. We need to get you to hospital. Be mad at me later.'

'I don't mean that. You need to get away from here. I called an ambulance. They can't see you here.'

I was now really confused.

'What do you mean?' I asked.

'The ambulance,' she stuttered. 'They'll ask what we crashed into. You're naked. You need to go.'

And the penny finally dropped. As the tears streamed down my face, I felt my heart break as the girl I loved more than anything was trying to save me … even though I had put her into a horrific accident.

'I can't leave you here!'

'Go,' she commanded. 'I'm fine. The ambulance will be here soon. I'll ring you.'

I stood up and could hear an ambulance siren in the distance. I didn't want to leave her, I couldn't just walk away from this.

'Terry, please … you have to go,' she pleaded again.

And like a cold, heartless monster … I walked away. I started to run and disappeared into the forest. I looked back and saw the ambulance speed up and halt next to the car crash. What had I done?

*

I waited until the ambulance had left, and soon enough, the police had arrived to investigate the scene. I started to run through the dark forest, away from the accident. I was completely naked, I was scared and I was confused … but none of that mattered right now. I needed to get home, I needed to get clothes and I needed to drive to Amy.

I ran for what seemed like an hour; my logic was to keep running uphill towards Mount Cudd. Sure enough, I started to get my bearings, and as I left the wood and reached the main road, I had to be more cautious of my surroundings (just in case someone was awake and saw a naked guy running through the street). It was unnervingly silent and the only noise was the sound of wind flowing through the trees. Once I felt it was safe to run, I did a final stretch to my house and made it to the gate without being seen … I hoped.

As I approached the front door, I had a horrible thought come into my head. Where was my phone? Did I have it when I was on my run? Did I lose it with my clothes when I blacked out? How would I contact Amy without a phone? I ran into the house, but my fears were short-lived, as my phone and keys were on my bed. I quickly changed into my clothes and turned on my phone to text Amy. I had kept my phone turned off a lot lately, as I couldn't bear any messages from Amy. As I opened up the messaging app, I had twelve texts from Amy unread, but I was shocked to see that the last one was sent today - less than an hour ago.

Don't come to the hospital. Wait by my house. I will text you when I am home.

She must have texted me just before the ambulance had arrived. I didn't know what to do. Did I listen to her? Did I just not go to hospital? Things were just so fucked up. I decided to listen to her and drove down to the Doories' street, keeping my distance. I sat and sobbed, restless in my seat, continually checking my phone. It seemed like hours before anything happened, but finally, just after four in the morning, I saw Michael's truck drive into the street and park on his driveway. He exited the truck and quickly opened the passenger door. It was Amy, whose arm was in a sling. I felt sick and felt like getting out of the truck and running towards her.

Lisa greeted them at the door and grabbed Amy into a hug as she sobbed. As the front door closed, I sat and watched the house, and another half-hour passed before the lights in the house turned off. As I started to question what to do next, my phone bleeped with a notification that Amy had texted me.

Are you awake?

I'm outside

Okay, I'm coming out. We need to talk.

Was she mad? She was barely home from the hospital and she wanted to go out already? I drove my truck down the street and outside of her house, scared that the sound of the engine would attract unwanted attention. Amy left her house and quietly opened the door and sat in the passenger seat.

'Amy, what are you doing? You need to rest.'

'I needed to talk to you,' she replied.

'Why aren't you in hospital? What did they say?'

'I'm fine, I've dislocated my arm and badly bruised my nose, but apart from that I'm fine. I was quite lucky really. Nick wasn't too good, though.'

'You were with Nick?' I asked.

I had never given the driver of the car any thought …

'Yes, but he'll be fine, they're keeping him in overnight.'

'Oh …'

'It's not what you think. I wasn't on a date or anything,' she replied, almost like she had read my mind.

'I wasn't asking if you were …' I lied.

I avoided looking at her. She looked tired, sore, and the huge white sling just made me feel like I wanted to crawl inside of myself and disappear.

'Can we go somewhere?' she asked.

'What do you mean?'

'To talk. I want to go somewhere quiet.'

'It's four a.m … it is quiet,' I replied.

'Drive me to the beach, we can talk there.'

I could have argued with her, but I didn't. I drove the truck to the beach and we both sat in silence the whole way there. I drove to a beach that was on the other side of town, where I remembered running before I blacked out last.

It was beautiful, it was quiet and it was out of the way. The sky was starting to light up and it was the grey and purple colour in the clouds that hid the sun as it rose. Amy got out of the truck and walked onto the beach. As I followed, I watched her as she stood in the sand and took a deep breath in.

'I needed this,' she said. 'I love the fresh air in the morning.'

I didn't reply, but took my shoes and socks off and rolled up my jeans. I walked ahead of her and into the shallow waves that rocked back and forth onto the beach.

'What did you want to talk about?' I asked.

'What do you think?' she replied. 'I want the truth, Terry. I want to know everything.'

I didn't want to do this. I closed my eyes and thought about what to do. I had ended my relationship with her to protect her, but that failed miserably. Did I tell her everything I knew? Or did I push her away? I wasn't doing a good job of protecting her … but I also felt extremely miserable without her. What the hell did I do?

'Terry, please … I have to know what's going on.'

'I don't know,' I replied.

'Terry, I have seen too much to know something's not right!' she shouted.

'No … I don't mean that, I just … don't know what to tell you.'

'You have lied about so much, why don't you tell me the truth? Start from the start, I want to know everything.'

I carried on walking through the water, and as the freezing cold sea hit my feet, it reminded me that this wasn't a dream. Was I really about to do this? I had feared this moment all of my life.

'I'm doing this to protect you,' I warned. 'I didn't want to split up with you … but you saw tonight how dangerous I am … If you're close, I can't keep you safe.'

'I don't need protection, I can look after myself. I just want to know what's happening to you. Why did you really leave me?'

I paused and contemplated what to do … Maybe she was right. Maybe she could make her own decisions. If I told her the truth, she would soon realise that I was a freak and she really did need to stay away.

'Okay … I'll tell you. But if you never want to see me again, I will understand.'

'You can tell me anything …' she replied.

I let out a fake laugh, as she really had no idea what I was about to say.

'Tell me that after I tell you the truth …
Okay. I'll start from the beginning.'

I turned around and looked at her and her
eyes were full of tears. She stood in the sand and
watched me like I was about to explode. I guess I
had nothing else to lose.

'I haven't lied about everything,' I began. 'I
do love your family, I do want to be with you,
and up until I ran away and hitched a ride to
Saundersfoot … all of that was true. When I
escaped to Saundersfoot, I only managed to live
on the streets for a few weeks. I didn't go and
find my uncle, because I don't have an uncle.'

'You … don't have an uncle? But where did
you go?'

'I was kidnapped.'

I stopped and looked over at her. This
sounded so superficial, so much like bullshit …
but for once, I was telling her the truth, no
matter how stupid it sounded, and it seemed to
be the most believable thing I had said to her.
When she didn't reply, I carried on.

'I don't know what happened, but I was
taken by two people and driven away. I never
saw the people, but I lived in someone's
basement for ten years.'

'Terry … what do you mean? Who were
they?'

'I don't know, but it was a very secure underground room … It was so hard to escape. Oddly, they really looked after me; I had a huge bed, I was always given new books, a TV, music … I just wasn't allowed the internet. If I hadn't been kidnapped, it would have been quite nice.'

'This isn't time to make jokes, Terry! This is serious.'

'Sorry … but you don't understand how weird it was. Whoever put me down there really wanted me to stay there. I escaped twice … I remember when I was fourteen I managed to escape and get away as far as Amsterdam. It took me weeks, but I felt like I was free … but they just kept finding me and taking me back to the room.'

'Why didn't you go to the police?' she asked. 'When you escaped?'

'And what did I say? Someone keeps feeding me and buying me gifts in an underground prison? No way … and I was fourteen years old, they would have forced me into care. I didn't want to be in care, I wanted to be free.'

'But you must have escaped eventually? You live here now.'

'Well, that's the strange part. One day I woke up … three months before I lived here and

I turned eighteen. In the middle of the room, there was a letter and a bag of items.'

'What were they?' she asked.

'A new life. I had a new background, the house in Byanbythe, a bank account with millions of pounds in it. They really went to town ... I had a new passport, a driving licence, national insurance number and a nice little farewell letter.'

'What did the letter say?' she whispered; her voice was scared and in shock.

'It said I was free, but I had to live under certain conditions if I wanted to stay that way. Whoever kidnapped me wanted to be sure I stayed in the house in Byanbythe and I had to live a quiet life. They said the money would give me a comfortable life and I needed to stay here if I didn't want to be kidnapped again.'

'Terry, this is insane! Why haven't you gone to the police?'

'Amy, these are scary and powerful people. In the documents they left me, they actually created a new driving licence and passport and all the documents making up a backstory about my uncle. They created a random identity for my uncle, the adoption papers, the death certificate and his will leaving me the house and money … Who does that? I just wanted to get away and be free.'

'And how would they know you actually lived here?' she asked.

'I don't know … I guess they keep an eye on me somehow. But the house has no cameras and I've always kept a look out … no one watches me.'

'Terry, this is too much …'

'I haven't even covered the worst part …'

'There's more?'

'You don't want to know why I go missing? Why your ex-boyfriend hit me and I didn't feel a thing? Why can a car crash into me, but take more damage?'

She looked me at me with more fear than ever.

'I am a freak, Amy. I do not feel pain and I cannot get hurt. I am freakishly strong. Nothing can even damage my skin, it's like I am inhuman … and I have no idea why or how? It's why I survived the car crash that killed my parents all those years ago or the one with you and Nick. It's why I don't ever get hurt.'

'But … why were you naked in the road?'

'Because I keep blacking out. I black out and wake up days later. I have no fucking idea what happens to me, but when I black out, I become something scary. Like a wild animal, I smash things and do really strange things until I wake up.'

She let out a gasp and stepped backwards in the sand.

'This is why you disappear? What do you mean? I thought you had migraines?'

I started to cry, I felt like a huge burden had come off my chest ... but I also realised how fucked up my story was. I was a monster, I was a freak and I was dangerous.

'No, every migraine has been an excuse for when I have blacked out. I don't know why, Amy ... It's happened ever since I was young. I have no idea what happens to me. I was so scared that I had a safe-room built in my house, similar to the underground room I was kidnapped in. When I moved back to Byanbythe, it was the first thing I had built, but instead of the safe-room keeping people out ... I made sure it kept me inside. I couldn't hurt anyone inside. As long as I could make it to the safe-room every time I blacked out ... everyone was okay.'

'And ... have you ever hurt anyone before?' she asked.

'I don't know ... I don't think so. I hope not. The worst I have done is destroyed my house, which was the night you called the police.

Thankfully, I had made it to the safe-room before I could do more than smash my house.'

'So you were underneath us the whole time?'

'Yes.'

'So why were you naked tonight?'

'I must have blacked out before I had a chance to get home. That's the first time that's happened. I can normally tell when I am going to black out.'

'Why naked though?'

'I can't explain it. I turn into an animal when I black out. I must have ripped off my clothes.'

'I don't … I don't know what to say.'

'This is the part where you should run away from me. I'm a monster.'

She started to cry and I couldn't bear to look at her. I turned away from her and walked a little bit deeper into the water. The water was now up to my knees and freezing cold. The sky had changed into a pale yellow and grey and it was getting lighter by the minute. The cold breeze of the wind swept my face like it was caressing me, telling me I was going to be okay, somehow. I wondered if Amy had run away. I couldn't hear her. I wouldn't blame her. That was the first time I had ever told anyone about my fucked-up life. If honest, it felt good and cathartic, but it also just made me realise how much of a mess I was and how I didn't deserve to have Amy in my life, or her family.

'You're not a monster.'

I turned around and Amy was right behind me, standing in the water.

'Amy … you haven't seen me. Look at what I did to you.'

'That wasn't your fault, Nick crashed into you.'

'But if I wasn't there …'

'Nick wasn't watching the road.'

'Amy …'

'Terry, you're not a monster. You've been through the worst experience in the world. You don't need to keep people away from you … You need people around you.'

'You really believe me?' I asked.

'Of course … I mean, it's fucked up, but that doesn't mean you need to stay away from me.'

'I don't want you messed up in my shit.'

'And I don't want to be without you … I love you, Terry, and I mean that.'

I looked into her beautiful dark eyes.

'You … love me?' I asked.

'I do, more than I could ever love anyone else,' she carried on. 'I had never felt so happy with someone before and you just made me feel complete.'

'But … I'm a freak.'

'I know you are … but so am I. We could be freaks together.'

We both laughed, but I quickly looked away.

'This isn't a joke. This is really serious,' I reminded her.

'I know. But I want to be with you.'

'I want to be with you. I've always wanted to be with you. Every day locked up in that prison, all I thought about was you. Your red hair, your eyes, your bossy attitude … When I moved here, I promised I wasn't going to get close … I wanted to see your family again so much, who were the only normal part in my life. When we met in college, it felt like fate. You and your family had made me feel normal for the first time in my life.'

'So why did you end it?'

'When you called the police and your parents came up, I realised I was kidding myself. I couldn't live a normal life, and that incident was going to be the first of many fucked-up events.'

'But now I know … we can look after each other … I can protect you.'

'Amy … are you sure about this?'

'Yes.'

'It isn't always going to be like it was, I could black out at any time, I could disappear,' I reminded her. 'The people who were kidnapped could come back.'

'We'll face them together.'

I looked at her and tears streamed down my face. She really was the most beautiful person in the world. She was so understanding, so kind and gentle. During the car accident, even though she was in danger, she only cared about getting me away from the incident. After I had stood here and told her about my horrible life, she just wanted to find a way to make our life work together.

'I want nothing more in this world than to be your partner,' I said. 'I want to be with you forever. I want to be part of your family. It's the only thing in life that makes me feel normal.'

'Then be with me. Be with my family.'

'I love you, Amy. I have loved you since the moment your dad took me home. You have been the only hope I have had through the darkest days of my life.'

She stood on her tiptoes and with her only functioning arm, grabbed my face and passionately kissed me. The sea continued to crash against our legs, the wind swept through our hair and we kissed like we had never kissed before. I loved this girl more than anything in the world and I never wanted this kiss to end.

'I love you, Amy,' I said and I kissed her nose, then her forehead.

We hugged, and after the worst night, I had somehow never felt happier in my life.

'Let's go home … before my parents wake up.'

The sun was now rising and the sky was yellow with bits of blue. I quickly drove Amy back to her house, but the whole journey we held hands, like we couldn't let go of each other. I stopped outside of her house and turned to her.

'What now?'

'I best sleep, but come round this afternoon. We can plan our next steps together.'

'What about your family?'

'We'll tell them. I want them to know about us.'

'Okay. I'll be back later.'

She gave me one last kiss and sneaked back into her house. I continued to watch the spot where she disappeared and slowly closed my eyes. Life really was a strange thing and my life in Byanbythe was certainly not turning out to be how I had planned. What should I do? I really did love Amy Doorie, with all my heart … but how could I keep her safe…?

…

'Terry?'

I woke with a huge shock. I turned to see Michael at my car window, standing with a steaming cup of coffee in his hands, dressed in his dressing gown. I opened the truck door and gave an awkward smile.

'Hey, Michael …'

'Why are you sleeping on my drive? You should have rung the doorbell! I keep telling you this is your home.'

'Michael, I'm sorry … I just -'

'I'm guessing you're here because of Amy?' he asked.

Did he see us in the truck? How did he know?

'Michael, I, just, um -'

'I'm guessing she texted you. Nasty crash, it was a boy driving. She's okay, though, I promise you.'

I felt a huge sigh of relief - he thought I was here because of the crash; I decided to play along.

'Ah, thank god, I was so worried.'

'Oh my lord, you have no idea! When I had that call, I thought the worst. Thank god she had so little damage. What was she doing with that boy though? Always hated that Nick!'

'I just wanted to check she was okay.'

'Ah, that's good of you, lad, but sleeping in the car! Lisa would kill you before the cold did if she thought you slept on our drive! Come in for a coffee,' he said, and I followed him into the house.

I looked at the grandfather clock in the living room and saw it was six in the morning. I sat down in the kitchen as Michael poured me a coffee. He sat down opposite me and gave me a huge smile.

'It was good of you to come down here to check on Amy,' he said, but there was something suspicious in his voice; was he questioning me?

'Of course, you're all family to me,' I replied.

We sat and spoke about football training for a little while, but the small investigation returned.

'Apart from football training … we haven't seen you too much down here of late. Lisa was worried something was wrong, is there?' he asked, with the same tone of ulterior motive.

I thought for a second before I replied … I had spent the night confessing all my lies and my sins; I felt good and compared my night to confessing to a priest and finally being absolved. If Amy and I were going to be together, Michael and Lisa were eventually going to find out the truth about us, and whilst I couldn't tell them the whole truth about my life, my relationship with Amy was the only truth I could give them that was safe.

'Michael, I need to talk to you about something,' I finally replied.

He looked over his small glasses and gave me a look of amused interest.

'Okay?' he replied.

'I haven't been around as much ... because I've felt awkward about something,' I began.

'Awkward? Terry, how many times -?'

'It's Amy.'

He stopped talking and looked at me with a confused look.

'I ... I think I have feelings for her. And I've felt awkward about it, like I've betrayed you and Lisa,' I admitted (but added a convincing tone of sadness to my voice).

He stared at me, and behind those glasses I had no idea what he was thinking. Had I messed up here? Had I judged this situation wrong? As I started to panic, I started to think about how stupid I was and how angry Amy would be, when Michael's expression suddenly changed - he smiled.

'My boy, did you think we had no idea? I was once a teenager too, you know ... The way you look at her, the way you smile at her … it was bloody obvious!' he laughed.

If only I could have seen my own reaction; I felt stupid, I felt like I had been discreet and acting like the Invisible Man, when it turned out everyone knew about my emotions?

'You … knew? You're not angry at me?' I asked, my voice raising a few octaves higher than usual.

'Angry?' he asked. 'Of course not! I think the real question is, does she know?'

'I think she does …' I replied, playing dumb.

'It's quite obvious she likes you too, if I'm honest. I love my daughter to bits, but she is a right moody cow. The only time I haven't seen her in a mood is when she is around you.'

I felt my face go red and I was suddenly staring at the ground, as I let out an awkward laugh.

'I really thought you'd hate me because of this.'

'Oh, Terry, you really do overthink things. I couldn't think of anyone nicer to date my daughter. I should feel sorry for you though, she does have a wicked temper.'

'Don't I know it …' I replied.

We suddenly started to laugh and I felt a little more comfortable to talk. Did Michael just agree to me dating Amy? I felt like I needed to slap myself - things were going way too smooth. Something was bound to go wrong. Good things didn't happen to monsters like me ... but they were and I was now wondering for how long?

AMY

I woke up and winced at the sudden pain I felt from various parts of my body. My arm stung, my nose felt like it was burning and my body ached like I had been at the gym for a solid month. Sudden images of the night before were flashing before my eyes. My first thought? Laura was dead to me and she owed me money. Nick was in bad shape, but was going to be in worse shape once my dad had got hold of him. And then ... then there was Terry ... the memories came flooding back, and suddenly, nothing hurt more than the overload of information I had from our conversation on the beach. What was Terry? What made him so strong? What caused him to not feel pain? Who kidnapped him? Who gave him money and a house? Why did they want him in Byanbythe? And the scariest part of all … what happened when he blacked out?

But as my mind tried to process all of this, none of those questions seemed to matter as much, because I then remembered how it all ended. Terry was finally back with me. We were going to face all this together and I could be happy again, knowing he was by my side. I slowly got out of bed and felt like I was limping as I walked out of the room. I knew I was about to face a hundred questions about last night, about what happened and why I was in Nick's car. Mom and Dad gave me the grace of needing rest when I arrived home from hospital, so did not ask too many questions … but this morning? There would be no prisoners. I was about to receive an interrogation. As I slowly lifted myself onto each step heading downstairs, I heard talking from the kitchen. I heard Mom and Dad laughing and then … Terry? Was I imagining his voice? I quickened my pace and entered the kitchen.

'Here she is!' my dad said. 'Good morning! How do you feel, Red?'

Terry, Mom and Dad all sat around the table eating croissants and drinking coffee.

'I'm okay, a little sore,' I replied. 'I didn't know Terry was here?'

'Oh, lover boy here couldn't keep away! I'm surprised he didn't bring roses!' my mom joked as she hit Terry on the arm.

'Shut up, Lisa,' replied Terry, but they were all laughing as if they were on a drunk night out.

'Am I missing something here?' I questioned.

'Oh, give up the act, Amy, we know you're both Romeo and Juliet,' my dad laughed.

I looked Terry in the eyes and he gave me a look of apology, but also at the same time a look of "just go with it".

'Oh … right,' I replied.

'He has our blessing. I told him I felt sorry for him really,' Dad laughed.

'Look, you're starting to put me off her,' said Terry.

'Okay, this isn't how I expected my morning to go,' I said, and they all continued to laugh and eat their breakfast.

'So, how long have you been courting each other?' Mom asked as she poured coffee into a mug for me.

'Courting?' Terry asked.

'Who says "courting" anymore?' I growled, cringing at the very word.

'You know what I mean!' Mom snapped back.

'Do we have to have the questions?' I moaned.

'I suppose not, but I guess I can show Terry your embarrassing baby photos now?' she replied.

I buried my head in my hands and let out a large groan.

'Take me back to hospital, I'd rather be there!' I shouted.

'Hey, maybe we could all go on a double date?' my dad suggested. 'Wouldn't that be fun?'

'You're doing this on purpose to torture both of us, aren't you?' Terry asked.

'It's a parents prerogative to torture their kids when they have a boyfriend or girlfriend,' Dad replied. 'It's just a little bit more fun because we know you so well, Terry.'

The morning passed ... smoothly, with lots of awkward jokes and questions from Mom and Dad. I explained what had happened at Emma Chanesse's party, about Laura leaving me in the lurch and Nick being my only option to get home safely - or so I thought. My mom threatened that I couldn't leave the house while I rested, but was grateful that I seemed to be acting normal. Eventually, Mom had to leave to take Tim to a swimming class and Dad had to go to town to collect some football stuff from a local supplier. Before he left, he made a final joke of booking a restaurant for our "double date" and finally left, leaving me alone with Terry.

'Wow …' I said.

'I take it back,' said Terry. 'The conversation on the beach wasn't the hardest conversation I had ever had, your mom and dad's awkward questions were a hundred times worse.'

'How did that even happen?'

Terry explained the events of the morning, and although I was horrified at how well my mom and dad took the news, I actually felt relieved that it was over and done with.

'So, what happens now?' he finally asked.

'What do you mean?'

'What do we do now?'

'I still don't get you?'

'I've never been in a relationship before, I don't know what to do,' he replied.

'Well … I guess we could do what we did before? Hang out, go on dates, kiss … you know, couple things?'

He laughed, but I could tell something was wrong.

'What's wrong?' I asked.

'I still feel wrong, like I'm putting you in danger. I'm scared I'll black out or something …'

I walked over to him and kissed him on the lips.

'I don't need protecting, you have to stop thinking you're here to look after me. I make my own decisions … and most of all, we're in this together.'

He laughed again and looked up into my eyes.

'You need to teach me how to be a boyfriend.'

'I will. Like today, I need to rest, so you need to get snacks, ice creams, chocolates and coffees. Then we need to sit on the sofa and watch terrible movies all day.'

'And that's what you do in relationships?'

'Those are the best times to have in a relationship,' I replied.

After continuing to kiss for what felt like an eternity, Terry finally managed to get out of the house to get supplies. I decided to attempt to have a bath and make myself semi-presentable (even days on the sofa required some level of looking decent). Just as I was about to go to the bathroom, the front door knocked. As I opened it, my good mood suddenly disappeared.

'I'm so sorry!'

It was Laura, who stood at the front door crying and apologising.

'You are the worst friend in the world!' I barked at her.

'I had no idea … I was drunk … I -'

'You just wanted to get laid with that old man, Ricky!'

'Amy, I'm so sorry … I really am. Are you okay?'

'No! I was in a car crash because I had to get a ride home with my ex-boyfriend!'

I slammed the front door shut, but I still heard her apologising from behind it. I wanted to walk back to the bathroom, but annoyingly couldn't leave her standing there. I reopened the door again.

'And you owe me money!' I shouted, and after thinking about how angry I still was at her, decided to slam the front door shut again.

I limped up the stairs and had my bath, trying to ignore the thought of Laura possibly crying at the front door still; she was a huge drama queen and quite possibly would have sat crying at the front door until someone asked her to come in. I knew it wasn't her fault that Nick crashed the car ... but she was still a shitty friend and as always put another guy as a priority over her friendships.

When Terry returned, I could confidently say that I had one of the best days of my life. He brought nearly every snack possible from the shop, twice as much as my mom would buy for an entire weekly food shop. We sat on the sofa and watched film after film whilst I lay on him. We hardly did anything, but it felt so good to be in each other's company, doing normal stuff, without drama. As we lay together, I couldn't help but wonder about the things Terry would worry about. What would I do the next time he was missing? Visit the secret safe-room in his house? And how would I explain to anyone if he never reached that room? What if someone had seen him naked in the road? These were really worrying thoughts, but I decided that they were all ifs and buts; worrying wasn't going to achieve anything and there was nothing I could do but face the issues if and when they occurred. I looked up at Terry and just thought how beautiful he was. He smiled and seemed to be happy-go-lucky again ... but underneath his smile, there was a very serious and sad side to him, one that had been plagued by tragedy and horror. It was funny how he thought he needed to protect me, when in reality, I needed to protect him.

*

College on Monday was everything I dreaded it to be, but like always, gossip came and went. News had spread fast about my car accident with Nick and when I arrived at college with bruises and my arm in a sling, it confirmed that everything was true. After a few days of people speculating what had happened, the general consensus was that Nick wasn't concentrating on the road and caused the crash. I did feel a little sorry for Nick; yes, he wasn't concentrating, yes, he was arguing and being horrible to me … but did I believe that crashing into Terry was entirely his fault? I started to feel conflicted about him taking the full brunt of people's judgements … but after remembering the way he acted in the car, my sympathy didn't last long.

Apart from the drama of gossip, I started to feel like a kid again when I was with Terry. Life just seemed to shift back to normality, as if nothing was wrong; in fact, my mom and dad seemed to get on a lot better with me since Terry was my boyfriend, as he was always round our house and around everyone. Terry and I were practically inseparable and I unintentionally started to display public affection with him when we were out. It started little; at first Terry and I didn't hang out together at college, but one day I just decided to hold his hand as we walked to class … which pretty much confirmed to all prying eyes that we were together. This did shift some thoughts to the gossip of why Nick crashed the car; was he jealous of Terry? Did he try and split us up? Either way, the whispers stopped after a while. Sometimes Terry and I would be shopping in town and he would randomly kiss me, which on reflection made me shudder at the thought of this public affection … but I guess I couldn't help myself. It felt too good to be loved and to love someone in return.

Laura had posted a card with my money through the front door and a "get well soon" card. After a few days of making her suffer, I decided to text her back, although I still didn't want to see her in person. When she had heard that I was officially dating Terry, she forgot that I wasn't talking to her and tried to text me for gossip. I gave her short replies and very little information.

The only other person I had not seen was Nick, who was rumoured to now be out of hospital. He still wasn't back at college and I didn't know if this was due to resting at home or through total embarrassment. One of the girls we were friends with was dating one of Nick's best friends, who had told her that Nick was refusing to talk about the incident. I guessed that once Nick had confirmed that I didn't tell anyone about the crash, he respected that and kept his silence too. At first, I really worried about what Nick would remember from that night. Would he remember crashing into Terry? Would I have to lie about what happened to save Terry (not that anyone would have believed Nick had crashed into him …)? The police visited me for a statement and gladly put my mind at rest when they said Nick couldn't remember anything. I made up a statement that we were arguing and Nick had crashed into a tree (which caused the big dent in the front of his car). They were satisfied with the events of the night and had given Nick a warning for reckless driving.

After a few weeks, my arm was much better and I no longer had to use a sling to support it. I was still bruised and I had the odd ache here and there, but I was just glad to have two functioning arms again. To celebrate, Terry had booked a date night at a very posh and expensive steakhouse on the beach, The Smoke House, which was a popular location for the rich and famous. I felt like this was too much of a grand gesture and insisted that I was happy with just a coffee date … but Terry wouldn't have any of it, set on a fancy night together.

Terry arrived at my house after getting dressed up in a plain white shirt, black jeans and boots, which he looked fantastic in. His hair was slicked back and he hadn't shaved (upon my request), which was starting to grow as a grey beard.

I wasn't very girlie, so didn't own a single dress, and most of my wardrobe was dedicated to black clothes, band tops and checked shirts. After stressing for a few hours, I had managed to find a black jumpsuit I had worn to a cousin's wedding last year and decided with a few accessories it would be acceptable enough for a date. As I was doing my makeup, I could overhear my dad in the living room talking to Terry.

'I cannot believe you are eating there! I have always wanted to go, but Lisa is a vegetarian … Ahh, Terry, why can't we go on a date instead?'

'You're just not my type,' Terry joked. 'And besides … you're like a dad to me, that's sick.'

'Ahh, I'm so upset, Terry. They have tomahawks there! The size of my leg, I've heard!'

'Michael, for God's sake, I have said we can go a hundred times before!' my mom had shouted from the kitchen.

'And do what? I'll eat steak while you watch? I doubt they even do vegetables there!' my dad shouted back, a tone of pure frustration in his voice.

I had always admired my mom for being a vegetarian and quite often joined her in eating meals with no meat. Meat didn't really bother me, but I ate it when it was on the table. My dad was a hundred percent carnivore and if he wasn't eating meat, he was talking about it. I knew my dad would be jealous of us going for this meal, but to hear him asking Terry on a date really put into perspective how much he wanted to go.

After I was finally ready and Dad had recommended hundreds of options to try off the menu, we arrived at the restaurant and took seats at a gorgeous window that overlooked the sea. The sun was starting to low, creating a beautiful sunset on the horizon. Without noticing, I was smiling at the sunset, which caught Terry's attention.

'What's funny?' he asked.

'My dad always told me when I was younger that the sun made a sizzling noise when it hit the sea … as if the sun went underwater when it slept.'

'Your dad is the funniest person I have ever met. Did you know he asked me on a date tonight, using me to get a tomahawk steak?'

'I heard …' I replied.

The restaurant was stunning. It was an industrial-styled restaurant, covered in dark wooden panels and black steel beams. A pianist sat in the corner of the bar area and played relaxing music, as the rest of the room filled with sounds of laughter and conversations. The smell was an intense smell of meat cooking from the open plan kitchen, where all the chefs could be viewed creating flames on the grill. The waiter took our order and instantly poured Terry and I a glass of red wine each.

'Would you like the wine menu to follow?' he asked.

'No, thanks ... can we order some soft drinks?' asked Terry.

The waiter looked almost offended, but took our drinks order and walked away, most likely about to scorn the two kids who didn't order off the wine menu.

'Why do people always think you drink wine?' I grumbled to Terry.

'I've never actually tried it,' he admitted, and took a small sip from the glass that the waiter had just poured. His face changed into a disgusted look, as if he had just bitten into a lemon. 'What the hell is that? It's like vinegar!'

'All alcohol tastes like vinegar,' I replied.

'So, is there a story behind why you hate alcohol? Or do you just like things that don't taste like shit?'

'Not really. I guess all of my friends have put me off drinking for life,' I replied. 'I remember my friends getting drunk from the age of thirteen, throwing up, drinking to excess … it just made me angry.'

'Wow, thirteen?'

'Yes, I just don't get why people *have* to have alcohol to have a good time. I don't mind people who drink because they enjoy the taste … but no one my age seems to drink for taste, it's always who can get wasted the quickest.'

'Is that what happened at your Halloween party?'

'Yes, I really enjoyed it until everyone got overly drunk.'

'Biggest perk of being kidnapped, you don't have to put up with drunk friends.'

'Wow … are you really joking about that?' I replied, and gave him a look of concern.

'Ah, come on, if I can't joke about it, what can I do? Besides, it wasn't like I was hard done by, was I? All things considered, I had a better upbringing than most … and I was kidnapped in a basement! They fed me good food, they gave me books, albums, everything I needed really. If the trip advisor did kidnappers -'

'Terry!' I barked. 'What they did was awful!'

'Could have been worse,' he laughed.

'Or you could have Stockholm syndrome … I mean, doesn't it disturb you how well they looked after you? And then bought you a house and gave you lots of money? At least with the kidnappers that treat people bad, it's obvious what they want … but this is something else.'

'I try not to think about it. I'm just grateful to have you and your family,' he replied and grabbed my hand.

'Do you remember much from before the car accident?' I asked. 'When I first met you?'

'No.'

'Nothing at all?'

'Nothing, I don't even know what my real parents look like.'

'Didn't your uncle ever show you any?'

'My "uncle" that didn't exist?' he replied, quoting the word uncle with his fingers.

'Oh, sorry ... it's a lot to remember. That's sad though, do you think you don't remember because of the accident?'

'Most likely.'

He started to look a little uncomfortable, so I changed the subject.

'What's your favourite colour?' I asked.

'What?'

'What's your favourite colour?'

'That's random.'

'Just answer it.'

'Purple. I think? What's yours?'

'Black, like my soul.'

'Makes sense ...'

'What's your favourite book?'

'*The Count of Monte Cristo*. But part of me wants to say *Harry Potter*,' laughed Terry. 'What about you?'

'*Wuthering Heights*, obviously,' I replied, and how could he not know that? It was a goth's bible.

'Okay, my turn. Favourite album?' he asked.

'*Disintegration* by The Cure. What about you?'

'*Shadows Collide with People*, John Frusciante. The greatest album to listen to when locked in a room.'

'Terry ...'

'Sorry. Okay, when was your first kiss?'

'When I was eleven years old, my first year of secondary school. His name was Ralph and he ate a tuna sandwich just before. What about you?'

'Outside your house after our first coffee date.'

'I was your first kiss?'

'Yes. I know I'm not allowed to make jokes, but you're limited on choices when you're locked on your own in a room.'

'Sorry … sorry … I'm still trying to take it all in.'

'It's fine. Who was your first boyfriend?'

'Chester Smith, massive hipster. I split up with him when he refused to listen to his favourite band when other people started to like them.'

'Wow, did he wear braces and have a gelled moustache?'

'No, he's asexual and protests on the beach to stop fishing, as it's cruel to the sealife.'

'Perfect, he's a contender against me for your most weird boyfriend,' Terry joked.

'You know, considering you black out, don't seem to feel pain and have this super strength … you're actually the most normal boyfriend I've ever had. I've done more normal things with you than I have with anyone else before.'

'Like crash into me with your ex-boyfriend?'

'No, like actually go on dates together, talking to each other, watching films … I've never had that before.'

'I really find that bizarre. How can people not want to talk to you? You're the most interesting person I know.'

'No, *that's* bizarre. I am boring compared to everyone else. I won't drink, I hate parties, I don't seem to understand people my age. I would be happy on a desert island listening to albums and reading books.'

'And that's what makes you interesting. You know, my first day of college, before I joined class, I saw so many girls. Every guy notices girls … but everyone just seems to be the same these days. Not one person stood out in the crowd, except for you.'

'That's because you knew me.'

'No, this was before I knew it was you. I saw you walking … your red hair, your style … the way you walked, it just … caught my attention. When I sat in class and saw you up close … I then knew it was you.'

I smiled and had no idea how to reply. Everything he said (when he wasn't making jokes) was always the perfect thing to say. He made me feel beautiful, even if I didn't see it myself. He noticed things about me that possibly no one else saw, but regardless of if they were true or not, it still made me smile.

The meal came and we kept firing questions and getting to know each other. He liked nearly every genre of music, which shocked me as he just seemed to have a great understanding of nearly every band I mentioned. We both had a passion for books, but he was far more diverse and in depth with his choices. The thing that shocked me most on the date was how much I laughed. I never laughed, I was miserable and moody ... but with Terry I just laughed non-stop and discovered laughs I didn't even know I had (and some quite embarrassing to hear).

I didn't want this night to end, and as always, he just said the perfect thing, like he could read my mind.

'How about we end the meal with a coffee?' he asked, and attempted to call over the waiter who judged us previously for hating wine.

TERRY

I felt like if I smiled anymore my face would get cramp. I could not stop smiling around Amy. I felt full, with the best food I had ever eaten, and thanks to Michael, a tomahawk steak was my new favourite choice. I decided to walk to the bar in the middle of the restaurant to order our coffees, as our waiter apparently didn't see me when I called him over (he was mortified when I had asked for mayonnaise for my fries previously).

The bar was extremely busy and it seemed like there were at least ten people in front of me waiting to order and get the bartender's attention. I crammed myself into the only gap at the bar and waited for the bartender to serve me.

'What a great place this is!'

A guy waiting next to me started to talk to me. At first I didn't acknowledge him, as I didn't think he was talking to me, but he soon spoke again.

'Your date is pretty hot. Red hair? I have a soft spot for girls with red hair.'

Red hair? Okay, he was talking to me and he now had my attention. I looked at him, disgusted with the tone he had as he described Amy. He also had red hair and was very tall and gangly. His hair was slicked back and he looked a little bit older than me. He was wearing an old, tattered leather jacket, and once I gave him a good look up and down, I realised he seemed out of place compared to everyone else in the restaurant.

'Thanks,' I replied, and turned away to ignore him.

'Does she know?' he asked.

His bright blue eyes didn't look at me once when he asked these questions, instead he seemed to be staring at Amy, with his back leaning against the bar.

'Does she know what?' I asked.

'What you are,' he said and I suddenly felt a little sick. What did he mean?

'Excuse me? Can I help you with something?'

'Surely when she crashed into you, she found out what you were?'

Fuck. He must have seen the crash. I started to panic and needed to think of a good excuse.

'I have no idea what you're on about, mate.'

I started to walk away, but he grabbed my wrist in a tight grip. He pulled me close and whispered into my ear.

'Don't lie to me. You can lie to her, but you can't lie to me. We have too much in common.'

'What the fuck do you want?' I growled and snatched my arm back, causing a few people at the bar to look at us.

He laughed like I had just told an extremely funny joke and put his arm around my shoulder.

'Don't cause a scene,' he whispered again. 'You'll regret it, trust me … and you don't want your red-haired girlfriend finding out what you are.'

'She already knows,' I lied, and pretended that I also knew what I was.

His face changed, and for the first time he looked serious.

'Bullshit,' he replied.

'Who are you?' I asked.

'Someone like you … but trust me, I know you're lying. Once people know what we are, they never stay around for long.'

'And what is it you think we are?'

He gave me a curious look and started to laugh, but this laugh seemed to be out of frustration. He ran his fingers through his hair and slowly rubbed his face.

'You're either a good liar or you're fucking around with me,' he finally said. 'Either way, I'll see you around … and your red-haired girlfriend.'

He slowly walked away and out of the restaurant. After thinking about what he said, almost in shock, I realised that I couldn't just let him go. I ran out of the restaurant, but it was too late. I watched him climb onto a motorbike and ride away. I thought he hadn't noticed me, but as he rode out of the car park, he saluted me.

I stood and watched until he was no longer in view. Who was he? Did he really know what I was? Was he really like me? Part of me wanted to climb into my truck and chase after him, but part of me knew he was trouble.

'What's wrong?'

I turned around and Amy was standing behind me, looking concerned.

'Sorry,' I said. 'I thought someone was trying to break into my truck.'

'Really? Where?' she replied.

'It was nothing. They're gone now.'

She smiled and grabbed my hand.

'Why don't we get that coffee at home?' she asked.

'Yeah, good idea,' I replied.

I suddenly became a zombie and felt like I had gone into autopilot for the rest of the night. I paid the bill and generously tipped by at least a hundred pounds without noticing and then drove back home to Amy's house. Whoever that was ... they were dangerous and I couldn't get them out of my mind.

*

I couldn't sleep. I felt paranoid. Who was that guy? So many thoughts raced through my head that I started to think he was watching me. I paced around my house and, for once, was grateful that I had very little furniture. I rushed over to the terrace above and looked everywhere in the forest ahead and the streets below, trying to see any signs of someone watching my house.

Such a perfect night ruined by that idiot ... and I let him get away. I was tempted to drive around and look for his bike. It was a very distinctive bike, it looked very old and was more of a chopper than a sports bike.

Was he really like me? I kept asking the same question over and over again, until the scariest question of all popped into my head. What if he was the person who kidnapped me? He didn't seem that much older than me … but what if he worked for them? It was starting to make sense and that scared me more. Did that mean the kidnappers were also like me? Were they monsters too? What if I was some horrible experiment that went wrong? But then again … I never even spoke or saw my kidnappers in person … How could they have experimented on me? So *many* questions. I head-butted the wall and didn't sleep a single second that night; I had officially driven myself crazy.

The sun started to rise and I decided to go for a run before I picked up Amy for college. I ran down my street and through the forest. I always ran through this area … I was sure, although I never asked to confirm, that the road closest to my house was where my parents' car crashed. Sometimes I would run to the side of the road, expecting to see something to confirm that this was the place they died. What was I expecting? A sign that said *"RIP Kelvin and*

Marie Haynes"? Maybe I was looking for signs of the car crash, some ruined road or stains on the ground? I didn't know, but I never wanted to read up old newspaper articles about it, nor did I want to ask people what they knew.

My run felt good and I built up a sweat. Running did not challenge me much, as part of my *"condition"* not only made me strong, but also made me feel super fast. I could run for miles and not feel out of breath. I had my limits, of course, but I rarely found them; the one time I really felt exhausted was the second time I had escaped from my kidnappers. I managed to make it all the way to Amsterdam (which was no easy feat). I felt safe after the fifth day, but sure enough someone started to follow me … I ran, they ran. I climbed over walls, over roads, up buildings … but whoever was chasing me managed to get me; that really did push my limits that day.

I arrived home and had a shower. By the time I was dressed, it was time to pick up Amy; time really flew when I thought about my past. I had almost forgotten my new problem, but sure enough, the ginger guy crept back into my head. I drove to Amy's and walked into the Doories' house. She caught my eye and every time I felt butterflies in my stomach. She was wearing a band top, tight black jeans and converse … I just felt so attracted to her. Her perfume was always so sweet, and when she had her hair tied up, I just noticed how white her skin was and how beautiful she was.

'Morning, you,' she said and gave me a small wink.

I wanted to kiss her so bad.

'Terry, did you take a picture of the tomahawk?!' Michael called from the kitchen.

Finally, a bit of normality. I sneaked Amy a kiss and sat down with Michael and Lisa for breakfast before college. As the day progressed, I slowly put the ginger guy to the back of my mind, trying to settle my thoughts. If he turned up again, I wouldn't let him leave without an answer. College finally finished and I waited for Amy outside of the car park. I waited for some time, and when she arrived, I grabbed her hand and started to walk to my car, finally feeling a little more relaxed and cheerful.

'You're running over,' I said.

'Don't even start me,' she replied.

'How was Film Studies?'

'Horrible. We're studying French cinema, which is really, really cheesy. That's why I'm late! We had to rewatch a scene over and over again.'

'Sounds easy,' I joked.

'Are you finally going to tell me what other classes you take at college?'

I refused to tell Amy what other classes I attended, other than English with her ... partly because I was embarrassed and mostly because it was cute how much it annoyed her not to know. Did I dare admit that, for some unknown reason, I took History and Philosophy? They were interesting subjects, I had to admit, but they were full of weird, hipster-like people ... and I didn't want to give Amy ammunition to call me a hipster.

'Nope,' I replied.

'I will find out what classes you take. I have people on the inside ...'

'You will never find out.'

'I think you study Dance ... or maybe PE? That's why you won't tell me.'

I stopped walking.

'Amy, go and stand by the car park entrance.'

'What?'

'Just go!' I ordered.

The ginger guy was back and he was lying down on my truck bonnet, looking like he was on the beach getting a suntan. The car park was mostly empty now, so he was wasn't hard to spot.

Amy slowly backed away, but I didn't look back at her; instead, I ran over to my truck.

'What the fuck are you doing?' I shouted.

'Ahh, here you are!' he replied, and slowly lay on his side to look at me. 'Nice car. I had no idea you went to college?'

'It's a truck and get off it! What do you want?'

'I want us to be friends. I've never met someone like me before.'

'What do you mean? You keep saying this, but you won't say what we are?'

'There you are, playing those games again. We are cursed! We are the gods!'

He quickly stood up on my truck bonnet and became animated as he shouted his words, like some dramatic actor on a stage.

I had to be careful, as there were already people looking over at us from the campus. I couldn't make a scene … but I felt so angry. I felt like I wasn't in control … I felt like I was going to black out. Without thinking, I grabbed his legs and pulled him, making him slip and fall onto the windscreen of my truck. He began to laugh.

'Wow, no respect for your car!' he laughed.

Thankfully, I must have acted so quick that no one seemed to notice the ginger guy falling onto my truck.

'Who are you?!'

'Fine … fine. I'm Joe. And you're Terry? Right?' he asked.

I didn't reply.

'Look, we need to have a heart-to-heart. I think your girlfriend needs to know what you are. She doesn't realise the pain you're going to cause her,' he continued. 'What's her name?'

'Leave her out of this …' I growled.

Joe looked over my shoulder.

'Terry's girlfriend! Come over here!' he shouted.

'Leave her out of this or I'll break your jaw,' I threatened. I felt venomous, I felt like I could kill this guy right here, right now.

Amy walked over and looked very confused.

'Terry, is everything okay?' she asked, and looked at Joe with concern.

'Amy, you need to stay back!'

'Amy! So that's your name,' said Joe. 'Poor Terry wouldn't tell me your name.'

He jumped off my truck bonnet and grabbed Amy's hand to kiss it.

'Get the fuck away from her,' I threatened again.

'Terry, calm down. I just want to talk to Amy!' said Joe, and he wrapped his arm around her. 'Amy, I think there are secrets about Terry you need to know ...'

'Who are you?' Amy asked.

'I am an old friend of Terry's, but I'm here to save you, Amy. Terry's a scary boy. He's not human. He's dangerous.'

Amy looked scared and she looked into my eyes for answers.

'You know about him?' she asked Joe.

'Know what?' replied Joe.

'I told you, she knows about me!' I shouted.

'Amy, do you know that Terry's not human? Do you know he has superpowers? That he's a killer?'

I looked at Amy and nodded to try and get her to agree.

'Yes,' she said. 'I know about him. How do you know?'

'Oh, he's not alone,' said Joe. 'We're very much the same ... but I'm worried how relaxed you seem about this. He could rip your head off with a single pull ... doesn't that worry you?'

'No, because I know him ... he's no monster ... but I can't say the same about you. What do you want?'

Joe looked annoyed and his laugh became fake.

'Amy, you're either stupid or Terry hasn't told you the truth.'

Joe pulled out a knife and thrust it into my chest. It all happened so quick, but the knife didn't penetrate my skin … Instead, it bent and blunted at the end. Amy let out a small scream, which attracted looks from people walking through the car park.

'Do you think this is normal? I've just stabbed your boyfriend and the knife didn't even hurt him! He's dangerous, Amy,' Joe whispered into Amy's ear. He looked feral, angry and like he was about to lose the plot.

I didn't feel a thing, but I quickly looked around to make sure no one was still looking. The people who reacted to Amy's scream must have presumed it was a fake scream.

'The only dangerous person here is you,' said Amy. 'I know all about Terry, so I don't know what you want me to say? I think you should just leave.'

This obviously wasn't the reaction that Joe was looking for and he seemed extremely annoyed with Amy's response.

'What the fuck is wrong with you? Are you that stupid? A knife didn't hurt him; he should be bleeding right now. Why aren't you freaked out?'

'Go. Away,' commanded Amy.

'You're just a stupid bitch, aren't you?' said Joe, who suddenly turned to me. 'I don't know what you did to brainwash this stupid redhead, but you've obviously been lucky. I don't know how many other people know what you are? Does the redhead's family know? We'll have to find out!'

I had had enough and clenched my fists as tight as I could. I was quick - but he was faster. I tried to punch him, but he jabbed a very powerful punch into my stomach, so fast I didn't see it coming.

I fell to my knees and grabbed hold of my stomach. I felt pain for the first time in my life. Someone punched me and I actually felt it … more painfully than any punch or any car crash I had ever brushed off in the past. I felt the wind get knocked out of me and suddenly was gasping for air.

'Don't *ever* think you can punch me. You think you're strong compared to these peasants that live in this town? You have no idea, I could kill you as easily as ripping a piece of paper in half.'

Amy fell to her knees by my side to check if I was okay.

'See you around, Terry … Amy, I will be seeing you very soon!' said Joe, who casually walked away.

'Terry!' Amy cried. 'Terry, are you okay?'

I took a few deep breaths and slowly stood back up. I looked over the car park and could no longer see Joe.

'Terry!'

'I'm … I'm okay.'

'Who was that guy? How does he know about you?'

'His name is Joe … I don't know him, though.'

She looked horrified and I hurried her into my car. When I closed my car door she started to cry.

'Terry, do you think -?'

'Do I think he's one of the kidnappers?' I interrupted, finishing her question. 'Yes, yes, I do. Or at least working for them.'

'Have you seen him before?'

'Last night … when I was at the bar.'

'That's why you were acting weird! Oh my god … Terry, is he … is he like you?'

'I think so … His punch was like nothing I had felt before.'

I grabbed her hand.

'Amy ... this is why I shouldn't be with you.'

'No! Do not do this again. We have to protect each other.'

I wanted to argue back. I wanted to tell her she was wrong ... but I didn't want to lose her. For the first time in my life, I felt vulnerable and I suddenly didn't feel so invincible.

'You need to make me a promise, then?' I asked.

'What is it?' she slowly replied.

'When he appears again, you get away as quickly as possible.'

'What will you do, though?'

'Shut him up for good.'

She didn't reply and she didn't question what I meant. I didn't really know myself ... but one thing was for sure ... he had to go away. I would need to find him and I would need to get him out of my life.

*

Amy asked a lot of questions when she was worried ... they were all valid questions, but none that I could answer.

'We need to find these kidnappers, Terry,' she said. 'I think we have to go to the police.'

'We've been through this. We can't go to the police …'

'Then what do we do? That guy stabbed you in the middle of the college car park!'

'I don't know yet.'

For the first time, we were sitting at my house, as we wanted to talk about Joe without anyone hearing. I hated it here, as I didn't have any furniture (which I still refused to buy), and it was very uncomfortable to sit in. I paced the room and thought over and over again through different plans; Amy was sitting on my bed and searching for something frantically on her phone, almost as though she googling the solution to our problems.

'Okay, I have an idea,' I finally said.

Her head snapped to look at me and her face lit up at the very idea that I could solve our problems.

'What is it?'

'I'll drive around and look for him. He can't be far and his bike is easy to spot. I'll find him, I'll talk to him and I'll pay him off. If he works for the kidnappers, he will only care about money.'

'You think that will work?'

'I don't know, it has to? Who doesn't want money? Even if I offered him one hundred thousand pounds? Who would turn that down?'

Amy sat and contemplated what I had said.

'Terry, what kind of kidnapper gives someone millions?' she asked again, changing the subject.

'A guilty one? Maybe they wanted to say sorry after years of being locked up?'

'This isn't normal ... I'm scared.'

'I did warn you I came with heavy baggage ... It's not too late to walk away.'

'No! I'm not leaving you ... it's just ... so scary.'

We both sat in silence, clearly deep in thought; there were no easy answers to any of our problems.

'So ... is your safe-room beneath us?' she asked.

I really didn't want to answer that question ...

'Yes.'

'Can I ... see it?'

I really didn't want her to see it ... but after everything, I realised I couldn't keep secrets from her anymore.

'If you must.'

I walked over to the radiator on the opposite side of the room. I turned the fake knob on the right-hand side and four wood floor panels next to me slowly lifted from the ground, revealing a metal staircase beneath.

'Wow ...'

'It has to be well hidden, otherwise it wouldn't be a good safe-room,' I explained.

She slowly walked to the stairs from my bed and stared at the new staircase in the floor, her mouth ajar as she looked at me.

'Go ahead,' I said.

Amy walked down the metal staircase to the thick glass door at the bottom. As I followed her, the door automatically opened to allow us to walk in. The safe-room was a huge, square glass room, lit up by floor lights. Behind the glass panes were the rest of the underground foundations of my house, pitch-black apart from the small illumination from the room.

'Terry ... this is incredible!' she remarked.

The room was completely empty, apart from a wall of TVs that showed CCTV footage of inside and outside the house on the left-hand side of the room.

'This was the first thing I had built before I moved in,' I said. 'The only modification I made was the locking mechanism ... Normally, a safe-room keeps people getting in … but this one keeps people getting out.'

'What do you mean?' she asked.

'I lock myself in here when I black out … or try to. That way, I can't damage anyone or anything. This room is pretty solid. I have to admit, the guys who installed it were pretty confused when I asked them to lock people in!'

'How do you get out?'

'It's programmed to open automatically after a day. I've never blacked out for longer than a day or so, so it's worked well so far.'

She continued to walk around the room and felt the glass walls as she walked around. When Amy reached the CCTV, she studied each screen that was dedicated to the different parts of the house.

I noticed she stared at the CCTV dedicated to the safe-room, which currently displayed both of us in the room.

'Have you ever …?' she started.

'Watched the CCTV when I black out? Yes. It's disturbing.'

She remained silent, but continued to watch. One thing I had to say about Amy was how brave she was. Even when she seemed scared, nothing would deter her. A part of me thought she was going to ask to see the CCTV, which I was ready to refuse. She finally turned to me and I was ready for an argument.

'I think we should go to the place you were imprisoned. The one you were kidnapped in.'

Okay. I wasn't expecting her to say that.

*

We debated for hours whether to go back to where I had lived most of my life. A part of me wanted to make excuses, I felt anxious at the very thought of being there … but a part of me was curious and knew it was a good idea. Amy's logic was to see if the kidnappers were there or if there were clues to who they were. If we did confront them, we could cut Joe out as the middleman and plead with the kidnappers or at least understand what they wanted. Eventually, I gave up and agreed to go.

'Do you know where it is?' she asked.

'Yes, it was in the Lake District,' I replied. 'The times I escaped really gave me a sense of my bearings.'

'Right, okay … I have a plan. We'll go this weekend, it's mid-November, so we'll tell my parents we're going to the York Christmas market. I was there last Christmas with Laura, so they won't suspect anything.'

'It's a long drive ... but we could do it in one weekend. Will your parents be funny with us going away together?'

'No, they trust you like a son. Plus, we'll be having "separate rooms" ...'

The plan was set and Amy very quickly settled things with her parents for our "Christmas Shopping" trip. I managed to book a bed and breakfast not far away from Lake Windermere and we planned to leave extremely early on Saturday morning.

The rest of the week passed and Amy acted very normal; we almost carried on like nothing was wrong. Without Amy knowing, I would spend each night after our encounter with Joe driving around and looking for his motorbike. I checked every hotel, every bed and breakfast, every street, every car park ... but his bike was nowhere to be seen. I felt anxious and felt frustrated that the very thing I didn't want to happen with Amy was now a reality. She was in danger and I had no one else to blame other than myself. Amy was trying to put on a brave face and she was determined to prove to me that I didn't need to protect her.

Saturday morning finally arrived and I arrived at Amy's house at six in the morning.

'Morning, Terry!' beamed Michael as I walked into the house.

'I will never understand how you are so happy this early in the morning, Michael,' I replied, and gave him a small hug.

'Ahh, it's the best time of the day, lad! Although, the sun seems to be long gone now. It's gone very miserable outside, hasn't it?'

November had turned very grey, very wet and very moody, almost as if the moment Joe had entered my life, the weather reflected the tone. Every day, the sky seemed to be a dark grey and it felt like things were getting more serious.

Amy dragged herself downstairs and looked like a zombie; she was not a morning person.

'Are you sure you can't have breakfast or a drink before you go?' Michael asked.

'No, thanks, we've got a long trip ahead!' I replied. 'I'd rather just head off.'

I packed Amy's bags into the back of my truck, and as Amy lifted herself into the passenger seat, I turned around to say goodbye to Michael.

'Let me know what the tomahawk is like!' I said, and handed him a small envelope.

'What's this, lad?' he asked, and opened up the envelope.

'It's a gift voucher for The Smoke House. You are booked in at eight tonight with Lisa and Tim.'

'Terry! You can't keep giving me gifts!' he said, but his face was bright with excitement.

'Hey, you trusted me to take your daughter away for a weekend in York. It's the least I could do.'

Michael insisted he would return the favour to me, but seemed over the moon to be finally visiting his dream restaurant.

We hugged again and I finally climbed into my truck, starting the drive towards the one road out of Byanbythe and through the road underneath Mount Cudd.

'You need to stop buying my dad things …' said Amy as she started to wake up.

'He's my best friend. I'm allowed.'

'Aren't I your best friend?'

'It's a very close second …'

She hit my arm, which set the tone for a long but very enjoyable journey to the Lake District. It was almost a six-hour drive, but it didn't feel long at all. The whole journey consisted of Amy and I laughing, talking and singing along to music. The highlight was Amy educating me on the cheesiest music from the '90s and performing karaoke to all the pop girl bands she loved (and she truly was a terrible singer). We didn't need to stop during the journey, as I brought enough snacks to last a week at least. When we finally reached the Peak District, Amy was in awe of the beautiful scenery all around us. The Lake District, in parts, was not unlike Wales. It was vast, empathetic and full of beautiful hills, mountains and lakes. We were both starting to feel tired and stiff from the long journey sitting down. Any sign of civilisation seemed to become less and less, until the roads were sparse and empty.

'Is it far?' she asked.

'No, it's just over this hill,' I replied.

'There doesn't seem to be anyone around?'

The place where I was trapped, for all those years, was well hidden, away from any human life.

'I guess they didn't want anyone around …' I replied.

The mood of the car changed and it suddenly felt very serious. The sky was still the mix of grey and black and it was raining lightly as we drove around a small mountain road. I took a sharp right turn into a small forest-like area and began to slow down. I finally saw the building ahead and suddenly felt a little stunned.

'Why are we slowing down?' she asked.

I understood her confusion, as the only building around was at the end of the road … and it didn't look like somewhere you would kidnap someone.

'That's it,' I replied.

She looked very confused. I parked the truck up on the small car park and eyed up the horrific building in front of me. For all intents and purposes, it looked like a normal office-type building. The entire front was glass and at the very bottom was a revolving door to the open plan reception area, bannered with the sign "Spartan Storage Inc."

'Terry … it's an office building?'

'It may look like one … but no one has ever worked here.'

She gasped, and as we slowly exited the truck, she looked up at the building in awe. I felt extremely anxious and a part of me now wanted nothing more than to climb back into my truck and drive away … as fast as I could.

'Terry … what's wrong?'

'I spent most of my life trying to escape this place. I dreamt every night about getting as far away as possible. I escaped twice and was dragged right back … and now I'm driving here on my own accord.'

Amy stared at me and I felt like it had just dawned on her how serious this was for me.

'Terry … I'm so sorry. I should have thought … come on, let's go back to the B and B.'

'No … we've come all this way now …'

I slowly walked towards the revolving doors at the front of the building.

'How are we going to get in?' Amy asked.

'It's open. It's never locked.'

I pushed the revolving doors and entered the reception area, with Amy right behind me.

'It's like it's a real office open for business?' she asked, as she walked around the receptionist's desk. 'All the lights are on … like it's a normal day. What's on each floor?'

'Just rows and rows of desks and computers.'

'Why, though? Has no one ever worked here?'

'I don't think so. I didn't really see anything when I was locked away … but the second time I escaped, I actually watched the building from afar for a few days before I ran away … no one ever used the building.'

Amy started to use one of the computers at the reception and I could see that she was watching some of the old CCTV.

'I'm skipping back days, weeks,' she said. 'The only people to enter the building are cleaners. Why would they have cleaners if no one ever works here?'

'Keeping up appearances?' I replied.

'This place is really, really freaky. What should we do?'

'There is a director's office upstairs. Maybe we could see if anyone has ever used one of the computers?'

I walked towards an elevator, which was just as smart as the rest of the building, made out of glass. We took the elevator to the top floor, and as each floor passed, we could see rows and rows of desks, computers, mini kitchens, canteens, seating areas and meeting rooms.

'It's like they've built a fake business that looks perfect … just to disguise the fact that they had you kidnapped downstairs,' said Amy. 'But why? Why go to all that trouble?'

'I've asked myself the same question since I was a kid,' I mumbled, returning to my zombie-like state.

As we reached the top floor, it was immediately noticeable that this floor was different to the rest. Instead of rows of computers, there was simply one giant desk, complete with a widescreen monitor and a small black leather sofa to the right of it.

'Wow, they obviously wanted the director to look like he was important,' said Amy. 'A whole floor just for one desk?'

We walked around the floor dedicated to the director and stood in awe at the beauty and detail dedicated to the fake office.

'Do you think this was ever a real office?' Amy asked.

'No, I asked someone local when I left earlier this year. I bought my pick-up truck not far from here. They said they had never heard of this place. There is also no such place as Spartan Storage Inc. on Google.'

'Do you think it's password protected? The computer?' she asked as she reached the large desk.

She moved the mouse of the computer around and her expression suddenly changed from excited to deflated.

'Nothing. There's absolutely nothing on this computer. What now?'

'Let's go down to my "room".'

We entered the elevator again, and instead of pressing a single number on the keypad, which would normally select a floor to travel to, I entered the combination of *2, 6, 5, 7, 1, 5*. The elevator sprang to life and we started to descend.

'How did you know that code?' she asked.

'The first time I escaped, I spent hours pressing every combination over and over again.'

'That could have been hundreds of combinations!'

'I had a lot of time to guess over and over again,' I reminded her.

The glass elevator travelled past the reception and now descended below the ground level. It travelled lower and lower and seemed to be double the amount of time it took to travel from reception to the top floor.

'How far down was your room?' Amy asked.

'I don't know, it has to be deep underground though …'

We slowed down and the glass elevator soon gave us a view to my room. The elevator was directly in the middle of the room. In front of the elevator doors was a small bed and a small sofa; on the opposite side of the room were several bookcases full of various films, books and music vinyls, complete with a small TV and chair in the corner of the collections. To anyone, this may have seemed like a great man cave; it was brightly decorated and looked tidy and cosy.

'This isn't what I expected …' said Amy.

'Did you expect a dungeon with dripping walls and shackles?'

'If I'm honest … yes, I did. This looks like a home.'

'It was my home.'

Amy explored the room, first looking at my old bed and then searching through the bookshelves and my old collection of personal belongings.

'The room is exactly how I left it … I don't think the kidnappers have ever come back.'

'They bought you so many cool things. They made you feel comfortable. They gave you lots of money and then they let you leave. Why?' Amy pondered. 'And why when you were eighteen?'

'Do you not think I have not asked those questions before? I don't know … I wish I knew.'

'None of this makes sense, and now that Joe person is involved, it makes even less sense.'

'I know … and it looks like we've come all this way for nothing,' I said, my voice starting to fill with anger. 'There is nothing here. I doubt they have ever returned!'

Amy continued to look around the room, searching for any clues possible.

'How did you eat?' she asked.

'The elevator would open twice a day with a tray of food. It was always good food too …'

'How did they know you weren't going to ride the elevator back up when they were going to deliver a meal?'

I pointed behind me at the wall in front of the elevator, which had fixed into the wall a small camera; around the room were multiple cameras pointing in different angles.

'I don't get it,' she admitted.

'The elevator would close if I was anywhere near it. They would wait for me to stand clear before closing it,' I explained.

'How on earth did you escape? And twice?'

'When I figured out the elevator wouldn't leave if I sat inside, I started pressing different number combinations. They can't have been close to the building, because I managed to guess the number code and escape without anyone trying to stop me.'

'What happened the second time?'

'They didn't take chances after that first escape. Every time food was delivered, they would cut the power off to the entire building until I was safely away from the elevator with my food.'

'This is so scary …'

She continued to walk around the room and was deep in thought.

'We should go. I don't like being here,' I admitted. 'And it doesn't look like we are going to get any answers.'

'Terry … what if you weren't kidnapped?' said Amy, completely ignoring what I had just said.

'I was locked in this room against my will!' I snapped back. 'What do you mean?'

'What if they weren't trying to kidnap you? What if they were trying to protect you?'

'Protect me? From what?'

'I don't know … from Joe? From whoever he works for? Think about it, they treat you well, they keep you entertained, they wait until you are eighteen, they give you money, tell you where to go? What if they wanted to meet you in Byanbythe … but Joe got there first?'

'Amy … you're speculating …' I said, but I had to admit … what she said did seem possible.

'Whoever kept you here didn't want you unhappy … in fact, they wanted to keep you here at all costs. And for what? Now suddenly Joe comes to Byanbythe to terrorise you?'

'I don't know …'

'Come with me! I have an idea.'

Amy quickly entered the elevator and prompted me to enter the secret combination.

As we returned to the reception area, she began to look at the CCTV footage again.

'What are you doing?' I asked.

'I want to see how far this goes back. When did you leave this place?'

'In June.'

She furiously clicked buttons and watched the various screens of CCTV.

'I can see you leaving.'

She pointed at the screen that focused on the car park, which played footage of the final time I had left this building.

'There you are ... you look so scared.'

'I was.'

She grabbed my hand and squeezed tight. I watched the footage as I carried my large bag out of the reception and into the car park, which had a small, empty car waiting for me outside. The footage showed how scared I was; every step I took, I hesitated, constantly looking around for any sign of the kidnappers. I remembered how I thought it was a trap; I had spent most of my life underground ... and now I had more money than I could imagine and was *"free"* to go live a life.

'Wait a minute ... how did you know how to drive? You can't have done your test whilst locked up?'

'That's because I haven't ever done my test,' I replied. 'The driving licence is fake.'

'What?! That's impossible! How did you know how to drive, then?'

'I guess it sounds stupid … but as soon as I turned sixteen, I had a new book and DVD on how to drive, which I watched nearly every day … After two years, I knew everything I needed to do in theory. Although, it was bloody scary driving in reality.'

'That's so dangerous, Terry!'

'Hey, I'm a good driver now, aren't I?'

'You have to do your test for real!'

'And what do I say? "Excuse me, can I replace my fake licence with a real one please?"'

'A fake licence … fake passport … who are these people?'

Amy continued to rewind the CCTV through the days before I left for good.

'What are you looking for?' I asked.

'Anything. Any sign of someone entering or leaving the building. That car had been there for a long time,' she explained. She rewound frantically, looking for any sign of activity on the CCTV. 'Hey, look, this must be the person who delivered your food?'

A white van pulled over outside of the reception and the driver carried in a box that must have been my meals. As he entered the building, the elevator would automatically open, prompting them to leave the food on the empty tray within. After the food was left, the delivery person would leave and drive away.

'The van … it's for a company called Commodore Caterers. We need to ring them up and see if they are real. Maybe they can give us a name of who made the order every day? Maybe they are owned by the kidnappers too?' Amy speculated.

She continued to rewind the footage, which showed the food delivery arrive twice a day every day. Sometimes the driver and deliverer were different, but it was always the same van and company. Amy continued to rewind, until she found what she was looking for.

'Look, a different car. Why does the screen go weird?'

She pointed again at the screen showing the car park. A large, black, and expensive-looking car had parked up … but it was at the very back of the car park, which made it difficult to make out what make of car it was, the registration or who was driving. I edged closer to the screen and the camera blacked out for a split second; when the screen returned, the black car was gone.

'What the hell happened there?' I asked.

'I don't know …'

Amy rewound the footage and watched again.

'Look!' I shouted. 'Look at the time before and after the screen goes black.'

Amy rewound for a third time and gasped.

'It skips time,' she said. 'They must have turned off the CCTV while they were here!'

Amy continued to rewind; the black car had appeared in May, but as she rewound further in time, it was clear the black car appeared frequently … but the CCTV would always black out and skip time.

'They really didn't want to be seen … it's so strange.'

After going back through the CCTV, with what seemed to be years worth of footage, Amy eventually stopped, concluding that the CCTV wouldn't give us any more answers.

'At least we've learnt a few things. There's nothing to suggest that Joe is related to the kidnappers … and we know the catering company who delivered your food,' she recounted.

'Let's go to the B and B … I'm tired and I just want to get out of this place.'

We left and I finally felt like I could relax. I hated it here and no matter what answers we had,

I knew they would just raise more questions. There was a sour taste in my mouth, and I thought to myself that if I never saw this building again, I would be happy. As we drove to the B and B, Amy continued to speculate and a huge part of me didn't want to listen. I was tired of talking about this, and although I knew she had good intentions, I wanted to forget this part of my life.

The B and B was small, a single house on the side of an old English pub. It was very dated, but had a cosy feel to it. After leaving the cold, miserable outside world, the rain gave way to allow the night sky to take over. It was very welcoming to walk into the pub to a blazing warm fire and locals sitting around talking and drinking.

'Can I help you?' a man said from behind the bar.

'Yes, I have a room booking. Should be until the name of Nick Palmer.'

Amy immediately looked at me with a confused look, but as the barman provided the key and directions to the room, I ignored her, trying not to laugh.

'Why did you use Nick's name?' she asked as we were walking to the room.

'I didn't want to use my real name … in case anyone local had anything to do with the kidnappers,' I explained.

Our room was on the bottom floor of the house next to the pub and we entered. It was just like the pub: dated, small, but somewhat cosy. The walls were a rich red and all the furniture, including the bed, was dark wood. The room didn't have much in it, apart from the bed, a small TV, a table with a kettle and mugs on, and finally, a door which must have led to a bathroom.

'Are you sure you don't mind sharing a bed?' I asked.

'I'm your girlfriend, of course I don't mind.' she laughed.

We settled into the room, and at my request, I asked Amy if we could relax for a small amount of time before we did any further *"investigating"* together. I didn't want to talk about my past anymore and just felt like being a couple, pretending we had no problems; Amy agreed, although I was sure she was already itching to research the catering company. I took my boots off and lay on the bed, feeling like I had run a marathon.

'Hey, I'm going to have a shower. Is that okay?'

I looked at Amy and just smiled ... but suddenly realised what she was alluding to.

'Oh, sorry! Yes, of course. Want me to turn around while you get changed?' I bumbled.

She laughed and slowly took off her top and then her bra. This was the first time I had ever seen a girl's breasts before and I suddenly felt like I couldn't look at anything else. They seemed bigger than I had imagined (I was a teenage boy, of course I had thought of Amy in that way) and her body was tiny in comparison. Her skin was still pale and everything about her oozed how sexy she was. I could see she was red in the face, possibly nervous, but also seemed like she had built up the courage to stand half naked in front of me.

'You keep forgetting we're a couple? If you can't see me naked, who can?' she reminded me, but her voice was high-pitched.

'Sorry ... I ... um ... I guess.'

She unbuttoned her jeans and then took off her underwear. Amy was now completely naked in front of me and I felt overwhelmed. A part of me wanted to push her onto the bed and kiss her like I had never kissed her before, but like she had read my mind, she slowly walked over and began to kiss me instead. My heart was racing, I had no idea where to put my hands. I felt her bum and then her back. The kissing became faster.

'What's wrong?' she asked, and suddenly stopped.

'I … urgh … I feel … nervous.'

'Why?'

'I've never done this before … have you?'

'No … but don't worry … don't be nervous.'

She started to kiss me again, but quickly stopped.

'Terry, what's wrong?' she asked again, and suddenly stood up off the bed.

'I'm sorry …'

'What for? We don't have to … I'm sorry.'

'Of course I want to! Look at you, I have never seen someone so beautiful in my life. It's just … I didn't expect it to be like this. I guess I didn't expect to lose my virginity in some dated B and B after spending the day looking for my kidnappers …'

She laughed and kissed my head.

'You're thinking about this way too much … but I understand, if it doesn't feel right, we don't have to have sex yet.'

'But I don't want you to think that I don't want sex with you!' I blurted out.

'I don't think that, I know we'll have sex when the time is right … Does that mean I have to put my clothes back on?' she teased, winking at me.

'No, I'm happy seeing you naked for now …'

We laughed and I couldn't help but stare until she disappeared into the bathroom. What had I done? Had I just messed up an intimate moment with Amy? The most beautiful girl in the world just showed me her amazing body for the first time and I rejected her! She had taken my rejection so well … I wondered if I had actually offended her? I started to worry and panic … but my emotions were all over the place. I didn't admit it at the time … but I felt like a wreck at the office building today. I felt chills running down my spine at the very thought of being there again. I sat on the bed, wondering how I could make Amy feel more comfortable around me … when a stupid idea popped into my head. I quickly took off my clothes and waited for her to finish her shower. As the bathroom door opened, Amy emerged with a towel wrapped around her; she looked at me and suddenly studied me up and down in shock.

'Oh …' she said, and was suddenly staring at the lower half of my body. 'Did you … did you change your mind?'

'I thought we could lie together for a bit?'

She smiled, and after removing her towel, she joined me in bed. We lay naked together and kissed; the kisses were different this time, they were slow and felt meaningful. We held each other, and although I felt so nervous holding her naked body, not knowing what to touch … it felt good.

'I love you, Amy.'

'Are you saying that because I'm naked?' she joked.

'No, although I may love you more now.'

She laughed.

'It's okay to be nervous, she said. 'And I love that you want to make it special.'

'I guess I ruined your plan for today, though …'

'I didn't really plan on it, I just thought it was our first time sleeping together alone. But I suppose after the day we've had, it wasn't the best idea.'

'I'm sorry … I guess today just emotionally drained me.'

'I should have thought of that before I suggested coming up here … I didn't think.'

'No … I had to face it one day. And I guess we got some answers … It's just … you don't understand how much I longed to get away. Every time I escaped, I felt so euphoric.'

'What happened the first time you escaped?' asked Amy, before quickly adding, 'If you want to talk about it, of course!'

I took a deep breath, lay on my back and thought back to my first escape.

'I was thirteen. I told you that I guessed the elevator code … When I reached the reception and noticed no one was there to stop me, I ran. I hid in the forest and watched, wanting to see who would come … but no one did. When I was sure no one was going to come after me, I ran into the local village. I slept in a bush the first night, stole food, robbed alcohol from a shop … I felt like a king.'

'You drank at thirteen?'

'I just wanted to feel normal. I had seen so many films about drinking and how people drank when they had a bad day … it was stupid, I didn't even feel drunk. Turns out that part of the monster I am, I don't get drunk.'

'Not the worst condition in the world. Anyway … what happened next?'

'I don't know, I slept in a tunnel one night, and when I woke up, I was back in the room with a note next to me.'

'What did it say?'

'It said *"Do not run away again!"* …'

'Wow … but you obviously didn't listen.'

'Course not. It was the next year I ran away the second time … I forced open the elevator door and climbed up the elevator cables, breaking out into the reception and into the real world. This time, I didn't wait. I hitched a ride on the motorway and just knew I wanted to get far away … where they couldn't find me.'

'Where did you go?'

'A truck driver was driving to France. From France, I travelled to Germany, Austria, Rotherham and finally … Amsterdam,' I reminisced. 'Ahh, Amsterdam was the best place of all. The further I travelled, the safer I felt. I lived rough, on the streets, stealing food … but I felt so alive. Amsterdam was full of the weird and wonderful.'

'How did they find you?'

'On my third day in Amsterdam, I felt like I was being followed. On the night, I knew someone was following me … but I couldn't see their face. I started to run … and they chased me. I ran so fast … but they ran faster. After an hour of running, the person caught me, hit me in the back of my head … and knocked me out clean.'

'Oh my god … that's so scary.'

'I was so mad when I woke up and I was back in that room. I smashed up everything around me. I ripped every book, smashed the

TV, snapped the DVDs … And when I woke up the morning after? The room had been restored, like I had done nothing.'

I clenched my fists and felt rage burn within me … rage I had not felt in years. Amy kissed my hand and held me tight … but it didn't ease the pain.

'You're safe now, it's okay,' she comforted me.

'I feel safe with you. Always.'

We lay holding each other in silence and I had never felt more comfortable in my life. Her body was warm against me, and although wild thoughts ran through my mind, I knew it was the right thing to do nothing. I held her and kissed her head. I loved Amy beyond comparison.

*

The night was pleasant, but I felt like I couldn't enjoy it; we had a beautiful pub meal and a few drinks next to the open fire. We sat and spoke for hours, and in reality, this was a perfect getaway, next to a warm fire whilst the world was raining heavily and freezing cold outside. We mostly spoke about everything other than the events of the day.

We had another setback when Amy phoned the catering company, Commodore Caterers. She used a fake accent to try and pretend she worked for Spartan Storage Inc. and she wanted to re-establish the food deliveries that were made for my meals … but they refused to talk to her unless she could provide the account number; they wouldn't even provide a name of someone they spoke to originally from Spartan. This certainly put a dampener on our hope for answers, and ultimately, we were left with very little reward from this trip.

I felt myself getting more angry. The more I thought about it, I felt like a puppet, used and dangled whilst other people planned my life for me. I had no say whether I was locked underground. I had no say whether I could leave. I wasn't allowed to know who kept me against my will and now I had Joe interfering with my life. I felt like I had no control and I wanted to go back and smash that office up!

Now, there was an idea …

I lay in bed with Amy at the end of the night. We lay naked together again and spent the rest of the night kissing each other like two madly in love teens (which, ironically, we were). After she fell asleep, I was alone with my thoughts. I stewed in my anger and poisonous thoughts …

and once I had the idea of smashing up the office, I could think of nothing else. I imagined smashing the room I was kept in. I imagined smashing every desk and computer. I wanted to smash every glass window at the front of that building. I imagined, I lusted … and then the most dangerous thought came into my head … why shouldn't I?

The building stood on its own, so no one would see me. I could smash the CCTV so no one would know it was me. I could even park my truck in the forest so they wouldn't see who had parked in the car park.

I shot out of bed, my rage replaced by passion. I quickly got dressed, and without thinking, I was driving towards a petrol garage.

I parked my truck on the opposite side of the road to the petrol station (to avoid the CCTV). I filled up a couple of empty jerry cans full of petrol and then bought some gas tanks that were sold and intended for BBQs. Although this looked very suspicious, the young guy that was working the night shift didn't seem to care and I paid without a single question or a raised eyebrow. I loaded my truck, and after what felt like another blink, I opened my eyes and found myself racing to the office. I blinked again and when I opened my eyes for the third time, I was now standing in the reception with the gas tanks and petrol. I was breathing heavily, almost panting. I was excited, I was anxious … but most of all, I was pissed off. This place had been my prison and brought nothing but misery to my life.

I ran around the building and smashed every camera with my baseball bat that I kept under the passenger seat of my truck. I checked the CCTV at the reception desk, and once I was sure every camera was destroyed, I really became unhinged. I smashed the desk of the reception, the chair, the screens, the CCTV. I ventured to every floor, I pushed every desk over, smashed every computer, every table. I would pour petrol on each floor evenly, and when I reached the director's floor, poured extra petrol on the desk, just in case the person who kidnapped me had ever sat there. Once I was sure that every floor was smashed and had enough petrol, I carefully placed gas canisters on each one … saving the best location until last … my room.

I entered the number combination and the elevator took me down. I felt like I had blinked again, and when I looked once more, I had destroyed the room. Every bookcase was in pieces, the TV was smashed and every book, DVD and piece of music lay in bits. I poured petrol, and just as I hit the elevator combination to return to the reception, I lit a match and threw it to the floor. As the elevator closed, the room ignited instantaneously with a blaze. As I reached the reception, I knew I only needed to set this area on fire, as the flames would eventually reach the gas canisters and other floors, finally destroying the building and everything in it.

I took one final look, and with a huge smile, I lit a match and threw it to the ground. I quickly ran out of the building and to the edge of the car park … and as I turned back, my heart filled with joy to see the reception area was consumed with fire. I stood and watched and didn't even blink when the first gas canister exploded. As planned, the explosion caused the first floor to set alight. As that floor was soon full of fire, the next gas canister exploded … and soon enough, the whole building was on fire and the flames were furiously destroying everything inside.

I sat and watched and felt like a huge burden had escaped my body. This office building … which had been a prison for me … a physical manifestation of hell … was now burning to the ground. I wanted to avoid coming back … but I was glad Amy had suggested it. I didn't care if the kidnappers knew it was me. I wanted them to know it was me who burned this place to the ground. Whoever kept me here, whoever was after me now … I needed them to know. I needed them to know I wasn't someone to be messed with and I would destroy anything in my path to ensure they had no control over me nor the people I loved. I watched the building fall apart. I watched my prison fall to the ground. I felt the anger leave my body like smoke from a fire, and for once, I felt in control.

AMY

I woke up and felt his warm body against mine. I had never slept in the same bed as someone before and certainly not naked. I felt vulnerable, I felt shy ... and yet, it felt so good to lie in his arms. I hadn't planned on coming on to Terry last night, but as we drove up together, it seemed like a good opportunity, as we were alone ... In hindsight, it was a stupid idea. I should have guessed that yesterday was going to be an emotional journey ... but as always, he acted like a gentleman. I turned around to look at him and he was fast asleep. He was a beautiful sleeper, he looked calm and he looked happy; inside, I knew, behind his smile, he was in a world of pain and fear still.

I quietly got out of bed and started to pack our things away in our bags. Terry must have sat right next to the fire last night, as his clothes smelt extremely potent of smoke, unlike mine, which hardly smelt at all.

'Good morning,' croaked Terry; his voice was tired and half asleep.

I turned around and he was stretching as he climbed out of bed. I couldn't help but still stare at his amazing body.

'Did you sleep well?' I asked.

'I did, considering you hogged most of the bed,' he joked.

'Oh, I like to starfish in bed. You'll have to get used to that or sleep on the floor in future? By the way, your clothes smell like you were actually in the fire last night!'

'Oh … I'll wash them when we're back,' he said, but he suddenly looked concerned.

'Are you okay? After yesterday?' I asked.

'I am. You know, I feel a lot better after confronting my fear. I feel like I have erased that place from my mind.'

I wasn't fully convinced, but pretended to believe he was okay. We were soon checked out of the B and B and back on the road in no time at all; the route back seemed to be different from the one we had taken before.

'We don't have to go straight back, you know?' I said, suddenly feeling like we had wasted a good weekend. 'We could spend time in the Lake District?'

'We're not going back,' Terry replied.

'Oh … where are we going?'

'We're supposed to be at the York Christmas Market, aren't we?'

'What do you mean?'

'There's no reason why we can't visit the Christmas market on the way back? Just means we'll be back home late.'

I felt elated. I was excited. It was like he had read my mind and the miserable weekend had turned into a romantic getaway, after all.

York was one of my favourite places on Earth. Before the *Harry Potter* films had come out, I imagined the tight, old-fashioned streets of York were exactly how the streets of Diagon Alley would be. I would also imagine that York Cathedral was what Hogwarts would look like. To this day, York captivated my imagination, as it still breathed like an old city of culture.

We parked right in front of the cathedral and slowly walked through the tight alleys of shops. From clothes to jewellery and old-fashioned pubs, it was everything I loved about the city. I felt like I walked into every shop, and Terry did not protest, as he was just happy to be with me. My mom's favourite bakery in the world, Betty's, was famous in York, so I made sure I bought her as many cakes as I could carry before we hit the market. In hindsight, I should have bought them after I walked around the market, but anyone who had been to Betty's before knew the queue could take hours to wait in. My mom regarded Betty's as her inspiration since she was a young girl and always wanted her own bakery to be just as famous. While she didn't have queues waiting outside her shop all day, she certainly never had cakes left at the end of her working day.

The Christmas market was full of excited families and locals, squeezed together whilst trying to walk around the various market stalls. The smells were overwhelming; at one moment, I could smell the strong perfume of mulled wine, but the next would smell the German hot dogs and burgers, which, of course, Terry bought. A small orchestra on the cold street corner played classical Christmas hymns, and as I looked around, not a single face had a care in the world. It was perfect, and for the first time this year, it felt like Christmas. I slowly turned around and watched Terry playing with some handmade wooden toys that made animal noises and felt so happy that he looked at peace, like everyone else, without a care in the world.

A small tearoom was hidden right behind the market and we decided to sit down and drink coffee before we journeyed back to Byanbythe.

'This has turned out to be such a great day. What do you think of York?' I asked.

'I think it's perfect. Almost as perfect as home!'

'I suppose you are right; you haven't seen Byanbythe at Christmas. The town really comes to life.'

'Do you have any family traditions at Christmas?' he asked.

'My nan always comes to stay. It's a pretty normal family Christmas. I have to help my mom at the shop as it's her busiest time of year.'

'That sounds stressful.'

'You have no idea …' I shuddered.

I thought about Christmas and felt a warm feeling in my stomach. I thought about Terry and wondered if he ever knew it was Christmas underneath that office? A part of me wanted to ask him, but why should I ruin a good day? All I ever did was bring up old wounds. We walked around the market until the sky was black, despite knowing we had a long journey back and college the next day. All the lights of the Christmas market illuminated the town and I did not want to escape this feeling of Christmas joy.

Unfortunately, we eventually had to pry ourselves away. We never stopped holding hands, Terry never stopped eating and we had never felt so normal without a single worry in the world - this is how things should have been. A part of me wondered if it could always truly be this way?

*

The next day at college was the biggest challenge of my life, with no exaggeration. We regrettably didn't arrive home until two in the morning. I was so happy travelling with Terry that by the time I had actually fallen to sleep, we were only a few miles away from Mount Cudd. I sneaked into the house and thankfully didn't wake up my parents, who would have really been angry at how late we were. I woke up like an undercover agent, wore an extra bit of makeup to cover the bags under my eyes, and attended college, almost running on empty.

College was starting to feel very festive; it was coming up to the last few weeks of November and the town would soon go all-out to decorate for the festive holidays. Although the walls were bare now, I could start to see the boxes in the hallways that were full of old decorations; pine and fir trees from the forest were begging to be delivered on site and an extra large one for the main courtyard would soon be erected.

Considering it was such an emotionally hard weekend for Terry, he seemed to be in the best mood, almost skipping down the hall to classes. When we spoke, it was about the Christmas market and nothing more. He acted like nothing else had happened over the weekend.

'Don't shut me out …' I warned him.

'I'm not,' he replied. 'We did what we needed to do on the weekend. As far as I am concerned, it's a closed book and it didn't give us any answers.'

'So where do we go from here?'

'We plan a fantastic Christmas!'

'Terry! You aren't taking this seriously!'

His face changed from jovial to serious and I knew he was becoming frustrated.

'There is absolutely nothing we can do, Amy. What do you want? Do we live in fear? Or get on with life and deal with the shit when and if it happens?'

If it happened … I didn't agree, it was one hundred percent a scenario that was going to happen. I wanted to ask more, as I felt anxious … but I knew not to pry. Terry must have noticed he was a little harsh and he grabbed me into a hug before our lunch ended.

'Listen, as long as I am with you, I will protect you. I have managed it so far.'

His words did not fill me with confidence, but I did feel safe with him.

AMY

I had spent the entire morning scouring the news, national news and local news to the Lake District. My fears came to a satisfying conclusion when the events of the weekend were finally mentioned, but in a non-suspicious way. A local newspaper (not even one of the most common ones) made mention of an office building that burnt down during the early hours of Sunday morning. It didn't mention the name of the company that occupied the building nor much else in regards to specifics; it merely mentioned that the fire had engulfed the building, but no one was hurt and police were not treating the incident as suspicious.

This was enough for me. No suspicion and no way of tracing the incident to me. I could safely enjoy my day and finally look forward to my first-ever Christmas that wasn't locked away in some prison.

I started to feel very comfortable with my life in Byanbythe. I was close with Amy and her family felt like my own. I was settled in at college and actually started to take a keen interest in my lessons and fellow students. I didn't particularly make friends, as most of my time was spent with Amy, but I was certainly on friendly terms with lots of other students. In my History class, we were currently studying American history, which I felt was an interesting (albeit politically heavy) subject. In Philosophy, I truly felt like I had the most fun of all. The lecturer, a very old, eccentric man called Truman Doo'che (seriously, that was his name), didn't really teach us much. Truman Doo'che questioned *everything*, and my entire experiences in class consisted of me and several other boys taking the piss out of him and asking him questions on subjects that we knew would get a huge response and tangent. A girl in our class, who clearly didn't find it funny that her Philosophy lessons were a joke, often shouted at Doo'che to actually teach her something, which hilariously generated a crazy reply like, 'MY DEAR GIRL! WHAT DO YOU THINK I AM DOING? I AM TEACHING YOU TO QUESTION ALL!'

When the girl replied, 'Okay, I am questioning what you are teaching us for an exam', Doo'che then ranted about the purpose of exams and their uses or benefits to life. Although I got on well with the guys from this class, I always rebuffed offers to hang out with them or do anything outside of college. I didn't want people to think that I was spending all my time with Amy, because that wasn't true; she had plenty of time without me with her own friends or on her own. I guess I spent so many years in isolation that I felt social anxiety to spend time with people. What would I say? What would I talk about? If they asked about my past, how many lies could I make and remember without being caught out?

No, I was quite happy and content with my time on my own and just as happy with Amy or my days with Michael. When I thought about it, with my time practising with the American Football team, Amy, college and everything else, I didn't have much time for making friends, and that was just fine with me.

After college that day, I drove home with Amy, who seemed to be a little distant with me. I knew she was worried and she thought I was brushing stuff off, but I really wasn't. Whoever my kidnappers were no longer resided in the place I was imprisoned. Joe, the piece of shit that was following me, could have been related to the kidnappers … but I had no way to prove it and I couldn't track him down, even if I tried. I couldn't keep living in fear and I certainly wasn't worried about Joe. He was scary and clearly knew something about me, but so far he was just trying to provoke me. The kidnappers themselves had not contacted me since I left the prison and so far didn't seem to have an interest in me (unless Joe was actually involved).

Hopefully, Amy would start to feel more comfortable as things became less eventful. Maybe a few more dates together and boring weekends would make her happy again?

As we arrived at Amy's house, something strange caught Amy's attention.

'Something's wrong.'

'What makes you say that?'

'Both my parents are home; that never happens at this time of day.'

Lisa's car and Michael's truck were on the drive, and I had to admit, this was a strange occurrence, even in the short time I had lived here. Amy ran into the house, and as I followed, I too sensed something wrong in the air.

Lisa grabbed Amy into a hug and began to cry. Michael looked at me with a glance of concern.

'What's wrong?' I asked, immediately thinking of several awful scenarios in my head.

'Your nan's been involved in a serious incident, Amy,' sobbed Lisa.

Amy began crying too and I looked at Michael, searching for answers.

'We think she was mugged outside of her home. She's currently in the University Hospital of Wales,' confirmed Michael.

'We have to go and see her!' cried Amy.

'I know, we've only just found out,' Lisa replied. 'But we need to sort out Tim first.'

'I can sort out Tim,' I volunteered. 'I can pick him up from school and look after him here.'

Michael, Lisa and Amy looked at me with surprise and I noticed Lisa and Michael glanced at each other before Michael smiled.

'That would be really helpful, Terry,' he said. 'Are you sure? I don't want to inconvenience you.'

'Of course, we're all family,' I replied. 'We'll be fine.'

The house burst into motion. Lisa quickly left money on the side so I could buy Tim a pizza and she quickly listed off activities, such as his time for homework, his bath time and when he needed to be in bed.

I didn't get a chance to say much to Amy; she was far too upset to speak, and if honest, I felt too awkward to know what to say. She asked if I was okay looking after Tim, but then quickly packed a few things to take with her to Cardiff.

As they left for Cardiff, I too drove away to pick up Tim from his friend's house (whose mom had kindly offered to take him in when Lisa wasn't able to meet him outside of school). I had to admit, in the heat of the moment, I stepped up to help out the family in a time of need ... but as the moment passed, I started to question my decision. I had never been alone with Tim and I had certainly never looked after a kid before. My experience as a kid was being locked in a prison with books and DVDs - did I lock Tim in his room and do the same?

As I pulled up at the friend's house, Tim ran merrily to the car and quickly jumped in, looking very excited about something. The parents of his friend quickly spoke to me in a very nosy and uninterested way, trying to find out what had happened to Amy's nan. Although

I protested that I didn't know much, she insisted on asking over and over again and even speculated what had happened - "I know, it's awful! You know what? She's old, maybe had some jewellery on? I bet they targeted her for days!"

After realising I wasn't going to give any information away, she finally left my car window and I was alone with Tim.

'Hey, Tim ...'

'Can we have pizza?!' he shouted, even more excitable than before.

Suddenly, my anxiety disappeared and I felt at ease looking after him; he clearly didn't know what was happening with his nan, and as far as he was concerned, it was a night with a friend.

'Of course! Shall we have a lads' night?' I asked.

'Yes!' he shouted, suddenly becoming animated.

'Maybe a few beers too?' I joked.

'Terry! I am only eleven years old!'

I forgot how much he reminded me of Amy.

*

The evening was fantastic. Whoever said that babysitting was hard? We ate pizza. We walked to the shop and bought lots of sweets. We watched films. We even had time for playing video games (which I am sure his mom would have discouraged, as the game was a mature-rated violent game).

I texted Amy a few times throughout the night, but got very little reply. It took over an hour for them to get to the hospital, and even after they arrived, they weren't able to find out much.

It was starting to get late and I realised that Tim hadn't even had his bath yet. He protested and argued that he didn't need one, but out of fear that Lisa would already be pissed off that I had fed him sweets all night, I needed to get something right. I ran upstairs and started to prepare the bath for him, as I was convinced that if I had left him to it, he would have faked his wash by merely running the water.

As the water began to fill the tub, I sat down on the toilet and thought about texting Amy again. After typing and deleting the same message over and over again, I decided against it, as I was sure she needed space to be with her nan. I finally shut off my phone and switched off the running water. As I walked to the top of the stairs, I heard Tim talking in the living room.

'Yeah!' Tim said. 'Are you serious?!'

'Of course!' a familiar voice replied. 'Terry will follow us! We can show you a game we play together.'

My heart stopped. It was Joe. I heard some footsteps quickly leave the living room and I immediately ran downstairs. My fears were confirmed as Joe was standing in the middle of the room, casually sitting on the armchair in front of the TV.

'What are you doing here?' I growled with the most vicious voice I could muster.

'Thought you could use some help babysitting the kid. He seems sweet,' he replied, with the most annoyingly smug smile.

'Get ... the ... fuck out of this house!' I said, and immediately walked within a inch of his face.

'Terry, Terry, Terry! You need to chill out, my friend!'

'Where is Tim?'

'He wanted to see my motorcycle.'

'Leave him out of this! We can deal with this right now.'

Joe looked at me and started to laugh.

'This is me dealing with it, Terry. Let's play a game with the kid.'

In a split-second, Joe hit me so hard around the face that I was knocked into the air and into the wall behind me. By the time I caught my breath, I heard a motorbike roaring in the distance.

I quickly got up and grabbed my keys. I could see Tim and Joe on his motorbike at the end of the street. I ran to my truck and started the engine, not even having time to put my seatbelt on or lock the house up. I drove as fast as I could, following the motorbike. This was seriously the scariest moment of my life. What was Joe going to do? Was he going to hurt Tim? He was driving so erratically on his bike and Tim didn't even have a helmet on … We drove through the dark forest and its winding roads, past houses and buildings. Where was Joe going? I rolled down my window as I finally started to catch up to bike.

'JOE!' I screamed.

His head turned and looked over his shoulder. I could imagine he was laughing. He stuck his arm out in the air and stuck his middle finger up at me, before kicking his bike into another gear and gaining speed.

'I SWEAR TO GOD I WILL KILL YOU!' I screamed.

I lost sight of the bike around a corner ahead. My truck was going as fast as it physically could without losing control. I drove and drove, thankfully on a one-way road. With a sigh of great relief, I was finally driving out of the forest and to the edge of the cliffs. Between the sea and the forest was a high cliff edge and a small narrow road that skirted around the entire edge of the trees. In the distance, at the highest point of the road, I could see Joe's bike had finally stopped. As I reached them, I pulled the handbrake of my truck as hard as I could and jumped out without turning the engine off.

Tim was fine, and to my surprise, he looked elated, like this was a big game.

'Tim! Are you okay?' I asked.

As I took a step towards him, Joe put his hands on Tim's shoulders.

'That was so cool!' said Tim. 'You didn't tell me you had a friend with a motorbike!'

I looked at Joe, who had a scary, deranged expression. His smile was gentle, but his eyes were focused on me. He didn't blink, but stared with an intense glare.

'What do you want, Joe?' I asked.

'How's the nan?'

I came to a sudden realisation and felt rooted to the spot.

'That ... was -?'

'Needed some time with you,' he replied. 'Figured it would be you and the girl ... but the kid's just a bonus.'

My fear became anger and I wanted to lunge towards him. This psychopath had gone too far. He had physically hurt Amy's nan to get me and Amy alone. He hurt an innocent old lady to get my attention. As I stepped towards him, my full intention was to murder him, but I needed to get him away from Tim. As I edged closer, he lifted Tim up on to his shoulders. I stopped walking towards him, scared of what he was going to do.

'Joe ... don't do this,' I warned.

What was he going to do? He was literally standing on the edge of the cliff.

'Hey, Tim,' said Joe. 'Remember I told you about a game me and Terry played together?'

Tim still seemed unaware that he was in danger and still seemed to think we were playing a game together.

'Hey, Terry ... can you catch?'

As I ran towards Joe, he threw Tim at me. As Tim reached my arms, I felt a hard kick to my back, throwing me over the edge of the cliff with Tim.

Tim began to scream and I had no time to lose. With great struggle, I twisted my body so my back was facing the rocks and sea below, holding onto Tim as tightly as I could. I had no time to think, and within moments and with a great thud, I smashed into the rocks and then into the water. I splashed around, not able to see anything, until I felt Tim's body. I pulled him out of the water and onto the rocks. I dragged myself onto the rock next to him and quickly rubbed my face, which burned with the salt water.

'TIM! Are you okay?' I screamed, slowly getting my vision back.

I thought the worst had happened, and as I opened my eyes, I could see he was also wiping his eyes. At first, he coughed and spluttered, but as he composed himself, he seemed unharmed.

'Tim!' I screamed.

He finally looked up at me and started to laugh.

'Oh my god, Terry! You do that for fun? Are you okay?'

He thought it was a game? *How* did he not realise how close he was to death? The fall, the crashing into the rocks, would have killed *anyone* in an instant. Had I not turned my back and took the impact, Tim would have been dead. Of course, being the monster that I was, it didn't even hurt me.

'Tim, are you okay? Tell me you are okay.'

'I'm fine! That was so cool, Terry!'

I looked at him. I was overwhelmed. I needed to think of something to say. What did I say? After taking a few breaths, I looked up at the cliff edge above and noticed that Joe was nowhere to be seen. After a few more moments thinking what to do, I decided to take control of the situation.

'You have to promise me that you will tell no one about this game, Tim!'

I had meant to come across gently, but realised that I had shouted at him. He suddenly looked confused.

'Why? Have I done something wrong?'

'No! Of course not … it's just … this is a really dangerous game that adults play at college. It's really dangerous and you should only do it if you are trained up. Your mom would *kill* me if she knew we were here.'

'But why did we play, then? Your friend said you had planned it.'

'My friend got it wrong; I said I wanted you to watch us playing it,' I lied. 'I didn't want you to do it with me! It's too dangerous.'

'Oh … okay, I understand,' he said.

I took a big breath and lay back on the rock. We needed to swim to the closest beach and then walk back to the cliff where my truck was.

'Terry?'

'What's up?'

'I promise I won't tell anyone about this. But … will you let me watch you in future? You know, jump off the cliffs?'

He was so innocent. I laughed and put my arm around his shoulder.

'Of course. Although, I don't do it often.'

'Does your friend?'

Joe … my friend? I had never wanted to murder someone so much before. The next time I saw him, I would make sure that he could never hurt my family again.

'No … he doesn't either,' I finally replied.

'Do you think you could teach me one day? I promise I won't tell!' said Tim, who was now more excited than I had ever seen him before.

*

Thanks to Michael being the great teacher he was, Tim could swim at an advanced level, so was able to swim with me with ease back to the beach. It took around an hour for us to swim back and then walk to the truck. It felt like no time at all before I managed to get Tim home, bathe him and quickly put his soaking clothes in the wash before Lisa would smell the sea salt on them and become suspicious.

I was absolutely sure that Tim would tell nobody, although it took me hours to calm him down. He had hundreds of questions about cliff jumping and I had to make up stories to get him to finally go to bed. He eventually fell to sleep, and strangely, he seemed to be my biggest fan, and asked if we could hang out again.

I was relieved that Tim was safe and felt good that he wasn't going to tell anyone … but that relief was shortly replaced by anger. I couldn't sleep; as the night became the early hours of the morning, I sat in the pitch-black living room, alone and in silence. I couldn't stop thinking about what had happened tonight, how close Tim was to being killed. How Joe had physically hurt Amy's nan to get my attention. I no longer cared who this Joe was, I just knew that I needed to kill him - and fast.

The clock struck two in the morning and the front door opened. Amy and Michael walked through the threshold and looked alarmed to see me awake.

'Terry! Did I wake you?' asked Michael.

'No, no, I was waiting up for you all. How is she?' I asked.

'She's a bit shook up, but she's going to be fine,' Amy replied.

'Her face is a bit roughed up, though! I tell you what, if the police don't find the scum that did this, I will!' said Michael through gritted teeth.

'Where's Lisa?' I asked.

'She's stopping overnight, then Nan's coming home to stay with us for a few weeks whilst she gets better.'

I felt sick. She was going to be closer to the person who attacked her.

'How's Tim?' asked Amy.

'He's fine, we had a good night together,' I lied.

Amy grabbed me into a hug and kissed my cheek.

'Thank you for looking after him,' she said. 'It really meant a lot for us to see my nan. Glad we had someone to keep Tim safe.'

Safe? She had no idea.

'Hey, I think we should all get some rest now,' said Michael. 'Terry, I want you to stay here in the spare room tonight. I don't want you driving home.'

'Honestly, it's fine, Michael. I could do with the fresh air and my own bed, if honest. I haven't slept much this past week.'

Amy shot me a concerned look and I was convinced she could see through my lie. Michael begrudgingly agreed and, after bidding goodnight, he left me alone with Amy.

'Is … everything okay?' she finally asked.

'Yeah, of course … why?'

'Why aren't you sleeping here?'

'I feel a bit rough; I was so worried and wound up about your nan being mugged.'

She seemed convinced and grabbed me into another hug.

'I love you so much, Terry. Are you sure you can't stay? Maybe you could sneak into my room and sleep?' she whispered.

I laughed and persuaded her that now was not a good time for her dad to walk in on me sharing a bed with his daughter. She walked me to my truck and finally ran to bed.

I had no intention of going home. I was going to find Joe.

*

I drove throughout the night looking for his bike. Every house, every street, every shop, every building … but there were no signs. It was a distinct-looking bike, almost vintage, jet-black, old wheels and a slim frame.

At around 7am, I decided that I could no longer stay awake, so drove home to get some sleep. There was no way I was going to go to college today, and knowing Amy would also have a day off to tend to her nan, I wouldn't face too many questions. I feared what Amy's reaction would have been to knowing how close her brother was to being killed. She was already worried ... what would this do to her?

As I awoke a few hours later, I didn't feel rested. I felt on edge, angry and like I would never rest again whilst Joe was alive. I decided that I couldn't just sit and wait for him to turn up again, so I would drive around again looking for his bike.

Hours passed by and there was no sign of him. I decided to drive deeper into the forest, to places that I may not have noticed before. In the deep forest, far away from the town, were random houses and huts dotted around; some houses were so rural that it was almost impossible to drive directly to them. Again, I had no luck finding his bike; just as I was planning to drive home, a huge bang against my truck made me lose control as I was driving. I slammed the brakes on and immediately jumped out of my truck to see what had happened. A huge dent was in the side of my truck. As I looked up, my prayers had been answered. It was

Joe, who was standing in the bush with another brick in his hand.

'Nice dent!' he shouted.

I didn't wait. I began to run as fast as I could in his direction. As soon as I ran, he ran and it became a wild goose chase into the forest. I could hear him laughing and shouting things, but I was too angry to care. I just wanted to catch up with him and slam his head to the ground. I was going to kill him. There was no doubt about it. I was going to commit murder today.

We ran and ran and the adrenaline just kept me going. He was faster than me, but I was determined I would catch up with him. I wasn't going to lose him, until … he actually disappeared out of my sight …

Where did he go!?

I continued to run in the same direction, through the trees and down the banks. I fought through the bushes and deeper into the forest. It felt like a good half-hour of running with no view of where Joe had gone. I started to slow down, feeling tired and exhausted (which was a rare occurrence). I didn't know if I was mentally defeated or my body was just giving up. I was running on no sleep and Joe was now tormenting every part of my life.

I leaned against a tree and banged my head against the bark.

'Stupid kid, you'll hurt yourself.'

I sprung around expecting Joe, but in fact it was an old man.

'I'm sorry?' I asked.

'You're stupid banging your head against the tree. You'll hurt yourself,' he repeated.

The man was very old and weathered. In his one hand, he held a fishing rod, and in the other, a bucket full of fish. He wore faded denim dungarees and a hat that looked older than he was.

'Thanks ... Guess I'm having a rough day,' I finally replied.

'You kids! Got no idea what a rough day is like,' he growled.

I smiled and began to walk away.

'This way, idiot,' the old man called.

I turned around and looked at him with confusion.

'Excuse me?' I asked.

'My cabin's this way. Come on, come tell me about your First World problems. I am sure we can sort whatever's going on in your idiot life,' he replied, and before I had a chance to decline his invitation, he began to hobble off into the forest.

I followed him, trying to stop him and tell him that I didn't want to talk to him in his cabin, but he hobbled so fast that I felt like nothing would stop him.

After ten or so minutes, a small, shabby cabin was in view. It was the only cabin around for what seemed like miles, and as the old man hobbled, I started to question why I was actually here.

'Hey, I really have to go …'

'Shut up and have a drink with me. Youth today, always in a rush,' he ranted. 'Rush, rush, rush, rush, rush, rush!'

When we got to the cabin, he quickly walked through the front door, but before I could follow, he slammed the door in my face. I stood back, a little bit in shock at how rude this old man was. Before I could open the door, he quickly reappeared, but with a kettle in one hand and two cups in the other. He hobbled past me like I wasn't even there.

'Sit down over here,' he commanded, and beckoned me towards two small crumbling wooden chairs next to a fire pit. I slowly walked towards him, sat down and watched him rant and fuss the fire pit, presumably to get it lit.

'Can I help?' I asked after a few minutes of watching him struggle.

'With what?' he snapped back.

'The fire?'

'What for? Are you a fire expert or something? No, no, no, I do this every day!'

As he continued to struggle lighting the fire, I felt like anything I said could offend him. I had to admit, the old man was peculiar enough to take my mind off Joe and I found myself suddenly amused at how crazy he seemed.

'I didn't catch your name,' I finally said as he started to make smoke with the kindle.

'Phil,' he quickly replied.

'Cool ... I'm Terry.'

He ignored me and finally lit the fire. He hung the kettle full of water precariously on a hook that dangled at the centre of the flame. Once he was satisfied, he looked around, sat down on his chair and stared into the forest.

It suddenly felt awkward. Not a word was said and the only noise was the crackling flames that heated the kettle in front of me. The fire was warm and welcoming, as the day was bitterly cold.

'Well, ain't you gonna tell me about your problems?' he finally asked.

'Oh ... well, it's nothing really.'

'Nothing? You said you were having a bad day and head-butting a tree. You were chasing another idiot, weren't you?'

'You saw the other guy?'

'I ain't blind, fool! Still got eyes, you know,' he grumbled back.

'Sorry ... Yeah, he's been giving me some trouble,' I admitted.

'What kind of trouble?'

I hesitated for a moment, before a revelation came over me. I needed to talk to someone ... I couldn't talk to *anyone* about this, not even Amy. I didn't know this old man and most likely would never see him again. I didn't need to give him the full truth ... but enough to get things off my chest.

'He's been ... harassing me. He follows me around, threatens me ... and my family. He took it too far the other day and now I want to get payback.'

'A school bully, eh? Well, that I know about! I was once the cock of the school, you know. I took shit from no one!'

I laughed, but he didn't seem to notice.

'What do you think I should do?'

'Kick his teeth out, son! You don't let a man give you shit and certainly not your family!'

He suddenly shot out of his chair, and in an animated fashion, pretended to fight an invisible man, throwing punches mid-air with a face full of fury. I laughed, but he snapped his neck around at me as if this wasn't a funny matter.

'I am trying to get him. That's why I was running after him,' I sheepishly admitted.

'Cowards run! But idiots chase. You an idiot, boy?'

'No.'

'Then stop acting like one!'

The kettle began to whistle and Phil poured boiling water into the two mugs he had laid out on a small table. He didn't ask me how I liked my tea and there was certainly no view of sugar or milk. He thrust the tea into my hands and stared into my eyes.

'I don't know how to get him to face me …' I finally admitted.

'You play him at his own game. If he finds you, draw him in, let him get close, then kick his arse! Make him eat the dirt beneath us until he's too scared to even think your name!' shouted Phil, and he again began to fight an invisible man.

Considering the old man was crazy, he had a valid point. Joe did always find me. I hadn't even come close to tracking him, and out of nowhere

he always appeared. I needed to draw him out …
I needed to get him to come to me so I could
finally fight him.

Phil sat down again and drank his tea, and
after a loud slurp, he finally said, 'Has that
solved your problems? Will you shut up
moaning?'

I finally started to look past his rudeness and
saw him for the man he was. He was old and
rude, but he was no-nonsense and straight to the
point. I had read books and seen films about
guys like him before, most likely fought in a war,
hated kids and lived in an age where men would
resolve problems with their fists.

It was suddenly silent again and both Phil
and I stared around the forest. It was very
private here; there was no path or road leading
out of the forest, and as far as I could see, no car
that belonged to Phil was parked close by. His
cabin was extremely old, and come to think of it,
extremely small; it surely had to be the size of
one small room.

'Nice place you have here.'

'Hmm,' he grunted.

'Have you lived here long?'

'I was born here over eighty years ago, lived
here until I got married, now I'm back.'

'Oh, wow, you don't look eighty,' I lied.

'And you don't look like a little bitch, but here you are needing a eighty-year-old man to solve your shit.'

He was so rude I could have laughed, and in a way, I found it quite refreshing.

'Do you live here alone?'

'I do now.'

'Oh, I'm sorry, I didn't mean to pry …' I said, realising he must have lost someone.

'Married for fifty-five years. My beautiful wife. I loved her dearly. Died ten years ago. Was rough. Lived here alone since.'

'I'm really sorry to hear that.'

'Did you kill her?'

'What? Of course not!'

'Then why are you sorry?'

It started to get painfully silent again, so I asked more questions to quickly change the subject.

'I noticed you fish?'

'Yup.'

'I've never fished before.'

'Course you ain't; youth never set time to separate themselves from their self-importance.'

'Yeah, you are right about that.'

'Gotta get the fishing in now before the lake freezes over!'

'Lake freezes over?'

'Are you stupid, boy? The Black Lake! Everyone round here knows it freezes over throughout winter. Eighth wonder of the world; no scientist can explain it. Just freezes solid for three months, at least!'

'Oh, wow, I didn't know that.'

'Are you foreign or something? Everyone knows about the Black Lake!' he repeated.

'I'll have to check it out; I've only just moved here.'

'Figures ... You know, I took Marie to ice skate every Christmas Day on the Black Lake. Just us two. Pair of crazy kids.'

'Wow ... that sounds nice.' I suddenly saw a sentimental side to him and felt like he wanted to talk about his wife. 'Were you good skaters?'

'She was majestic. Like an angel on the ice.'

'She sounds beautiful.'

'She was.'

'Do ... do you still skate now?'

'Don't be stupid, idiot! Does it look like I can still skate?!'

Okay ... the sentimental side was now gone.

*

It took a while, but the conversation with Phil flowed all afternoon. He made me tea, he told stories, and the moment he became sentimental about his wife, he would quickly snap back to the hard man he was. Phil was an interesting person, whose life was dedicated to his wife, Marie.

Marie was a lecturer at whatever version of college was in Byanbythe all of those years ago; Phil ran a business on the pier taking tourists for rides on his boat (but admitted that he spent most of his time fishing). They had a modest life in Byanbythe and lived on a separate boat at the pier. They struggled to conceive a child, which broke Marie's heart, but they lived the best life possible. Sadly, Marie had stage four cancer and quickly died before Phil could wrap his head around the news. Without dealing with his emotions, Phil gave up on society; he didn't even sell his boats, leaving them at the pier, and moved to his dad's small cabin in the forest. If I dared show him any sympathy, he would call me an idiot and move on to a different subject quickly.

It felt like a breath of fresh air talking to someone about my emotions and fears; as I didn't know Phil and he didn't know me, it felt easy to give a small portion of my reality. He listened, he gave harsh advice, and the strangest part - he made a lot of sense.

I finally left as the sun started to settle in the sky, and by this time, I had completely forgotten about my morning with Joe; I no longer felt angry and I felt like I had a clear mind to think with. As I started to walk away, he quickly shouted at me in the distance,

'Meet me at six in the morning on Sunday. We'll go fishing! Ya idiot!'

He didn't ask, he didn't even check if I was free, he just told me when to meet him. I agreed and thanked him for a great afternoon.

I liked Phil, he was good to talk to and he didn't feel sorry for me; he was straight to the point and gave me advice I needed to hear. He would listen to me, but did not seem to cast judgement. This was what it was like to have a friend ... and I could talk to him about the stuff that I didn't want to burden Amy with. I wasn't a big believer in fate, but I felt like meeting Joe was the closest thing. I needed something to calm me down and someone to talk to. Phil seemed to be one and the same. Even though he acted miserable, he must have been lonely in this cabin and clearly missed his wife with all his heart; he needed someone to talk to and that's where I came in. We were the perfect odd couple.

AMY

I was so relieved to be holding my nan's hand in the back of my dad's truck. What a horrible few days it had been for her. Every time I looked at her, I wanted to cry, as her face was red and black where she had been attacked. What sick person could attack such a sweet and innocent old lady? She insisted she couldn't remember anything about the incident, just that she was walking home from the shop, and the next thing she knew, she was in hospital. The police were going to continue the investigation, but it seemed hopeless to track down the scum who did it.

Nan seemed in good spirits and she certainly hated to be fussed; it took both my mom and dad to persuade her to come live with us for a few weeks. Whilst I was relieved to have her home with me, I couldn't help but move on to my next worry, which was Terry. He hadn't texted me all day and I still thought it was really strange that he wouldn't sleep at our house last night. I was even more worried that Laura hadn't seen him or his truck at college when I texted her at lunch. I thought he seemed okay after our trip to York, but like a fan blowing hot and cold, his mood changed like the wind; at least Tim had a great time with him, who hadn't shut up about how much fun he had had with Terry.

When we arrived home, Mom and I arranged the spare bedroom so it was comfortable for Nan and then we baked her favourite cake to cheer her up.

'Amy, make sure Terry is coming tonight for our family meal,' my mom called from downstairs.

I had texted Terry a few times, but so far had heard nothing back. I was starting to worry, and as it got closer to dinner, I feared he wasn't going to turn up. I sat with my nan to keep myself occupied, but I couldn't help but think the worst. What if he had blacked out? What if he was stuck in his safe-room? I was starting to plan walking up to his house, when a knock at the door distracted me.

'Terry! Where have you been?' called my mom, who embraced him as he walked through the front door. 'Are those for me?'

She was referring to three large bouquets of flowers in his hands, one of which was given to my mom, who made a noise of affection.

'Sorry, I had a long day at college,' he replied. 'Nan! How are you?'

Terry came over to Nan and fussed over her, giving her a kiss on her non-bruised cheek and placing a bouquet of flowers on her lap.

'Oh, Terry, you are a sweetheart,' she said.

Finally, Terry turned to me and gave me the final set of flowers.

'I've missed you,' he said.

I was confused and knew he was lying about the long day at college … but seeing how happy he was and the fact he made my nan smile was enough to prevent me from asking too many questions. I grabbed him in a hug and whispered in his ear.

'I was worried. Did you black out?'

He looked at me and just smiled; I didn't know if this was a yes or no.

Terry spent the next hour talking to my nan and he even held her arm as we walked to the dining room table to eat together.

If I didn't have so many worries, this would have been a perfect scene for me. Everyone was talking and joking, my nan was here (who was in constant conversation with Terry) and it was starting to feel like Christmas. This should have been perfection, but all I could feel was anxiety and like something was wrong.

'How was college, Terry?' asked Dad.

'It was good! I actually made a friend.'

'Oh, that's brilliant! Anyone we know?'

'Well, it wasn't actually at college. I fancied a walk this afternoon as I had a free period. On my walk, I met an old guy in the forest. We sat down and spoke for a long time.'

'An old man in the forest?' said Mom. 'How random! I wonder if we know him? What was his name?'

'Phil, he's a big fisher.'

'Old Phil Freeman?' shouted my dad. 'My goodness, I didn't think he was still alive!'

'Who's Phil Freeman?' I asked, intrigued about this new friend of Terry's.

'He used to teach all the boys in town how to fish on his boat,' Dad explained. 'Everyone loved Phil!'

'His wife, Mrs Freeman, was actually a cooking teacher at the school,' said Mom. 'She was one of the first people to inspire me to bake.'

'He told me about his wife,' said Terry.

'Such a bloody shame. She was the most wonderful lady … Horrible thing, cancer.'

'Where does Phil live now, Terry?' asked Dad. 'I haven't actually seen him since his wife's funeral. His boats are still on the pier.'

'He lives in an old cabin in the forest. He's on his own, but he fishes a lot on the black lake. He seems happy … lonely, but happy.'

'I am so glad you spent your afternoon with him, Terry; how lovely!' Mom praised.

'I must come with you to see him,' said Dad. 'I hope he remembers me!'

'He actually wants me to go fishing with him on Sunday,' said Terry. 'Maybe you could come?'

And so I was losing Terry and Dad on Sunday to a fishing trip. Dad was over the moon to be seeing this Phil guy and my mom was immediately planning on making some cakes that were recipes of his wife.

The evening settled down and I finally managed to get Terry alone by asking him to join me on a walk.

'Finally! We can talk,' I said as we reached the end of our road.

'I've missed you.'

'Really? You haven't texted me once today …'

'I'm sorry. I guess I needed to clear my head.'

'So you really did go for a walk?'

'Yeah. Sorry, I should have said something to you. I guess you worried that I had blacked out.'

'Yes, I did!'

'I'm sorry, Amy, I didn't mean to worry you. I guess so much has happened that I needed to get my head straight.'

'I know how you feel.'

'Hey … I really am sorry about putting all my shit on you. It's been so much for you lately. I just want you to know that you can leave me at any point; I'd understand.'

I stopped walking and looked at him; is that what he was worried about?

'Terry, you have kidnappers and mysterious guys following you around … and you are worried about me?'

'Yes. I can deal with my shit. I can't deal with adding to yours.'

'You have nothing to worry about. I can deal with this. I'm more worried about you.'

'Wow, I guess we can worry about each other, then?' he laughed.

We carried on walking down the steep road, along the forest edge.

'It sounds like you had a nice afternoon with Phil.'

'I did. He's really cool to talk to.'

I often worried that Terry had made no friends since living in Byanbythe, and whilst it was an unconventional friendship, it was a friendship all the same.

'It's nearly December, you know; I feel like we should stop worrying about everything and just enjoy the run-up to Christmas. Few dates together, decorating, baking … normal stuff.'

He again stopped walking and turned to me before kissing my lips.

'That sounds perfect,' he replied. 'Some normality.'

His reply sounded like a sigh of relief; normality was all he seemed to want.

*

It was beginning to look a lot like Christmas. November shortly turned into December and all seemed to be well. We spent the weekend decorating our family home; every year, Dad would take us to a special area of the forest that sold freshly-cut Christmas trees. The tree was always too big for our living room and its crown would fold and bend at the top. Our wooden house that was usually very brown and beige was now full of every rich colour you could imagine, golds, reds, greens and silvers. Not a single part of the house was left undecorated without tinsels, beads and ribbons. Mom would be playing old Christmas music in the kitchen whilst baking festive bakes for her bakery and my dad would enforce a list of Christmas films we *had* to watch before Christmas Day.

Nan had decided to extend her stay with us until the new year, which was a dream come true to have her here for the festive holidays. The house was certainly a busy place full of life, as Terry may as well have lived here too, only returning to his own home to sleep or get changed.

Terry and Dad had their fishing trip with Phil and both seemed to have a great time. Dad wanted to arrange more trips and Terry seemed to visit Phil a few times a week, forming a very good friendship. It was good to see him have someone to talk to and bond with. I tried to spend time with Laura on the days that Terry would see Phil, but nothing had changed there;

she was hard to deal with and all she spoke about was her new relationship.

It wasn't just home that felt festive. Like Halloween, Byanbythe went all-out decorating the town and houses with the festive lights and decorations. There were festivals planned, parties, and just in case Christmas wasn't enough, a street party was planned for New Year's Eve.

College continued the motif of festivities and it tried to one-up the town on decorations, almost making it a little too overbearing to see. Classes were starting to wind down for the end of the second term. To keep in line with the season, Louise had set us a task of dissecting *A Christmas Carol* by Charles Dickens. Unfortunately, if you have studied English Literature at college, you would understand that you could never take any book at face value. Instead of loving Dickens for what he wrote, we had to objectify his themes, think of alternative themes and question what characters represented. Why couldn't someone just write a book and mean what they wrote? Did everyone have to be so cryptic that they never actually meant what they wrote? Terry certainly thought so, as he was almost completely zoned out of studying English. He attended every lesson, but rarely got involved; he didn't answer questions and every time I looked over at him, he was writing something in his notepad that I was confident was unrelated to the class. I often asked him if he regretted taking English as a subject, but he gave a sweet reply that it was worth it purely for meeting me. I wondered if he enjoyed his other lessons? I would never know, because he still refused to tell me what his other subjects were.

Things were better than ever between me and Terry and life had almost felt normal over the last few weeks. I was a little disappointed that he didn't want to decorate his house; the house was still bare, unfurnished, and very unhomely. Whenever I tried to encourage him, he would argue that his home was with my family and his house was just somewhere to sleep.

We had decided to take my family back to York for another weekend at the Christmas market and it felt especially special as we were all together. I managed to start buying some presents whilst I was there, but I was struggling to think of what to buy Terry. As far as I knew, he didn't have any particular hobbies; he loved his truck, he loved playing American football and now he seemed to be a passionate fisher, but all of those weren't gifts that I wanted to buy. I wanted to buy something sentimental, and considering it was our first year together, it had to be perfect. Terry had money, so technically could buy himself anything, but he wasn't bothered by anything material. This was certainly a difficult gift to buy.

Mom was her usual self and bought too many gifts for too many people. She constantly reminded my dad that all these gifts were a perfect way to test the size of his pick-up truck boot, but he seemed unconvinced. I had the pleasure of watching my mom spend an obscene amount of money in Betty's and constantly lament that her own baking was nothing in comparison.

We all drank hot mulled wine from the market, ate sugared nuts and a small German section of the market was selling huge tankers of beer to accompany foot-long hot dogs. Unfortunately, as both Terry and my dad were driving and my mom had had a few too many mulled wines, no one was able to enjoy many beers (apart from Nan, who found it hilarious to hold a tanker of beer that was bigger than her head). It was the perfect Christmas experience with my family and I couldn't have been happier.

*

It was the week running up to Christmas and I still had not thought of a gift for Terry. We had so much planned and it was officially the week that my mom became crazy, as it would be the busiest week at her bakery and also her week to plan and achieve the perfect family Christmas; she would go into ultra military mode and none of us dared disturb her flow.

I was working a few shifts at the bakery to help Mom and her staff with the Christmas rush. I wasn't cut out for working in a shop and I was sure I messed up more customers' orders than I actually got right; in the end, my mom asked me to serve at the front counter and take money from people instead of the responsible stuff.

College ended on the twenty-third of December and Terry had managed to book tickets for an amazing event on Christmas Eve; the local cinema was hosting an outdoor cinema on the beach playing a marathon of festive films. After messing up too many customers' orders, my mom was more than relieved to excuse me from working on the bakery's last day before Christmas, which gave me a whole day to enjoy the outdoor event.

The cinema seemed to attract every single person I knew from college; the beach was lined up with rows and rows of cars in front of a huge screen by the pier. A couple of cars away was Laura and her new boyfriend, Todd, who seemed to be less than interested in watching films. When Terry disappeared to get food, I sat talking to Laura through the passenger window of Todd's car.

'So, did you buy anything for Terry yet?' she asked.

'Some little things, but I really couldn't find anything big to get him. I kinda wanted to make it special for him as it's first Christmas here and our first Christmas together.'

'Buy some sexy underwear! That's what all guys want!' intervened Todd, who had suddenly decided to talk to me for the first time.

'No, Todd, that's what you want from me … and I'm not even seeing you on Christmas Day!' shouted Laura.

'Whatever, no drama …' he replied, and lost interest in our conversation.

'Hey, there's Terry!'

Laura pointed. In the distance was Terry; at least, I thought it was Terry, as I couldn't see his face. He was holding at least ten different items in his hands, barely showing his face as he walked.

'Oh my god, Terry, did you buy the shop?' joked Laura.

'Have you seen the stuff they sell here?' said Terry. 'Tango Ice Blasts, gingerbread men, Nutella hot chocolates and donuts!'

'Hey, don't fill yourself up too much,' I reminded him. 'Remember my mom does hot pork rolls on Christmas Eve for all of our neighbours?'

'Your mom, she's so crazy,' Laura laughed. 'Who does a big roast the night before Christmas, and then a bigger roast Christmas Day?'

'Yo, are we invited? Ain't your mom a chef or something?' reappeared Todd.

'Ew, no! You can't just invite yourself to someone's house, Todd. You don't even live in Byanbythe!' replied Laura, looking disgusted with her boyfriend.

'Where do you live, Todd?' asked Terry.

'Yo, it's sick man!' replied Todd. 'Past the mountain and a few miles towards Clendugahe, there's a holiday home complex.'

'You live in a caravan with your dad, Todd,' Laura corrected him, further retreating into her expression of utter disgust; something told me that this relationship was not going to last. We finally wished Laura and Todd a merry Christmas, and I gave Laura her Christmas gift before I left her.

Terry had kitted out the back of his pick-up truck with two sleeping bags, plenty of blankets and several pillows. It was extremely cute, and as he lay down, I cuddled up to him and felt the warmth of his beautiful body, which battled the cold crisp air from the sea blowing in our faces. I was shocked to discover that Terry had seen very little Christmas films before meeting my family. I still found it extremely sad to think that he had never celebrated Christmas properly before. Although we rarely spoke about his time before Byanbythe, he did occasionally come out with little snippets of information, such as how he "celebrated" Christmas. The kidnappers would strangely deliver a Christmas dinner and a wrapped-up gift every Christmas to him. It was always something weird like a hand-knitted jumper or hat; what kind of sick people would give such a homely present? I found it extremely sad to think how lonely he was, which made me more determined to make this Christmas special for him.

When the films had finished and we had escaped the large queue to drive off the beach, we drove to my mom's bakery to help her close up the shop. Watching Mom leave the shop was like watching an actor leave the stage; she looked at the front door after she locked it, took a deep breath and turned around with a huge grin.

'Let's have the best Christmas!' she declared.

Her moment of relief soon ended and she returned to a crazy lady as she entered our home. She had the largest pork joint to take out of the oven and over fifty bread rolls to prepare for the party she was about to host. I must admit, even through the chaos, it was very warming to have all of our neighbours over on Christmas Eve. We didn't always speak, but when we did, it was always to wish each other well and talk about life in Byanbythe and all of its wonders. Slowly but surely, the house began to fill out and Terry, Tim, Dad and I were on a patrol to make sure everyone was well fed, with not an empty glass in sight. My nan would play her usual tricks and pretend she didn't receive a top-up of wine, but after playing my dad and Terry off against each other, it was soon apparent that she was very drunk indeed.

It was a sight to behold, and after too many rolls were consumed and far too much mulled wine was drank, everyone began to sing

Christmas carols in harmony. When I was young, I hated this and found it very cringey (just like Tim, who had ran up to his room once the singing began) ... but as I grew older, I appreciated how wonderful it was to sing with my neighbours and bring in the Christmas cheer. Terry, bless him, didn't know a single word of any Christmas carol, so hummed along merrily whilst watching everyone sing around him.

One by one, the neighbours slowly retreated to their own houses ready for Christmas Eve night and my family was finally ready to settle for the night. It was a Christmas tradition to all wear the same tartan pyjamas on Christmas Eve and enjoy a mince pie and a glass of sherry together. My mom, who struggled to relax even after the party, was wrestled by my dad to leave the turkey alone until tomorrow.

'Will you just enjoy a drink with your family Lisa?! The turkey does not need to go in yet!'

My mom had convinced Terry to sleep over for the rest of the Christmas holidays, as she refused to let him be alone in his house during the season. Tim was extremely excited that Terry would be sleeping in his room on the floor and Terry seemed just as excited to play Tim's Xbox with him.

'Right, everyone, off to bed!' shouted Dad. 'We don't want to be awake for Santa!'

'Aww, come on, Dad, can we watch just one more film?' begged Tim.

'No! We need to put a plate out for Santa and carrots for Rudolph!'

Tim rolled his eyes and slumped his way to the kitchen, almost trying to convince Dad that he didn't think he was too old to believe in Santa.

The once bustling house of laughter and singing powered off and everyone was in bed, ready to sleep the night before Christmas away. The house was deadly silent and all that could be heard was the rustling of trees outside, rocked by the cold winter wind. Once upon a time, I remember that I found it impossible to sleep on Christmas Eve; now I found it impossible to wake up early the next day. As I started to slowly fall asleep, a creek at my door startled me.

'Hey …' whispered Terry.

He crept into my room and slowly climbed into my bed, wrapping his warm body around me under the blanket. He kissed my neck and then my cheek and whispered into my ear.

'Merry Christmas. Thank you for making it so special.'

We kissed until we finally fell asleep in each other's arms.

*

It was a very typical Christmas morning; Tim woke up at six a.m ready to open his gifts. He first burst into my mom and dad's bedroom and then my nan's room to wake them all up.

'Wake up! It's Christmas!'

He didn't dare come into my room, as he knew it wasn't worth his life. I was extremely relieved that Terry had set an alarm to sneak back into Tim's room, which didn't seem long before Tim had actually woken up.

We all congregated in the living room and it was my job to divide the presents under the Christmas tree into individual piles for each recipient. My mom was in the kitchen making cups of tea, coffee and hot chocolate and also to begin initial preparation of the big Christmas feast. My mom's rule of not eating anything big before dinner was strict, as when she lay down a small plate of croissants in the middle of the coffee table, she gave us all a look of warning to not fill ourselves up.

'Don't open anything yet!' called my dad.

My dad had his own tradition of filming everyone open presents on Christmas morning; although this was annoying when I had bed hair and no makeup, it was cute that we could watch every Christmas back. It was strange to see myself grow up, but also embarrassing how excited I would get over dolls and toys. When he finally pressed record on his camera and said go, everyone burst into action opening presents. Tim had his usual video games (which excited him), and some clothes from my nan (which didn't excite him). Dad was pleasantly surprised that my mom had bought him a brand-new fishing rod for his new hobby with Tim and Phil. There was a cute moment where both Dad and Terry opened the same gift, which was a New England Patriots jersey with their names on the back; they both high-fived and stared in awe at their gifts (which were both from me). Mom had the usual gifts of perfumes, clothes and a beautiful necklace from Dad. My nan seemed to have acquired packs of dried fruit ... but she seemed over the moon.

'Where is your gift from, Terry?' Dad teased.

I had opened the standard gifts: notebooks (my favourite), stationery, perfume, some makeup and clothes … but I realised that I hadn't received anything from Terry.

'It's a surprise,' replied Terry, who grinned cheekily.

'It's not a car, is it?' joked Mom.

'No, a motorbike,' said Terry (to which Mom punched him in the arm).

Once all the gifts were opened, Mom and Dad moved to the kitchen to work on the Christmas dinner. Tim ran to play his games and Terry was talking to my nan about her obsession with dried fruits.

'What's Phil doing today, Terry?' called my mom from the kitchen.

'I don't know, he said he didn't care for Christmas much.'

'That's a shame … his wife loved it. Did you buy him anything?' asked Dad.

'I bought him some nice whiskey. He told me to shove the present where the sun doesn't shine … but he still managed to open the bottle,' laughed Terry.

I started to wonder what Terry had bought me for Christmas? I wonder if it was better than my surprise for him?

*

The day was beautiful; I sat with Terry and my nan watching Christmas Day television. The beautiful aromas of the kitchen made everyone in the house feel very hungry and excited for dinner.

'Everyone, start getting ready! Dinner will be in an hour,' warned my mom. 'Good gracious, there's enough here to feed a table of ten!'

Another tradition that I had to teach Terry was my mom insisting that we wore our very best clothes for Christmas dinner; we could wear pyjamas all day, but dinner had to be shirts, ties or dresses (to which Terry offered the dress). As we were all getting ready upstairs, I heard Terry speaking to Mom.

'Oh, Terry, of course! I should have thought of that. Please, you must!'

After a few moments, I heard the front door open and close, and as I left my bedroom, I noticed Terry had left the house.

'Mom, where's Terry gone?'

'You'll see,' she replied, and walked downstairs and into the kitchen.

I was intrigued, but knew I was not going to get much more information out of her. I continued to get ready and then walked into my nan's room to help her with her makeup.

'I wish you didn't wear such dark eyeshadow, Amy!' she barked. 'You look like one of those moths!'

'It's goth, Nan, not moth,' I laughed.

'Is that what Terry likes? Goths?' she questioned.

'I wouldn't care if he didn't. I like being a goth.'

'That's my girl! Don't change for no man! Although, I have to admit, I like Terry a lot. He seems very old fashioned, not like that prick lad you were with before.'

'You mean Nick?'

'I know what I said …'

We both laughed and I grabbed her into a hug.

'Oh, Nan, can you live with us forever?' I begged. 'We have the space. I have loved having you here.'

'I have loved it, but I have a home, my dear, with all my friends too. I miss moaning about everyone with people my own age.'

We hugged again and I looked at her beautiful face, which was now almost totally healed. She no longer seemed on edge and back to her normal, sarcastic self.

Mom called us down to lay the table for dinner and I was starting to wonder where Terry was. I poured a glass of wine for my mom, dad and nan, a glass of Shloer for Tim (who liked to think it was wine), Mountain Dew for Terry, which seemed to be his favourite drink, and Pepsi for me, as I was boring. As I neatly placed the Christmas crackers on the table, the front door opened and Terry called in.

'Hey, everyone, I'm back.'

He wasn't alone, as he welcomed into the house a small old man.

'Mr Freeman!' my mom called, and paced from the kitchen to give him a hug. 'Thank you so much for accepting our invitation.'

'I appreciate the offer, although I told the lad not to bother,' growled the old man. 'Christmas is for families and drunks … and I ain't neither.'

'Shut up and sit at the table, you grumpy old git,' laughed Terry. 'No one should be alone at Christmas.'

'Phil!' screamed my dad in surprise.

'Let's hope you are a better cook than you are a fisher, boy!' barked Phil.

Terry stood back and watched the scene with a warm smile on his face and I slowly walked over to his side to whisper to him.

'So this is Phil?' I asked.

'Charming, isn't he?' Terry sniggered. 'I hope you don't mind him coming over?'

'Of course not! I'm just surprised.'

'He has no one ... and spends every day alone. I asked if he wanted to do something for Christmas a few weeks ago and he shouted at me ... but I couldn't stand the idea of him being alone when we had such a perfect family Christmas here.'

'It's such a beautiful idea, Terry. You're right, today isn't the day to be alone. But I don't know how you persuaded him?'

'He's a gentleman at heart. I told him your mom insisted and he begrudgingly accepted. I think he was secretly happy, though.'

I put my arms around Terry and hugged him tight.

'You really are the most thoughtful person, Terry, you know that?'

He smiled at me and then the family. My dad walked over and placed his hand on Terry's shoulder.

'This is a great, idea lad, well done,' he praised.

Phil was grumpy but funny as I watched him talk to my mom and then Tim. It wasn't until he reached the table that he met my nan.

'My god! Someone who actually looks like they know what they are on about!' said Phil as he shook my nan's hand.

We all sat down at the table and I poured Phil a glass of red wine.

'Ah! So you're the one who's got the boy on a tight lead?!' asked Phil as I poured into his glass.

'Erm … yes … I mean…' I honestly didn't know how to reply.

'Well done, girl! Every lad needs to be told what to do, otherwise they get lazy!'

I laughed and watched Terry place his head in his hands.

'Don't embarrass me, old man,' begged Terry. 'It's Christmas Day.'

'I couldn't give a flying hoot if it's Judgement Day! The girl deserves recognition for putting up with a layabout like you!'

I immediately started to like Phil.

A small pinging noise from the kitchen indicated for everyone to fall silent and my mom slowly arrived with a large silver tray in her hands, holding the largest turkey I had ever seen. Everyone clapped their hands in appreciation and my mom began to carve the meat and place slices on each plate on the table. Once everyone had a serving that almost filled their plates, she beamed a huge smile of relief and sat down.

'Help yourself, everyone! Dig in.'

The noises of clanking and chinking soon filled the room; plates were full of crispy roast potatoes, pigs in blankets, stuffing, cranberry sauce and a small pile of vegetables (because I felt like I had to); the gravy was thick and rich, and if all of that wasn't sickly enough, my mom brought in a huge pile of mash potato and cauliflower cheese which she had forgotten in the kitchen. We all ate like we were starved, and Terry, in his passion for food, even tried some of my mom's nut roast, which he agreed tasted good (but not as good as turkey).

I spoke to Phil a lot during dinner and he was a very interesting man. He spoke harshly, but you could tell his heart was always in the right place. It was sad to know that he had not celebrated Christmas since his wife had died, instead spending every year alone in his cabin. He tried to play it off like he wasn't bothered, but it was clear how alone he was and how much he loved his wife.

I looked around the table and saw a picture-perfect scene. Everyone was talking, smiling, eating, drinking and it seemed like there was nothing wrong in the world. I looked at Terry, who seemed to be the only person not engaged in a conversation; he watched everyone talk and slowly ate his food.

'Are you okay?' I asked.

'More than okay. I've never felt so happy,' he replied.

I grabbed his hand and smiled at him. To hear this was the greatest present of all.

*

Dinner ended with a game of "Who Am I?" in the living room, which was a game where you wrote a name of someone famous on a sticky note and placed it on someone's head who had to ask questions to find out who they were. Mom brought in the most delicious trifle she had made to date (which specifically impressed Phil as it contained a lot of sherry).

The day started to slowly close and it was suddenly pitch-black outside. Nan and Phil were engaged in a conversation of their yesteryears and the rest of my family half-listened to them and half-watched some Christmas TV specials. I was lying on Terry and felt myself slowly falling asleep, which wasn't good as I still had my present to give to him; as I resisted, Phil called over to Terry, which took me by surprise.

'Boy, aren't you supposed to be somewhere?'

'Yes! It seems like the perfect time now. Come on, Amy!' said Terry in an excited tone.

We quickly got up and Terry told me to wrap up warm. As I retrieved my coat, I heard Phil say to Mom and Dad, 'I'll explain to you when they are gone', which peaked my attention all the more.

'You know where to go?' asked Phil as we walked out of the door.

'Just like you said,' replied Terry.

Terry refused to say anything to me and wrapped a scarf around my eyes so I could not see where he was driving. It felt like a long time to be sitting in the dark, but every time I asked where we were going, he laughed and told me to wait. Minutes felt like they were turning into eternities and Terry continued to drive. Where were we going? What did he have planned? And what did Phil know about it?

'Okay, we're here,' said Terry. 'Don't take off your scarf, I'll guide you.'

Terry opened my door and held my hand as he helped me out of the truck. I could tell we were in the forest as the ground beneath me crunched with frosty leaves. Wherever we were, it was freezing cold, colder than anywhere I had been in a long time.

'Stay here, I won't be a second,' said Terry.

I heard rummaging in the background and it sounded like Terry was on the floor. I was trying to listen to what he was doing, when he suddenly fell silent and it became very eerie.

'Okay. Take off your scarf.'

I ripped off my scarf in anticipation. When I opened my eyes, I felt overwhelmed. I didn't know what I was expecting, but it wasn't this.

'Terry ...'

We were at the Black Lake, which was famous for being mysteriously frozen over every winter. I was standing on the edge in the forest and Terry was standing in the middle of the lake with ice skates on his feet. I looked to the ground next to me and wrapped neatly was a brand-new pair of purple ice skates.

'Do you like it?' he asked.

I didn't know what to say. I felt like I wanted to cry. The lake looked like the most beautiful thing in the world; the frozen water glistened like a bed of diamonds under a pitch-black sky. It was peaceful and I could see my breath before my very eyes. As there weren't many houses by the Black Lake, the stars above could perfectly be seen here, which reflected on the frozen floor below.

'Is it safe?' I asked.

Terry didn't reply, but skated towards me whilst extending his hand out to help me onto the ice. I slowly put my new ice skates on and hoisted myself up to the ground. I gently walked towards the ice's edge and Terry grabbed my hand.

'I haven't ice skated since I was a girl,' I admitted.

'Just hold onto me,' he whispered.

We steadily skated away from the edge and I held Terry's hand tight. This was the most beautiful moment of my life. I was clumsy and almost fell over a few times, but Terry never let me fall. He skated so gracefully and I felt like a chicken in a swan dance ... but he never let me feel bad. We laughed, we kissed and we had the whole lake to ourselves. This felt like our place and we danced all around the lake together, skating back and forth, never letting go of each other. We hardly spoke, but just skated through the crisp cold air. It felt like we had skated for an entire evening and I didn't want it to stop, however, I was slowly losing the feeling in my fingers and my cheeks were so cold that I felt like they were starting to burn. When Terry kissed me, he started to laugh.

'Your lips are as cold as the lake! Come on, let's head back.'

I suddenly thought about my present to Terry and started to feel nervous.

'Can we stop at your house first?' I asked. 'I want to give you your gift.'

He looked back at me with a look of curiosity.

'Okay.'

We skated back to the edge and Terry helped me take off my skates before taking off his own. As I finally felt the much-welcomed heat from the truck heater, I started to feel more anxious; I needed to talk through my nerves.

'Who taught you to skate?' I asked.

Terry began to laugh again.

'You won't believe me.'

'Who?'

'Phil.'

'Okay, you are going to have to explain that one.'

'So, skating on the ice wasn't my idea. Phil used to take his wife to skate every Christmas Day. He told me it was always the best moments of his life and that I should do the same for you … if I truly loved you.'

'I'm glad you truly love me. He was right, it was the single most amazing moment of life. I didn't want to leave.'

'Good … 'cause I've been called an idiot around six hundred times whilst Phil taught me to skate. He hasn't got a lot of patience.'

We both laughed, but I started to think about Phil and his wife.

'He really did love his wife, didn't he?' I asked.

'Until the very end and beyond,' said Terry. 'That's why I know I love you, because I want to love you until my last breath. I want to grow old with you.'

I grabbed his hand and squeezed tight; he had a way with words and it only made my present to him feel more right. We finally reached his driveway and we walked into his lonely, empty house.

'Wait there,' I told him.

Terry sat on the bed as I walked into the bathroom. I was either going to create the second most beautiful moment of my life or do something very embarrassing.

TERRY

I sat on my bed and wondered about my present, although I couldn't possibly think of a single present that Amy could buy me that could make this day any more perfect.

I looked around my house and it only solidified the values I was starting to appreciate in life. This house was big, but it was empty, it was cold and didn't have a family feel to it. I would live with the Doories any day over this place. Their house was full of memories, full of laughter and full of love. Now more than ever did I appreciate and value those feelings. Everything about this Christmas, from the family, the friends and the neighbours was everything I wanted in life ... and it felt like I was slowly achieving it.

'Terry?'

I turned around and for the second time in my life, I saw the most amazing body. Amy walked out of my bathroom naked and stood in a nervous way.

'Amy?'

She walked towards me and kissed me.

'I think we're ready,' she said. 'I couldn't think of a more perfect moment than our first Christmas.'

I suddenly felt sick with worry and very, very anxious. I was a virgin ... but I guess so was she. I didn't know what to do. I didn't know how to initiate this. She kissed me again and I decided to stop thinking about it. She started to undress me and I gently threw my clothes to the floor. The kissing was slow and gentle. I whispered that I loved her and she kissed my chest. When I was finally fully naked, my nerves suddenly disappeared. Strangely, this moment was not unlike skating on the lake with Amy. She was beautiful and natural and I felt awkward, but she wouldn't let me feel that way. It wasn't perfect, but we laughed when I did something clumsy or something wrong.

I had seen enough films in my life to see college kids having sex … but they never really showed how things really happened. Neither of us knew what we were doing. It didn't last for hours and I didn't do as much as I thought I should have done. I tried not to think where to hold her, where to kiss her, what to do next … but somehow, the imperfections made it perfect. I didn't possibly think I could love Amy any more than I did already, but in this moment I felt like I was physically one person with her. I felt like I had discovered another way to express my love and I didn't want to stop. When we did stop, we stared into each other's eyes and laughed nervously together. It felt like we had achieved a huge milestone together, but she was right - this was the perfect moment. After today … after the beautiful moment on the lake, making love to Amy couldn't have been more perfect.

'Wow,' I whispered.

Amy began to turn red, but her body was glowing in my dark house. She turned and lay in my arms and her warm body felt like an extension of my own body. I stroked her hair and kissed her neck.

'I really couldn't think of a more perfect day,' she said.

I agreed and felt like the luckiest man alive.

*

Amy fell asleep in my arms, but I couldn't sleep; I felt too happy. I slowly turned to look at my clock and noticed it was almost eight o'clock. I needed to drive Phil home and it was getting late.

I woke up Amy, who slowly got out of my bed. I took another look at her perfect body and began to kiss her again.

'Don't, otherwise we really will be late,' she teased.

She was right and we both got changed.

'Your present won,' I joked.

She turned red again and turned away from me, but I could see her laughing. We locked up my house and drove back to her house.

'Amy!' called Lisa as we walked through the door.

'Well, did you mess up, boy?' asked Phil. 'Did you trip?'

Amy retold the events of the lake to her family, who Phil must have explained to already. Lisa and Amy's nan sobbed little tears and Michael placed his hand on my shoulder.

'What a beautiful idea. Well done, Terry,' he confirmed.

I looked at Phil, who too seemed to be a little emotional. I walked over to him and hugged him, thanking him for the great idea.

'Carry on the tradition, kids. Just because I can't doesn't mean you shouldn't. Ahh, Marie would be so proud,' said Phil as he wiped a tear from his eye.

Amy walked over and kissed Phil on the cheek, thanking him for sharing something so intimate with us. Phil quickly cleared his throat and straightened up.

'Okay, okay! That's enough emotional shit for today! Take me home, Terry, I need some peace and quiet from all this mushy stuff.'

We all laughed and everyone bid Phil goodbye. Lisa wrapped up a container of leftover Christmas dinner and insisted Phil should come again for dinner; Phil agreed and quickly hobbled through the door.

I drove Phil home and he was completely silent on the way back. I wanted to ask if he enjoyed his day or if he enjoyed his dinner or the company, but I knew him well and knew that even if I asked, I would get a sarcastic reply hiding his real emotions.

As we were driving through the forest lanes, something caught my eye. In fact, it caught my eye so much I almost lost control of the road.

'Whoa, boy!' barked Phil. 'Have you drunk some sherry or something?'

'Sorry,' I replied, but continued to look in my rearview mirror.

I had just driven past a hut. It was extremely shabby, older than Phil's. I could see the glow of a small light coming from the inside, which was good because without the light, you would think it was derelict. None of this caught my attention as much as the motorbike parked outside - it was without doubt Joe's motorbike.

I hastily picked up my speed to drive Phil home; I parked as close as I could to the forest's edge and walked with him to his cabin. I wanted to get him home quickly so I could drive back to Joe's hut.

'Did you enjoy your day, Phil?' I asked.

He turned around and looked up at me, and for the first time since I had known him, smiled a genuine, warm smile.

'Thanks, kid. It really did mean a lot. I haven't felt like that in a long time.'

I smiled back and watched him enter his cabin. Once I knew he was okay with the lights on, I ran back to my truck.

I couldn't let Joe escape. I raced my truck as fast as I could, retracing the roads to where I saw the hut. I felt excited, I felt ready for whatever was about to happen. I could see the bike in the distance! I slowed my truck and parked a little bit away. I didn't have a plan and I certainly wasn't ready for a fight, but if he was there, I would fight him and I would kill him. I crept to the window and saw a small dim light from within. I peaked around, not taking any chances, in case this was some twisted trap from Joe. I didn't know what I was expecting, but as I looked into the hut ... it wasn't what I saw.

There must have been at least fifty empty bottles of cheap whiskey on the floor, the type you brought from an off-licence with petty change. The hut was bare and empty. It looked like it had been abandoned for some time; the walls were dark and damp and the wooden beams looked like they had rotted from a hole that leaked water in from the roof. Amongst the empty bottles was Joe, sitting with his back against the wall and crying.

I suddenly had mixed emotions; through all my anger, my hatred and my fury to want Joe dead, I never once thought I could feel anything else for him, yet I suddenly felt pity, like watching a man who had reached rock bottom. I didn't know what possessed me, but I felt like I needed to speak to him. Maybe it was the Christmas feeling inside, after a beautiful day with the family? But a part of me wanted to reach out to him and give him a chance. I walked to the door at the back of the hut and walked inside.

'Joe?'

I stood a few metres away from him, still prepared that this could have been an ambush again.

'Come to rub it in my face?' he slurred.

He was drunk. I was genuinely surprised; if we were the same monster, with the same curse, then he had achieved to get drunk, something I had never done before.

'I've never managed to get drunk before,' I said in surprise.

'Takes a lot. It used to take a lot more than this, but hey ... when you drink every day!' he proclaimed and took a huge gulp from another bottle in his hands.

I had never drank more than a few bottles of hard liquor, but it seemed that a mystery was finally solved - I could get drunk; it just took enough to quench a full town.

'Is this where you live?' I asked.

'Once upon a time. Sorry, I didn't get a mansion like you,' he sneered.

'We need to talk, Joe. You have the wrong idea. I didn't choose a mansion. Or this life. And I really have *no* idea about what we are!'

'We are cursed.'

'Do you even know what we are?'

'We are in hell. We were born to suffer.'

'Joe, what aren't you telling me?'

'That you will be miserable like me, once they all know what you are.'

'How can they know what we are if we don't know?'

'I'll make sure they all know what you are … just like they did to me,' he replied, but he wasn't looking at me. He stared at his whiskey bottle like he was talking to it.

'Why are you doing this, Joe? I haven't done anything to you. Neither has my family. You could have killed that little boy.'

'Family?!' he shouted, suddenly looking at me. 'You think you have family? You think they will love you forever? Love you when you are nothing like them? I cannot wait for them all to know!'

My pity for him faded and my hatred returned.

'They all know about me,' I lied.

His face changed. He looked confused and angry. His face screwed up, disgusted by what I had said. He began to pace the room, muttering under his breath, but I couldn't tell what he was saying.

'I can help you, Joe …'

'Help me?! I don't need your help, you piece of shit! I am here for one reason only and that is to make your life miserable! I don't give a shit if your *FA-MI-LY* know. I'll tell every fucker in this town until they realise that you are dangerous.'

'If you come near me or my family again, I will kill you,' I growled at him.

Joe laughed and attempted to throw a punch at me, but it was the most pathetic punch I had ever seen. It was slow, almost in slow motion, and if he was aiming for me, he missed me by a few metres. Joe stumbled forward with his punch and fell to the ground. I began to laugh and realised I did pity him, after all.

'You're pathetic. I can't believe I was scared of you. You're just a drunk loser, jealous that no one likes you. You're jealous that I have a good life and you're alone on Christmas Day in a hut, drinking yourself to sleep because your life is too much of a joke to face. I'm not scared of you and the next time you come near me or my family, I will kill you.'

Joe began to sob on the floor, but I felt far too angry to show any compassion. This man wanted nothing but to watch my life fall to pieces and had no moral compass; he attacked old women and young kids for his pleasure. I started to walk away, but felt like I had one last thing to get off my chest.

'We are nothing like each other. You may think we're the same, but we're not.'

I left him on the floor sobbing and returned to my truck. I felt like I had some closure by seeing him in the state he was in. I didn't need to be scared of him and he certainly wasn't a threat.

*

The only sad part of a perfect Christmas was the days to follow. Unfortunately, nothing could compare to Christmas Day, and even though the days were fun, they seemed like a comedown in comparison. Boxing Day was a quiet affair, with a buffet dinner of all of the leftovers from Christmas dinner. The Doories planned a big walk through the forest and to the beach, which was hosting the National Boxing Day Dip (an annual event where people would swim from the coast in fancy dress for charity). Michael and

Lisa were planning to take part dressed up as ducks, which Amy found both amusing and embarrassing.

Amy's nan was driven by a neighbour down to the beach to get a good viewing spot on the pier, whilst the rest of us took part in our walk. The walk was pleasant, as Lisa spent the whole journey asking Amy about ice skating on the lake.

'You were gone for such a long time!' said Michael.

I could see Amy turn slightly red in the face, which made me burst out laughing. Michael gave me a confused look, but thankfully, didn't ask any more questions. After a few miles of walking, Tim got tired, so was lifted onto poor Michael's shoulders, who already had a strenuous event ahead.

As we walked, I looked up at the tall, dark trees of Byanbythe and started to think of its beauty during winter; the wind was crisp, the town was alive and everyone seemed to get together in community spirit. I was so proud to be part of this community and revel in its hidden gems like the Black Lake.

When we arrived at the town, I could see the first decorations for the big New Year's Eve party planned in the town.

'Is it a big party?' I asked.

'Huge!' replied Michael. 'People dancing in the streets, singing at the top of their lungs. There are lots of bands playing too.'

The Boxing Day dip was a very unusual but fun event to watch. Michael and Lisa changed into their duck costumes and joined an army of dressed-up members of the community. I could see cowboys, sharks, aliens, ballerinas, gangstas … everything that you could imagine! We stood and watched the event go ahead, which didn't seem to last very long, and it looked extremely cold, going by the reactions of people as they jumped into the water.

After the big dip, a BBQ was hosted on the beach for all the brave souls who swam (and the brave souls who stood and watched in the cold). We eventually met up with Michael and Lisa, who were wrapped up in big, warm towels.

'Well done!' I congratulated.

'Next year, Terry, you best take part,' said Michael. 'Awfully refreshing!'

I laughed and half-promised I would take part. We split up into the crowd, which seemed to fill the whole beach with everyone and anyone from the town.

'Hey, can we go back?' asked Amy.

'Of course, why?'

'I'm not feeling so good.'

She seemed fine to me, but I put my arm around her and found Michael and Lisa to tell them we were heading back.

'Can we get a taxi home?' she asked.

'Okay …' I agreed, further perplexed by her sudden illness.

She didn't say much to me during the taxi back, and when we finally reached home, she couldn't wait to get inside. I paid the taxi and followed her to the house.

No sooner had I closed the door did she wrap her arms around me and begin to kiss.

'Wait, I'm confused,' I said, not understanding how she could go from being ill to furiously kissing me.

'Everyone will be at the beach all day. We have a empty house,' she said as she was taking her hoodie off and throwing it to the ground.

I suddenly understood and joined her in taking advantage of having a free house. The strangest things in life were experiencing things for the first time. It seemed like having sex for the first time was a big event, something that took a long time to build up to. Now we had gotten the first time out of the way, it was like we were uncontrollable. We must have had sex five or six times in the time we had the free house. Amy was like a different person and I couldn't keep my hands off her. We did it in many rooms, in different ways, learning what we liked and what we did not like. I still did many things wrong and at times so did she, but that made it more exciting. As we attempted to begin the seventh time, we heard a noise from downstairs and Amy pushed me off her and onto the floor.

'Get changed! Quick!' she said.

'Okay! Okay!'

I heard multiple voices downstairs, some I didn't recognise.

'Amy? Are you upstairs?' called Lisa.

'Oh no! She's gonna catch us!' I panicked.

'Out the window!'

'What? Are you being serious?'

'You survived a car crash! Jump. Out. The. Window!' she whispered in a furious tone.

I finished zipping up my jeans and began to climb out the window. Lisa began to open Amy's bedroom door, which panicked us both more. Before I could get my second leg through the window, I was pushed out and fell to the ground.

I looked up (unscathed, of course) and quickly saw Amy check if I was okay before turning around and talking to her mom.

I was glad that she knew that I could survive being pushed out of windows …

*

The days between Boxing Day and New Year's Eve were quiet and uneventful. We sadly said goodbye to Amy's nan, who returned home to visit her friends that she had missed over Christmas. In the days that followed, I had arranged another fishing trip with Phil and Michael, who was extremely excited to try out his new fishing gear. Phil seemed to be more upbeat than usual, and during our fishing on a small lake by his cabin, he recounted story after story about adventures during his life. Maybe the Christmas spirit had awoken a happier Phil? I was over the moon to see someone I saw as my best friend come to life with joy and stories.

In the times that I wasn't fishing or doing something with the family, I was having sex with Amy. Whether or not it was the fact that it was something new to us, we could not stop having sex. It was at her room, my house, her living room (when everyone was asleep), the spare room; we had even experimented in the shower. We were young and free and expressing our love in the most physical way possible.

New Year's Eve eventually came, and in no time at all, we were all walking to the big party in town. It wasn't long before the loud music could be heard and the bright lights from the pier were blasting into the sky. As we reached the town, it was plain to see why everyone was so excited for this night. A huge stage stood on the pier, where a band was playing for all to see. On the beach were fairground attractions with all the rides you could imagine. People were drinking and dancing, and if they weren't doing that, they were eating at one of the many fast food stalls that were dotted around. I didn't let go of Amy's hand and it was so strange to feel like we were a brand-new couple again. Michael and Lisa took Tim to the fairground and Amy wanted to see her friends who were drinking under the pier.

'Come with me and keep me sane?' she asked.

'Of course.'

I knew Amy hated hanging out with the people from college, but for the first time, I actually saw her enjoying herself. Yes, people were drinking, but they weren't excessively drunk. People were just having a good time, laughing and enjoying life for all it had to offer. Laura came over, suddenly single after a

Christmas breakup with her most recent boyfriend, but even she was happy, and after no more than three drinks did she start dancing and singing at the top of her voice.

Every so often I would catch eyes with Amy in the distance when she was talking to her friends. We smiled at each other in a way that made me want her more; I was literally on cloud nine and wanted to spend every minute kissing her. I was talking to different people that I hadn't spoken to before and mingling with different people from college. Could life feel any more perfect?

The night felt a lot like Christmas, but with a different group of people. We all partied under the pier with the sound of music and screams of laughter from the fair above. As it got close to midnight, everyone started to congregate towards the middle of the town for the big countdown to midnight. On the stage walked a very small but official-looking old lady, who Amy informed me was the mayor of Byanbythe. She gave a big speech about the community and recapped a few big events that had occurred throughout the past year.

As she spoke, something caught the corner of my eye, but I tried to dismiss what I thought it was. I continued to watch the mayor on the stage; we were quite far back in the crowd, but she could still be heard crystal clear. The same thing caught my eye again and I couldn't dismiss it. Everyone in the crowd stood still where they were as they watched the mayor ... which made it more difficult to ignore the only moving figure. Drifting between the crowd was a slim, ginger figure in his usual biker jacket. Joe drifted from left to right in the crowd, smiling at me as he walked. Before I could react, he disappeared ahead. I let go of Amy's hand and started to follow.

'Terry, where are you going?' she whispered.

'I just need the toilet. I'll be back in a second.'

'It's almost midnight!'

'I'll be back.'

I drifted into the crowd in the same direction as Joe. He was up to something and I had to stop him before he hurt someone. I sidestepped through the crowd, squeezing between different gatherings of families, but without another sight of Joe. I looked around and got closer to the front, but couldn't find him. I started to head back towards Amy, when in the distance I could see Joe again ... but this time he was very still. I felt sick, I felt like a single wrong move could end in a very bad way. Joe stood behind Lisa, Michael and Tim. Of course, they had no idea, he was just another person behind them in a large crowd.

Joe just stared at me in the most peculiar way; he looked deranged again. I didn't know what he had planned, but it wasn't good. I wanted to walk towards him, but was scared how he would react. I started to think of the best tactic to take, when the wise words of Phil echoed in my mind. I needed Joe to chase me for once. He was trying to draw me in, trying to get a reaction; every time I chased him, I walked into some elaborate trap. He was still staring at me, waiting for me to walk towards him. I took my opportunity and started to walk out towards the town and away from the crowd. I kept looking back at him and he was obviously unhappy with my reaction. It took me to reach the edge of the crowd for Joe to finally start following.

I continued to walk to the edge of town, far from the happiness, the grand speech of the mayor talking and from all my family and friends. Joe continued to follow me, and as I reached the forest, I stopped and waited for him to join me.

'What do you want, Joe?'

'I was joining in the New Year festivities.'

'I told you to stay away from my family.'

'Or what? What was it you said? You would kill me?'

We started to circle each other on the edge of the forest; in the distance, the party could still be heard.

'Don't push me. I *will* kill you.'

'Take your best shot!'

We began to fight, but for once I had the edge. I punched him in the face, and before he had a chance to react, I then grabbed him by his shoulders and threw him to the ground as hard as I could.

Joe quickly jumped and ran at me, pushing me into a tree full of brute force. I struggled, but he had me a tight grip.

'Who said it was your family I was after today? No. Not this time. I'm looking for someone a little older,' he whispered into my ear.

Phil …

In the distance I could hear music and the countdown began to ring in the new year. The crowd was all shouting in unison. I felt strange … something I had not felt for such a long time. I felt hot, I felt like I was going to be sick. The world around me faded to black, but I fought with all my strength to not black out.

'TEN!'

I pushed Joe away and tried to wrestle him to the ground. I was fading.

'NINE!'

I couldn't black out now. I needed to save Phil.

'EIGHT!'

Joe was on the ground. I punched his head as hard as I could and as fast as I could.

'SEVEN!'

Joe pushed me away.

'SIX!'

I faded into the darkness. I was losing control. I couldn't resist much longer.

'THREE!'

I regained a brief moment of consciousness and saw Joe running away in the distance. I chased him as fast as I could.

'TWO!'

I leapt and tackled him to the ground. I hit harder than I had ever hit something before. I hit him like I was trying to punch through him and to the ground.

'ONE!'

I couldn't resist anymore.

'HAPPY NEW YEAR!'

The sky burst with the loud explosions of fireworks, which illuminated my final moments in the world as I blacked out. My final moment was in the dark forest, illuminated by hundreds of different colours showing the last thing I saw. I had done some serious damage to Joe, as his face was bloody and cut open. He looked scared … but not as scared I was.

NO!

I had to resist. I had to fight this!

My eyes opened again, but I was alone on the forest floor. I had to get to Phil's. I kept drifting in and out of consciousness, running for my life in the direction of Phil's cabin in the woods. I had never fought for something so much in my life. I faded again, but when I regained consciousness, I could see Phil's cabin in the distance.

'PHIL!' I screamed out.

I stumbled to the ground, resisting to fade with every fibre of my body. I heard noises coming from Phil's cabin.

'Get out of my cabin! I have a gun!' I heard Phil shout.

I drew closer towards the cabin, shouting out for Phil.

'PHIL!'

'Terry! Get in here! Quick!'

I heard the noise of a smashing plate and the sound of some struggle inside the cabin. I needed to get inside the cabin.

'P-Ph-Phil,' I stuttered; I couldn't hold on much longer.

The door of his cabin opened, and to my horror, Joe emerged with a terrifying look on his face.

I crawled on the ground towards the cabin and finally over the threshold. Inside, Phil lay on the floor, clasping his chest. There were no marks on him. He was having a heart attack, gasping for breath.

'Phil … I'm … here.'

I was fading again. There was nothing I could do. I needed to stay awake. I needed to save his life. I needed to call an ambulance.

Phil stared me in the eyes with such panic and fear as he struggled for breath. With his other arm, he reached out to me. The last thing I saw was his face, his eyes, his fear.

*

I woke up in the same place that I had blacked out, on the floor of Phil's cabin. In front of me lay a cold, lifeless body. I slowly got up and walked next to Phil's body. I didn't need to check his pulse; it was too late. I slowly picked him up and lay him on his bed, which was a few metres away. The cabin was a single room, not unlike my own home. I looked around the room and admired how minimalist Phil's life was. There was nothing more than a bed, a toilet, a basin and a chair. I took a quick look in the mirror on the wall and I was unmarked. I needed to phone an ambulance for Phil, but I couldn't have anyone turn up if I had blood or marks on me; that would have looked too suspicious. I kept looking over at Phil's body; I couldn't erase the last image of him out of my head. I knew that his face would scar me until the moment I died.

I didn't want to think about Joe. I felt like I was in shock, but strangely, I didn't feel much else. I sat down on the armchair and thought about the best thing to do. After sitting there for a while, I felt like I finally had a plan in my head. I also thought how fucked up it was that I had to think up a lie to cover up my best friend's death.

I removed my phone from my pocket and saw that I had hundreds of missed calls from various people; Amy, Michael, Lisa. Amy was the closest, as her latest text was asking me if I had blacked out. I needed to call for an ambulance before I spoke to her.

I dialled 999 and it was the most surreal call of my life. They didn't ask too many questions once I confirmed he was already dead. I lied that I had come to visit him this morning and found him in bed. They were sending an ambulance and sent their condolences for my loss.

Now I needed to call Amy. I knew that I could tell her that I blacked out and not need to tell her much more, but what about Michael and Lisa? I took some more time to think about it before I called Amy.

'Amy …'

'Terry! Are you okay? I've been so worried! Did you black out?'

'Yeah … I'm sorry. I needed to get away from the crowd. I blacked out and woke up in the early hours of the morning near Phil's cabin.'

'Oh, Terry! It's been such a long time since the last blackout. Are you okay?'

'No. I need to tell you something.'

'Okay …'

'I wanted to see Phil this morning, to wish him a happy New Year.'

'Terry, what's wrong?'

'Phil's … dead.'

It was almost as if saying the words made it real. As soon as the words had left my mouth, all my emotions came crashing back. I suddenly felt overwhelmed by grief. The tears escaped my eyes and I couldn't stop myself crying.

AMY

It was the worst way to start a new year. I had never seen Terry cry, and quite frankly, it was the most heartbreaking thing to watch. By the time we arrived (Mom and Dad alongside me), the ambulance had already arrived and took Phil. The police naturally had to come to take a statement, but Terry could hardly talk to them.

We were all so upset to lose someone out of our lives, especially someone that had become so prominent of late. Just over a week ago, we sat down with Phil and enjoyed Christmas dinner. He was fishing with my dad and Terry, telling stories of days that had passed … and yet, days later, he was dead.

I had told Mom and Dad that Terry had to rush home with a migraine last night and came to see Phil early this morning to wish him happy New Year. They were both just as upset as Terry and I felt like I needed to support them all. Terry had lost his best friend, someone he loved to hang out with and confide in … and to find them dead? It was beyond comprehension.

The next few days seemed to blur into one; Terry spent a lot of time on his own, and although I didn't like it, I knew he needed the space. My mom insisted that he stayed at our house, but again, Terry declined and said he needed some time to take everything in. My mom and dad wanted to be there for Terry as much as I did, but this was the first time they witnessed Terry dealing with grief; he had become withdrawn from the world. The hardest part for me was the huge change from before Phil died; Christmas had seemed so special and it was the happiest I had ever seen Terry. Dancing on the lake, all the sex, the parties … to go from that happy place to now, it was hard to adjust.

The police didn't treat Phil's death as suspicious and he didn't have a will, not that he had any possessions other than his boats and his small cabin. It was decided that all of Phil's possessions could be sold to settle the bill for his funeral, but Terry insisted he was going to pay for everything. It was really hard to arrange the funeral. Although Terry felt so close to Phil, he felt like he didn't know enough about him; in the end, Terry felt the best thing to do was to scatter Phil's ashes on the beach, next to his boat where he had so many fond memories with his beloved wife. Terry didn't know if Phil had any friends, and going on the fact that he had not spoken to anyone since his wife passed away, the funeral was planned to be just our family.

I had only been to one funeral in my life, which was my granddad's when I was very young. I didn't know quite what to expect, but Phil's funeral was very quiet and over quickly. We all drove to the crematorium which was located in a town a few miles away from Byanbythe. No music was played and a few small prayers were said as the curtain was drawn around his coffin. Terry had not spoken once all day, and after the funeral, we all drove back to my house to have a small "wake" in Phil's memory. Terry was told that he would be able to collect the ashes the next day, so it was decided that we would all go down the beach tomorrow afternoon to finish the ceremony.

I felt like I was hopeless in this scenario; I wanted to support Terry, but he didn't want to talk about it and he continued to be on his own. When he left early on the evening of the funeral, I expressed how concerned I was to my mom.

'He just needs time,' she said. 'It's always hard losing someone you care about.'

'I just wish there was something we could do for Terry. It was really sad that no one came to Phil's funeral. I think Terry feels he has let Phil down …'

My mom's face lit up and she immediately grabbed the house phone.

'I have an idea. Leave it with me.'

I was confused, but didn't have a chance to question her as she was immediately on the phone to someone I didn't recognise.

I thought long and hard about something I could do for Terry and thought about Terry talking about preserving Phil's cabin and boats in his memory.

'Dad?' I called.

'Yes, Red?'

'Does the locksmith still do engravings?'

'Yes. What are you thinking?'

I had a great idea to have a plaque with Phil's name on that we could place on the cabin. My dad thought it was a great idea and we set out to drive to town to get the plaque made. It felt like everything was done so quickly, as within an hour my dad was driving me to Phil's cabin to see if Terry was there.

'Are you sure you don't want me to come? What if Terry's not there?' said Dad.

'He will be. He's been there every day since.'

Dad dropped me the closest he could before I had to walk through the forest. It was pitch-black outside, so my dad wasn't comfortable with me walking on my own. After persuading him that I would be fine, I began to walk towards the cabin and hopefully Terry.

I felt relieved to see a small light emitting from the small wooden cabin, and as I entered through the door, I saw Terry sitting on Phil's bed, his arms wrapped around his legs and in deep thought.

'Terry?'

He looked at me as if he hadn't heard me walk into the cabin.

'Is everything okay?'

'I just wanted to check on you. We're all worried about you.'

He slowly climbed off the bed and walked towards, grabbing me in a gentle hug.

'I'm sorry. I'm just struggling to process everything.'

'Don't be sorry. It must have been horrible to find him.'

'I wish I had done more for him.'

'Like what? You already did so much.'

'I couldn't even throw him a half-decent funeral. Five people and a priest.'

'That's not your fault, Terry.'

He dismissed my comment and sat back down on the bed.

'I've brought you something.'

I walked over and placed the plaque in his hands.

In memory of Phil Freeman
A fisher. A friend. A teacher.

Terry stared at the plaque like it was more than a hundred words. I was worried that I had done the wrong thing, but when he finally looked at me, his tears were accompanied by a smile.

'It's perfect,' he said.

He grabbed me into another hug and sobbed into my shoulder.

'I thought we could put it on the cabin's front door. This would always be a place in his memory.'

He sobbed into my shoulders and my heart was breaking.

*

We spoke late into the night; Terry was finally opening up to me and talking about his feelings. He was dreading the next day, scattering Phil's ashes, but mainly because he felt like it was a poor example of celebrating a man's life. Terry felt responsible for Phil's death and I didn't know why.

I persuaded Terry to sleep at ours that night, so he could be with us the next day when he collected the ashes. It was a quiet journey, and again, Terry didn't say much as we drove back to Byanbythe and towards the beach. The only person acting stranger than Terry was my mom, who seemed to be glued to her phone most of the day.

'Here we are, everyone,' said my dad as he drove around the corner to the main town.

It was the most peculiar scene. The whole street, which was the stretch of town towards the beach, was lined with people, all dressed in black. I don't think Terry realised at first, but when he did, he looked around in shock.

'Who are all these people?' he asked.

'Terry, I hope you don't mind,' said Mom, 'but I extended the invite to a few friends … and

I guess they extended the invite to most of the town. Everyone knew Phil and Marie and wanted to give him a proper send-off.'

We got out of the car and Terry stared around at the crowd in shock. It felt like the entire town had turned up to give Phil his final send-off. Terry grabbed my mom into a hug, and although he tried to hide it, I could see he was crying again.

The crowd walked to the beach and I could see that Terry was trying to thank as many people as he could as held Phil's ashes. It was a beautiful day and I truly believed it gave Terry the closure he needed. It turned out that both Phil and Marie were very popular people back in their day for Byanbythe. Phil was so highly thought of, he was even asked to run for mayor, but in typical Phil style, he told them to piss off. Many people thought Phil had passed away years ago or at least moved away, as he hadn't been seen or spotted since the funeral of Marie. People were exchanging stores with Terry about their fondest memories of Phil and it was great to know that so many people were as fond of him as Terry was.

Terry walked to the water's edge and addressed the crowd in a feeble, croaky voice, obviously very moved by the turnout of the crowd.

'I was an idiot to think that no one would turn up today. I just want to thank Lisa for showing me the error of my ways. Today has been a great day, because I have shared so many stories with other people about a truly special man. He didn't want attention and definitely spoke his mind ... but he always knew the right thing to say. I will miss the fishing trips and the stories about his wife, but most of all, I will miss the way he shouted at me or called me an idiot.'

The crowd laughed and clapped as Terry raised the urn of ashes in the air.

'To Phil!' called Michael.

The crowd repeated "To Phil!" in unison as Terry scattered the ashes into the ocean. It was a beautiful end to a beautiful day. I was so proud of my mom for making this happen with such little time and it relieved Terry of any guilt he once had. To hear all the stories portrayed Phil in a different light and gave Terry the story of Phil's life that he needed. Despite all his bravado, Phil was a beautiful soul, who dedicated his life to his wife, who made an outstanding career as a teacher. It was a sad tale that they could not have kids, but with the absence of blood came bonds, and Phil acted as a father figure to so many in Byanbythe.

A few of the older men from the town took Dad and Terry to see Phil's boats. It was unanimously agreed that the boats should be handed to Terry, but being the man that he was, he had quickly decided that he wanted to fund a fishing school business with the boats, which some of the local fishermen were honoured to host and help with.

As the beach started to clear, I had a moment on my own to reflect on what the new year had dealt already. Last year had ended with so much joy; I felt like I was living out a dream come true. This year felt like the polar opposite, and the man Terry ended the year as was not the same one that this year began with. I was worried that the man who took me ice shaking on the lake, who I was having sex with like there wasn't a care in the world, now carried a sadness that he had not known before. Terry's life had seemingly been plagued by tragedy, losing his mom and dad, being kidnapped for most of his life and haunted by mysterious kidnappers and that strange ginger man. All of that sorrow seemed like nothing compared to now; Terry had a serious side, but most of all he seemed very happy-go-lucky ... until Phil's death. I could see something in his eyes that disturbed him. Could it be the fact that he was the one to find Phil dead? That seemed like an impossible situation to handle, but something told me it was something more, something Terry wasn't telling me. He was accustomed to having secrets, I literally had to pry things out of him at times. Would he start to open up more to me the more serious our relationship became? Or would he hide things from me? Could I live my life always guessing what was on his mind? I felt selfish for thinking all these things at such an unnecessary time like a funeral, but these were important questions nonetheless. For the first time, I had serious concerns about the future and I wondered if love alone would be enough to get me through.

TERRY

The next few months felt like they passed in a giant blur. I could hardly remember what had happened, but I guess I didn't need to; every day and night felt like the same things happened over and over again.

I didn't sleep. I couldn't get the image of Phil out of my mind. I couldn't get Joe out of my mind. I couldn't get rid of the anger that I felt, something so deep in the core of my stomach it felt unnatural to hold on to. I tried to work on my emotions, but the more I thought about Joe, the more obsessed I became. If the sleep wasn't bad enough, I had started to black out again, but it came back with a vengeance. At one point, I had blacked out almost every night. I wasn't quite sure, but I had a suspicion that the blackouts had something to do with my anger and the lack of sleep. The less I felt in control, the more I blacked out, until I felt my life was in autopilot.

My obsession drove me to go looking for him every single night. In the day, I tried to be as normal as possible. I attended college, spent time with the Doories and tried to maintain a normal relationship with Amy; we had dates, we kissed, we even started to have sex again, but it didn't feel like before. I didn't feel like I did before. I wasn't the same person anymore. I felt guilty the moment I felt happy; how could I feel happy after what I had done to Phil?

If I hadn't have met Phil, Joe wouldn't have targeted him. I couldn't stop thinking about those final moments in the cabin. What would Phil have been doing? Was he in bed? Was he drinking a cup of tea? Knowing him, he probably didn't even know it was New Year's Eve … and yet, out of nowhere, a random guy was in his cabin. His voice sounded scared; what did Joe do to him? It must have been the worst possible thing to cause him to have a heart attack. Phil must have got so worked up, he … he …

I had to stop thinking about it!

I couldn't.

But his face. Those eyes. The way he reached out to me.

Every night, I looked for Joe. I travelled to his hut. I looked around every street, every house, every pier and every cliff. I spent every moment alone, looking for the smallest sign. I dreaded to think about his next plan. How far would Joe go next?

This question drove me to the edge of insanity, so much so that one night I had planned to run away. If Joe was targeting everyone I loved, then it was only a matter of time before he did something to the Doories. So far, he had no regrets over attacking an old lady, a small child … and even leaving an old man for dead. All because he wanted to expose me. Torture me. Make my life a living hell. Everyone close to me was in danger and I was moments away from driving somewhere far. The only thing that scared me more than Joe attacking the Doories was the thought of him attacking them whilst I was somewhere far away; at least in Byanbythe I could try to protect them. Unfortunately, there were no signs of him. Days became weeks and weeks became months.

My relationship with Amy was starting to feel strained. She knew something was wrong, but I couldn't tell her why; she always knew I had had a blackout the morning after, but she stopped asking about them. At least she was only angry at me; I knew telling her the truth would worry her to a state worse than the one I found myself in. I had become a shit boyfriend to her and that became apparent on Valentine's Day, when I decided to spend the night looking for Joe instead of giving her the romantic evening she deserved. How different things had changed from ice-skating on the Black Lake to suddenly stooping to a five-minute visit with flowers and then disappearing for the night. With every stupid mistake came a stupid argument, until Amy started to feel a little distant to me. Without the friendship of Phil, the love of Amy and no sleep to live my life, I slowly drifted into a deep depression. I dragged my feet everywhere I walked. I didn't participate in classes and I just didn't enjoy anything anymore. I used to skip to go see the Doories, I used to be obsessed with eating and spending time with Amy. Now I just had one purpose and it felt shit.

*

Winter began to fade from Byanbythe and the cold crisp days started to be drowned out by the smell of spring. The flowers began to come to life and brighten up the paths around the forest. The sunshine cracked over the horizon to brighten up the forest and seaside, and slowly but surely, tourists began to visit the village behind the mountains. It had now been three months since I lost Phil; my anger began to fade and all I felt now was misery. I still searched for Joe, but started to feel that he was never going to show his face again. Was it safe to go back to normal? Could I start to feel once more?

I thought of Phil every single day; although the last image of him still burned behind my eyes, I felt like my memories had a little more room to think of the good times too. I brought myself to start fishing again with Michael, who was making a conscious effort to spend time with me (at the request of Amy, who often expressed her concerns). The fishing trips were quiet at first, but after some time, we began to speak about some of our fond memories of Phil, and Michael would recount some of the times he learnt to fish with him as a kid.

The fishing business seemed to be doing well, and as the better weather came, more and more lessons for sea fishing were booked. I didn't have to put too much money into the business, as it was mainly giving Phil's boat a lick of paint and some safety equipment for the fisherman running the lessons. Yes, I didn't want to admit it, but some light was beginning to shine in my life. I felt myself slowing gripping reality again and just hoped that everything could go back to normal.

Unfortunately, not everything could go back to normal that easily. I began to worry that my relationship with Amy was damaged beyond repair. We started to see each other less and when we did see each other, we started to argue. She would ask me what was wrong and then call out my lies when I gave an excuse. Eventually, it felt like she just gave up caring, to the point it didn't even feel like we were friends. This only made my depression worse, and one day, it became too much.

I had stopped turning up to college, I didn't answer my phone, and I didn't want to see anyone. Amy must have presumed at first that I had blacked out, as she didn't seem concerned, but after days of not responding, her worries must have got the better of her. I had locked myself in my safe-room, scared of blacking out again and ending up somewhere naked like before. I felt exhausted, I felt like I no longer knew the difference between falling asleep and blacking out. I lay against the glass wall of my prison and just began to cry. I didn't know how long I cried for, but it felt like hours.

'Terry?'

Her voice felt like a dream calling me out of a nightmare. As I turned my head, Amy stood at the bottom of the stairs behind the clear door.

'Amy …'

'Let me in.'

I slowly got up and unlocked the door for her. She looked me up and down and gave me a look of concern. I didn't want to look her back in the eye, so sat back down on the floor and rubbed my eyes.

'You look like shit,' she said.

'Thanks.'

'I'm saying it because I care, Terry. You look awful. What's happened?'

What lie could I tell her again? No matter what I said, she would see through it and it would cause another argument. I didn't know what to say and, embarrassingly, started to cry again.

'Terry?'

I didn't look up at her. It broke my heart to know I had ruined this relationship.

'I'm fine,' I lied.

'I can't do this anymore, Terry! You won't tell me a single thing. You lie to me all the time and nothing's the same anymore. I can't live like this. I love you more than you could ever know … but you clearly don't feel the same! Otherwise you would open up to me!' she shouted in a burst of frustration.

'I am the reason Phil died …' I whispered.

Maybe it was the lack of sleep? Maybe I had just given up … but against my better judgement, I decided to just tell her the truth. Maybe she'd split up with me, maybe it would worry her to death … but I just couldn't keep up these lies anymore.

Amy looked at me in shock. Her moment of frustration had vanished and she now seemed stunned.

'What do you mean?' she finally said.

'The night he died. It was my fault. I was there when it happened. I watched him die, Amy, right in front of my eyes, and there wasn't a single thing I could do.'

'Terry, you're not making any sense.'

'It was Joe, that ginger guy that was following us around. He's been tormenting me for weeks. On New Year's Eve, I was chasing him down … he was going to Phil's to provoke me. I started to black out … but it was too late. When

I got to the hut, Joe was there … and then Phil had a heart attack. He must have been so scared … and I couldn't save him in time. I blacked out.'

A single tear streamed down her face, but she was speechless. I decided to carry on.

'I have wanted to stop Joe for a long time. I have spent every night searching for him, patrolling the town, making sure he doesn't come back.'

'And … is he … is he here still?' she stuttered.

'No, he's disappeared completely.'

'What does he want, Terry? Why does he keep doing this?'

'I don't know … he wanted to hurt me bad and he got what he wanted. I'm broken. It's ruined everything. I can't get Phil's last moments out of my head. I can't stop worrying about you. I can't stop thinking if he'll come back and cause more issues.'

'Oh, Terry, why haven't you told me any of this before? I can't believe what he's done, what you had to witness.'

I sobbed. I sobbed harder than I had ever sobbed before. Amy sat down beside me and pulled me into her arms.

'Amy, I can't be with you without bringing you danger. I can't live with that.'

She stroked my hair and held me tight. I had told her most of the truth, but left out the part about Tim and her nan. I had done what I swore not to do and that was to give her something to worry about. For a moment, I was starting to think she agreed with me, as she didn't say anything back.

'I told you before, it's not your job to look after me. Nor is it your choice whether you're the right person for me. I can make my own decision.'

'But Joe -'

'You said he was gone? If he was planning something else, he would not just disappear. And if he does come back, we deal with it then.'

'But if he gets to your first? Or your family?'

'It's not your role to protect us all. If he comes, we will deal with it then.'

'How can you say that, Amy?'

'Because if my choices are to definitely lose someone or potentially lose someone, I know which is the easier choice.'

'Amy -'

'Stop fighting back. Stop trying to make choices for me. We love each other, don't we? Joe isn't the problem in this relationship. It's you keeping things to yourself. Secrets. Lies. All because you think you are protecting me, when in fact you are making things worse.'

'I'm sorry.'

'What you have been through is unimaginable. You need people around you to support you. You can't do this alone.'

I looked at her beautiful face, in her beautiful eyes and just wondered how she could be so brave? I was inhuman. I was indestructible … and yet, she was the one who stood with no fear.

'Amy … I'm so sorry. I really am. For everything.'

'Just be the Terry I knew at Christmas. Tell me everything that goes through your mind, everything that worries you,' she begged. 'You have been through so much in life already; we need to enjoy life when we can.'

'I want to, but -'

'What would Phil say to you right now? Shut up, boy and man up!'

We both started to laugh. I almost forgot what it was like to laugh. I stood up and grabbed her into a hug.

'I promise I won't keep things from you.'

'Good. Because if you do it again, I promise you that Joe isn't the one you need to worry about.'

And that was that. Amy, my strength, acted like Phil would have in this situation - a slap to my face to bring me back to earth. I still felt guilty for putting this on Amy, and in truth, I was sure under her bravado she was worried ... but she was acting as the strong one to pull me out of my low. We walked out of the safe-room and locked the door behind us.

'I don't want to see you in this room again unless you really need it Terry. I hate this room and we're going to find a way to stop you blacking out.'

'I can't control it, it's become really bad again,' I admitted.

'There was a time you hardly blacked out last year. We'll figure it out.'

She grabbed my hand and led me back up to my house, taking me to the bathroom and forcing me to get showered and changed.

I was amazed. For months I had pushed her away, falling into this pit of despair that I felt like I couldn't escape ... and yet, with one frank conversation and a bit of honesty, I felt like there was a little hope again in my life.

That night, Amy took me for fish and chips

and a long walk on the pier. We didn't discuss anything about Joe or Phil, just random things. Our night ended up in the arcades and I was suddenly laughing again with Amy, feeling normal like the teenager I should have been. When I laughed, I looked in her eyes and suddenly valued how lucky I was. If I felt guilty, I reminded myself that Phil wouldn't want me to feel guilty, but to live my life to its fullest. Like his love for Marie, I needed to cherish every moment with Amy until my last breath. If I carried on with my misery, Joe would get exactly what he wanted. I needed to carry on, and like Amy said, if he ever showed his ugly head again, I would have to deal with it then.

AMY

After what felt like the worst few months of my life, things finally felt like they were looking up. I still suspected that Terry was patrolling for Joe; I soon discovered about his run down in the forest ... but the patrolling was certainly a lot less, and he was definitely more attentive to everything else in his life.

I had to admit, learning about how Phil died really disturbed me and I was worried about Joe. Was my family in danger? This only added to my doubts about my future with Terry and our relationship.

My doubts didn't take over too much, and soon enough, I felt like I was slowly returning back to normal. Terry was back at college and playing American football with my dad and we were dating and enjoying life as much as we could.

It was my mom's birthday towards the end of April, and although she wanted a quiet affair, my dad had organised the first BBQ of the season with all of our family and friends. To everyone's surprise, Terry had offered Michael to host the party at his house.

'Wow, a BBQ up the Great Western Way? Are you sure, Terry?' asked Dad. 'We wouldn't want to intrude.'

'You're my family. It's a huge house and it's never used. I literally take up a few metres and the rest is blank space,' admitted Terry.

When I asked Terry what spurred on using his house, his change of attitude shocked me more than the gesture itself.

'I guess I should start making my house a home.'

'Wow, only nine months too late!' I teased.

'Maybe you could help me decorate it? Add some things in … you know, a sofa? Rugs?'

'That's what constitutes making something a home? A sofa and a rug?'

'Okay, we'll go off your bedroom. Posters of goth and grunge bands. Maybe a coffin or two?'

'Now you're talking! Maybe I could put you in one if you ever pissed me off?'

He winked at me and kissed my forehead. He still gave me the butterflies that I felt the moment we first kissed and I loved that we were flirting again.

I spent the morning of Mom's birthday decorating Terry's house ready for the BBQ. Dad wasted no time at all bringing his grill and setting it up on Terry's garden terrace on the first floor (Terry had to pretend to struggle carrying the grill up the stairs when helping Dad). We pushed Terry's only possessions (the bed, TV and boxes), to the empty garage joined to the house, creating a completely empty house and ground floor for the guests.

The sun was beaming, the smell of BBQ food was perfuming the air, and slowly but surely, friends and family were walking up the long private drive of Great Western Way. For many people, the houses in Terry's street were a big talking point that people only dreamed of visiting. Today was an open house invitation and Terry seemed over the moon to be sharing his house with them. There were the obvious whispers and questions about how Terry could live there alone or afford such a large and lavish home. Although it was my mom's birthday, she excelled herself at making cakes and light bites for the party. I was doing my best at acting as a host, to allow my mom to enjoy her party, hardly noticing who was walking around, when a familiar voice called out behind me.

'I never thought I'd see the day you were acting as a host!' teased Laura.

'You came! Where's your mom?' I asked.

'I think she's taking a selfie in front of the house. I can't believe this is where Terry lives! How have I never seen this place before?'

'He's hardly here, in fairness. He's mainly at my mom and dad's.'

'Wow, if I lived here I'd never want to leave.'

This was the sort of house that suited Laura to a tee; big, luxurious and perfect for showing off. She followed me through the house (which was now full of people both inside and out) and onto the terrace.

The afternoon was a great occasion and it made me smile to see Terry's house full of life and laughter. The house's beauty had always been overshadowed by how empty it was and the love it lacked. If I ever thought of Terry alone in this place, I often thought of when he blacked out and the times he had made it to his safe-room hidden beneath the house.

Laura was the only person I had invited from college, but I was glad she was there; when my hosting duties were no longer required, I managed to catch up with her and talk. For once, she was single, and as we spoke, we discussed the upcoming end-of-term exams.

'Can you believe our second year is almost over?' she asked.

'I know. I've actually kind of enjoyed college this year,' I admitted.

'I'll say! You haven't been as much of a miserable bitch this year,' Laura joked. 'Maybe having a boyfriend you like has helped?'

'I really wasn't happy before. I guess I realise that now because I am happy,' I admitted. 'I haven't really seen Nick since the car crash.'

'He's still around college, although he's not as cocky. Heard he had a new girlfriend who was in Year Eleven at school.'

'Makes my skin crawl. He's eighteen and he's dating a sixteen-year-old?'

'I can't knock him. I was dating eighteen-year-olds when I was sixteen.'

'Laura, you were dating thirty-year-olds when you were sixteen.'

'Cheeky bitch!' she laughed.

I noticed Terry mingling with a few friends of my dad, every so often looking over at me and smiling.

'You really love him, don't you?' asked Laura, catching me smiling back at Terry.

'I do.'

'It's really good to see you happy. I never thought I'd see the day. Who knows, I may see you drunk this year?'

'Don't push it,' I warned her. 'I'm in a happy relationship, not a mid-life crisis.'

'I'm joking. Although, it would be nice to go to a college party sometime soon. I feel like Emma Chanesse's Halloween party was the real last big party.'

'And look how that turned out. You left me and I was in a car crash …' I reminded her.

'You can't hold that against me forever!'

'I can try.'

Laura rolled her eyes and leaned on the glass banister that overlooked the whole of Byanbythe.

'It's a shame we never have college parties up in these houses. Can you imagine?' Laura pondered.

'Emma Chanesse's was a big house,' I reminded her. 'I heard that it was wrecked after the party. I heard her mom and dad paid hundreds of pounds to fix the swimming pool around the house.'

'Yeah, I guess it's easy to be a guest at a party. I wouldn't want to be the host. I've been to some pretty tragic events. Remember Alex Sawyer's house?'

The event that Laura was referring to was a party in our tenth year of secondary school. Alex Sawyer hosted a garden party for a few girls from school, which turned out to be the entire class of Years Ten and Eleven and even a crowd of college kids that Alex didn't even know. The party became so out of control that several police vans turned up, all windows in the house needed replacing and I was sure a fight broke out in the street between two drunk kids.

'What happened at Alex Sawyer's house?' said Terry, who had finally joined us.

Laura exploded into several stories about the infamous party and even managed to dramatise some of the stories to be even more extreme.

'Wow! Sounds like I missed a good night,' laughed Terry.

'I was trying to explain to Laura that this is why it's not a good idea to host a party,' I explained to Terry.

'Why? Who's hosting a party?' asked Terry.

'No one; that's the problem,' moaned Laura. 'No one has arranged a party for months. There isn't even a party planned for the end of the college year!'

'Have the party here.'

'Have you not listened to anything Laura said? Your house would be destroyed,' I snapped at him.

'Come on, everyone's in college now, it can't be that bad. And even if they do wreck the house, it doesn't matter.'

'Oh. My. God. Terry, you're being serious?' screamed Laura.

Before her imagination ran away with her, I had to stop Laura from texting every household in Byanbythe.

'Hold on, Laura! Before you start sending the invitations out, Terry, can we discuss this first, please?' I pleaded.

'Amy, come on! Don't be boring,' begged Laura. 'Terry said it was fine!'

'I'll talk about it with Terry first!' I snapped.

Laura knew she was overstepping the mark and quickly changed the subject to Terry and college, faking an interest in how he found his lessons (which he still refused to reveal the identities of). When she realised that she wasn't going to get an answer today, she began mingling in the party, rejoining her mom, who was entertaining a group of her clients from the hairdresser's. As I was finally alone with Terry, I knew now was my chance to discuss the party with him.

'Are you sure you know what you're hosting, Terry?' I asked.

'It's only going to be the same as now.'

'You have no idea. This is a party of people in their fifties and over, all very respectful to people's properties and not going to drink excessively until they cause chaos.'

'Honestly, I don't mind if they do. Like I said, I need to start acting like this is a home. If I have to replace a few windows, so be it. I don't even have furniture for them to wreck.'

'Are you sure, Terry? 'Cause once Laura knows, the whole of college will be invited,' I reminded him.

'Only if you don't mind. I want to make friends and it is the end of my first college year, at least.'

I gave a big sigh. I wasn't fond of parties and I certainly wasn't a fan of hosting a party at my boyfriend's mansion … but Terry seemed to be making the effort and I suppose he was right - what could they wreck? I asked Terry one last time and sighed as I walked over to Laura to give her the news she wanted. After a scream that could only be associated with someone being murdered (and attracting a look from everyone at my mom's party), Laura began to jump up and down with excitement.

'Can I help plan it? Please, please, please!' she begged.

'I suppose, but Terry has the final say on everything! Do you understand?'

She agreed (but I wasn't entirely convinced that she was going to respect what Terry said). She threw hundreds of ideas at him, but Terry seemed to find it amusing and didn't particularly agree or disagree with anything she said. When Laura left the party (practically skipping away to plan the event of the year), I looked at Terry with a look of deep regret.

'You have no idea what you have let yourself in for,' I forewarned him, dreading to think the lengths that Laura would go to.

*

The next few weeks were unbearable. I had to warn Laura almost every day that she could only invite people we knew and certainly no more than fifty people. She agreed, but again, I doubt she was listening. She was planning themes, drinks, buffets, music, lighting.

'Laura! This is a college party, not a wedding!' I reminded her.

Her imagination had no limitations, but Terry still didn't seem to mind at all. Soon enough, Terry was becoming a very popular person around college and not just because he was the guy who fought my ex-boyfriend. People who had never spoken to Terry before were walking up to him at college and asking about his party. People from the first year to the third year were all talking about the party at the mansion at the top of Byanbythe. I heard it in lessons, during breaktimes, in the library and even in the car park walking to Terry's truck. I used to love the fact that not many people knew who I was at college, but now I was Terry's girlfriend, the girl who was dating the guy in the mansion (which I really hated).

When I cornered Laura on how many she had invited, she denied inviting many at all and blamed it on word of mouth for the "party to end all parties". Soon, the rumours were becoming outlandish and out of control, from famous DJs attending to hot tubs and swimming pools. During a lunch break at college, I sat down with Terry to discuss the rumours.

'Maybe I should buy a hot tub?' joked Terry.

'Don't joke … please. I thought you hated people thinking you were rich?'

'I do. I must admit, I'm sick of people asking about my parents or who I live with or how I afford the place. Someone even asked to lend fifty pounds from me the other day.'

'God, I hate people!' I growled.

'Don't worry, I presume after the party, people will forget who I am again.'

'Will you now admit that you regret hosting a party?' I asked.

'No. I will admit that I regret involving your best friend, Laura … and that her party planning is making the idea of a party regretful,' said Terry.

'Speak of the devil …' I muttered, as I saw Laura walking towards us.

'Terry!' she called. 'You are going to love me!'

'You've cancelled the party?' replied Terry.

'You are such a joker!' laughed Laura, oblivious to Terry's sincerity. 'No, even better! I have sorted out the alcohol!'

'What alcohol?'

'It's a college party; obviously, there will be alcohol,' she replied in a matter-of-fact tone.

'Whoa, I don't think I'm comfortable about that, Laura. There are going to be first-year students there and I know for a fact that most of them aren't even eighteen yet. I ain't breaking the law for a party.'

'Come on, Terry, everyone practically drinks from the age of thirteen!'

'No way, Laura, I'm putting my foot down on this one,' insisted Terry.

'You can't have a party without alcohol! And I've already paid the guy now.'

'What guy? What do you mean?' I interrupted her.

'Listen to this! So, I was on a date with a guy I kinda knew from a few years back. His friend owns a brewery and had crates of beer that he was selling off cheap! This guy offered to deliver them and everything! I've paid him as a thank you for hosting the party.'

'But what about the people underage?' said Terry, sounding like he felt very awkward.

'If you are that insistent on it, I'll make sure that I ask Liam Hanningon to make sure he doesn't serve beer to anyone underage.'

'Wait, who's Liam Hanningon?' said Terry, now more confused than ever.

'He's going to be running the temporary bar we're setting up at your house!'

'What temporary bar?'

'For the booze, of course!'

'Oh ... okay.'

'So, I've said to this guy that we could store the barrels in your garage? Then we could set the bar up next to the door in your house that leads to your garage? Clever, isn't it?!' concluded Laura.

Terry's face looked confused and like he hadn't quite taken everything in. He agreed with Laura, but did not look entirely convinced with what he was agreeing too. When Laura finally skipped off, I grabbed Terry's hand and gave him a look of concern.

'Hey, she's getting out of control. It's not too late to cancel this party,' I reminded him.

'No, I don't mind really ... just don't feel comfortable with people underage getting drunk at my party.'

'If it'll make you feel better, I'll be sober and I'll kick out anyone drinking underage.'

'That won't make you very popular at college,' joked Terry.

'I have never wanted to be popular in my entire life,' I insisted, and we both laughed. 'Are you sure you want this party?'

'I'm sure. We'll have a great time! Just maybe lock Laura in the toilet so she can't cause drama.'

'Maybe your safe-room?'

'I need to make sure people don't accidentally find the button to open that room.'

'They won't, you really have to know what to press to open it up,' I reminded him.

I could see he was concerned, so started to joke around about locking Laura in the safe-room for a few weeks to make things right. I started to realise that Terry was a lot like me and had no desire to ever attend parties, never mind host them. After the bad start of the year, I felt like he was desperately trying to get some normality into his life and fit in more with what people our age were doing. I could see he was uncomfortable about the party, but wanted to make this effort, maybe even to prove to me how much he was trying. He had come a long way since Phil's death, and even started to black out less, the last time being last week in his safe-room (in which he was more successful in trapping himself before he blacked out).

'Hey ... you know, we don't have to go to the party,' I said to him as we were walking to our next class.

'What do you mean?'

'Well, I don't like parties and neither do you. Maybe we could show our faces and then go to the beach and leave everyone to it?' I joked.

'But it's my house, I can't just leave everyone.'

'Damn. Thought we could get away with it …' I laughed.

'Oh, you're joking. I thought you were being serious then!'

'Okay, maybe I was being a little serious. I can't help it that I want you on your own all the time,' I said, winking at him as I walked into the classroom.

As I looked over my shoulder, I was almost positive that Terry had gone red in the face.

*

It had been weeks and weeks of rumours and planning from Laura. Slowly but surely, the plan was coming together and the whole town was becoming aware of some great party; even my mom and dad had caught wind, but to my disappointment, they were excited for us.

'Ah, lighten up Amy, it sounds like a great party!' said Mom. 'And Terry's house is huge!'

'But if there's too many people there and drunken idiots, the police might come.'

'Don't be silly. The police will only be involved if there is trouble. We were all young once upon a time.'

Was I the only one who hated parties this much? I guessed one good thing about the party was how much I was preoccupied by it. I was so busy trying to rein Laura in that it completely took my nerves away for my end-of-year coursework and exams. College officially ended on Friday 28th May, but most people had exams right until the very end of the day. Maybe it was a good thing that they had a party to look forward to? Because of the exams and revision, I spent most of the weekend before the party decorating and preparing Terry's house. We had to borrow painting and decorating tables to make a makeshift bar and DJ table in the house. On the first floor and on the outdoor garden balcony, we placed lots of chairs and empty barrels for people to place drinks and food on. For decorations, it was very minimal, and against Laura's wishes, we placed a string of fairy lights in the garden that ran throughout all of the house. It looked very beautiful and something I asked Terry to keep up even after the party was over. A guy from college who owned his own DJ kit set up a giant booth in Terry's kitchen area, with speakers almost as large as the fridge-freezer itself. On the Thursday before the party, Laura's new boyfriend had driven up with thirty barrels of beer and plenty of bottles of spirits to store in Terry's garage. Terry had an American football training session that night with my dad, so bravely gave Laura the keys to his house to help her boyfriend. When Terry returned home that night, he was relieved that the garage was full of metal barrels and bottles and nothing outlandish that Laura wanted for the party.

'Hey, Joey said to focus on drinking the barrels closest to the door to the house, okay?' said Laura.

'Why?' I asked.

'He said the ones at the back of the garage aren't that nice, but still drinkable. I guess those were the barrels his friend was desperate to get rid of.'

I was hoping that people weren't going to be drinking enough to reach the back of the garage, but I didn't have much time to think about it. Tomorrow was my last exam for Media Studies, which I knew focused heavily on a piece of phone hijacking and undercover journalists; I needed to study at least five examples to be ready for the exam. I spent the night alone in my bedroom and read every source I could. I didn't get nervous for exams, but for some reason, this one was keeping me up. Media was always such an easy subject to do, but the exams were brutal in their questions. I felt like I didn't get any sleep, as every time I started to drift to sleep, I would wake up thinking about something I needed to revise a little bit more.

The final day of college was full of everyone talking about Terry's party, but I couldn't think of anything apart from getting this exam out of the way.

'Haven't you got any exams today?' I snapped at Terry, who seemed very relaxed during our lunch.

'No. I did History on Tuesday and Philosophy doesn't have an exam, just shit loads of coursework,' he replied, but as soon as he had finished, his eyes widened with shock.

'Oh my god, you do History and Philosophy!' I screamed. 'You finally told me!'

Terry was extremely annoyed with himself that he accidentally told me his courses and I spent the next forty minutes mocking him for his subject choices.

'English, Philosophy and History, aren't you a little hipster? What do you want to be when you grow up? A student until you are sixty?'

'Says you!' he snapped back. 'What good jobs come out of Film and Media?'

'Like all the best jobs in film and TV?'

'Yeah, and most of them spend years doing freelance work and eating pot noodles to pay their student loans. No, thank you!'

We bickered until the end of lunch and I was so grateful, as it took my mind off my exam. After dropping one more insult to him, I kissed Terry goodbye and walked to my final exam, which was being hosted in the auditorium at the college. I was glad to see that I wasn't the only person nervous for this exam and could see other people from class cramming in last bits of revision before they walked into the auditorium to take the exam.

It was worse than I thought. None of the questions seemed to be exactly what we had prepared for. I looked around the room and could see people scratching their heads or their faces full of confusion. I wrote pages and pages of content, rambling on about everything and anything I knew about each question and topic. My hand started to cramp and I felt like I was physically and mentally exhausted as I finished my fifteenth page of written material. As the examiner called for all pens to be put down, I breathed a huge sigh of relief. What was done was done. I didn't feel particularly confident about what I had written, but it was in my nature to always doubt my ability. I got up out of my chair, stretched and walked out of that auditorium, knowing that it was now beyond my control and college had officially broken up! I had a party to get over and done with and then I could enjoy a whole summer with Terry, without a care or plan in the world.

Over the last few days, Terry and I had discussed our plans for the summer. We decided we wanted to go on holiday together, somewhere hot, somewhere private and somewhere where we could just eat, drink and have sex without a care in the world. I tried to remind myself to lighten up for tonight - yes, it wasn't my cup of tea, but it could be fun and it would literally be for one night only.

Terry and I drove to his house with Laura and we spent the next few hours getting the house finished for the party. Laura and I got dressed in Terry's bathroom together. My ritual was simple and easy; my makeup was the same (black) and I always wore the same perfume. Laura, on the other hand, had different makeups for different occasions, with different shades for different dresses. After fretting for an hour, the first voices of people joining the party could be heard from outside the house, so Laura quickly finished getting ready, made sure her boobs were pushed up and visible, and got ready to show her body off.

'Joey's coming tonight, I want you to meet him!' she said to me as she was bagging up her makeup.

'I have met literally hundreds of your boyfriends, Laura, why should this one be any different?' I asked.

'I like this one a lot. He's mature and a bit of a bad boy.'

'Aren't they all?'

'I really think you'll like him, Amy, I promise.'

I nodded and walked out of the bathroom and into the house. I could see a handful of people talking to Terry and admiring his house, all pointing at the large windows and high walls. The DJ began to play some music and I felt the same uneasy feeling in my stomach that I always felt before events like this. I took a deep breath and reminded myself that this would all be over in a few hours.

TERRY

I remember thinking Lisa's party had had a lot of people at my house, but that was a small group compared to this party. It hadn't even been an hour and the bottom and first floor of my house was full to the brim, with people overflowing onto the driveway at the front of the house and the garden terrace above.

It was loud and I couldn't hear anything that anyone said to me. The main comment that I got was "Cool house, man!" and "Oh my god, is this really your house?" As I looked around, I felt like I didn't recognise hardly anyone at all and yet here they all were, drinking and eating in my house. I felt like I was too socially awkward to

399

play the host that mingled, so I gave myself the job of working. I carried barrels of beer out of the garage to the bar, I cleaned up plastic cups off the floor and mopped up drinks that were spilled here, there and everywhere. Amy, my rock and soul, was pretty much doing the same as I was, although I felt like I had hardly seen her as the night carried on.

I was grateful that I had had the common sense to pre-warn my neighbours about the party. Although my closest neighbour's house was a fair bit away, the music was extremely loud and I feared it could have been heard all over the town, far and wide. It was official, I hated parties and this was literally my idea of hell. I hated how disrespectful people were to other people's property and hated how stupid people acted to show off and drink themselves out of control. I agreed to this party because I wanted to feel like a kid my age and fit in more, but all it did was confirm that I was more Phil's age in my head instead of a teenager. If only Phil was alive, I could have been fishing with him right now on some quiet lake, having a real conversation about something that mattered. All the conversations that happened at this party were about who was having sex with who and who was drinking and who was going to the beach after the party to drink more. My main form of entertainment was watching Amy shouting at people who were clearly underage and drinking. I remember seeing one crowd of boys all have their drinks snatched out of their hands and Amy marching them out of the house to move on to somewhere else whilst being shouted at by her.

After walking around aimlessly, not feeling welcome in my own home, I thought about how much I wished there was another entrance to my safe-room. Even though it was a room I associated with one of the worst parts of my life, the blackouts, I started to think it wasn't so bad, a room on my own locked away from everyone. I even started to appreciate blacking out; maybe I could black out and wake up when the party was over? Oh, how ironic this moment felt.

I thought about where I could stand and be out of the way, when I finally bumped into Amy.

'Nice party!' I shouted.

'I know! Why didn't we do this sooner?' said Amy, who pretended to throw up and then started to laugh.

'Fancy running off to the beach together? There's still a bit of sunlight left!'

'Are you being serious?'

'Absolutely! Let's get out of here. They can wreck the house, for all I care.'

Amy's face was filled with excitement and I grabbed her hand as I led her through the crowd of the party.

'Oi! You two! Where do you think you're going?' called Laura.

I turned around to look at Laura, who was running over to us.

'We're just popping to the shop,' lied Amy.

'Liars! Hey, don't go without meeting Joey. Please?' begged Laura.

Amy looked at me to see if I wanted to meet Joey and I smiled and agreed. We followed Laura through the crowd and towards the bar.

'Joey! You have to meet my best friends, Amy and Terry!' Laura screamed over the loud music and crowd.

As Joey turned around, I stopped walking. I felt sick. I was rooted to the spot and I could feel that Amy was the same. Laura gave us a look of confusion and walked towards us with her boyfriend.

'Joe …' I whispered.

It was Joe. Standing in my house. At this party. Dating Laura …

'Oh my god? You know each other?' screamed Laura.

'Terry! Man, I didn't know this was your house,' laughed Joe. 'Small world! I had no idea I was delivering beer for your party!'

His voice was different. He sounded like he was mocking Laura's voice and tone. I was speechless, I didn't know what to say. I felt like all my worst nightmares were coming to life.

'Terry! You look like you've seen a ghost. Oh my god! I'm so excited you know each other; we can double date!' said Laura, completely oblivious to the look of fear that clearly was on my face.

'That's an amazing idea, Laura!' agreed Joe. 'Hey, Terry, now I know it's you, can I show you some of the beer I dropped off? There's some special ones in there I think you'll love.'

'Sure … Amy, why don't you go with Laura?' I replied. I was speaking slowly; I had never felt so scared in my life.

I looked at Amy, who had gone white and looked just as scared as I did. She hesitated, but moved when Laura started to walk away with her. Laura was laughing and practically jumping up and down, ignoring the fact that Amy didn't take her eyes off Joe as they walked away.

I followed Joe past the bar and through the garage, and as he closed the door behind him, his grin quickly faded.

'Over there on the floor is a wire with cuffs on the end,' said Joe. 'Go and put them on.'

'What are you doing, Joe? Please, I'm begging you, I'll do whatever you want, but leave everyone out of this,' I pleaded.

'Shut up and put those handcuffs on,' he said in a gentle tone.

I walked over to the back of the garage, and behind a metal barrel was a strange electrical device with a wire coming out of it that had handcuffs attached to the end. I did as he asked, and once the handcuffs were on, he used a key to lock them before throwing the key across the room, far out of my reach.

'Listen and don't interrupt me,' said Joe, who looked more deranged than I had ever seen him before. 'If you don't do what I say, a lot of people are going to die. Do you understand?'

Something was terribly different today; this was more serious than any other interaction with Joe; it was planned out in great detail. He had delivered the beer to my house, planted some weird device with handcuffs and began a relationship with Laura just to get to me. I nodded my head and Joe began to pace the room.

'This room is filled with metal barrels,' said Joe. 'The one closest to the door is beer. The ones at the back of the room are filled with an explosive material that is highly reactive. The device linked to your handcuffs will cause the explosion to happen prematurely, if you move away from the device and pull the wire.'

'What the fuck are you doing, Joe?!' I shouted at the top of my voice. 'Why are you planning to kill innocent kids?!'

'If you listen to me, no one will die. All you have to do is not move,' he said calmly.

'What are you doing, Joe? Please don't do this,' I begged again, desperation in my voice.

'Stop talking. Like I said, if you move, everyone in this house dies. If you sit tight, I will make sure everyone is out of the house before the barrels explode.'

'Why would you do that? You know it won't kill me!'

'That's the point, Terry. This house will explode into pieces, falling onto you and crushing your body. Everyone will see you survive and realise what you are. They will see you like they see me. Inhumans. Freaks.'

'Joe, this is insane! Please, please, please, I am begging you. I will move away. I will disappear. I'll do anything.'

'You have no idea what insanity is yet. But you will soon. Like I said, don't move or people will die.'

'Joe … please!'

Joe left the room. The music was booming from the party. I couldn't hear anything but a hundred voices and music. I couldn't believe what he was doing. I needed to stop him somehow! How could I get out of this? How would he make sure the people would be out in time?

The music stopped playing and Joe's voice echoed through a microphone.

'Everyone, get out! There's a huge fire in the garage! Quick! There's a car in there! It's gonna explode!' Joe shouted in a convincingly terrified tone.

The music was replaced by people screaming and the sounds of hundreds of feet running. I could hear random people shouting "Get out!" and "Quick! There's a fire!"

I wanted to run with them. I was so scared to move. The wire from the strange device on the floor was tight with little give. If I made one move, the barrels would explode. I had never been so petrified in my life. I wasn't worried about me and I wasn't exactly worried about the aftermath. I was worried about someone being caught in the house. What if someone didn't make it out? Joe could kill hundreds of people who were innocent!

I sat there and sobbed, scared for what was about to come. The screaming continued and the room beyond my garage sounded like chaos. It felt like I had stood there for hours. Time had slowed down and I was motionless, too scared to even move an inch. Gradually, the screams and shouts faded, I could hear less people behind the door and more people in the distance somewhere.

What was going to happen next?

The electric device on the floor began to beep. At first, it was gradual, but then it began to speed up.

It was a strange thing to be at the centre of an explosion and live to tell the tale. The sound was deafening. The light was so bright I felt like it burned my eyes clean out of their sockets. The heat was like having pure fire poured onto my body. And then the house. It felt like heavy rocks were landing on top of my head, but it wasn't just one, it was one after one after one after one. In what felt like a flash, the noise, the brightness, the heat and the feeling of everything dropped onto me stopped. Chaos turned to silence and not a thing could be heard.

AMY

The explosion was the single scariest thing I had ever seen. I ran with hundreds of people away from Terry's house, not knowing what was going to happen. Everyone filed onto the main road, which felt like a safe distance away. As I turned around, the last few people were running away from the house. When it looked like no one else was leaving, that was when it happened. It was the loudest noise I had ever heard. The explosion was bigger than the house and pieces of rubble went flying into the air. People began to run away further from the house, but were stopped by Joe who was running towards the explosion.

'WAIT! TERRY HAYNES! HE'S INSIDE THE HOUSE STILL! EVERYONE! QUICK!'

Suddenly, a large group of people joined Joe and everyone else began to gather at the end of the drive, staring in horror. I could hear whispers, people crying and people quickly panicking that someone was in the explosion. The group that joined Joe ran towards the destroyed house, which lay in ruins and ablaze. Black smoke was billowing into the air and the heat from the explosion was extreme, even from this distance. The sound of sirens quickly echoed in the air and in no time a fire engine, a couple of ambulances and police cars came racing from both the town and from the tunnel under the mountain. I could hear someone explaining that someone was apparently in the house when the house exploded. The paramedics and firefighters ran towards the house.

None of this mattered. I couldn't move. I felt like I was truly in shock for the first time in my life. I felt frozen, unable to blink, unable to move and unable to think.

'OH MY GOD! IT'S TERRY! HE'S ALIVE! HELP ME MOVE THESE BRICKS!' screamed Joe.

The firefighters ordered the group from the party away from the rubble, including Joe, and they started to remove large concrete blocks from a mound where the garage used to be. As they removed the rubble, I could see Terry emerge unscathed; the firefighters quickly picked him up and commanded the ambulance drivers to get the stretcher ready.

People were frantically talking around me and the whispers spread through the crowd about Terry surviving the explosion. Joe ran from the scene ahead and back to the crowd.

'Everyone!' he called. 'Terry Haynes was inside the house when it exploded! He's alive and he's not hurt! It's a miracle! How has he survived?'

The crowd suddenly became wild with talk and amazement. At this exact moment, I felt like I had breathed for the first time and realised the severity of the situation. I pushed past Joe and ran towards Terry.

'I don't need to go to hospital!' shouted Terry. 'Please leave me, I am fine!'

'Sir, you need to calm down!' said one of the paramedics. 'You have been involved in a serious incident.'

'I am fine! Let me go!'

'Sir, you don't know that! You took a serious blow to the head. You've had a house fall on top of you! Please just come with us!' pleaded the second paramedic.

As I ran towards Terry, a police officer tried to stop me.

'That's my boyfriend!' I screamed.

The officer looked unsure, but let me through. I grabbed Terry in a hug and leaned on him, crying my heart out.

'Miss, you need to step back,' said the first paramedic.

'She's my partner! Leave her alone!' barked Terry.

'Terry, we should go to hospital. People will talk more,' I whispered into his ear and he seemed to understand.

'Can we just get this done with?' Terry conceded.

They carried Terry on a stretcher into the back of the ambulance and I took a seat next to him. The firefighters were working hard to put out the fire and the police were talking to various people in the crowd who stood and watched the disaster. I felt like I couldn't think straight, like what had just happened wasn't real. I couldn't look at Terry and we didn't talk during the trip to the hospital.

*

The nurses in A&E did some quick tests on Terry, but were absolutely stunned to see he was in perfect health. After a few hours of tests, they checked his temperature, his blood pressure and did cranial nerve checks with a torchlight and a stethoscope. They couldn't quite believe that Terry had been inside a house that had just exploded and crashed down on him, but his vitals all checked out. They placed me and Terry in a small private room whilst they organised an emergency X-ray and further tests. I had still not said a word to Terry, instead sitting there in silence, thinking about what had happened.

'Amy.'

I didn't look at him.

'Talk to me. Please,' he begged.

'What do you want me to say?'

'Anything. Please. What's wrong?'

'What's wrong?!' I shouted. 'That sick bastard could have killed everyone! What does he want, Terry?'

'I don't know … I really don't know. I think he wants everyone to hate me. I think he wants to expose me.'

'Well, he's done a good job, hasn't he? I saw it on national news when we were walking into the hospital. You are literally the main headline! Local boy survives house explosion.'

There was a small TV in the room and I switched it on and changed it to the news channel. Lo and behold, a reporter was standing outside Terry's house.

'Less than an hour ago, a house party celebrating the end of college was ruined by an explosion not seen before in this quiet town. Terry Haynes, a local eighteen-year-old boy, was involved in an explosion in his own home. We have reports that Terry is, by some miracle, completely unharmed. We have an eyewitness, can you tell me what happened?'

Joe appeared on the TV as the camera turned to him.

'Yes! Terry Haynes was hosting a party. A fire broke out and suddenly everyone was running outside and screaming. I think Terry was trying to make sure people were out the house and safe, but it was too late … but he survived! He was actually right next to the explosion! And the whole house fell on top of him! It's a miracle. He's actually come out without a single cut!' reported Joe in a very upbeat tone.

'Thank you, sir, and I believe you have provided us with a picture of the victim and his girlfriend?'

On the screen flashed a picture of me and Terry standing on the pier together. I felt sick - this was a picture from my bedside table. It was the only copy.

'Terry, how does he have the picture from my bedside table?' I said in a furious tone.

I looked over at Terry. If I thought I was angry, nothing compared to how angry Terry looked right now. His fists were clenched, he was red in the face and he looked like he was about to kill someone.

'I'm going after him. Now!' shouted Terry, who stood up to leave the room.

'You are not going anywhere until you tell me what's going on!'

I tried to stop him, but he grabbed my hand to push me away.

'Amy, I have to kill him! He nearly killed everyone at our party. He's done stuff you don't even know about!' Terry seethed.

'More secrets? Terry, you are not leaving this place!'

'Amy, he was the one who attacked your nan! He did that to get at me and get your attention. He tried to attack your brother! Nearly killed him by throwing him off a cliff! This guy is dangerous and he needs to be stopped!'

I felt like I was going to faint. I felt weak at the knees and began to tremble.

'What do you mean? Terry ... what do you mean, he attacked my nan? What did he do to Tim?'

'It doesn't matter right now. I just need to stop him now!'

'What else haven't you been telling me, Terry? I thought we didn't keep secrets from each other anymore!'

'And how was I supposed to tell you that a scary guy attacked your nan? How was I supposed to tell you he threw your brother off a cliff? Please tell me in what way I could have told you without ruining your life with worry?'

'No, just ruin my life by putting my family in danger and getting blown up in front of me!'

As Terry began to leave the room again, I began to sob.

'I don't think I can handle this anymore,' I said. 'I thought I could ...'

'I'm going to sort this now.'

'By killing him? You'll be just as bad as he is then. You'll be a murderer.'

'What's the alternative? Let him kill someone? I will be saving lives by ending his.'

I continued to sob uncontrollably in the hospital chair. Terry took another look at me, sighed and walked out of the door, escaping the hospital and leaving me behind.

TERRY

I walked for miles and miles and hours and hours towards Byanbythe. I kept trying to hitch a ride from every car that drove past me, but no one took any notice. I had no phone and I was walking around with a pair of plain joggers and a t-shirt that the hospital had loaned me (as I refused to wear a hospital gown). I had no idea where I was going, but thankfully managed to steal a hoodie off someone who wasn't paying attention from the back of their chair at a restaurant. At the very least, I was now a little bit warmer than walking around in a t-shirt. I was deep in a city I didn't know, but I didn't care, as

I only had one thing on my mind and it was to kill Joe.

I began to get desperate, and in the distance, I could see a motorbike ticking over whilst its owner was talking to a friend on the street side.

I walked over, and without thinking about my actions, I punched the owner of the motorbike and stole it without a moment's hesitation. Within moments, I was riding off into the distance, looking for any signs that said Byanbythe.

I drove for some time, until I started to recognise signs of cities and towns that I knew, eventually on the long road to Mt. Cudd and Byanbythe.

It was the early hours of the morning now and the dark sky began to show signs of dawn. As I drove through the tunnel under the mountain, I formulated a plan in my head. I would go straight to Joe's hut; he was either going to be there or potentially come back there. Would he run away again? I didn't have the answers, but I had to try something.

As I finally exited the tunnel and reached the top of Byanbythe, the first left would have been my house. As I rode past, I could see that the police were still there and the long driveway that was my private street was closed off with police barrier tape. I didn't have time to think about my home. I was on a mission. Judging by the sky, it had to be the early hours of the morning, maybe four or five o'clock; that would mean it had been around five hours since the explosion. That was plenty of time for Joe to run away or disappear. I felt apprehensive and drove as fast as I could to his hut.

My heart leapt when I saw his bike outside of his hut. I skidded to a halt and jumped off the bike. I kicked down the front door and burst inside the hut. He was there. He was lying on the floor, crying, but this time without any bottles of alcohol around him.

'You piece of fucking shit!' I screamed, and kicked his face as hard as I could.

He didn't react, he didn't even try to stop me. He let me kick him in the face and continued to lie on the floor.

'No one even cared,' he mumbled.

I kicked him again.

'No one even questioned how you survived,' he sobbed.

I stamped on him with all my weight. I wanted to kick him into the ground. I wanted to break every single bone in his body.

'Not a single person thought it was strange. No one thought you were a freak,' Joe continued, almost in a trance.

I picked him up off the ground and threw him through the hut window, smashing the glass and the wooden frame. He crashed to the ground outside and barely lifted himself up. It wasn't enough; I didn't care if he wasn't fighting back. I jumped out of the window and quickly picked him up off the ground, throwing him against a tree with a loud thud. I punched as hard as I could, over and over again. With all my might, I continued to punch his impenetrable skin, until it started to feel weaker. I kneed him in the stomach and punched his face until, by some miracle, I drew blood from him. Blood was pouring from his mouth. Did we have limits? Were we not as invincible as I thought? I didn't care. I kept punching him and more blood came out of him. Joe started to raise his arms to stop me, but I threw him with all my force to the ground. I picked him up again and threw him so hard he landed a good distance away and into the road.

'YOU PIECE OF SHIT! YOU DESERVE TO FUCKING DIE!' I screamed.

I ran over to his body that lay in the middle of the road and climbed on top of him. I began to punch his face again, punching it so hard that I wanted it to merge into the ground. Every punch felt like it was taking a little bit more of his life away. He was bleeding a lot now and it felt fantastic. His face was full of panic, he looked like he was scared of me, he looked like he was dying. At last, I was going to kill his monster.

'TERRY!'

I quickly looked to my left and Amy was running towards me with tears running down her face. Behind her was a car and two people that I did not recognise.

'Get off him!' she screamed.

'Amy, he has to die!"

'Terry, you have to stop!' she cried.

I began to punch Joe again, whose blood now spilled onto the road. Amy screamed, but before I could punch him again, one of the strangers that had travelled with Amy picked me up and carried me away from Joe.

'Get off me!' I screamed.

Whoever this guy was, he was extremely strong ... stronger than I had imagined. When you were as strong as I was, it was shocking to ever think someone else was strong.

'Please, you need to calm down,' said the man.

He had a deep voice with a foreign accent and was dressed in a smart suit. He carried me further away from Joe, who was being tended to by the other stranger, who was a small, dark-haired lady.

'GET. OFF. ME!' I screamed.

The man pinned me against the wall of Joe's hut with such force that I felt like it knocked the wind out of me.

'Listen to me! You need to calm down,' said the man.

I felt breathless. I stared at the man with great fear. He was bald and dark-skinned with a large beard. He was extremely tall, possibly over six and a half feet.

'He's going to be okay,' called the lady who was kneeling over Joe; she, too, had a foreign accent.

Amy came running towards me, but the man still had me in a firm grip against the wall of the hut.

'If I let you go, will you be calm?' asked the man.

I slowly nodded and the man gently put me down.

'Can we use this hut, Terry? We have to talk to you,' he said.

I looked at Amy, who nodded at me with a look of approval; I, too, nodded and the man beckoned me to walk through the door.

'Bring the other one in with you,' called the man to the woman.

The woman was so small I expected her to drag Joe, struggling to lift his weight, but to my surprise, she picked him up with great ease.

I felt like I was still in shock. So many questions were running through my head, too many to think straight. As we entered the hut, the man gathered a few wooden crates from the corner and placed them on the ground as seats.

'Sit. Please,' he commanded.

I did as I was told and sat down on the small crate. Amy sat down too. The lady had now entered the hut and gently placed the blood-ridden Joe on the ground. Joe was conscious, but looked like he could have passed out at any moment. When the lady was satisfied that Joe was safe, she turned to the man and nodded. The man sat down on the final crate, looked at me and gave a large smile.

'I never wanted to see you again, but I cannot deny ... I am so happy to see you, Terry,' he said. 'You have grown into such a beautiful man.'

'Who are you?' I whispered.

'My name is Casper and my partner here is Milkaia. We have known you all of your life.'

The questions in my mind only got more extreme. I had never felt more confused in my life. I had never seen this man or woman in my life.

'Terry … say something,' begged Amy.

'I don't know either of you. Where have you come from?' I asked.

'When we saw the news of the explosion of your house, we had to come immediately,' replied Casper. 'When we arrived at the hospital, you had already left. Thankfully, we met your beautiful partner.'

'They said you were in danger, Terry,' said Amy. 'I had to bring them to you. I knew you would be here.'

'Danger?' I repeated. 'What do you mean?'

Casper gave Milkaia a look of concern.

'What I have to tell you is a lot,' said Casper. 'It will overload your mind and almost be incomprehensible at first, but you must listen. We do not have much time and we need to move fast.'

I remained silent.

'You obviously know already that you are not a normal man? I must ask, for my own curiosity, what do you remember? What do you know?'

'What do you mean? About what?' I replied.

'The fact you survived an exploding house? The fact that nothing can hurt you? Surely you have realised that you are stronger than the average man?'

Again, I stayed silent and realised that all the questions of my mysterious life could be about to be answered.

'This is a long story and I cannot tell you everything today, but you must trust me. Milkaia and I have loved you dearly like you were our own family. We have dedicated our life to protecting you.'

'How can that be?' I replied. 'I've never met you.'

'We have always been there in the background. We kept you away from the world as a boy and, when you were a man, gave you everything you could need for a comfortable life and a fresh beginning.'

'You're my kidnappers?' I said and stood up and backed away in shock.

'Sit down, Terry,' begged Milkaia, who walked towards me and tried to grab my arm. I snatched my arm away from her and quickly grabbed Amy by the arm to back away too.

'Terry, please ...' said Casper.

'Fuck you! You kept me in a prison as a kid!' I screamed.

'Please listen -'

'Get away from me!'

'Terry, we had no choice! We had to keep you safe! SIT DOWN AND LISTEN!'

I stared at him, but I refused to sit down. After a good few minutes staring at my two kidnappers, Milkaia began to talk.

'You were in grave danger,' she said. 'Had we not hidden you, you would have been killed.'

'Why?'

'You were just a child and your parents were killed,' said Casper.

'In a car crash?'

'No, they were murdered. The car crash was faked to hide you in Byanbythe. We had planned for you to be hidden here, adopted, and to live a normal life'

'Whoa, whoa, whoa!' I screamed. 'What do you mean? You are not making sense!'

'Let me start from the start. Please, Terry, I am begging you. You will not understand unless I start from the start.'

'Someone start fucking talking, then!'

Casper cleared his voice and stood up. He looked nervous and began to pace the room, looking like he was thinking hard of where to start.

'You belong to a great race of people, Terry, thousands of years old, from the early days of time. Our people are not like any other. We do not have limitations nor any weaknesses. We are as close to a god as you could ever imagine. Your father was one of the first men of our kind. He was a founder and a ruler. Your father was the king and the greatest ruler you could ask for. He led our people to a life of safety. He kept peace in the world. He kept balance. He ruled for thousands of years ... until he was murdered in cold blood. Jealousy and greed ... They murdered your parents to overthrow the throne. We had to get you to safety. We needed to put you somewhere safe, out of sight, somewhere where they couldn't find you. If they killed you, the throne was available to take ... but alive, they couldn't take over. Me and Milkaia did the only thing we could; we hid you, created a life for you that should have been so normal that no one would have found you here ...'

'Are you joking? Normal? What part of my life was normal? You kept me in a jail!'

'Not by choice! You ran away. We staged the accident. Fake parents. Fake accident. You were going to be fostered, adopted and then have a normal life. You ran away, so we needed to keep you hidden until you were old enough to be safe on your own. We did everything we could.'

'You're lying! This is bullshit. If any of this was true, I would remember my parents! I would remember life before the crash.'

Milkaia looked at me and began to cry.

'My dear, sweet boy … I cannot apologise enough,' she sobbed.

'What do you mean?'

'I … I had to take your memories away. I wanted to give you the most normal life possible. You needed to forget everything. Please … forgive me, Terry,' she begged.

I stared at her and then at Casper. I honestly couldn't piece together a single thing they had said. My mind felt like it was going to explode.

'Who are you people? Fake car crashes? Kidnapping? Fake office buildings to hide a prison? Millions of spare cash? How the hell can I trust a word you are saying?!'

Casper became enraged.

'Because without us, you wouldn't be alive today! You would be dead!'

'How can I trust that's even true?' I shouted back.

'Because you have no other choice!' Casper spat back. 'You are hours away from the gravest danger you could imagine!'

'Please don't argue, both of you,' Milkaia begged. 'Terry, please, we love you …'

There was a long, deafening silence that preceded Milkaia's plea. I stared at Casper, who stared back at me, just as furious.

'Why is Terry in danger?' said Amy, suddenly speaking for the first time.

I looked at Amy and she stood there, white as a ghost, staring at Casper.

'Terry was hidden,' said Casper. 'He was safe here. He had a normal life here … until he was on national news. Local boy survives an exploding house? A boy who is the spitting image of the dead king? It was more than enough for the ones who murdered the king and queen to find him. If they aren't in Byanbythe already, they will be on their way.'

'But why?' said Amy.

'Dear girl, have you not listened? They want to take over the throne! As long as Terry is alive, they cannot do this. They have to kill Terry and Livia before they can take the crown.'

'Who's Livia?' I asked.

Casper and Milkaia both gave each other another look.

'Livia … she is your wife-to-be,' said Milkaia.

'Wife-to-be?' I repeated. 'No! No! I can't handle this! This is too much! What do you mean, *wife-to-be*?'

'It is … a custom to be part of an arranged marriage in our culture. You and Livia have been betrothed to each other long before you were born.'

I grabbed my head and began pacing the room.

'This is fucked up!' I shouted. 'This is really, really fucked up. This can't be real.'

'Terry, please, there is no time. We have to act fast! You must listen to me!' shouted Casper.

'What do you want? You cannot possibly fuck me up any more than you have already. What have I learned today? My house has exploded, I was kidnapped because my mom and dad were a king and queen. They were murdered and as a result, they want to kill me? Anything else? Oh yes, I have an arranged marriage!' I shouted, but stopped when I looked over at Amy.

Tears streamed down her face as she stared into nothing, completely engrossed in what she had just heard. I walked towards her and tried to hold her, but she pushed me away.

'Amy, this means nothing. I didn't even know she existed. You are still the love of my life.'

'How ... how old are you, Terry?' she asked.

I looked at her, confused. What did she mean?

'I'm eighteen ... why are you asking that?'

'But how old are you really?'

'Sweet girl, he really is eighteen,' said Milkaia. 'He is not hundreds of years old, if that is what you fear?'

'Is he one of the people who are trying to kill Terry?' asked Amy, who pointed at Joe lying on the floor.

Casper looked at Joe and quickly picked him up off the ground and stood him up.

'Who are you, boy?' he said.

Joe did not reply.

'You don't know who he is?' I asked.

'No, but he is definitely one of our kind ... aren't you, boy?'

Joe stared at Casper with tears in his eyes.

'I ... don't know.'

'Of course you are, boy!' said Casper.

'He's dangerous. He has been trying to kill me since I moved here. He is the one who destroyed my house!' I barked.

Casper's eyes widened and he quickly grabbed Joe by the neck and slammed him into the wall.

'Are you working for Rainforth? Are you one of those murderous traitors?' growled Casper.

'N-n-no …' croaked Joe, barely able to breath.

'Who are you, then?!'

'I … don't … know.'

Casper let go of Joe, who dropped to the ground.

'Start talking, boy! If I think you are lying, I will kill you.'

'I don't know. I really don't know,' cried Joe, who began to sob as he lay on the floor.

'Where do you come from?' asked Milkaia.

'I don't know … I have always lived here. I don't … I don't know who I am, honestly. I was left here as a baby.'

Casper turned to look at Milkaia again, almost like he was starting to realise something he had not known before.

'How old are you?' asked Casper.

'One hundred and five,' replied Joe, still crying.

Casper did not stop staring at Milkaia, almost as if they were having their own private conversation telepathically. After a few minutes, Milkaia began to cry, but Casper ignored her and picked up Joe from the floor.

'Do you want to know your past? Do you want to know who you are?' asked Casper.

Joe began to furiously cry and he dropped to his knees and looked up at Casper.

'That's all I've ever wanted. Please ...' he begged.

I had never seen Joe look so ... pathetic. He was on the floor, begging a man he had just met.

'Do as I say and in time I will tell you,' said Casper. 'You must follow my every order. Do you understand?'

'Yes! Anything, please,' cried Joe.

Casper turned away from Joe and walked towards me.

'Terry, we have no more time. The man who murdered your father is called Rainforth. He will not be alone. He has a small army of separatists who believe in his cause and want Rainforth to be king. You have to get out of here. Now!'

'I'm not going anywhere,' I said.

'Terry! Please. We have no time for this.'

'You haven't even told me who you both are. Why do you care so much?'

'We are lifelong servants to the king and queen,' explained Milkaia. 'We have dedicated our lives to your parents and to you. When they died, it became our one and only purpose to serve you and protect you.'

I was shocked by the reaction of Milkaia. There was so much I wanted to know, but felt like I had little time.

'And where will I go?' I asked.

'You will go to Scotland and find Livia. You must watch over her, but you must not speak to her. As far as we know, she is living a life as you were; she knows nothing. It must stay that way! All you need to do is watch over her and make sure she is safe.'

'Scotland? Are you mad? I am not going to Scotland!'

'You need to be as far away from here as possible. We also need to make sure Livia is safe. They may have found her. We just don't know!'

'She's not my wife. She has nothing to do with me!'

'That does not matter!' snapped Casper. 'Even if she has nothing to do with you, she is still someone in danger. Does that mean nothing to you?'

I paused. I didn't know how to answer without sounding bad.

'What about Amy?' I asked.

'It is too dangerous for her to be with you. You need to be as far away as possible. Please trust me, boy. Rainforth is extremely strong and extremely dangerous.'

'I won't leave Amy unprotected.'

'We will protect her with our lives! We live to protect and serve you, Terry.'

I looked at him and then I looked at Amy. Amy continued to cry, but stared at the floor as if she wasn't listening anymore.

'I need to talk to Amy alone,' I said.

'There really isn't time -'

'If I can't talk to her, then I'm not leaving her.'

Casper sighed a huge breath of frustration and looked at Milkaia again before agreeing. I grabbed Amy's hand and walked with her outside. I had no time to think and I had no time to take anything in. All I cared about right now was her.

'Amy …'

She still wouldn't look at me.

'That was … a lot,' she said.

'Yeah … I know.'

'You're … not human.'

'He didn't say that -'

'You have a wife.'

'She's not my wife. I don't know her.'

'You're a prince.'

'I'm not -'

'And someone is on their way to kill you. And it's not Joe.'

'Yes, but -'

I tried to grab her hand, but she again snatched it away from me.

'Terry, this is too much,' she said. 'I cannot do this. I thought I could, I wanted to … I have tried so hard, but I can't. It's too much!'

'Amy, I know, I know … I promise I am going to sort this.'

'How? I don't even know who you are! And back then, you were going to kill Joe. I didn't think that was you. I was so scared.'

'Amy, I … I didn't know what to do. I wanted to protect you. I needed to make sure you were safe.'

'It's over, Terry. I can't do this. I don't need this in my life. This is all too much. It's dangerous and I'm scared.'

She was sobbing as she spoke and still couldn't look me in my eyes.

'No one's going to hurt you. I'll lay low for a while, I'll go to Scotland. I'll watch over this woman … then, when it's safe, I'll come back to you. I promise.'

'I don't want you to come back to me! It's over, Terry! Aren't you listening to me?' she shouted, her voice suddenly full of anger. 'Your life is completely different to mine! We shouldn't be together!'

'Amy ... please ... don't say that. Don't do this.'

'Terry, it's over. Just ... just go.'

'Amy -'

'JUST GO!'

I tried to hold her, but she shoved me away. As she cried, I cried. I couldn't take this all in. I was losing everything that mattered to me.

'I ... I love you, Amy.'

'It's not enough, Terry. Please ... just go. If you loved me ... you would walk away now.'

AMY

I stood as far away from Terry as possible. Casper and Milkaia quickly made arrangements with Terry, but whenever I looked at him, he didn't seem to be listening. The plan they laid out seemed quite simple; they gave Terry the address of where this Livia lived and asked him to monitor her from afar, explicitly no contact or interaction. Casper and Milkaia would stay in Byanbythe and protect me from afar, although I soon planned to tell them to pack their bags and leave me alone.

What was Terry? An alien? A creature? A prince? These things didn't happen in real life. These were the writings of bad fiction, sci-fi stories and the silver screen. This did not happen to real people.

But then again … what was normal about Terry's life? A car crash where he ran away? Being kidnapped for ten years? Blacking out? Super strong? Invincible? If all of that was true … how could I call anything else far-fetched? I felt like I no longer knew what was real in life, but I did know one thing - I had no intention of getting involved. I wanted Terry gone and Joe and these two new strangers. It was too extreme for me, a girl from a small Welsh town.

'Take your motorbike, Terry,' instructed Casper.

Terry looked at the bike and slowly responded.

'It's … stolen.'

'We haven't got time,' said Casper. 'Take the A roads, avoid the motorways. Avoid stopping unless you need petrol. It will take you around seven hours to get to Livia's house.'

Terry nodded, no longer arguing back or asking questions. He looked like a broken man. Part of me wanted to grab and run away with him … but the other part knew better. I didn't belong in his life and we clearly weren't meant to be. Maybe Terry would meet his arranged wife and fall in love? If she was like him, then they were a lot better suited together.

Casper turned to Joe and said, 'You, what was your name? Joe? Go with him. It's unsafe to go alone.'

Terry's face finally came back to life.

'What? No, no, no!' he shouted. 'Absolutely no way! I'm not going near him!'

'Terry, please, stop arguing,' said Casper. 'Rainforth and his men are dangerous. If they are in Scotland, you can't be there alone. Joe is one of us, whether you like him or not.'

'No! I refuse!'

'Please, stop arguing! Whatever has happened between you and Joe, this is a lot bigger. You are in danger!'

'Yesterday, I was in danger - because of him!'

Casper rolled his eyes, sighed and turned to Joe.

'Boy, if you want to learn about your past, you're going to do as I say! Aren't you?'

Joe looked very sheepish as he stared at the ground.

'Yes …'

'I can't hear you! Are you going to do as I say?'

'Yes,' said Joe, a little louder than before.

'And are you going to cause any more trouble for Terry? Will you travel to Scotland and fight *alongside* him if anything should happen?'

'Y-yes.'

'Good, because if you want to know *anything* from me, you protect him with your life!' shouted Casper, who pointed at Terry.

'Casper,' Terry began, 'I am not -'

'Terry, I am not asking! You will both go to Scotland. You do not need to speak. You do not need to be best friends. Go! Now!'

Terry looked like he wanted to argue, but the way Casper spoke, only a fool would say something back.

'Joe, do you have a car?' asked Casper.

'I … have a bike,' replied Joe.

'Good. Get on it and follow Terry. Remember - guard him with your life!'

Joe quickly walked away and jumped on his bike. Terry hovered and looked from Casper to Milkaia and finally to me.

'I have so many questions,' he said. 'None of this makes sense.'

'Dear boy, I know,' said Milkaia, who grabbed Terry's arms in a loving way. 'I don't expect you to understand yet. I promise, when this is over, we will never leave your side. We will explain everything, I promise.'

Terry hesitated, but turned his attention to me one last time.

'Amy, I don't want to end things like this.'

'I need space … I need to get my head around things.'

'I know you don't love me anymore. I know this is too much for anyone to bear, but I can't just leave you like this.'

'Terry … I … Just go … please.'

'Can we speak again when this is over?' he begged. 'Just one more talk and then you never need to see me again.'

'I don't know … Just give me some space. Please.'

Terry looked like he wanted to say more and tears began to run down his face. After staring at me for a few more moments, he finally climbed on top of his bike and looked at Casper. He gave Terry a small bag of items.

'This is a satnav. It won't attach to your bike, but you put headphones into it and it will guide you. This is also a mobile phone with my number saved into it. It's secure, so please call me and provide regular updates. Last but not least, there is a folder with information about Livia and photos from a few years ago.'

'Okay,' said Terry. 'Just promise me you will guard Amy with your lives. If you care about me, then you will prioritise her safety over mine. Do you understand? Amy is your primary care now.'

'With our last breaths, she will be safe,' said Milkaia.

Terry took one final look at us all and ignited his motorbike. He drove off into the distance and Joe followed on his bike.

I waited until the sound of the motorbikes were all but a distant noise before I finally turned to Casper and Milkaia.

'He's gone now, so you can go,' I said.

They both looked at each other with confusion.

'I'm sorry, dear, I don't quite understand what you mean,' replied Milkaia.

'I don't need looking after. I don't particularly want two strangers following me around. I'd rather you just go. Like you said, these people aren't after me; they want Terry.'

'We have promised Terry that we will guard you with our lives and that is what we will do,' said Casper.

'You won't even notice us, dear,' said Milkaia.

'I just want to be left alone!' I shouted.

'Let us take you home. We'll find somewhere to stay and give you our phone number. How does that sound? We'll protect you from afar.'

It sounded like a shit idea, but I was pretty sure that no matter what I said, they were going to watch me from afar anyway. I was worried that they were going to rent a house in my street or somewhere close by. I didn't want them near me.

'I know somewhere you can stay,' I said. 'It was a friend of Terry's.'

'Okay,' said Casper. 'Is it close to you?'

'Yes, very close,' I lied. 'I'll take you there now.'

I sat in the passenger seat of their car and directed them to where Phil's cabin was and then guided them back to my house.

'This isn't very close, Amy,' commented Casper.

'It's close enough, okay?'

'I don't feel comfortable protecting you that far away.'

'Please,' I begged. 'I'll have your number anyway. I just need some space.'

Casper agreed, although something told me that he was never going to be far from my house. As his car parked outside of my house, he wrote his number in my phone and insisted that I wrote mine in his.

'We'll be in contact,' he said. 'You must ring us if you think something is suspicious, Amy. Do you understand?'

I agreed and left the car, watching them drive away until they turned the corner out of my street. I gave a huge sigh of relief and started to walk towards my front door.

'She's here! Michael! She's here!' shouted my mom.

'WHERE HAVE YOU BEEN?! WE'VE BEEN WORRIED SICK!' screamed my dad.

And then all my worries and fears about Terry and his strange new world disappeared. I suddenly remembered that since the explosion and going to hospital, I had not spoken to my parents once.

*

There was a lot of shouting and very little chance for me to explain. Eventually, once my dad had stopped turning red, I explained that I was rushed to hospital with Terry and that my phone had died (which was true). I then had to bend the truth, but as far as I was concerned, I wasn't lying too much. I explained how upset and restless Terry was and that he discharged himself from hospital and ran away. As I had no way to get back and no phone, I had to rely on some kind strangers to take me home .... so I wasn't exactly lying too much.

I felt bad for my mom and dad. They had been up all night worrying about me and Terry. They were woken in the early hours of the morning by the explosion, and in fairness, I wasn't surprised that the whole town heard the bang. After I had left in the ambulance, hundreds of parents gathered to see what the commotion was and, of course, to make sure their kids weren't involved. After apologising over and over again, my mom and dad's concern turned to Terry.

'Where did he go? He can't just discharge himself!' shouted Dad.

'I don't know. He hasn't got a phone and he didn't come here. I've checked Phil's cabin already.'

'Michael, you have to find him,' my mom begged.

'How? We have no idea where he is,' I insisted.

'I don't know,' said Dad. 'I'll start at the hospital and go from there.'

My dad grabbed his coat and quickly left in his car; I couldn't stop him. How would I stop him? "Oh, sorry, Dad, Terry's actually driving to Scotland to make sure his wife that he didn't know about is okay"? This was the exact reason that I couldn't stay with Terry anymore. I was sick of the drama. I was sick of lying to people.

My mom checked me from head to toe to ensure I was okay before ordering me to bed to get some rest. I sat and worried about my dad, who was now going to waste the day searching for Terry, who he wasn't going to find.

*

The next few days were rough. My mom and dad were extremely worried about Terry. Dad spent every day searching for him in every city, town and village this side of Wales. The atmosphere was just awful in our house and I was worried that it would be this way forever, especially knowing that Terry would never come back.

Every day, I received a text from Casper checking that I was okay. I replied, and although I was annoyed at first, I did start to feel a little settled knowing that two extremely strong people were around the corner looking out for me. Having the days at home had given me time to reflect on everything that I had learned, and the more I thought about it, the more questions I had. It was so much to take in, and although I knew I was doing the right thing by separating from Terry, I realised how hard I had been on him. I mean, anyone would have reacted the way I did! To learn all of that stuff after witnessing a house explode? I was almost impressed by how my head had not exploded already.

Terry's house explosion was all around town and still on local TV (national news had got bored with the story). It was thankfully confirmed that not a single person was involved in the explosion; apart from shock and trauma, everyone got out okay. Many rumours were flying around about what caused the explosion, but each one was more outlandish than the truth. Thankfully, the questions about *how* the explosion happened far outweighed the fact that Terry had survived without a scratch and not many people were speaking about that part.

Laura constantly texted me, wanting answers and to check how Terry was. I decided that I was only going to text her once and that was to tell her that I was okay, but wanted some space to rest. Seventeen texts later, she seemed to have got the point.

My curiosity had gotten the better of me, and once I had had time to digest everything that I had learned about Terry and his past, I had pressing questions that I wanted answered. I decided to walk down to Phil's cabin one day and pay a visit to Casper and Milkaia.

When I arrived, both Casper and Milkaia were sitting outside of Phil's cabin in silence; when they saw me walking towards them, they both stood up.

'Amy, is everything okay?' said Milkaia.

'Yes, everything's fine. I was hoping I could talk to you both?'

Casper nodded and Milkaia gave a warm smile. I had to admit, I really liked Milkaia. From the little I knew about her, she seemed very gentle and mother-like; she was also very beautiful. She had dark hair and dark eyes and beautifully-tanned skin. Her accent suggested she was possibly Italian, but she spoke perfect English. Casper was very similar in looks, skin tone and accent, but a lot taller and broader than Milkaia; I started to think they were brother and sister.

'How may we help?' said Casper.

'I, erm, just wanted to apologise for the other day. I was quite rude to you both.'

'Dear girl, what you heard from us would scare the strongest of people. You are brave and clearly care for Terry,' replied Casper. I ignored the comment about Terry.

'I was hoping you could tell me a little more about … your … kind?' I asked.

'Well … you have to understand, no one outside of our people knows about us. This is very strange for me to be telling a human, but clearly, the prince trusts you … I am sure we can trust you too?'

'Of course. Although, even if I told people, who would believe me?'

Casper laughed and agreed with me.

'Very well … what would you like to know?'

'Wow … so many questions … I guess what you are would be a good start?'

'Ah, I'm afraid the answer will disappoint you … only three people know the answer to that question and they are the three original founders of our kind.'

'The king and queen?' I asked.

'The king, yes, but not the queen. You see, King Trajan was a Roman warrior back in 100BC. His two best friends and right-hand men were the other founders, Atticus and Cassius.'

'How do you not know what you are?'

'Our lives are full of secrecy. Our trust in the king has helped us survive for thousands of years, generation after generation of family.'

'Wow ... so you can ... have kids? How many of you are there?'

'Well, it's a little complicated having kids ... but yes, we can. King Trajan has had *many* rules for our kind. There are only around ten thousand immortals living at one time. Every family is three generations only. If the last generation wants children, the oldest generation must die ... and so and so forth.'

'And how old are you two?'

'Wow, so many questions from such a young lady. Milkaia and I are twins, both born eight hundred years ago. We were both orphans of a war ... our parents were killed, so the king took us in as his own and raised us as his loyal protectors.'

'He sounds like a good king.'

'He was.'

Casper was sad when he mentioned the king and Milkaia put her arm around him to comfort him.

'Why was he killed? Why are they after Terry?' I asked, not wanting to pause for breath.

Casper sighed a deep breath and looked away from me.

451

'People don't change, Amy. The king received criticism of his rule since the dawn of our people. Many people think that our place in the world isn't alongside humans. They believe we should rule above them. The same people that killed the king and queen want to rule our people to carry this out. They wish to rise up and rule the world like great tyrants.'

'That's awful!' I shouted.

'Indeed. The only thing that stops them taking over is Terry's right to the crown. If Terry is dead, the crown is theirs for the taking.'

'Did you really believe that Terry would never be found?' I asked.

'Yes, we did. In fact, if it wasn't for the national TV news, he would have stayed hidden here and he would be safe!'

'Who are these people, though? Did you say his name was Rainbow or something?'

'Rainforth. He is a very, very nasty man. He was once the general of the king's personal army, but even the king saw him to be too extreme. Rainforth is like a poison to the mind, like a cult leader. He has always been vocal about ruling humans like slaves,' said Casper through gritted teeth, and as he finished speaking, he spat on the ground with utter disgust.

'But … after all this time? Ten years?'

'Time is nothing when you live forever,' said Milkaia.

I paused for a moment, taking in all the new information I had. Once I felt like I had digested this information, I wanted more.

'So ... what can you do? Do you have powers or something?'

Both Casper and Milkaia began to laugh.

'No, we are not superheroes,' said Milkaia.

'But you are super strong? You don't get old? You can't get hurt?'

'All because of the same reason. What we are is a result of what we are. We don't all have super strength. Because we cannot die and we have no weaknesses, we can get stronger and stronger without the limitations of a normal man.'

I felt like the only other question I had was the most curious one of all.

'Okay ... my last question, I promise.'

Casper chuckled and looked amused at all of my questions.

'Please, go ahead.'

'Can anyone ... become one of you?'

'I was waiting for this question,' he admitted. 'Milkaia, why don't you answer this one?'

Milkaia's face turned serious and she looked at me with great intensity.

'It is the greatest secret of our kind. Only one man can make someone immortal or change an immortal to a mortal again.'

'Who?' I asked.

'Atticus, one of the original founders,' she confirmed.

'Why only him?'

'Again, no one knows, just like our origins. Whatever happened during the first days of the three men's immortality, Attitcus was the one with the knowledge to change people. The king wanted Atticus to be the only one with this knowledge to ensure that the population control was in place.'

'I think I understand,' I admitted. 'I guess it's a clever way.'

'Atticus has spent the last hundred years training Milkaia about the process. Milkaia was lined up to be the next Atticus!' Casper said in a proud voice.

'What happened?'

'He … disappeared right before the king died.'

'Oh … do you think -?'

'I would rather not talk about it,' interrupted Milkaia, who stood up and turned to face the opposite direction. After a few minutes, she attempted to change the conversation. 'I presume you are asking because you wish to become immortal with Terry?'

I froze on the spot. I felt awkward answering. How *did* I answer? Isn't this what most people dreamed of? To live forever? I felt weird to admit it, but the thought hadn't crossed my mind once and I had no intention at all of ever becoming immortal.

'No ... not exactly,' I finally concluded.

I truly meant it from the bottom of my heart. I didn't want to be involved in this life. It was fascinating and truly amazing what I had learned today. It answered so many questions about Terry that I thought would never be answered, but this life wasn't for me and I would never wish to be like them.

TERRY

It was the longest journey of my life, but somehow we made it to Scotland. We only stopped twice and that was only to get petrol. We rode all day and late into the night, finally reaching the destination that Casper had given us in his satnav. I hadn't said a single word to Joe the entire time, and if honest, I didn't plan to either. Hours ago, I was punching his face into the ground, almost killing him … and now we were having a road trip to Scotland. If my life wasn't already fucked up enough, this turn of events was a true testament to it.

The place in Scotland where Livia lived was … scary. It was a very rough neighbourhood and almost every house was either boarded up or had graffiti on the front. Whilst this wasn't an ideal location to live, it was a perfect location to hide. Directly opposite the house that was Livia's was a seemingly boarded-up and abandoned house with "WARNING - DANGER" signs plastered all around it. We parked our bikes outside and broke down one of the panels at the back of the house, which gave us safe entry inside.

I could see why the house was marked as dangerous; it was practically falling apart inside, with rusted support beams temporarily put in place to hold up the ceiling and structure. I walked around the bottom floor and then the top and confirmed it was totally empty. Without saying a word to each other, Joe walked into one empty bedroom and I walked into the other. The room I had chosen was at the front of the house, which, after breaking a small piece of wood away from the boarded windows, gave me a perfect view of Livia's house.

I was glad to finally be alone from Joe and gather my thoughts. The long journey on the motorbike had given me a lot of time to think and reflect on everything that had happened. I felt like I accepted everything I had heard from Casper and Milkaia, although I still had millions of questions to ask them still. What amazed me most of all was the fact that all the truly incredible things I had learned didn't seem to matter. I was more bothered about Amy. I continually told myself that she was in shock and, of course, emotional after the house exploded. Maybe she didn't mean what she had said? Did she truly want to split up with me? Or did she just need space? I was scared beyond belief of what the reality was … I felt myself welling up, but also very tired. I retrieved the phone that Casper had given me out of the small bag and dialled the only number saved in the contacts.

'*Are you safe?*' said Casper.

'Yeah. We're here. Is Amy okay?'

'*She's perfectly fine. Get some rest, my lord. I will phone you tomorrow.*'

Without waiting for a reply, Casper hung up the phone. I started to yawn and thought that if I didn't sleep soon, I would end up crying myself to sleep anyway. I lay down on the hard, damp wooden floor and tried to find any position that felt comfortable. In the end, I took off the hoodie I had stolen and lay it on the ground as a makeshift pillow. I was cold, I was hungry and I was heartbroken. I lay for what felt like hours, but eventually, the exhaustion finally kicked in.

As I fell asleep, I continually thought of Amy and wanted nothing more than to hold her.

*

The next day seemed extremely dull compared to the last few; from explosions to life revelations to suddenly sitting in an abandoned house, very much alone. Joe did not leave his bedroom once, although I heard the occasional noise of wincing from him as he moved or the occasional floorboard creak.

I had no plan of what to do in Scotland, nor did I think that Casper and Milkaia had planned much either. Did I stare at the house over the road forever? What if no one came? What if absolutely nothing happened at all?

I decided the best I could do was go through the items that Casper had given me regarding Livia. The items were scarce, nothing more than a few photos and a folder full of facts and information. I was ashamed to think about it, but my initial reaction to Livia was noticing her beauty. She was dark-haired and blue-eyed and very curvaceous. Had she had lived another life, she would have looked like a model, but life had not been that kind to her. She looked tired, downtrodden, and by the looks of her partner, like she was in a bad relationship. Her partner was huge and very scary-looking, dressing as if he was part of some gang: tattooed head to toe, a leather jacket and it looked like a knife attached to his belt buckle.

According to the fact sheet, Livia's adopted name was Kate Robinson. She was placed in Scotland and put up for adoption under dramatic circumstances. Kate's fake mom apparently died of an overdose, and as a result, Kate was staged to have been taking the drugs as a result of her mother, which created a perfect explanation for why she had no memories.

I had no idea who Casper and Milkaia really were, but they were clearly well connected. Who had the power to forge lives and create birth certificates for the sake of placing a baby? When I thought about it more, who had the power to own an office building, completely for the guise of ensuring I was imprisoned? Who just created a fake ID, driving licence and gave millions of pounds and a mansion to someone? This was bizarre and everything in my life seemed more bizarre by the moment.

As I read over Livia/Kate's information, an important question suddenly dawned on me. Was Terry my real name? I wondered if I had another name? Before I could think any more, a noise in the next room caught my attention. I quickly placed the photos of Livia on the floor and ran to the hallway; Joe was walking down the stairs.

'Where are you going?' I asked.

Joe ignored me and continued to walk down stairs.

'Hey! I'm talking to you!'

'I'm getting something to eat,' he replied.

'Oh … okay. I guess we'll take it in turns going out.'

'Whatever.'

Joe continued to walk away and finally out of the back door of the house. I started to feel angry, but then I quickly reminded myself that it wasn't that long ago that I was pounding his face and splattering his blood over the ground.

I spent the next few hours watching out of the window at Livia's house. Just as I started to question if Casper had got the right house, a car had parked up outside the decrepit and run-down house. Climbing out of the car was Livia and her partner … and I was sad to see my suspicions were correct. Livia continually stared at the ground whilst her large partner constantly shouted at her as they walked into the house. I was quite a distance away, but I could have sworn that Livia had bruises on her face and down her arm.

I felt extremely sorry for her, and although she had nothing to do with me, part of me wanted to run over there and hit the guy - how could he hurt a woman? But, then again, why didn't Livia hit him back? If she was like me, then she should be super strong? She should have been invincible? If she was bruised, then someone would have had to have hit her over and over and over and over again? Why didn't she fight back? I was confused, and like everything else in my life, more questions seemed to be raised instead of answers.

*

A few more days passed and not a lot happened at all. I had my daily check-in with Casper, but the calls were brief and to the point. Before I could ask him any more questions, the call would be over and I would sit there, disappointed. The days were boring and I continued to watch Livia leave her house day in and day out. Sometimes, just to get some variety in my day, I would leave to go and find something to eat or go for a walk whilst Joe stayed behind. I didn't, for one moment, think

Joe would be on the lookout at Livia's house; he would just confine himself to the second bedroom.

Outside of Livia's street, Scotland actually seemed to be a beautiful place. It was a shame that Livia didn't live in the mountains or lochs, as I had heard that was where Scotland's true beauty was, but the city we were in was lovely enough. I loved the accent and I loved how much life was in the streets and people.

After another day of hardly anything happening at all, my boredom started to play with my emotions. I had resisted texting Amy from the temporary phone, but was grateful that I could remember her number. I argued with myself that she wouldn't want to hear from me ... but when you had little else to do, emotions always beat logic. I caved and texted her a simple message.

Hey. It's Terry. Just wanted to check you were okay.

I didn't know what I expected. Was she going to text me straight away? Would she text back at all? Unfortunately, it seemed to be the latter. I had to remind myself that the relationship I once had with Amy no longer existed. The girl that would text me back almost instantly and talk to me every day wasn't in my life anymore. Hours passed by and I continued to stare at the phone, waiting for a sign that she wanted to talk to me. As the day began to close, I started to feel hopeless. I was wondering if I should have called her? Maybe text her again? Before I could decide, the loudest noise in the world made me jump to my feet. The house started to shake furiously, not unlike my own had as it exploded. When the house stopped shaking, I ran out of the room and was in shock at the scene before me.

The house had collapsed, and what was previously the room Joe was sitting in was now in pieces on the ground floor, along with Joe underneath the rubble. I now realised why the house was boarded up and branded as dangerous.

'Are you okay?' I shouted down.

'Course I'm okay!' he shouted back.

I quickly ran to my room to peer outside and see if anyone was out in the street. It looked like no one had reacted to the large noise from the house.

'I don't think anyone noticed,' I called down.

'Great,' he sarcastically replied.

As the stairs had been severely damaged, I had to jump on top of the rubble that was on top of Joe. I moved the piece and lifted him out.

'You'll have to come into my room,' I said to him as he stood up.

'I'll stay down here,' he said.

'Don't be stupid. You'll cause more damage. Just stay upstairs. We don't have to talk.'

He wanted to argue back, I could tell, but instead he walked past me and climbed upstairs, and into my room; I rolled my eyes and realised how much worse my situation had become.

*

I didn't know pain until I had sat in a room with my enemy. It was beyond awkward silence! We sat at opposite corners of the room and the atmosphere felt like it could have been cut with a knife. Joe sat on the floor with his arms wrapped around his knees and his head facing away from me as he stared at the back wall. I had never felt more awkward in my life, and when Casper gave his daily call, I answered like my life depended on it. I was desperate to speak to someone, but as always, Casper kept his conversation short and sweet. Silence filled the room once again. I was absolutely sure that the silence slowed down time! The minutes felt like hours and the hours felt like days! I was absolutely sure that nightfall would never come and I felt like Livia was taking a holiday between leaving in the morning and returning at night. I was never more grateful than in the moments I would leave the house for food, and if I could get away with it, I would stay out as long as I could or take my time walking back. I truly felt like I was descending into madness.

At times, I wanted to poke Joe in the arm to make sure he was still alive. He hardly moved, nor made a noise unless he was going out. At the end of our first week in the abandoned house, our opportunity to speak to each other came as he returned from his lunch. As Joe sat down, he made a loud wincing noise that indicated he was in a lot of pain. I mustered the courage to finally talk to him.

'Are you in pain?' I asked.

'I'm fine,' he quickly replied.

'You don't sound fine.'

'I'm fine.'

Silence fell onto the room again, and after a few moments, I refused to fall into the madness again.

'This is ridiculous! I can't stand this silence no more.'

Joe ignored me.

'We're trapped in this room together, we should at least talk.' I begged.

'What about?'

'Anything!'

'Last week, you were moments away from killing me … we could talk about that?' he said, still refusing to look at me.

'Maybe because you blew up my house before that? Or threw Amy's brother off a cliff? Attacked her nan? Or maybe when you killed my best friend!'

'You should have finished me off. In fact, kill me now if you want to; it would beat this boredom.'

'What the fuck is wrong with you? Why do you hate me so much? I have done nothing to you!'

'You wouldn't understand. Just leave it.'

'You think you are the only person who has suffered? I have felt pain you couldn't imagine! Before I lived in Byanbythe, I was stuck in a prison for ten years! I supposedly lost my parents in a car crash, only to recently find out they were murdered! Tell me what I wouldn't understand, please?' I shouted.

Joe didn't seem to react and he still refused to look at me.

'You really, really don't understand,' he repeated.

'Explain to me, then!' I shouted, but after a moment, paused and gently said, 'Please … I need to know.'

Joe took a deep breath, and to my surprise, he turned to look at me with a face full of tears. Once he started to talk, he didn't seem to stop.

'You're not the only one who was dumped in Byanbythe. I, too, was dumped there as a baby on the doorstep of the hut I lived in. Back then was a simpler time; you didn't need to adopt someone properly, you could be just left on someone's doorstep and hopefully someone would take you in. My parents were good people. They took me in and treated me like their own blood and they gave me a great childhood. They taught me everything - to ride a push bike, to play football and rugby. I attended school, college, got a job … got married.'

'What happened?'

'This curse that fucks up our lives … that's what happened.'

'What do you mean?

'Back then, I had no idea that I was a freak … but soon enough, everyone else did. I stopped ageing at twenty. My parents died, and after years and years, my wife started to look more like my mother than she did a wife. Like everyone else, she couldn't understand why I stopped ageing … They all shut me out like I was a disease. My wife left me, too scared that I was some kind of monster.'

'I'm … sorry to hear that.'

'Do you want to know the worst thing of all? I watched her die, Terry. Even though she wanted nothing to do with me, I always stuck around. I lived in the forest, close to my hut where she continued to live. She aged … she grew old … but that didn't kill her. No, she suffered, she had the most severe cancer plague her … and you know what? Even in her weakest moments, she wanted nothing to do with me; she would rather have died alone, in pain, than be with a monster like me! I wasn't allowed at her funeral; apparently, her dying wish was to keep me away. I lost her … and then all the friends who shut me out? They all died too. Everyone I loved and cherished died and I was frozen in time - my own personal hell to live with the consequences. I could never make any new friends. I could never love anyone again - not after my wife. I couldn't keep a job without someone becoming suspicious. I had everything that mattered to me taken away. I had no one in my life. No one understood what I was. I just ceased to exist, but lived forever with no escape!'

'Why didn't you move away? Start fresh somewhere?' I asked.

'I couldn't leave her. I don't even know where she's buried … but her memory lives on in Byanbythe. I could never leave her.'

'I'm so sorry, Joe…'

'Me too. Sorry I didn't die, instead of her.'

'I still don't understand what I did wrong. Why do you hate me so much?'

'Have you not listened to a single thing I have said? I lived for over a hundred years being rejected from everyone and anyone … and then you come along from nowhere. It was so obvious you were like me … The first time I saw you was during that car crash your girlfriend had. You just stood there naked in the road, shaking like some freak … but you were unharmed. She clearly knew what you were, but did not reject you. She didn't hate you, fear you, think you were some freak. She loved you! So I thought … maybe she's the odd one out, so I decided to show her brother. He didn't care, nor did he tell a single soul. Your old friend? He didn't seem to give a shit when I told him what you were before he died. Out of desperation, I thought my only resort was to show the world what you were. If the ones closest to you did not care, then surely the world would? But no … no one questioned how you survived. No one thought you were a freak. No one questioned a single thing that was suspicious about that explosion. They all cared about you and wanted to know you were okay. Why you? Why didn't you get the same treatment I did? Why did no one shut you out? Everything I had to endure and suffer … and yet everything I wanted was offered on a plate to you. It made me realise something … people didn't reject me because of my curse; they rejected me because of me … I am the curse, it has nothing to do with what we are. And that is why you will *never* understand the pain I have been through.'

The silence that now filled the room was a completely different silence than the last few days. I truly felt pity for him and had never realised the pain he had been through.

'I hope you never have the woman you love look at you like you are a freak. I hope you never have to see your wife reject you because of what you are and rather die alone than be with you,' Joe concluded.

'I'm really sorry for what you have been through.'

Joe looked away from me again.

'I never asked for this life, Joe … I know you have been through a lot, but the world has changed. A hundred years ago is a completely different place to the world today,' I continued. 'Regardless of what you have been through, it doesn't justify what you did to me. You killed my best friend.'

'I never meant to kill him …'

'You scared an old man enough to have a heart attack! What did you expect to happen?'

'I just … wanted you to be miserable like me. I wanted him to know what you are … I'm … I'm sorry.'

I was not expecting an apology, which completely derailed my train of thought or the next thing I was going to shout at him. After a moment's thought, I could only say what was on my mind.

'I can never forgive you for what you have done. When this is all over and you learn about your past from Casper, we need to sort things out.'

'What do you mean?'

'I can't let you live for what you have done …'

Joe turned to look at me with a face full of shock, although he didn't look angry; instead, he looked like he accepted what I had said.

'Do what you need to do ... I don't even care about my past anymore ...'

'Then why are you staying here with me, then?' I asked, and when he didn't reply, I continued, 'Don't act like you don't care. I saw you cry. You want to know your past more than anything in the world.'

He didn't reply and continued to look away. I saw through his bullshit, and even before he spoke to me today, I had realised that Joe was just a lonely man, desperate for answers. He had lived a life of rejection because of what he was, and when he saw that I had a happy life, he wanted to inflict the same misery on me. What a sad life to live.

AMY

I tried to spend as little time as possible with Casper and Milkaia, but I felt massively guilty about it. They were both the kindest people I had met and reminded me a lot of my own mom and dad ... and Terry (who I was trying not to think about). They were also the most interesting people I had spoken to and I felt myself wanting to ask more and more about them and their world; this was the exact reason I had to stay away.

It felt wrong to split up with Terry and not want to be part of his world and then ask hundreds of questions and show an interest. Casper and Milkaia still checked in with me over the phone and even asked if I wanted to see him again, but after I declined, our conversations would then become brief. I felt like my life had taken a dramatic change for all the wrong reasons, and I hated to admit it, but I really missed Terry. My family had slowly given up searching for him, admitting that if Terry wanted to be found, he would come back. My mom blamed the stress of the house explosion for causing Terry to run away, maybe some sort of PTSD. Of course, if she knew the real extent of drama in Terry's life, she would have known that a house explosion was pretty mild in comparison.

I had spent almost every day writing a text back to Terry ... but I honestly didn't know what to say back. One of the last things he said to me was "I know you don't love me anymore". Of course I still loved him ... I would always love him. But what could I reply back with that wouldn't cause him more pain? Maybe it was easier this way? I could be distant with him to make the breakup easier? But then I thought about the pain I would be causing him right now, never mind the future! I was so confused! Just as I started to think of something to say to him, I received another text from Terry, but this time from a different number.

Had to swap phones. Something bad has happened and I have had to come back. Can you meet me at the Black Lake on your own? I don't trust Casper and Milkaia.
Terry x

What did he mean by "something bad had happened"? Why was he back in Byanbythe? I felt scared. I was worried. I quickly texted back that I was on my way to him and ran out of the house to begin the long walk to the Black Lake. It would have taken me a long time to walk, but how could I ask for my mom or dad to drive me? "Oh, Mom and Dad, could you drive me to meet Terry at the Black Lake?" I walked as fast as I could.

Maybe it was the fear, maybe it was because my mind was going a hundred miles an hour, but the thirty-minute walk seemed to pass by in moments. Before I knew it, I was standing outside the sign that labelled the lake ahead. I texted Terry's new number when I finally arrived to say that I was there. The lake was now a beautiful blue colour, a huge contrast to when it was frozen during winter. It was very peaceful during the summer, and sadly, not enough people spent time here, instead opting for the beach. I looked around for a sign of Terry, but couldn't see a single soul. As I began to worry, I heard a rustle in the trees and turned around, expecting to see Terry.

'You are more beautiful in real life than you are on TV,' said a cold, raspy voice.

I didn't recognise this person, but whoever they were, they were very scary to look at. The man was tall, broad and had scars all over his face. He was bald and the scars on his face covered all of his features - one across his one eye, one across the other, one down his lip and several across his throat.

'Who ... who are you?'

'My name is Alexander Rainforth. I believe you are the girlfriend of my friend? Terry Haynes?'

Rainforth ... How could I have been so stupid?

'I know who you are! You are no friend of Terry's!' I shouted.

He began to laugh a cold laugh.

'I didn't think you were that clever. You humans amaze me.'

'I'm not alone! You need to go before you get hurt! Terry and a whole army of people are not far away!'

'Is that why you planned to meet him here? Sweet girl, maybe you are as stupid as the rest of them,' he replied.

'What do you want with me? I don't know where Terry is!'

'I don't want to know where he is. I want him to come here. Now … I wonder, how does one encourage someone to come out of hiding?' he laughed.

'I split up with Terry. He won't come back for me. You're wasting your time!'

I was panicking like never before. If I was ever worried about Joe, then Joe seemed like a mouse compared to Rainforth. His whole demeanour was petrifying, like every word was an attack ready to happen.

'Perhaps,' he concluded. 'But I have to take my chances. If he doesn't come for you, I can find uses for you elsewhere.'

'Leave me alone!'

I ran in the opposite direction from him, but it was no use. He ran with such speed it took less than a second for him to grab me. Before I could realise what was happening, he punched me in the face with such force that all the light in the world faded in an instant.

TERRY

Joe's story continually played on my mind. I hated feeling sympathy for someone I hated so much ... but his story was so sad. For the little bit of life that I had had in Byanbythe, it was full of love, happiness and fond memories. Joe, it seemed, had the complete opposite and had turned into the bitter and twisted man he was today. It begged the question: was he evil? Or was he the by-product of the fear of others?

Another question that came to mind was the fact he, too, was abandoned as a child in Byanbythe. Was Byanbythe the pit stop for abandoned inhuman babies? Then again, the reaction from Casper and Milkaia made me feel that they weren't involved. Yet again, more questions were raised by the little answers I gained.

My talk with Joe didn't seem to resolve the awkward silence; in fact, I was sure it had made it worse. Instead of sitting in silence avoiding each other, we now sat in silence avoiding each other with the added awkwardness of me feeling sorry for him and Joe knowing I still wanted to kill him.

Every day, I saw Livia leave the house and return, and each day I saw the torment that her partner caused her. She looked like an empty shell of a human and I felt guilty at how our lives compared. When I was placed in Byanbythe, I was left millions, a mansion and everything I could need to live a great life. Livia was in a shithole and looked like she had no money. My life had love, and Livia's seemed to have hate.

On the Sunday, my emotions got the better of me and I did something very stupid. Livia was outside, cleaning the windows of her house, when her partner, seemingly drunk, came out in a furious rage. I couldn't hear what was being said, but the situation seemed to escalate quickly, and within a blink he had struck her across the face and knocked her to the ground. I felt rage overcome me and I wanted nothing more than to run over there and hit him back. The thing that shocked me the most was that even though she was on the ground already, the monster continued to shout at her. I watched Livia cower in fear at her partner and raise her arms above her face to protect herself. He was clearly going to strike her again, and without thinking or waiting a single moment more, I ran out the house and onto the street.

'Oi! Leave her alone!' I shouted.

The partner quickly turned to me in great confusion and anger.

'Who da fuck are yew!' he shouted back.

I stood in front of Livia and directly in front of the thug.

'If you hit her again, I will break your hand!' I threatened.

'Who da fuck do yew think ya are? Shut ya puss before I shut it for ya!' he replied.

From an outside point of view, this guy was three times my size and looked like he would eat me alive.

'You think it's okay to hit a woman?' I said.

'Yer aff yer heid lad!' he shouted, and tried to push with great force.

When I didn't move an inch, he stood back in shock. He tried to push me again, and when I didn't move, his anger overtook his confusion and he threw a mighty punch towards my face. I grabbed his fist and twisted it back, making him scream in pain.

'Do. Not. Touch. Her. Again! Do you understand?' I ordered.

When he didn't reply, I twisted his arm as far as I could without breaking it, making him scream more and finally agreeing. I let him suffer a little more, making him squirm in pain.

'Terry!'

I turned around to see Joe in the middle of the road. I looked from him to Livia's partner and finally let go when I realised what I was doing. Had I lost my mind? What kind of person had I turned into? A few weeks ago, I would avoid confrontation and violence … now it seemed to be my first and only reaction to anything. I didn't know this guy; I didn't even know Livia officially and yet here I was intervening and attacking someone. Yes, he had been hitting a woman, but was more violence the answer? I started to feel like I was the real monster right now. I turned around to Livia and offered my hand to help her off the ground. She hesitated, but finally took my hand and let me pick her up.

'Are you okay?' I asked.

'Who … who are you?' she stuttered.

'It doesn't matter. Listen, no woman should be hit by a man. Don't take shit from this thug. You're stronger than you know, you know that?'

I looked into her blue eyes and it felt like she understood what I really meant to say. Did she know she was super strong? Maybe she realised that I was the same?

'Terry, let's go,' said Joe.

I followed Joe down the street and away from Livia and her partner. I didn't even bother to look back and see the end result of my intervention.

Joe and I walked for some time until we were a good distance away from Livia's street. When it felt like we were a safe distance, Joe turned to me and pushed me against a wall.

'What the fuck do you think you were doing?' he shouted.

'He was hitting her!'

'We're not here to get involved in her life. We're here to make sure she's not being stalked by your fan club! God, you are such a kid!'

We stared each other in the eyes, both furious and ready to kill each other again. As I stared, my phone in my pocket began to ring. I didn't answer straight away, but after a few moments staring at Joe, I slowly took the phone out of my pocket and answered, still not breaking eye contact.

'Casper,' I answered.

'*At last …*' said an unfamiliar voice.

'Who's this?'

'*Do you know how long I have longed to hear your voice? Dear, sweet prince, it is an absolute honour to hear your voice.*'

'Who is this?'

'*I could announce myself as many things. Once upon a time, I was a loyal servant to your father. A leader to an army, proficient at war, but maybe I should just announce myself as something a little closer to home? My latest title is the protector of Amy Doorie.*'

'Rainforth?'

'*I love it when people say my name. It makes me feel like an honoured man.*'

'Where is Amy? If you have hurt her -'

'*Prince Claudius, I have no desire to hurt a single person today. All I want right now is to see you.*'

'Where is Amy?'

Joe now looked at me with confusion and was mouthing to me to ask who was on the phone.

'*She's safe. Come back to Byanbythe and we can talk. That is all I want to do. Talk.*'

'Don't think I don't know why you are looking for me! You want to kill me.'

'*I don't know what fables have been fed to you, Claudius, but I think it's only fair you listen to my side.*'

'Leave Amy out of this!'

'*Come to me and I will let her go. It really is that simple.*'

'So you can kill me?' I argued back.

'*Regardless of what I plan to do, I don't think you have much choice … if you want to guarantee Amy's safety.*'

I paused. He was right. No matter what I wanted to argue back, he already had Amy.

'Okay. If I see Amy is safe, I'll come willingly.'

'*Good.*'

'Where are Casper and Milkaia?'

'*They are safe too, although, they won't be much use to you. You will find them in the cabin they were in.*'

'Where am I meeting you?'

'*My friends have scouted the area. There is a college that seems to be unused at the moment. Do you know of it?*'

'Yes.'

'*Then we will meet there. How quickly can you get here?*'

'Tomorrow …'

'That is not quick enough. Do not try to fool me, Claudius. Whatever you try to plan will fail and I will kill her.

'No! I'm being honest. It will take a day to travel. Honestly!'

Rainforth paused.

'Very well. The college, tomorrow night. Come alone.'

He hung up the phone.

'Who was that?' asked Joe.

'They have Amy!'

'Who does?'

'The people that want to kill me! We have to go!'

Joe didn't reply and we ran together, back to our motorbikes.

*

We rode as fast as we could, again only stopping for petrol; we were in such a rush that we took the motorway home, not caring that I was driving a stolen bike or about the possibility of getting caught. I felt sick, but I was so scared that I couldn't actually think. We drove long into the night and the early hours of the morning, until we finally reached the tunnel underneath Mt. Cudd and into Byanbythe. My first port of call was to find Casper and Milkaia; Rainforth mentioned a cabin, so I assumed that he had meant Joe's hut.

My back and bum were numb from the long journey, so it was a welcome relief to finally jump off as we reached Joe's hut. I quickly ran inside, but was petrified to see that it was empty.

'They're not here!' I shouted.

'Do you know of another cabin?' asked Joe.

'Only Phil's …'

'Then let's try there.'

We were back on our bikes and we rode towards the forest by Phil's cabin. We ran through the forest and finally reached the small cabin. With a big sigh of relief, I saw a light coming from inside. I burst through the door and saw Casper and Milkaia in the strangest condition. They were badly beaten, both covered in cuts, bruises and blood with their mouths gagged by duct tape. They were both trapped, confined by chains that were so tightly wrapped around them and connected to several parts of the cabin it was practically impossible for them to break free, even with super strength.

'I'm here. Are you both okay?' I called.

I carefully removed the tape from their mouths and started to unwrap the chains from their bodies. Whoever had wrapped these chains knew what they were doing. They were strategically wrapped in such a way that not even Houdini could have escaped them. They were interwoven, wrapped, knotted and linked. I tried to undo what had been done, but became desperate and started to rip the chains apart. Joe helped, and as soon as Casper and Milkaia's arms were free, they began to rip the chains too and then the duct tape.

'Terry! You came!' cried Milkaia.

'Are you okay?' I asked, putting my hand on her shoulder and checking her over.

'You should not have come! They are here!' shouted Casper.

'They have Amy! I had to come.'

'This will not end well in any scenario, sir. Rainforth does not make deals and he cannot be trusted.'

'What else could I do? I can't let Amy die.'

'But they will kill you, my prince,' Milkaia warned.

'It doesn't matter. I would gladly give my life if it meant saving Amy.'

'You do not understand. If he kills you, then there will be a lot more than just Amy in danger,' said Casper.

'I DON'T CARE! It's Amy's life that is in danger. You either help me or get out of my way.'

Everyone looked at me in silence and I suddenly felt very alone. I didn't care; if I had to go to that college alone, I would.

'What are you thinking, Terry?' asked Milkaia.

'I don't know ... I don't think I have many options. I think I need to hand myself in, but not before Amy walks away safely.'

'Sir ... I don't think Rainforth will honour the deal. It is very unlikely that Amy will walk away safely.'

'Then we make sure she's safe!' shouted Joe.

I turned around, in shock. I looked at Joe, questioning if he really meant what he just said.

'What do you mean?'

'We're going to college with you, Terry,' replied Joe. 'I don't know the full plan ... but whatever happens, we make sure Amy gets out safe.'

'It's not going to be easy,' said Casper. 'He has around ten men with him, all loyal and ready to fight to the death. We are outnumbered.'

'We're not there to fight them,' I said. 'We won't win and it's too risky. Joe's right … I need you to focus on getting Amy out of there safe.'

Casper looked at Milkaia, who began to cry.

'But, Terry … you will die. Please …' she begged.

Milkaia grabbed my hands and fell to her knees, sobbing uncontrollably.

'Milkaia, what choice do I have?' I asked. 'I can't let Amy die.'

'My prince, we could run away,' said Casper. 'We could make a better plan to take Rainforth down. Your father still has many loyal followers who would fight in his honour!'

'If we don't go tonight, they will kill Amy!' explained Joe.

I was shocked at how much he was acting like he cared about Amy's safety.

'She would not die in vain,' said Casper. 'She would be saving the world. We cannot let Rainforth take the throne; he would kill millions of innocent people.'

'Any scenario where Amy dies is *not* an option!' I shouted.

Casper and Milkaia were lost for words and both looked down in defeat. Milkaia still sobbed on her knees and Casper looked away in fury.

'Are you with me or not?' I asked them.

The room fell silent, and for a moment, I thought they wouldn't join me. In this weird scenario, suddenly the people who were supposed to be my loyal protectors were against me and my sworn enemy was my only ally.

'We are … with you.'

'Casper, no!' Milkaia begged. 'We swore our lives to protect him.'

'We also swore to follow his rule. If this is how he wants to do things … we have no choice.'

Milkaia continued to sob into her hands and it was now starting to sink in that I had signed my own death sentence. I was hours away from death, and strangely enough, I was willing for it to happen, all to save Amy.

*

The next few hours were awful. Milkaia eventually stopped crying and Casper suggested several plans that were too risky to follow; eventually, he got the idea that Amy's safety was my priority and there was nothing we could do that would risk that. The plan, in the end, was very simple. We would walk through the college and locate Rainforth and his men; once Amy could walk away with Joe, Casper and Milkaia, I would accept my fate.

As Casper and Milkaia argued inside the cabin, I stepped outside, where Joe was waiting for us to travel. I sat down next to him in Phil's favourite outdoor chair and took a deep breath of the beautiful summer evening air.

'It's peaceful here,' said Joe.

'It is. Phil loved it here,' I mused.

Joe looked at me and gave me a small, awkward smile.

'I really am sorry …'

'For what?'

'Everything. For taking away your best friend. For causing your family so much pain.' I wasn't expecting this and I was suddenly lost for words. After stuttering, he continued, 'I was wrong for doing what I did. I guess I wanted to make you suffer like I did.'

'Why are you saying this?' I asked.

'Because you have reminded me what it really means to be human today.'

'I don't get you.'

'You would willingly die for that girl, the same way I would have done for my wife. No questions, no hesitations. All you have ever done is try and protect the people you loved.'

'Wow. I thought you hated me?'

'I do. I hate you more than anything in this world … but it doesn't mean you can't teach me something.'

'Why are you fighting for Amy, then?'

'Because if I could have saved my wife, I would have … and because she didn't deserve everything I put her through. I have to do something right.'

I nodded at him and we had a small mutual agreement; whilst it didn't make up for anything that had happened, helping Amy today was a step in the right direction.

'Are we ready?' asked Casper.

I turned around and Casper and Milkaia were standing outside Phil's cabin, fully dressed in cloaks.

'Let's do this.'

'Terry … are you sure?' asked Milkaia. 'You don't understand how valuable you are to our world.'

'And you don't understand how valuable she is to my world. She is my world.'

'Very well.'

'I did want to ask something before we left, though.'

'What is it?' asked Capser.

'I wouldn't want to die without knowing a few things.'

'Of course. Anything, my lord.'

'On the phone call with Rainforth, he called me Claudius? Is that … is that my real name?'

'It was the name you were given at birth, yes.'

'So it's my real name, then …'

'No, it's not,' replied Casper. When I looked confused, he walked towards me and put his hand on my shoulder. 'Dear prince, what is in a name? As far as I am concerned, you have grown into the perfect gentleman. You have a great life here with someone you love, and from what she told us, a family who loves you dearly too. You have done all of this as Terry Haynes. That is your real name.'

'But as a child -'

'You have grown up to be a better man than we could have ever hoped for, Terry,' said Milkaia, who embraced me with a hug. 'Your mother and father would be so proud.'

'Thank you,' I said, suddenly feeling very emotional.

'Did you have any other questions?' asked Casper.

'Livia … in Scotland. Why didn't she get a good life like I did? I don't know if you knew, but she's got it pretty rough up there.'

Casper looked at the ground and suddenly became very sad.

'As much as we try, there is only so much we could have done to help you and Kate,' he said. 'We gave her the same opportunities as you, including money and family.'

'So what happened?'

'We have tried to keep an eye on both you and Kate ... but Kate did not make the right choices,' said Milkaia. 'From what we could tell, she mixed with the wrong crowds, shunned her family ... and blew the money we had given her.'

'I don't know how. She lives in an awful area ... She doesn't look like she has much money at all.'

'Like we said ... there is only so much we can do for people,' Casper concluded.

I thought about Livia (or Kate); so, she had had the same money as I did, and by the sounds of it, was placed with a good adopted family ... to see where she was now was very sad.

'Was there anything else, sir?' asked Casper.

'Yes, only one more thing and it's not a question ... it's something I need from you.'

'Anything you ask, Terry,' said Milkaia.

'When I d- ... When I'm with Rainforth ... I want Amy and her family to have all of my money. I want Amy to have the best life possible with every opportunity she could ever want. I also want to make sure she is watched over and protected.'

'She will be guarded with my life, sir,' said Casper.

'I promise, Terry,' Milkaia confirmed.

'Thank you … I don't think I have said it yet … but I'm sorry for how I have treated you. It sounds like you have had my back my entire life, going above and beyond to make sure I was safe. My mom and dad were lucky to have you both.'

Before they could react, it was my turn to embrace them and I gave them both a hug. Milkaia welcomed my hug like she was hugging her own son, but Casper suddenly became very rigid and awkward.

'Let's go.'

The walk through the forest and to the car was in silence; we all walked together with our heads low, which only made me feel more apprehensive about what was to come.

'Would you mind if I drove?' I asked. 'If it's my last …'

Casper agreed and gave me the keys to their car. Again, we were all in silence, but this time I took my time as I took a long detour. I drove past the Doories' house and thought about Michael and Lisa, who had been like parents to me; what I would give to have one last warm hug from Lisa … or maybe a final word with Michael, who always said the right thing and gave the best advice.

I drove through the town and past the American football training ground where I would have spent most of my time with Michael and the lads from the team. I then drove past the pier and beach and thought of New Year's Eve with everyone from college or Phil's wake and the immense kindness from the town. Next to the pier was the restaurant that I took Amy to on our first date and I remembered how much we laughed during that night; the vision of Amy at that table, with her beautiful laugh and smile … I was going to miss that most of all.

I turned the car around and stopped to take one final look at the beach and pier. The sun was setting on the most beautiful evening and the sky was a dull gold and blue. Next to the pier, I could see the two boats that had once belonged to Phil.

'Those boats there at the end, make sure they continue to be funded and looked after? Please?' I asked.

'Of course,' agreed Milkaia.

'Thank you. I'm done with asking for favours and saying goodbye. Let's go.'

I drove back through the town and through the forest, through the roads that led towards the college. I was finally ready to accept my fate.

It was very eerie to see the college car park empty. I parked as close to the front of the car park as possible and we slowly got out of the car.

'We need to be careful,' said Casper. 'Rainforth's men could be dotted around the college. It could be an ambush.'

'We're in this together,' said Joe.

I smiled and nodded at him before turning around and walking into the college. I had no idea where to expect Rainforth, as he had not explicitly said where to go. I wasn't sure if it was the nerves, but I started to feel very warm and sick, like I was going to throw up. We walked past the several buildings that were dotted around the campus and past the huge main building that held the reception and main hall.

'No sign …' said Joe.

I started to think where they could be … there were no signs of any break-in or disturbance; where could they be? I thought hard, of all the locations that would be open enough to hold a group of people, potentially strategically dotted around for an ambush. The answer was so simple and there was only one place they could be.

'The park ... in the middle of college. They have to be there.'

We all began to walk towards the park, which wasn't too far away.

'How are you feeling?' Joe asked in a low voice.

'I'm fine.'

'I promise she's going to get out safe.'

'Thanks, Joe.'

'You know ... if we didn't hate each other so much, I bet we could have been friends.'

'You don't have to be nice to me just because I'm going to die,' I joked.

'I'm just jealous I didn't get to do it myself ...'

We both laughed and it was a welcome feeling as we approached the park. I looked ahead and in the distance I could see a group of people standing around the water feature, which was at the very centre. As we walked closer, I looked around the park and could see people dotted around. Everyone stood in silence and all stared at me with great intensity. There was no sign of Amy yet, but as we got closer, the crowd gathered around the centre began to separate, leaving two people standing alone ... one of whom was Amy.

Casper quickly grabbed my arm and pulled me back before I had a chance to run to Amy. I tried to rip away from him and I felt pure rage take control of me. I had lost all sense of reason - Rainforth had hurt Amy! Her face was bruised and she looked barely conscious, with her hands tied behind her back.

'You said she would be safe!' I shouted.

Both Casper and Milkaia held me back now, struggling to stop me from running forward.

Rainforth grinned a large, twisted smile and slowly walked forward before bowing before me.

'Your Highness,' he mocked.

Several of his followers began to laugh and shout their own insults, but I ignored them, still focusing on Amy.

'You lied to me. You said she would be safe!'

Rainforth looked back at Amy and she opened her eyes in a dazed way.

'She is alive, is she not?'

'Let her go!'

'All in a good time ... all in good time. Please, allow me an audience with the prince?'

'What do you want? Can we skip the theatrics?'

Rainforth glared at me through his scarred face; he was revelling in this moment and I knew he was going to perform for his audience.

'I have waited all of your life for this moment; please don't deny me this.'

'Let Amy go! I'll do whatever you want.'

'Entertain me?'

I didn't reply. I watched Rainforth walk around the water feature, smiling around the park at all his male and female followers. When we spoke, he addressed them, instead of me.

'King Trajan. Do you all remember him?'

The crowd began to laugh hysterically.

'Manically obsessed with us all living in the shadows like slaves of society? *Embarrassed* of our gifts?'

The crowd booed and jeered in unity. A familiar hot feeling began to bubble in my stomach, but I tried to suppress it. I tried not to look at Rainforth, who seemed to love every minute of his own performance. I instead looked at Amy, who looked back at me with fear in her eyes.

'And do *we*, the true visionaries of the immortal race, accept the vision of *our* king?' Rainforth called out.

'NO!' the crowd chanted.

'Of course not! This is why we killed the king!'

Rainforth laughed as the crowd cheered and applauded.

'And do we accept this prince as our new king?'

'NO!' the crowd chanted again.

Rainforth walked towards me and finally addressed me directly.

'Prince Claudius, you are sentenced to death!'

'On what grounds?' I asked through gritted teeth.

Rainforth smiled once more, but his eyes were gleaming with fury.

'Obstruction to progression,' he finally answered with a lowered voice.

'Listen to me, Rainforth. My three friends here are going to take Amy away; once she's away from the college, you can do what you want to me,' I reasoned.

Rainforth began to laugh uncontrollably in a very dramatic way.

'You are *no* prince of mine! You do not give me orders! You think your friends can escape? I will take her head off her body right in front of you, then take yours back to the council. I think your head will be proof enough that the throne is up for taking.'

'You promised! Don't do this, Rainforth. I will come with you. I'll give you the throne right in front of your council! Just let them go!'

The pain in my stomach was becoming too much to bear. It was happening at the worst time possible! I couldn't black out now … I had to save Amy. I couldn't let the same thing happen like it did with Phil.

Rainforth walked towards me, close enough that only I could hear what he said.

'On the other hand … she's rather beautiful. Maybe I could give her the touch of a real man before I kill her?'

'NO!'

I wanted to hit him, but it was too late. I fell to my knees with the most severe pain spreading throughout my veins. This blackout was different, like nothing I had ever felt before. The heat burned more and my body was uncontrollably shaking all over. I hit the ground and started to spasm furiously, unable to stop what was about to happen.

'Terry!' Milkaia called out.

'What is happening to him!?' shouted Rainforth.

I felt like I was going to shake until I exploded. The light from the world was fading away, and before I left the world, surely the last time I would see the world, I took one last look at Amy. Even before death, she was the most beautiful sight that my eyes could be honoured to see before they closed forever. I fell into darkness with a broken heart, knowing that I could do nothing to save her. I had failed her, like I had failed Phil. I loved her so much and my final thought was how lucky I was to have loved someone like her.

*

I didn't open my eyes. Was I dead? If I was, I could hear a sound that sounded like heaven. The birds were singing in the trees, the wind was rustling through the trees and somewhere in the distance, I could hear the noise of seagulls, no doubt above some beach. I had not given much thought to the afterlife, neither had I thought much about religion, but if this was it, it seemed a good place to start. I didn't want to open my eyes, but I could feel the hot sun on my body and it was magnificent.

What was the last thing I remembered? I thought long and hard …

'AMY!'

I opened my eyes and sat up.

I was lying in Phil's bed in his cabin. I looked around the room and to my left was Amy, who sat and stared at me, crying …

'Amy?'

'Are you okay?' she asked. She was smiling at me whilst crying. I was so confused.

'Are you okay? What happened?'

'Relax … you have to take it easy, Terry.'

'Amy, are you okay?'

'I'm fine, thanks to you.'

'What happened?'

Her face was still bruised, but apart from that, she looked perfectly fine. Was this a dream? Maybe this was heaven?

'You … saved us. All of us.'

'I … don't understand? I blacked out.'

'You did, but it was the freakiest thing I had ever seen. You were on the floor in a spasm - it was really scary, I had never seen anything like it.'

'And then what happened?'

'You just … stopped.'

'Amy, put me out of my misery. What happened?'

'I don't know. You stopped having a fit and then you just … changed. You got up, but it wasn't you. It was like you were a completely different person. You were ... feral, like some wild animal.'

'What happened to Rainforth?'

'You fought him ... and nearly all of his followers.'

'How? I ... don't ... I don't remember any of this.'

'I didn't think you would. It was like you were possessed and a hundred times stronger. With the help of Casper and Milkaia, they literally didn't stand a chance. I have never seen something so incredible or scary before in my life. You should have seen the look on Rainforth's face ... he was so shocked and scared. You beat him within an inch of his life.'

'What about you, though? How did you get away safely?'

'As soon as the fighting began, Joe grabbed me and ran as far away as possible. A few of Rainforth's followers tried to get me first, but Joe saved my life.'

I felt like this was an information overload, and so overwhelming. Amy was alive and safe; it had to be a miracle.

'And ... are you okay?' I asked.

'I'm fine, honestly. How do you feel?'

I felt weak, like I hadn't eaten or slept in days (and to some extent, that was most likely true).

'I'm okay. I'm just glad you're safe.'

'Casper told me that you were going to give your life for me. You're an idiot … do you know that?'

'I love you, Amy; no matter what has happened or will happen, that will never change. You mean more to me than life itself.'

'I love you too, Terry. Regardless of what has happened, I love you more than anything else,' she said, and finally climbed onto the bed and kissed me.

As she leaned on me, I felt a sharp pain in my stomach and side. So this was what it was like to feel battered and bruised.

'Where is everyone else?' I asked.

'They're dealing with Rainforth and his cult.'

'What do you mean?'

'Well, you killed quite a few of them … so Milkaia's dealing with the bodies.'

'I killed -?'

'Well, considering they were going to kill us and you were possessed during a blackout … I think you can be forgiven.'

We both laughed and she wiped away the single tear that had streamed down my face.

'What about the rest? Did Rainforth survive?'

'Just about. Around eight survived, including him.'

'What's going to happen with them?'

'Well, for once, I had a great idea,' she said, with a big proud smile on her face.

'What do you mean?'

'Casper mentioned imprisoning them once they were put in front of some council? But he said that could take some time ... so I came up with a great idea. Why not imprison them in your safe-room?'

'What? How?'

'Well, no one knows about the safe-room underneath your house ... and it's practically hidden under an exploded house. Casper thought it was a great idea once he made a change or two ... he was going to chain them all up and imprison them in there.'

'Oh, wow ... is that safe?'

'Casper seemed sure enough they would never leave. He mentioned something about chaining them up the same way he and Milkaia were chained up?'

'That makes sense.'

Amy slowly lifted herself off the bed and stretched as she walked towards the kitchen area.

'Do you want a cup of tea?' she asked.

I was flabbergasted at how calm and relaxed she was; after everything that had happened over the last few weeks, how could she be this calm?

'Amy … you seem so … relaxed?'

She laughed and filled the kettle up with cold water.

'I guess things seem a little better now. The worst is over, right?'

'But what about everything else? My past …?'

Her smile faded and she turned and walked towards me again, sitting on the edge of the bed and grabbing my hands.

'You know I love you?' she began. 'More than anything in this world … I will love you like no one else could.'

'But …'

'But our worlds are so much different. I'm not strong enough, Terry … I'm not the right person to stand by your side when you're a king.'

'I don't want to be king!'

I suddenly got out of bed and stood above her.

'Terry, you have a life out there waiting for you. It sounds like you have to lead people like you to a safe life.'

'I have a life here! With you. Your family. I don't want to be a king.'

She looked sad ... but she also looked like she had made her mind up. No matter what I said, I was not going to convince her. Amy was disturbed by my past, with good reason. Now that she had seen this side of me, she couldn't see me as the same person as I was before and it was something I needed to accept.

I felt like I was moments away from begging her to stay with me or trying to convince her I was no king, so I decided to change the subject.

'Where's Joe?'

'He was outside last time I saw him.'

I turned away from her and walked out of the cabin. Joe was sitting in the exact same seat as he had been the night we travelled to college, staring into the distance and into the forest.

'Hey ...' I said as I sat down in Phil's chair.

'Had enough beauty sleep?' he joked.

'Why? Do I look beautiful?'

'No, you look like shit.'

We both laughed and then stared at the beautiful forest again that was illuminated by the golden sun that ruled above the tall trees above.

'Thank you,' I finally said.

'What for?'

'You kept your promise. You saved Amy.'

'Hardly. You turned into Shakin' Stevens and then started a bar fight!'

'You know what I mean.'

He looked at me and smiled, nodding his head as if to say "you're welcome".

'Isn't it mad …? A couple of weeks ago, we were ready to kill each other,' he reflected.

'Strange what a trip to Scotland and fighting a rebellion does to change perspective, isn't it?'

Joe nodded again and slumped lower in his chair.

'What now, then?' he asked.

'I need to see Casper and Milkaia.'

'You're in luck, then …' he said and looked behind me.

I turned around and saw Milkaia running towards me, before grabbing me into the tightest hug I had ever felt.

'Terry! Oh, Terry! You're okay!'

Over Milkaia's shoulders, I could see Casper walking towards us too, beaming at me.

'Sir, you are awake,' he said.

'Is everything okay?' I asked when Milkaia finally released me.

'Everything is in its right place.'

'Any issues?'

'Nothing that isn't sorted now, sir.'

Amy opened the cabin door and walked outside.

'What happens now?' I asked.

'Well … I need to gather a council meeting,' said Casper.

'I'm glad you said that. Rainforth mentioned a council. What is it?'

'It is a meeting that your father held with over a thousand people of our race. Normally, one representative from each family would meet once a century.'

'And what happens there?'

'Well, normally your father talks business, news and updates for the community … however, it can be used for important and race-changing decisions. I deem it important that everyone sees you are alive and well and then we can plan the next stages of you taking the throne.'

I ignored this comment, as I wasn't ready to drop my next bombshell. As Casper mentioned the throne, I could see Amy look away.

'And what about Rainforth and the others?'

'We will present them in front of the council and sentence them to death or life imprisonment,' Milkaia explained. 'You will make the final call when you are king.'

'Okay … how quickly can you gather a council?' I asked.

'I have already begun the work, sir,' said Casper. 'It will take a few months, at least, to spread the word and prepare so many people to get together.'

'Good … because I'm going to abdicate.'

Casper's eyes widened and Milkaia clasped her face to her hands.

'Sir, surely you don't mean that!' Casper cried.

'Please do not joke about such things!' begged Milkaia.

Amy and Joe both looked at me too, in shock.

'I'm not joking. I have never said that I was going to be king.'

'But it is your birthright!' Milkaia argued. 'The king is dead!'

'I have never wanted this life … I'm sorry, but it's the right thing to do. I wouldn't be a good king anyway. It sounds like this race needs someone who knows what they are doing to be in charge.'

'Terry, please reconsider this!'

'No, I have made my decision. I have a life here now … I don't have any desire to be part of your world.'

'This is … unprecedented …'

'If you abdicate, then the next in line would be Livia, as your betrothed … but with her life in Scotland, it would fall to the council to nominate and vote on a new king or queen,' explained Casper.

'Could I make one of you king or queen as my first and only command?' I pondered.

'Absolutely not, sir! If the rightful heir cannot take their place, then democracy must decide the rightful ruler.'

'Please don't be mad at me … this is what I want.'

Casper and Milkaia gave the usual look to each other that they did when something bad was said. Again, Casper sighed and began to nod.

'We cannot force you to be king, sir, if this is what you really want?'

'It is. I will do everything that is needed to support the process, but once I'm out, I'm out.'

'Very well,' Casper concluded in a defeated tone.

'There is so much to do,' said Milkaia.

'Where do we start?' I asked.

'Leave it with us. You need to lay low in Byanbythe for the time being. Is there somewhere you could stay?'

'I suppose I could stay here,' I said, as I looked at Phil's cabin.

'Or my house?' offered Amy.

Everyone looked at Amy, who had finally joined in on the conversation.

'What about Joe?' I asked as I turned to him. 'What happens to him?'

Casper turned to Joe and gave him a serious look.

'Joe … I promised you I would tell you everything you wanted to know about your past. I still intend to keep that promise. With everything going on, will you help and support me over the next few months? Once we deal with the … abdication of the prince … my time will be fully dedicated to you and your past.'

Joe looked at me and Amy and finally back at Casper.

'What do you need me to do?' he asked.

'All in due course, boy. Will you help me, then?'

'I suppose I don't have a choice.'

'Very good,' said Casper, before turning to me. 'I don't suppose I will change your mind on any of this, sir?'

'I'm sorry … I really am.'

Casper nodded and turned to Milkaia.

'Come, Milkaia, we have plenty to do.'

'Indeed,' she replied. 'Joe, will you watch over Terry's old house? Rainforth and his group are safely and securely locked away … but I'd feel better knowing someone was watching over them whilst Casper and I are away.'

'No problem,' agreed Joe.

'Where will you both go?' I asked.

'Where all things in our race begin and end. Italy.'

After a few moments where nothing was said, Casper and Milkaia began to walk away, but I felt like I had so much more to ask them.

'Wait!'

They both turned around and looked at me; Casper looked excited, almost as if he was expecting me to change my mind.

'There's … there's still so much I want to know.'

Casper's face became sad again, but in contrast, Milkaia beamed at me.

'I know,' she said. 'We can talk some more when we're back? We'll only be gone a month or two.'

I smiled back and nodded at Milkaia. There was so much I wanted to thank them both for and tell them how much I appreciated their love and support. I felt like my decision to walk away from my destiny had betrayed them and broken their hearts all in one conversation. I slowly walked over to Milkaia and gave her a hug, which she seemed to greatly appreciate, as she let out a small sob. Finally, they both walked away through the forest and out of sight. When they were gone, I turned to Joe.

'Will I see you around?' I asked.

'Apparently, I'm the new guard dog at your house. You know where to find me,' he said, and walked through the forest in the same direction as Casper and Milkaia.

At last, I was alone with Amy. I turned and looked into her eyes, trying to gauge how she was feeling.

'Wow … I didn't expect that conversation to go that way,' she admitted.

'I wasn't lying when I said I didn't want to be king,' I said. 'I don't want anything to do with that world; my life is here.'

'Maybe … I don't think you'll get out that easy, though, do you?' she asked with reservation in her voice.

I shrugged my shoulders. She was probably right; on paper, what I had asked for seemed like a simple task, but in reality, it was probably a nightmare. At least Casper and Milkaia were off to start the arrangements and I had some time to rest and get my head around everything that had happened.

'Will you stay with my family until you go?' she asked.

'If you want me there.'

'We'd love you there,' she replied, but slightly emphasised on the "we". 'We should go back ... I'm surprised there hasn't been a police search through the woods yet. I haven't been home in over three days. My mom and dad are going to be worried sick. I've put them through enough already ...'

'I'm sorry. You're right; I do cause a lot of problems.'

'It's okay. It was worth it in the end to know you are safe.'

We both smiled at each other and began to walk towards the main road.

'What will we tell them?' I asked.

'Well ... I was already in a lot of trouble for disappearing after the house party explosion ... I guess I will just say that I went looking for you and found you. I'm half hoping the fact you will be with me, safe and sound, will distract them enough to not punish me for life,' she joked.

'Hmm, I'm not so sure about that.'

'Why?'

'Because when we turn up at your door, I'm going to be standing with you and that black eye you have. I don't think they'll be too glad to see me if they think I have given you a black eye.'

'They won't think that you did this!'

'Well … we'll need to come up with a good excuse, then.'

We both laughed a little, but soon enough, the slow walk back through the forest and down the main roads was in silence. It wasn't an awkward silence; in fact, I felt so comfortable around Amy that, even though we had broken up, I still felt comfortable being quiet by her side. The birds still continued to sing, the sun was beaming a beautiful heat up in the sky, and if I closed my eyes and daydreamed a little, this was just a beautiful walk with my beautiful girlfriend on a warm summer's day. Oh, how I wished that dream could still be a reality.

As we slowly began to get closer to the Doories' house, Amy began to talk to me.

'Have you thought what you will do after all this is over?'

'What do you mean?'

'Well, if the abdication goes well … I guess the world would be your oyster.'

'Wow … I had never thought of that. I never thought I'd get to a stage in my life where I would have some answers about what I was … I also never thought I would ever feel truly free.'

'Well, maybe that day's coming soon. What would be your dream?'

'I don't know … I don't know much about the world. Maybe I'd see it a little? I've always thought Byanbythe was the perfect place, but it might be a little awkward to stay around here. I might just see what's out there and what the world has to offer. Maybe I could find some warm beach where I can listen to my favourite music and not have a care in the world?'

'That sounds perfect, Terry.'

We finally reached Amy's street and I could see the Doories' house in the distance. All the cars were on the drive, which gave me the unsettling realisation that we would have some explaining to do for Michael and Lisa shortly.

'Best get this over with,' I sighed.

I began to walk towards the house.

'Terry?'

I turned around and Amy was still standing at the edge of the street.

'What's wrong?' I asked her.

'Do you think, one day, I could join you?'

'What do you mean?'

'On that perfect beach … listening to music and not having a care in the world?'

I gave her a warm smile and grabbed her hand.

'It's the only way it would be a perfect beach.'

I didn't quite know what she was getting at; was she suggesting that, one day, we could be together again? Maybe she meant as friends? Whatever she meant, I didn't feel like I was emotionally ready to know the answer. We held hands as we finally walked down the street together, ready to face her mom and dad.

AMY

There was a lot of shouting. And then some crying. And then some more shouting. I really had put my parents through the worst experience of their lives over the last few days. If it wasn't for Terry walking through the front door by my side, I was sure my parents would have chained me to my bed and never let me leave the house again. We gave them our story, and in my mind, I was hoping it would be the last lie and cover-up I would ever need to tell my parents. I made the story up that someone had seen Terry on the streets of Cardiff and, not wanting to scare him off, I decided to go alone (and thankfully, they didn't ask how I managed to get to Cardiff on my own). This was where the story became far-fetched, but through the drama and emotions (I thought my parents were beyond the state of logic and reason), I explained that before I reached Terry, someone tried to mug me, hit me in the face and took my phone (which was a perfect cover-up for my missing phone, which Rainforth destroyed after using it to call Terry). Thankfully, they somehow believed the story, and as I explained about finding Terry in an emotional state of shock, the firing line somehow came away from my direction.

It was quite comical, if honest, like watching Jekyll and Hyde switching in the same conversation. One minute, my mom and dad would be crying and hugging Terry, and the next, they would be shouting at me for doing something so reckless and dangerous. In the end, we were all a happy family again; Mom and Dad begged Terry to live at our house whilst all the affairs with his own house were sorted. My mom and dad extensively spoke to Terry about his trauma from the explosion and begged him to take some kind of therapy to deal with what he had been through; they also insisted that he return to the hospital to get checked over. Terry agreed, although I could see that he wasn't one hundred percent thrilled about it. I knew my mom was going to be over the top to Terry for the next few months, checking up on him and making sure he was okay, but secretly, I thought Terry enjoyed the love he received from her.

'There is one other thing, Terry,' said Dad.

'What's that?' Terry replied.

'The police still need to speak to you about what happened at the party ...'

Mom and Dad had explicitly avoided talking to Terry about the party. When they questioned me last week, I had said I didn't know anything until the house was evacuated, but of course, they wanted to know what caused the explosion. Terry agreed and my dad arranged for the police to come around that evening and get everything over and done with.

One thing that concerned me with all the lies and cover-up stories that were being told was how much easier they became to tell. Like Terry, I was becoming more comfortable with making up stories to cover up for the strange and supernatural truth. How long did someone have to tell lies for before they didn't know the difference between fact and fiction anymore?

When the police arrived, Terry pretty much denied any knowledge of what had happened at the party. He said that some random kid was shouting about a fire in the garage. Terry said he tried to get as many people out of the party, and when he ran back to the house to check that everyone had gotten out safely, the explosion occurred. The police seemed dubious about Terry's lack of knowledge, but his tale of events seemed to match all the other stories from the partygoers that had been interviewed. The one police officer explained that the size of the explosion could only have been caused by a high amount of explosive material in the house; again, Terry denied all knowledge of any explosive material in his house and the police begrudgingly accepted his story, based on a lack of evidence.

That night, my mom did her thing and made a fantastic meal to welcome both Terry and myself back home. As we ate around the table, I looked around and everything ... seemed back to normal. It was strange and very, very surreal. I reminded myself that this was the very reason why I was walking away from the life that Terry had. It didn't stop myself feeling guilty, like I was abandoning him to face his demons alone ... but I honestly wasn't strong enough. In less than a year, so much had happened, and in the last few weeks, even more than the year in total had occurred ... and yet, after everything, after nearly dying more than a few times, we were now sitting at my mom and dad's table, eating a family meal. How could everything feel so normal?

After dinner, I went upstairs to take my makeup off. I felt so naked without a phone; normally, I would listen to music when I took my makeup off or call Laura or, once upon a time, Terry. I put on some comfy clothes and walked downstairs to see where he was. I wondered what it was going to be like living with Terry now we weren't together. Was it going to be awkward? What would be talked about? Would it become obvious to my mom and dad that we had split up?

As I walked downstairs, my dad was in the living room watching TV on his own. Maybe Terry was in the kitchen with my mom? I walked inside, expecting to see Terry helping her wash up or baking bread, but found my mom on her own, reading a magazine at the table.

'Where's Terry?' I asked.

'He wanted some fresh air,' Mom replied. 'I think he's gone for a walk down to the beach.'

'Alone? Are you sure that was a good idea?'

'We have to respect his wishes. Maybe some fresh air will do him good?'

I thought about where Terry could have walked to. Maybe the pier? Or Phil's boat? After thinking of other possibilities, I finally realised where he would be.

'Mom, do you mind if I walk down to Terry?'

'You're not grounded, Amy,' she reminded me.

'I know … I just don't want you worrying where I am again. I'm sorry I put you through that.'

'Oh, don't worry, I'm sure the tracker we'll have installed will sort out that problem,' she joked, although I was sure there was some truth in there.

I walked out of the house and down our street, taking a short cut through the forest and towards the beach.

As I walked, I started to recount the year that had passed and what had happened. I started off as such a different person to who I was today. I laughed at how much I used to long for adventure and something bigger than Byanbythe once upon a time; now that I had had a true taste of the real world, I had never appreciated the small town around me more.

It was strange; before Terry came back into my life for the first time, I realised that I had been miserable and had no control over my decisions. I was with a boyfriend that I didn't like, doing things that I didn't enjoy and felt so pessimistic about the future. Terry walked back into my life that day in college and so much had changed since ... even without all the weird stuff. Terry had shown me how to love someone ... and I meant truly and utterly love someone. I began to live, instead of just exist, and found someone I could share it all with, not only as a boyfriend, but a best friend as well. Terry had shown me how to find my inner strength and that no matter what happened, there was always a solution. After everything we had been through, we proved that nothing could not be overcome.

I thought back to all the beautiful moments we had shared together and felt sad that life couldn't be simple and like that anymore. I remembered skating on the Black Lake with him and how that felt like it was always going to be the most beautiful moment of my life.

As I walked through the trees, I could start to hear the seagulls and the rushing of the waves ahead. Although I was thinking of all the positives, I also began to think of the struggles that we had overcome together ... and possibly the ones that were yet to come. There were so many questions left unanswered about Terry. Why did he black out? What would happen to his betrothed fiancée in Scotland? There were also questions about the immortals - would they accept Terry's abdication? And if they did, who would take the throne? If it was someone like Rainforth, then it was very scary to think what the future could be.

As I reached the edge of the forest, I crossed the road and finally reached the beach. I saw Terry ahead in the exact spot that I imagined he would be in. At the edge of the sand were his shoes and socks and I could see his footprints that led all the way down to the water's edge where he stood. Terry was standing in the water, in the exact spot he stood on the night he told the truth about who he was. That was the night he admitted his love for me and that was the first time I told him he wasn't a monster. I stared at him, and although he had his back to me, I could imagine that he had his eyes closed, whilst he took in the last part of the sunset. The sky was the most beautiful pale yellow as the day came to a close.

He was the most inspirational person I had ever met. After everything he had been through, he was still standing tall. I thought about the life that could have been for him - the chance to be a

king and to rule a race of people just like him …
and yet, he rejected this life in favour of the one
he had in little old Byanbythe. Instead of
wearing a crown, he just wanted to stand on the
beach, with his toes in the sand and the water
wrapping around his legs.

I didn't want to disturb him, so instead I
waited at the edge of the sand and watched him.
As if he had some sixth sense, Terry slowly
turned around and looked over to me. His face
looked sombre. I smiled and looked into his eyes,
which even from this distance were beautifully
warm. Terry smiled back at me and we just
stared at each other.

I wasn't sure what the future held for us both.
What was today would be different tomorrow,
and maybe one day we could find that perfect
beach together without a care in the world.
Maybe the best was yet to come.

EPILOGUE
LIVIA

I stared at my phone, not quite sure what to think about what I had just heard. I wasn't crazy. Everything that I had thought was an illusion in my mind was finally real. The last few days had been crazy … first the strange boy who had defended me outside of my house and now this phone call from a complete stranger … I had no idea what was going on.

One thing was for sure. The girl that answered that phone call was not the same person who put down the phone. A fire ignited inside the pit of my stomach. That boy was right! I had spent most of my life as a pushover. I had let the brute that I called my boyfriend beat me black and blue. He took all of my money and lost it gambling or buying stupid things like motorbikes and drugs! I had *nothing* in life apart from the feeling of a heavy fist or a kick to my stomach.

No more.

I was better than this … and that phone call had all but confirmed what I once thought was crazy.

Before I could think any more, the front door of the house slammed open and Johnny came rushing in.

'I told you to stay away, Johnny!' I screamed.

'Yer think I'm gonna listen to yew, ya slut!' he shouted back, fists clenched and face red with fury, 'I've stayed away long enough … and it's given me good time to realise what a slut ya are!'

'What the fuck are you on about?'

'The boy who tried to break my arm. Yav been cheatin' on me wid him, ain't yew? I should have known, yer a whore!'

'How dare you?! Have you ever thought that someone was showing me kindness? Maybe stopping some big ugly brute from hitting a woman in the street?'

He punched me in the face and I fell to the ground. It was true … I didn't actually feel physical pain. All the pain he had put me through for all of these years … every punch, every beating … it was never real physical pain. It was emotional pain. The torture he had put me through destroyed my soul and destroyed my confidence. I lived in fear … and yet … I didn't need to. I was invincible! All of this time, I didn't need to take a single punch.

Now was the time to stand tall.

'Hey, Johnny … you know you always said I could take a good beating? Remember you bragged to your friends that you need to punch me for hours and hours before I started to bruise?'

He kicked me and threw in another punch for good measure.

'What da fuck are yew on about, crazy bitch?! I'll beat you fucking black and blue today, if that's what yer want!'

He tried to throw a punch at me, but like the boy who saved me before, I grabbed Johnny's fist and quickly snapped it backwards, causing the most gut-wrenching noise I had ever heard. Johnny screamed and fell backwards onto the floor.

'Ya stupid cow! You've broken mar wrist! Call an ambulance!'

I stood up and towered over him; years of his wrath were about to be served justice.

'It turns out there's a reason you could always beat me for hours. Turns out ... you never actually hurt me that much at all. IT TURNS OUT THAT I'M PRETTY FUCKING STRONG MYSELF!'

I stamped on his stomach and then kicked him in the groin as hard as I could. He screamed and then he began to cry. I picked him up from the floor and pinned him to the wall. He looked petrified. He looked confused. He looked like he was wondering how the woman he had beaten for years and treated as a slave could be answering back to him right now.

'K-Ka-Kate?'

'My name isn't Kate! It's Livia.'

'W-w-what?'

I put my head close to his ear and began to whisper.

'Oh, and that guy who met you the other day? He's my fiancé. Turns out I could do better than you.'

I grabbed his head with both hands and twisted it around as hard as I could. I thought it was going to be difficult, but it was as easy as twisting off the cap of a bottle of pop. His neck snapped clean and he was dead in an instant. I dropped his disgusting, lifeless body to the ground, which made a large thud.

I walked away from Johnny and looked into the mirror in the hallway. I looked awful. Underneath these rags that I called an excuse for clothes was a beautiful and sexy body. I was strong. I was ready to take on the life that I was destined for! I was ready to meet my future husband and take over the world with him, as king and queen.

I walked out of the house and thought about my plan of action. Maybe I could rob some money from someone? I certainly didn't have any of my own. I also wanted a better car ... I wasn't going to drive around in Johnny's piece of shit. I thought about the stranger on the phone and how much one conversation had changed my life. I was a new woman. I was the woman I was meant to be.

I just needed to find out where Byanbythe was.

Printed in Great Britain
by Amazon